Treasures in a Bottle

by

April Henley

Enjoy the fantasy
and believe!

April Henley

Treasures in a Bottle

First Edition

Published by arrangement with the author.

For information, contact:

https://henleyapril.wixsite.com/bay-horse-press

Manufactured in the United States of America

ISBN: 979-8-9895614-0-7

DEDICATION

To my grandma, Esther Johnson, my biggest fan, who never gave up on me and told me never to give up on myself. You encouraged me and always asked, "When do I get to read it?" Thank you for believing in me.

To my dad, Neil Henley, who passed away before I could finish this story. You were always a pillar of strength and a great role model in my life. I learned by watching you and seeing your achievements to always seize my dream and never let go. You always believed in me and said you were proud of me. I hope you are proud of me still.

To my mom, Ellen Henley, who instilled in me a love for fantasy, enriched my imagination with folklore and mythos, read me fairytales and fables, and encouraged me to read, read, READ! You never let me down, and I owe you more than I can say. Thank you for giving me life, as well as an appreciation for the written word, and planting the seeds of creativity and belief in me.

I love you all.

CONTENTS

PRONUNCIATION GUIDE TO THE CHARACTERS

Aerwyna (Air-wee-na), Serena (Seh-ree-nah), Cari (Car-ee), Kai (Kye), and Lorelai (Law-ruh-lai) – Mermaids, Qoral's sisters

Annora (Ah-nor-a) – A griffin, Glendor's mate

Aquila (Ah-que-la) – Winged horse matriarch

Arthur (Ar-th-er) – King of Camelot

Azrael (Az-ree-el) – A basilisk

Bantuck (Ban-took) – A giant

Brom (B-r-aa-m) – A centaur

Cadmus (Kad-mus) – A dragon

Corvina (Kor-vee-nuh) – A harpy

Dove (Dove) – A harpy

Dirus (Dry-us) – Lord dragon

Flint (Flint) – Crown phoenix

Francis (Fran-sis) – Royal assistant to King Arthur

Glendor (Glen-door) – Lord griffin

Godan (God-en) – A dragon

Guinevere (Gwi-nuh-veer) – Queen of Camelot, Arthur's wife

Haco (Hay-coh) – A phoenix

Hamel (Ha-muhl) – Boss giant

Honeysuckle (Huh-nee-suh-kl) – or Honey for short, a fairy scout

Isla (Eye-s-la) – A dragon, Drius' daughter

Kadel (Kah-dell) – A dragon

Liliana (Lily-ah-nah) – Fairy queen

Lira (Lee-ruh) – A dragon

Madera (Mah-deer-ah) – Harpy queen

Marigold (Meh-ruh-gowld) – or Mari (Ma-ree) for short, a fairy

Meribella (Mer-ih-bell-ah) – A mermaid, Qoral's mother

Merlin (Mur-luhn) – A wizard

Mira (Mee-rah) – A dragon, Drius' mate

Nimueh (Niy-muw-ey) – Merlin's former love

Nora (Naw-ruh) – A centaur, Ulysses' mate

Nutmeg (Nuht-meg) – A fairy

Nyneve (Nih-neh-vay) – A nymph

Obsidian (Uhb-si-dee-uhn) – A unicorn, Opala's mate

Opala (Oh-pah-la) – Unicorn matriarch

Orpheus (Or-fee-uhs) – A winged horse

Picard (Puh-kaard) – A merman

Piper (Pai-pr) – A cuttlefish, Qoral's pet

Qoral (Kaw-ruhl) – Mermaid queen

Ragnar (Raag-naar) – A dragon

Sli (Sly) – King sea serpent

Silzer (Sil-zhr) – King basilisk

Tana (Ta-nuh) – A phoenix, Flint's mate

Ulysses (Yoo-li-seez) – Centaur chieftain

Vesper (Veh-spr) – A dragon

PROLOGUE

In olden days, when knights fought for glory, and kings ruled from great stone castles, fairytale creatures, both beautiful and frightening, roamed the land and sea. Everything fantastic was alive and well, and anything mythical and mysterious was real. It was the age of magic, and a wizard named Merlin set out to make a young boy king of Britannia.

The pair – Merlin and his ward, Arthur – journeyed to the enchanted stone that held the famed sword, Excalibur. Into the blade were inscribed the irrevocable words: "Whoso pulleth out this sword of this stone is rightwise King of Britannia." Many strong, noble men had tried to free the sword and failed. Yet Arthur, small as he was and not very old, drew Excalibur from the stone and was crowned king.

Under his rule, the country prospered. He strengthened alliances with neighboring kingdoms and fended off Britannia's enemies. His greatest achievement was building the city of Camelot, the capital of his realm, from which he ruled for many years. People from all over would visit and marvel at his castle and court, revel at his festivities and jousts, and leave with praises on their tongues. Arthur was well-loved by the people, but time and again, he credited Merlin, his advisor and wise man, who was ever faithful to counsel him in his responsibilities as king. As the country's right-hand man, nothing that had come to pass was possible without the wizard.

Arthur reigned for twenty-five years, and to rule so long and fare so well tempted fate. And there is the old adage, nothing lasts forever. A challenger came, threatening war and destruction if Arthur did not surrender the crown. So the King engaged his enemy on the battlefield, and they slew each other. Camelot and country were left without a ruler, and chaos ensued.

Nations and lords took up arms against each other. Wars broke out, fighting for the crown and the right to rule the country. Many died, yet none succeeded in claiming the throne. Relentless in their quest for power and kingship, they sought more drastic means to win. They sought to possess magic.

Merlin, heartbroken over the loss of his king, fled Camelot. He traveled north, for he had grown tired of people, befriended a colony of dragons, and went to live amongst them in their mountains.

In the cave he called home, the wizard spent his days writing the history of his life – a series of wonderful adventures. He wrote of clashing with evil kings, conversing with giants, helping the unicorns with their great migration, enjoying a tea party with the royal fairy court, and so much more. Most of the stories he penned left him satisfied, for he had not realized how much he had done in his 187 years of living till seeing his memories scrawled on paper. Perhaps, should he ever venture south again, he would share these stories with wayward travelers. Stories were all he had left to give, for there was little need for his magic anymore. He determined himself to be a retired wizard in a world that was moving out of the dark ages.

Years passed, and the wizard's name faded into legend. For a long time, no one knew what happened to Merlin, and he may have been happy to keep it that way. But now, dear reader, here in this book, a new chapter of the wizard's life is shared. It is a story that must be told to save the lives of many. I only hope my words read true, and you believe.

CHAPTER ONE

A Favor

It was a fine mid-summer day when Drius, the leader of dragons, paid the wizard, Merlin, a surprise visit at his cave.

A reptile of immense size, Drius was a formidable beast. His scales and plated underbelly were tougher than steel – manmade weapons suffered to wound him. A swipe of his claws would cut down horse and rider, and his teeth, set in a jaw that had the strength to crush stones into dust, rendered armor useless. His strength was matched by his speed, for Drius was the fastest flier of any dragon in the colony, able to turn, swoop down, and lift back up again with flawless action and agility. And, like most dragons, he could breathe fire, the flames so intense, they could melt a knight's shield and sword. It came as no surprise then that Drius was undefeated and thus had ruled over all lesser dragons for over a century. Unless he was caught in a fiery mood, the dragon lord was otherwise beautiful, regal-looking even, with scales like emeralds, and wings fair like gold. And, despite his fierce reputation and appearance, Drius kindled a tender heart toward most, and he was one of Merlin's oldest and dearest friends.

Peering inside the cave, Drius called his name. "Merlin?"

The wizard was at his desk, quill in hand, scribbling away. He was an old man, tall and thin, but looked well for 187 years of age. The wrinkles on his face made him look wise and friendly. His spectacles balanced on the bridge of his nose, and behind them, his deep blue eyes concentrated. His long white hair was tied back with silver thread, and his beard fell to his chest. He wore beautiful blue robes, embroidered with shimmering stardust, and there was an aura of kindness around him, with overtones of mystery and intrigue, so that he was approachable but also inspired admiration.

He did not stir at the sound of his name, so Drius called again, a little louder, "Good day to you, Merlin."

"Hmm?" Merlin lifted his gaze. His eyes twinkled at the sight of the dragon, and he smiled. "Drius! Good day, my friend."

"Sorry to interrupt—"

"Save your sorry." Merlin put away his quill and ink pot. "You are not interrupting."

"What are you working on?"

Merlin came outside, for Drius was too big to enter the cave. "I was drawing sketches of the baby dragons that hatched yesterday. You know the ones – they were born to Lira and her mate, Ragnar. Cute little tikes. Though, one surprised me when he sneezed and caught my beard on fire." Merlin patted his beard and laughed. "No harm done though. But uh, tell me, Drius,"—Merlin folded his hands behind his back and peered up at the dragon—"what brings you here? Often I enjoy our visits, but today you have a worrisome look, and I see…yes, I see concern, maybe even fear in your eyes."

"Always perceptive, Merlin. But then I hide little from you. I wish this was nothing more than a friendly visit, but I have received troubling news from afar. News that concerns humans and many, if not all, magical beasts."

Merlin frowned. "I see." He sat on a boulder and removed his spectacles, letting them hang by the silver chain around his neck. "Please tell me what news this is, Drius."

The dragon lord laid down, crossing one clawed foot over the other, and said, "I spoke with Aquila early this morning. I believe you know her. She is lead mare and matriarch of the winged horses."

Merlin nodded. "I know her." He thought back:

I met her three years ago. A foal suffered a snake bite, and she came to me, asking me to heal it. I brewed a potion that soothed the foal back to good health, and Aquila declared me a friend to her herd from that day forward.

"I hope she is well."

"She is troubled, just as much as I am," said Drius. "She had returned from visiting Opala, lead mare and matriarch of the unicorns. Some of her own were roaming the western countryside the night before, throughout the region where Camelot once stood."

Merlin winced.

Ten years after Arthur's death, there was a great siege. Camelot was razed to the ground with fire and hate. Merlin remembered the night he heard of it. When he left Camelot and hid away so no one might find him, he had done his best to shun the whispers of the wind and all the voices of nature that tried to tell him of his former home. He did not want to know its fate. But still, one night, as he lay asleep, a breath of wind spoke softly in his ear, and he awoke with a start and tears.

Arthur's great city, gone. His legacy, gone.

He tried not to believe it, but soon after, word came to him from beasts and birds who had passed that way. All that was left was rubble, a graveyard of stones and masonry.

Merlin brought a hand to his chest. The pain, old but familiar, gripped his heart.

"Merlin?" Drius' voice was soft with concern.

"I am sorry, Drius. The loss still has its sting after all this time. A hundred years, and it still hurts to hear Camelot is gone. Do you find that strange?"

"Not at all. It is never strange to mourn for what was lost, no matter if a hundred years pass or even a thousand. We always mourn for that which was a part of ourselves."

And I am all that is left of Camelot, thought Merlin. *Me, and my memory of it.*

He sniffled and inhaled sharply. "But enough with the past, when you have more pressing matters at present. Please continue, Drius."

"You are certain?"

"Yes. Please."

Drius paused, then said, "Aquila brought me word from the unicorns. They say that humans do not believe in magical creatures anymore. They leave us out of stories and songs, and they hinder their imaginations so that they no longer dream about us. Dragons, unicorns, mermaids, fairies – so many fantastic beasts are being forgotten." The dragon gravely stared at Merlin and lowered his voice. "You know what will happen if this continues."

Merlin paled and nodded. "Yes, I do. If humans stop believing in magical creatures, then those creatures will disappear into nothingness. They will no longer exist. You will disappear, Drius, you and all the rest that are wondrous. You will disappear from this world and never return."

He rose and paced the cave entrance, wringing his hands and muttering inaudibly under his breath. When he finally stopped, he turned to the dragon with a desperate face.

"Drius, how can we be sure? What certainty is there this news is true? Perhaps the unicorns are mistaken. I cannot fathom how people can forget you, you or any other wondrous being. Your kinds have been around for centuries, and so many have seen you. Surely those sightings leave a lasting impression."

"Seen us?" Drius stared at him in disbelief. "Have you forgotten, Merlin?" He rose to his feet. "Or has time passed you by?"

Merlin's brow rose, and he thought, *It often does when you are as old as I am and magical.*

"Perhaps you have spent too much time hiding yourself away from the world," said Drius. "I know you closed your ears and mind to most of what happened after the death of your king, so I will remind you."

Merlin frowned but said nothing.

"During Arthur's reign, there was peace, not only between the people but between humans and the realm of magical beasts. Your king respected magic because of you, and so he revered the magic-born. But when he died, his rule and all he stood for died with him. The wars started, and so did the wild hunts.

"At first, it was for sport – men hunted magical beasts, if not only to brag, then in the pursuit of titles and honors and knighthood. But when, after five years of fighting, there was still no one on the throne, the pretenders thought magic would give them what they wanted. Their hearts swelled with greed for great power and splendor. They coveted what they could not have and wanted it all and magic too. So they hunted the magic-born in hopes that they might possess our magic.

"Do you not remember? I do. I remember the hunts, the humans' hot fury, desperate to have us, and clinging to the foolish notion that if they had us, they had our magic."

The dragon lord rumbled from within, a warm glow filling his belly. His lips curled back, and whiffs of smoke seeped through his sharp teeth.

"The lords and their hunting bands came after the magic-born in mad pursuit. Nowhere was safe. With their hounds and horses, they chased, ran down, and killed a great number of wondrous creatures over fields and through forests. They took their ships to sea, cast their nets and hooks, and speared countless lives. And even in the skies, the hawking parties brought many down in a shower of arrows.

"They cut us down, taking all they could from us, but our magic was never theirs to possess. Still, they did not accept this, and driven by madness, malice, and greed, they went on killing – always their greed, a terrible sin that blinds most, so they never acknowledge their wrongdoing.

"So many lives were lost to their villainy. How many dragons did they slay in hopes of finding treasure? How many unicorns did they murder for their horns? How many griffins or centaurs or fae did they put to death? How many—"

Flames leapt from Drius' mouth, his anger ignited. Merlin dove behind the boulder to escape the scorching heat.

"Drius!" He yelled over the roaring blaze. "Calm yourself before all that's left of me is charred."

The dragon lord closed his mouth and blew a thick cloud of smoke from his nostrils. "Forgive me, Merlin. My own memories are still too painful, and time does not heal all wounds."

Merlin stepped out and shook the soot from his robes. His eyes wandered to a jagged scar along Drius' right wing. It was a mean-looking scar, one which had come from a blow of anger and hate.

"I understand, Drius."

The dragon folded his wings and continued in a calmer voice: "The killings lasted five long years. I met you toward the end, but you were not the same person then as you are today. You were broken, desperate to be irrelevant to the happenings of mankind. And our friendship was new, so I did not involve you. But I knew it was never going to end, not till the lords and their hunting parties wiped us out or those of us that remained did something to alter our fate.

"So I called a meeting between the leaders of those magical beasts that shared my feelings, those that were determined to survive against our common enemy. Never before had such a gathering taken place. Friend and foe put aside their differences to help each other. Some demanded we fight the humans. Others with more tender, peaceful dispositions and sage wisdom counseled that spilling blood for blood would solve nothing and bring only more death. In the end, it was decided that we should take our own and go into hiding and avoid all contact with humans."

"Drius?"

"Hmm?"

Merlin was sitting on the boulder again, his hands folded in his lap. "Did no one think to talk to the people? To try to reason with them or make peace? It seems strange to me that you, being intelligent and able to speak, did not try as much."

Drius sighed. "I did try, Merlin. But there are limitations to who can and cannot understand the speech of magic-born. You can because you are magic yourself, and only those people who are willing and want to listen can hear us. All others have their ears closed. The moment I approached an offending party, I was assailed, and though I fled, its ruffians took chase and followed me home." A flash of anger blazed in the dragon's eyes, and Merlin frowned.

"But what about the fae? They are so close to being like people. Not even they had a voice?"

"Some tried and lost their lives for it. Merlin, you know how humans are when it comes to conquest and seizing power: they stop at nothing till they have what they want, or they die trying to possess it."

Merlin nodded. He did know, all too well.

"We went into hiding," continued Drius, "and the humans could not find us. Time passed. The lords disbanded their hunting parties, believing we were gone, that we were all slain. Then finally, a new king wore the crown, and the wars were over.

"We had peace again and could raise our families without fear. But a hundred years have come and gone, and our absence has made the humans forget the wondrous beasts they almost destroyed."

Merlin inhaled deeply. The fog of time lifted, and he remembered. It all came back to him, like a long-forgotten dream, as Drius spoke it to memory. He stood up fast. "So then come out of hiding. Let the people see you so they may believe once more."

Drius shook his head emphatically. "No, Merlin. The risk is too great. If we reveal ourselves, what guarantee do we have that the wild hunts will not begin again? Humans may come after us, spurred on by fear and an unwillingness to understand those who are different from them. Or for lesser reasons, for sport, title, and honors. I will not endanger my kind with such recklessness and lead them to a bloody fate. I am certain the leaders of other magical races feel the same.

"Yet, I do not wish to be stagnant, to do nothing and vanish from this world. I want to live. I want my own to survive. We, the leaders, all want that for our races. We have every right to, but as of now, we are not sure what to do. We face certain death in one form or another with little hope. That is why I have come to you."

Merlin pointed at himself. "Me?"

"Yes, you. Merlin, you are a dear friend. You have done so much for me and other magical creatures over the years. You have proven yourself to be a loyal and trustworthy ally. You are our only tie to the humans, and you know so much about them and beasts alike.

"As I said, I did not involve you before because of how you were then. But I know you. You would not see us disappear. And enough time has passed that I think you should want to be relevant again and help us. Perhaps you can think of a way to save us, preserve our memory, and make humans believe in us again without endangering our lives."

"But Drius, look at me." Merlin patted his chest and stepped forward, his face desperate with worry and doubt. "I am an old man."

"An old wizard."

"Yes, an old wizard who has not used powerful magic in a long time. What could I possibly do? Worse yet, what if I try and fail? If I let you down and lost you, I...I could not bear the guilt."

"If you do nothing, you will still lose us, and then how will you feel?" The dragon lord frowned but spoke gently. "I know I ask a lot of you, Merlin, but the truth is you may be our only hope."

"I will ask the leaders to meet again, and I am sure the same suggestions will be made as before, but to show ourselves could be our undoing, and if we fight back, both sides will lose great numbers. But if we do nothing, we will fade."

Merlin sat down and brought a shaky hand to his beard. He continuously ran his fingers through the long white hairs, his gaze fixed on the ground. For a while he said nothing. He waged an argument with himself while beads of sweat peaked on the back of his neck.

If I fail...but then it is better to try and fail than to do nothing. He is my oldest friend. I could not live with myself if I did not try...And if I do not save him, or the others, I will be alone again.

Merlin swallowed, his throat dry as sand. He looked at the dragon lord with uneasy eyes. "What you ask of me, Drius, is daunting, and I fear I may be of no help. Yet, I know you are right. I could never live with myself if I did not try to alter your fate. I promise I will think of nothing else but this."

Drius nodded his approval. "That is all I ask, Merlin."

The dragon lord spread his wings. They gleamed with golden splendor in the sunlight. He then turned and dove off the cliff. Merlin ran forward and gazed over the edge, watching the dragon rapidly descend toward the earth, his wings folded in. Faster and faster he fell till suddenly he opened his wings and caught the air, lifting himself back up again. With each flap of those powerful wings, Drius put more distance between himself and the earth. He ascended past Merlin, soaring toward the heavens until he was lost in the clouds. Merlin gaped at the awe and majesty of the sight, wondering all the more how a creature so marvelous could be forgotten.

CHAPTER TWO

Beach Treasures

Merlin sat at his desk and silently puzzled over the problem laid before him. His gentle blue eyes stared ahead at nothing, his thumbs twiddling, as his mind turned one idea after another on top of its head.

We could try – No, that will not work. Or maybe I can – No.

He fiddled with trinkets of magical potency – healing crystals, soothing stones, and lucky amulets, all strewn about his desk, in hopes that one of them might help calm his nerves. It was to no avail. He grabbed hold of one trinket, tossed it aside, seized another, and let it go as well. None of those fabled charms gave him any clarity of mind to find the answer to this terrible riddle. In fact, if he did not know any better, he might suspect the baubles were doing the opposite, rousing his frustration to greater heights.

"Oh, blast it all!" He rose from his seat in a huff and began to pace about the cave.

There has to be a way, a way to change their fate. I have cheated fate before. Why can I not do it again?

The warm light of day brightened the place Merlin called home. It was small but cozy, and Merlin had done his best to transform the drab cave interior into a charming place of color and warmth.

At its center was a fire pit circled by four stones. Into the cavern floor was carved a compass – the pit at its center and the stones at its four points, with north pointing toward the back of the cave. The easterly wall was Merlin's workstation. There was his large mahogany desk – the redwood panels were carved with spirals and leaflets, and the legs were griffins supporting the top on their wings. Behind the desk were several stacks of books next to a large whitewood curio with glass doors. Half its frame was set within the cavern wall, and behind the glass was a colorful, if not unusual, assortment of potion ingredients – mermaid tears, unicorn hair, mandrake roots, mushroom spores, teeth of wooly-eyed toads, and the like.

To the left of the curio and desk was a large pine table, its legs carved into the likeness of a stag, a lion, a wolf, and a bear. Upon their shoulders sat the large pine slab, its surface cluttered with oddly-shaped bottles, stirring rods, a mortar and pestle – these and other assorted tools of the potion-making trade, as could be inferred by the large volume of potion recipes at the edge of the table, open to page seventy-two, entitled *Weed Wilt*. The use of such a humdrum potion was for the humble garden, set into the westerly wall of the cave, with those rarer plants – star flowers, ghost orchids, jade vines, and fairy roses, to name a few – the wizard needed for his potions. This was a clever greenhouse of Merlin's own construction and design. The garden sat off the ground, framed by a rock wall of washed river stones. The roots of the plants poked through tiny gaps in the stonework, reaching down into a crescent pool carved in the cave floor. The water was enchanted to help the garden grow without fail. And just above the garden, a hole in the cave ceiling let sunlight cascade through to nourish the budding flowers.

At the north end of the cave was Merlin's large, four-post canopy bed. The blackwood posts were carved in the likeness of dragons, holding in their jaws the red drapery which crowned the bed. Around the foot of the bed laid several fine red silk carpets, and on the back cavern wall hung a tapestry showing "The Peaceful Gathering." One of Merlin's most prized possessions, it was an exquisite work of weaving over a thousand colorful threads to illustrate a great feast between humans and magical beasts.

This was Merlin's home, and should anyone dare try to find it, they would fail because the wizard used his magic to render the climb up the mountainside impossible for humans. It was supposed to be a safe place, far away from people and the troubles with them, but now those troubles had crept their way here. Through forests, across rivers, and over mountains they had snuck, such a long way for them to slither, and now Merlin had to find the answer to quash them.

Or I fear more innocent lives will be lost.

Suddenly, some invisible force pulled at Merlin's psyche. It was soft, like a child tugging his robe, yet the intent behind it was strong, not something to ignore. The strange sensation would be unfamiliar to those of the non-mystic discipline, but Merlin had felt it once before, a long time ago. A shadow fell over his mind, imparting fear and uncertainty, and though he tried to shake it off, the force kept pulling at him with growing insistence. Perhaps, dear reader, you sought something out that was once lost. You searched high and low and were just about ready to give up when this stray thought – more like a feeling – dawned on you, compelled you to look in the one place you never thought to pay any mind, and there it was – the lost something that was then unlost. That may be the only way to give an inkling of this strange phenomenon that happened to Merlin – only, this something was not lost. It was almost in plain sight. Before, he had deliberately ignored its existence, taught his eyes not to see it at all, but now it was calling to him. This thing emitting its force was of the magical variety, and thus, it was pure enchantment that pulled at the wizard's psyche, both mind and spirit, begging him to notice that which he had put away.

Merlin reluctantly glanced over at the dark marble podium that stood off to one side of his desk. A red velvet cloth was draped over its crown, and a discernible four-cornered shape lay beneath it. To even acknowledge its presence gave the force a new wave of strength, and Merlin felt compelled to walk over and seize the fabric that lay between him and that thing it hid.

I promised…but these are desperate times.

With a sharp breath, he pulled the cloth away, stirring up a thick cloud of dust, and revealed the resting place of his Spell Book. This voluminous text of 242 spells, charms, and curses was bound in aged brown leather, with its title painted in gold scrawling letters, and the pages were worn from the ages and elements – it seemed they might fall apart at a careless turn. But even in its fragile state, it was something beautiful.

Merlin stared at his Book. Fear rolled over his eyes like a dark fog as his trembling fingers traced the spine. He opened the front cover and silently read the lovely penmanship scrawled over the first page – *Liber Carminum Magicorum*, which was Latin for "Book of Magic Spells", *Merlin Ambrosius*, his full name. Beneath his name was Merlin's sigil – a blue shield with three white stars and a crescent moon, held up by two silver dragons. A gray rook tower sat atop the shield with a silver crown around its middle, and a wreath of black and white leaves fringed either side. Beneath the shield was a banner with the words, "Magic bound by wisdom, valor, and honor." Merlin's eyes lingered on his motto, and he let out a heavy sigh before turning the page.

Animation – To give life to the inanimate, be it a common object, stone, tree, or mere illustration – a thing which has no soul. The first spell.

The calligraphy was a work of art. There was the ornate "A" and bold colorful block letters of the title, followed by the subtle red scrawl of its definition, and below this, the sharp black ink strokes that composed the spell – and all of this was framed by a florid border of swirling leaves tinted blue, green, and red, with gilded flowers. This decorative penmanship and staging were present throughout the Book, and if the truth be known, it was Merlin's skillful hand and hardy quill that penned and garlanded each page, for it was a time-honored tradition that a witch or wizard author their own book of spells. In such manner, the enchanter left their personal mark of magic in the pages, binding the book to them exclusively.

Below the words, there was a drawing of a blue sugar bowl, short and round, with its handles resting on its hips. A spoon lay at its side, with a monarch butterfly poised on its tip. If one stared at the picture long enough, the butterfly's wings fanned open and closed, and the bowl came alive. Unfurling an arm, it grasped the spoon, which startled the butterfly to leave her perch and flutter overhead. Curiously, the bowl lifted its cap, revealing the delicious sugar cubes that were its charge, and spooned one out. It dropped the white morsel to the side and motioned the butterfly to settle. Without hesitation, the butterfly came to the ground and happily licked the tasty treat. An animated illustration.

Merlin turned the page.

For a time, he stood silently over his Book, fingering the pages one at a time and skimming the titles.

Asphyxia – To suffocate an opponent by means of an invisible force.

Aventari – To impart unto oneself or another the ability to fly.

Benefi – To bestow favor and protection.

As he did this, he felt a growing sense of discomfort. His mouth became dry, and his breathing accelerated. After the "B's", he skipped a few pages at a time, and beads of sweat peaked on his brow. A thoughtful voice echoed in the back of his mind, and from the crypts of his memory, he recalled an image of himself, younger with a shorter beard, and his ward, Arthur, still just a lad and not yet king. They were sitting beneath their favorite willow tree as Merlin recited the boy's lesson for the day.

"Magic," he said to Arthur, "is a force of unimaginable potential. It can be used for good.

Remedium – To remedy or cure (most wounds and ailments).

"Or great evil.

Malum – To harm or wound, maim or mutilate.

"It can make your wildest imaginings come true.

Transforma (Animal) – To transform into a beast of air, water, or land.

"And it can breach the dark recesses of our nightmares.

Phanta (mal) – To create hallucinations, or phantoms, of a foe's worst fears. Guaranteed to drive insane or scare to death.

"Never take it for granted, or it may very well fail you."

This memory was followed by another which prodded Merlin along. He flipped through the pages more quickly, more earnestly, his composure failing with a miserable frown. He felt a growing pain in his side. He became a man possessed by desperation as he made the pages fly back and forth, the titles of spells morphing together in a blur. Every now and then, he would stop to look – *Invisibility, Wishes, Disguise* – and in a huff carry on. All the while, his frame shook, and a tear gleamed in the corner of his eye.

"Oh, this is hopeless," he cried, slamming the Book shut. He collapsed in his chair and dropped his face into his hands.

"I am supposed to be done with magic. It has been so long since I cast anything powerful, and I…I am so old and out of touch with my potential."

He took several deep breaths, trying to calm himself, and rubbed his temples to chase his headache away.

"I thought I was done with the world, but the world, it seems, is not done with me."

For a time, he sat in silence. The only sound was a light wisp of the wind outside his cave that made the forest shake and clamor below. When he chanced to glance up, he saw his sandals and satchel bag hanging in their designated spot at the edge of the cave, and a new light filled his eyes. He stood up and with a careful breath said, "I think I shall go for a walk to clear my head. A stroll along the beach may be nice."

When he reached the shore, Merlin removed his sandals and dug his toes into the warm sand. He smiled to see the waves rolling in and breathed deeply the salty air. He loved the sea, so he often went to it to soothe his inner turmoil and calm his troubled heart. Many was the time he walked barefoot along these sands, as he was apt to do so now, to clear his mind to better think on what ailed him.

The cool waves gently lapped over his old, worn feet, ever so slightly pulling at him as if to encourage him to play in their aqueous body. The wizard looked at his feet, all wrinkly and withered, much like the rest of him.

My feet bear the weight of many journeys and adventures. How far they have carried me, I cannot count the miles. I thought it was time to rest, but now I wonder, with this new task set before me, if I will be venturing out again.

He shook his head.

Seems ridiculous.

Every now and then, he gazed out over the crystal blue waters, wondering what it would be like to venture beneath the surface. There was a place he had never been before, and it would not require a great deal of walking, he imagined.

This absent thinking meant he was not really paying attention to where he stepped, and with sudden surprise—

"Ouch!"

He stubbed his toe on something hard. Grabbing his sore foot, Merlin soothingly rubbed the pain away and seethed sharp air between his teeth.

"What in the seven realms…"

He searched the sands and saw something peculiar and gleaming poking out. Grabbing hold, he unearthed a cork-sealed bottle covered in barnacles and dried seaweed. He brushed off the granules and debris and studied the found treasure.

"Something is inside."

It was a couple of rolled-up parchments, and he was careful to pull them out. The bottle had preserved them well. They were still clean and crisp to the touch, and when he unfurled them, Merlin caught his breath. They were drawings. The first was of a knight engaged in battle with a dragon. He rode gallantly forth upon his noble steed, his spear aimed at the dragon's heart, while flames leapt from the beast's mouth. Though well-drawn, it was too close to the heart of Merlin's present worries, so he put it away. But the second drawing was more to his liking: it was of a little girl sleeping in a bed of flowers, and a unicorn stood over her, protective and ever vigilant.

"Whoever the artist is, their work is impressive."

He considered the details of the drawing and the skill of its creator. He also wondered about the would-be story behind it. It captured his fascination. The innocence of the child and the devotion of the unicorn to protect its charge created a perfect harmony. It was then that an idea struck Merlin.

"Oh my…"

Yes, yes! Why did I not think of it before?!

"That's it," he joyously shouted. "I've got it! I've got it!"

He hurried back to the dragons' mountains and went straight to Drius' cave. The dragon lord had been resting when Merlin entered, proclaiming with much excitement, "Drius! Drius! I have it! I have an idea!"

His voice reverberated off the cave walls, causing a great echo that startled the dragon awake, and he bumped his head on the cave ceiling.

"Ouch! What is it, Merlin? What is wrong?" Drius frowned and rubbed his aching skull.

"Nothing is wrong, Drius. Actually, everything is right, or at least I think it is. I am sorry, but can you call a meeting between the leaders as soon as possible? I have an idea that may save you all."

A new light filled the dragon's eyes, as he swelled with hope. "Really? What is it, Merlin?"

"No time to explain. I must plan accordingly. But call them together. The sooner the better." And with that final word, Merlin hurried off to his cave.

CHAPTER THREE

The Great Circle

It took three days. Drius sent seven dragons to find the eleven magical creatures that made up the rest of the council. His message invited them to come together, peacefully, in a secret place to discuss their plight, and made mention that the wizard, Merlin, friend and ally, wished to help them.

On the fourth day, the council met in a glade at the center of an enchanted forest. The space was lush and green, with a pond at its edge, and encircled by tall pine, oak, and elm trees. At any other time, it was a quiet place, charmed only by songbirds and prancing deer. Now it echoed with the growls and mutterings of twelve fantastic creatures. This gathering was known as the Great Circle.

Some bowed to one another in greeting, while others simply nodded. A few frowned and quietly observed the rest. None had overlooked, however, the presence of a thirteenth party, an old man dressed in blue and silver robes, who stood close to Drius.

Merlin's heart pounded against his chest and into his Spell Book. He clutched it tightly and took a couple of deep breaths to calm his nerves. No person had seen the Great Circle before, a gathering of magic-born, friends and foes, in one place, but there he was. It was a great honor to be a part of it, though he wished it were under different circumstances.

He struggled to maintain his composure. So much was his excitement to be in the Circle, to see the twelve, that his nerves were taught and charged, and he tried not to smile too much. They had come together to resolve a serious matter, and he thought it better to look thoughtful and somber, but it was difficult. His eyes twinkled, and his own magic reached out to touch theirs.

A few of them he knew quite well. Others he had never met but had interacted with fellows of their race. And then there were some whose representations he had only seen in books of lore. He knew their names, and their reputations preceded them, either in stories told by the dragons or in the whispers of the wind.

To Drius' immediate right was Aquila, lead mare and matriarch of the winged horses. Unlike her non-winged cousins found in the stable, this equine creature was quite large – Merlin, himself a tall man, stood level with her withers. Her muscles bulged, and her veins swelled; to be sure, she was a strong beast to be able to fly great distances. A chieftain mare not easily intimidated, yet she carried a constant grace in her appearance, in the way she moved – how now, with Merlin looking on, she tossed her grand head, her long white mane dancing in the air, and her starlit eyes conveyed glimpses of heaven. She was as white as the first winter's snow. She had no markings, no blemishes, and when the sun shone on her, she gleamed. She pawed at the earth with silver hooves and shook bits of cloud from her white-feathered wings, the span of them twice that of her body. To her right was her unicorn cousin, Opala, and the two magical equines nickered softly to one another.

When he chanced to look at the unicorn, Merlin put a hand over his heart to make certain it was still beating. Not to be misunderstood: the wizard had seen a unicorn more than once in his lifetime, but his reaction was no less the same. Opala was a creature so simple in appearance but with a beauty so profound – to look on her was to look on that which was most pure and innocent in all creation, that any man good of heart was to feel a wave of conviction fall over him, as he suddenly became aware of how unworthy he was to stand in the presence of something so good and blameless. She was milky white, with pale, sun-kissed hooves and long mane and tail – those white tresses so long, with colorful flowers braided in them by fairies. Protruding from the crown of her forehead, her long ivory horn, with its spiral twist, came to a point and was the root of her magic. Her dark jeweled eyes glinted with the sophisticated wisdom of an immortal with a century on this earth.

It was when the unicorn lifted her gaze that Merlin looked away, not wanting the chaste creature to know he had been staring. He instead fixed his attention on the solemn figure to her right, that of Ulysses, the chieftain centaur. Half-man, half-horse, from the waist down he had the body of a brawny bay stallion, with copper-brown hair that turned black down his sturdy legs. His long black tail irritably swished at the morning flies, and his large black hooves – the strength behind them could crack a dragon's skull with one well-aimed kick – were firmly planted as he stood tall and alert. His equine hair faded at the naval, and from the waist up, he was a strong man with thick arms crossed over his bare chest. There was fine dark hair on his breast and trailing down, but not enough to hide his scars. Those angry battle wounds, long-time-healed, gave proof to the stories Merlin heard about this bestial warrior – tales of his bravery and victory over many adversaries, both man and beast. One strange mark – a crescent line of several pits in his left forearm – came from a bear that bit down and then lost its life to the centaur's sword. That great sterling weapon, now sheathed and strapped to the chieftain's back, had several war tokens tied to its hilt – among them, a bear's claw. Despite his rugged form, he had a pleasant face with a strong jaw, an aquiline nose, and eyes the color of warm maple. His curly russet beard was well kept, and his short auburn hair barely hid the tips of his pointy ears. He stood off to one side, quiet and watching the others. One might venture to guess the centaur was unfriendly, but Merlin, who could still recall his time amongst military figures, thought to himself, *He is keeping a close eye, ready for anything.*

A soft light came to the edge of Merlin's vision then, and he looked to see Liliana, the fairy queen, float over to the center of the Circle, a radiant glow about her, and slowly descend toward the ground. As she came down, new growth sprung from the soil. A single stem rose above the grass, with a mature bud that unfurled into a beautiful white lily to receive her. She sat upon the lily with royal formality, her posture upright, hands folded in her lap, legs together, and bare feet dangling over the petals. Her golden dress framed her small waist in a floral bodice, and its bubbled skirt spilled around her ankles. Her train was made of lace like butterfly wings, delicate and flowing all around her, and embroidered with golden florals. Her translucent wings curved into several fine points and teased fractions of colored light when kissed by the sun. For one so small – seven inches from wing tip to toe, she was quite powerful. There was so much magic in her tiny body that her fine skin shimmered, and rivulets of light traced her flaxen hair. Upon her brow was her golden circlet crown with a small opal at its center. She looked around at the gathering, a pleasant smile on her angelic face. Then her eyes settled on Merlin – those enchanting eyes, earthen with streams of gold buried in them, and though he was dazed at first, the wizard quickly noted the warmth grow in her smile. She politely bowed her head to him, and Merlin reciprocated, but not before removing his blue silk cap.

On Drius' left sat Hamel the giant. An impressive fellow: when standing, he was fifty feet tall, so he towered over lesser trees but not the pines. He was thickset but not quite fat, though it was clear he never missed a meal. He wore tall seven-league boots of dark suede with crossing laces, and his clothes were homemade – brown cotton pants, a green tunic, and a brown leather vest with a giant sunflower fixed in its lapel. He was a humble-looking giant with a round face, rosy cheeks, a button nose, and eyes that were blue like the sky on a cloudless day. His bushy brows moved up and down with fluid expression, like big fuzzy caterpillars at play. On his head was a crop of golden hair that was combed and parted down the middle. He had a warm, infectious smile and hardly seemed the fierce monster of bedtime stories. Merlin noted the dirt under the giant's fingernails and the light smudge just beneath his chin. *He must have been tending to his garden before he came here.* Like others of his tribe, Hamel was a farmer, a great tiller of soil, and his crops grew many times the size of those in a common man's garden. As if to prove the point, the giant pulled a luscious red apple from his satchel and took a bite, the crackle of it like snow. He wiped the sweet juice dribbling down his chin with the back of his sleeve and offered some to Flint the phoenix, who was perched on his shoulder. The avian shook his head, and the two carried on with what must have been pleasant conversation, for every now and then, Hamel laughed. His jolly laughter not only shook his whole person but made the ground slightly tremor. A great fellow, this giant was – friendly, to be sure, but when Merlin finally noticed the large club lying behind him, he had no doubts that if the giant felt threatened, his prompt response would be to bash the offender.

As for the magnificent bird on his shoulder: Flint was the first phoenix Merlin had seen in his life. He had the body of an eagle, only larger. His plumage was red, except for his belly which was gold. His golden-scaled feet ended in sharp black talons that gently clutched his perch on Hamel's shoulder. When he stretched his wings, the span of them was great, and underneath the feathers looked like many tongues of fire. His tail had many feathers – most of them long ribbons fading from red to yellow, but a few crimson ratchets branched out amongst the ribbons, and being a male phoenix, he had three feathers that looked much like those of a peacock, only these were gold with red eyes, that fanned out over the rest. His face was fierce like an eagle but also beautiful like a swan. His black beak was sharp and hooked. Upon his head was a crest of iridescent feathers. Beneath his golden feathery brows were obsidian eyes, perfectly round and deeply set in his dark skin. When those eyes looked at Merlin, the wizard saw neither malice nor curiosity but rather careful observation, and something else. Merlin looked on, and the thing sparked in his mind. *Fire.* Fire burned there in the phoenix's eyes. *The fires of time and wisdom. Time is his slave and wisdom sits at his right wing.* Merlin became suddenly aware that the air was fragrant. It smelled of cinnamon, myrrh, and sage, and he knew at once that these delightful aromas came from Flint. *The kindling from his funeral pyre. Drius said that at the time of the last Great Circle, Flint was 375 years of age. It has been a hundred years, and he looks well for a bird of 475. He must be nearing his end though. He looks tired. If it were not impolite to ask, and also it being a sacred thing, I would ask to see his rebirth.*

To Hamel's left, upon a large, flat rock laid Glendor the griffin. Half-bird, half-beast: he had the head, wings, and forefeet of an eagle and the body of a lion. The golden brown feathers yielded to the tawny fur at the valley between his wings and below along his chest. His avian forelegs, rough and golden, were crossed, the talons dangling over the lip of the rock, while the powerful feline hindquarters stretched out and over its end. His long tail, with its tuft of black hair on its end, swished. His feathered ears twitched. He held his proud head high, and those sharp, golden-rimmed eyes surveyed the council in the same manner a king observes his court. He was nothing short of magnificent, but he was immense. So large was he – he was at least half the size of Drius, and just as strong, and his wings, the breadth of them was impressive, that it was no wonder he was called the king of beasts and birds, for he was the best of both. Yes, he was formidable, *But,* thought Merlin, *he is also noble.* When Glendor fixed his sights on Merlin, the wizard instinctively bowed his head. The griffin paused, then looked on at the others. Merlin grinned. *He remembers.* He would not soon forget it either – the first time he met Glendor and almost lost his life. *His feather completed the potion* – Merlin had entered the griffin's cave, hoping to find no one home and a spare feather lying about. But the griffin was there, newly returned with his fresh kill, a wild boar. Glendor charged, claws open, ready to tear Merlin to pieces, when the wizard dropped to one knee and humbly bowed in submission. *Glendor said I was daft, but it was enough to stop him and give me time to explain myself, and besides that, he gave me the feather.*

A sudden *SPLASH* pulled Merlin away from his thoughts, and he saw a shower of water pelt the griffin's hide. Glendor hissed and glared at Qoral, the mermaid queen. She ducked her head beneath the pond surface to stifle her laughter in bubbles. Merlin also brought a hand to his face to hide his smile. *Impetuous sea nymph.* She had come there by way of an underwater cave that led from the pond all the way back to the ocean, affording her the chance to sneak up and surprise the griffin. She surfaced with a lovable grin, looking quite pleased with herself, and swam this way and that without a care. She was a youthful beauty, her loveliness still veiled by innocence, and the blush of mischief only started to tease. Her fair skin rivaled the whitest sands, and her eyes were of the deepest, most unsettling blue that the sea might ripple with envy. Translucent cerulean scales lined the sides of her face and faded at her pearly smile. She had long, wavy silver-blonde hair dressed with pearls and pinned behind her pointy ears. Her gills, found just beneath her lobes, fanned open and closed to let her breathe. Her maiden form was small and slender, and she wore a top made of aquamarine sea glass that, by the stunning craft of her mer-smiths, was shaped to resemble a pair of seashells. She traced the water with her webbed hand and raised her tail to threaten Glendor with another splash. Her flesh turned to shimmering blue-green scales below the naval, and at the end of her long elegant tail was a large golden tail fin. Gracing the sides of her tail were golden fins with spines, each spine armed with a poisonous barb. The power of her venom, Merlin had studied, rivaled most jellyfish and could stun a shark or even kill a man; but, like most creatures with such a delicate weapon, she could inject it at will and only if threatened. *Beautiful but deadly,* Merlin thought as he looked on at her horseplay.

She was poised to strike the water again. Her mischievous grin showed she was not swayed by Glendor's growls. But then she hesitated and grew quite rigid. Her smile faded, and fear clouded her widening eyes. Her spines stiffened, pulling the fins taut, the dangerous barbs glistening. Qoral looked back over her shoulder and hissed at the growing shadow beneath the water. She retreated from it, swimming to the pond's edge, close to Glendor, who also eyed the shadow with cautious dislike.

Merlin's stomach quivered, but curiosity held his gaze. The dark shape was dispersed by a soft, eerie glow, like drowned lightning. Then a massive head broke the surface, not with a splash or sudden surge, but with quiet, undulating grace. Sli, the king sea serpent, rose above the council. There was silence as they all watched the oppressive beast – the last to arrive – hover with his eyes closed. Merlin, his mouth agape, stared in frightened fascination. He had seen a couple of sea serpents in his time, but Sli surpassed them, not only in size but in terror. *Great heaven, he must be the length of three longships* – and most of him was still beneath the water, stretching some ways back through the underwater cave. He was thick, powerful – a breathing line of muscle. Merlin shuddered to think how easy it would be for the serpent to wrap his length around a ship and, with a great squeeze, reduce it to splinters. His topside was coated in golden scales, tightly knit together, like the formation of a shield wall – impenetrable, and he had a pale-plated underbelly. A razor fin, translucent and spiked, crowned the length of his back. It glowed a strange hypnotic luster that started to fade. His face, eyes still closed, was menacing. A row of sharp teeth rose over his lip. Two horns protruded from the top of his head, and his giant gills were behind fanned fins beyond the jawline. His great nostrils snapped open and blew forth a spray of seawater, and then those eyes opened. Those eyes – they were like dusty, faded glass, but viscous, and behind them, the large black pupils swam in murky water. Those eyes beheld the council, and at once, Merlin felt weak in the knees. *So it is true,* he thought, remembering a sailor's tale: *Those eyes, they were awful. When it looked at me, a net of thought caught me fast, and I knew I should die. For a moment, I forgot where I was and who I was, and even in my terror, there was an underlying calm, for it would all be over soon.* Merlin did not look away. He stared at the sea serpent and closed his hand into a fist. *Only a strong mind anchored by a strong heart can break free of his trance.*

"Welcome, Sli." Drius' voice broke the silence, as well as the haze that seemed to grip everyone, and Merlin suddenly lowered his gaze.

Sli only nodded to the dragon lord, and the assembly continued to mutter amongst its parties.

Merlin did not look at the sea serpent again but instead looked across the way at the last two leaders in the Circle. It was then that he thought, *Sli is only the beginning of scares.* These final members, being unsavory creatures with a strong distaste for the sun and its light, concealed themselves in the shadows of the trees. They had no friendly cohorts here and only conversed with each other. Merlin could hear the faint wisps of their whispers and the sharp pitch of their hisses. One of them, the smaller of the pair, was up in a tree, and Merlin felt the stab of seething hate when she trained her piercing gaze on him, and he shuddered.

Madera, the harpy queen, looked out from her perch at him. Merlin had never seen one of her kind before, and her appearance spurred great fear and disgust. She was a winged horror. *The antithesis of an angel.* From the waist up, she was a thin woman. Her pale skin clung to her bony frame – her ribs and collarbone stuck out in a sickening way. She was raked with scars. Joined to her long, skinny arms were the black, oily feathers of her large, imposing wings, which originated from her shoulder blades, and her over-callused hands had long, extra-jointed fingers with sharp black nails. Black feathers fluffed out over her chest. Below the navel, her wide hips turned to large avian legs, with black feathers descending to the knees, and from there black, scaly feet ended in great black talons. Those talons clawed at the thick tree branch Madera stood upon, over and over again in silent frustration, sending little curls of tree bark fluttering to the ground below. Her face was a fright, sharp and triangular, with hollow cheeks and cracked, faded lips that peeled back in a silent hiss to reveal her razor-sharp teeth. Her greasy, matted hair, red like blood, fell about her shoulders, barely hiding her pointy ears. Beneath her dark feathery brows, her unsettling eyes – the whites of them a deep red, the centers a pale blue – looked at Merlin like trained daggers. A light breeze blew through, and on it, he caught a whiff of something foul. *Carnage.* The smell of rot and decay, and he was certain it came from her. *For her kind neglects to bathe.*

Without taking her eyes off Merlin, Madera tilted her head and inaudibly whispered to the creature beneath her perch. Merlin looked down, and a sudden chill laced with dread seized him. It ran down his spine, made him tremor, and for a moment he forgot to breathe. *Steady, Merlin,* he cautioned himself.

Beneath the tree, hidden in shadow and partly coiled, was Silzer, the basilisk. A colossal serpent, his body was thick and heavy, a deadly force of muscle. His underbelly was smooth and gray like ash, while his backside was a threatening sequence of keeled scales, serrated and edged, and black as ink. The scales were more prominent at the back of his neck, dissuading beasts from biting that sensitive mark. Merlin could not see the basilisk's face. His head was high, but he looked south, away from the council. *Beware the basilisk*...A verse from an old poem drifted through Merlin's memory...*and his deadly sight*. Then Merlin's own thought: *Yes, it is better he looks the other way.* The basilisk carried death with him wherever he slithered. Silzer was the first Merlin had laid eyes on, and he recalled all the terrible things he had read about these serpents. *Scorching venom — withering breath — eyes that kill with one look. And the last is why he looks the other way. Drius said he and the council insisted a hundred years ago that if the basilisk was to be privy to their talks, he must look away, though he is hardly vulnerable this way.*

This was the Great Circle. Twelve creatures. Some gentle, some fierce. Some good, some less so. Beauty and terror, friend and foe. All draped in mystery, all of them magnificent. Each of them born of magic.

Magic, Merlin thought, *that fickle, untamable force plays by its own rules. It can give us such wonders—*

He looked around at each creature again, then down at his Spell Book.

But it can also snatch them away. And why?

His thoughts interlaced – a thought within a thought. The second was a faint echo bolstering the first. So behind the *why* was, *(If humans stop believing…)*

He envisioned a woman, white and ethereal, bright, and without a face.

Because magic is a mother, and if her rules are not followed…

(…these creatures will disappear into nothingness.)

She takes back what is hers. Sadly, the penalty falls on them too, her children.

Merlin looked at the twelve and put to memory the sight of them here, together, in this place.

Such an odd gathering, all for a higher purpose. It has been a hundred years since the first Great Circle, and I wonder, if my plan works, will this be the last time it meets?

CHAPTER FOUR

Merlin's Plan

Merlin wondered how they would start. He eagerly drummed his fingers along the spine of his Spell Book. His nerves were settling, but his magic still leapt within him, desperate to know them who were also magic. He became still when Drius stepped forward, his head high and eyes looking over the whole of the Circle. Perhaps it was his prowess as a leader and authority that captured their attention, for the gathering fell silent, and they waited.

"You all know why we are here," said Drius. "Some of you are friends, others enemies, but in this place, at this time, we put aside our grievances with each other to be united in our struggle to survive. Some of you are new faces, taking the place of the leader who came before you and was here a hundred years ago, and some of us, myself included, were here that first time.

"When first the Great Circle gathered, we sought a way to survive human tyranny and their insatiable greed for our magic. It was decided that we should go into hiding, and for a hundred years, we had peace. But now a new threat faces us, born of our decision. We have been gone for so long that humans are forgetting us. Without their faith, we will fade into nothing. We will be gone from this world, and no one will know to mourn us."

Merlin saw fear ripple through the Circle. Even the bravest and fiercest of them faltered, unable to mask their worry. They were afraid, not of death, but of being undone, unmade, and forgotten.

"So we have come together again," continued Drius, "to try to alter our fate. I am sure some of you have thought as much as I have, that if we stop hiding and make our presence known, the humans will hunt us again. I admit I am not sure which fate is worse – to die by a sword or to do nothing and fade away. Both cause me great fear and dread and turn my inner fire to ice. I only hope we come to some resolution today and can leave here with hope in our hearts.

"That being said, I will do most anything to save my kind, and I am certain each of you feels the same about your own." He eyed the gathering, and some nodded while most remained stolid and waiting. "So I went outside our Circle and asked Merlin to help us." Drius gestured to Merlin with an open claw and encouraged the wizard to step forward.

Merlin did so, feeling the warm, exposing sunlight, as he left the safety of Drius' shadow. So many eyes were on him at once. His blood paced, and he thought his face might redden. Butterflies leapt in his stomach, and he gripped his Spell Book tighter.

"Some of you know Merlin well, and others know only his reputation. He is a wizard, was King Arthur's advisor, and is one of my oldest and dearest friends."

Merlin smiled, and the butterflies settled. He cradled his Spell Book under one arm, crossed his hand over his heart, and bowed low, first to those leaders directly south of him – Liliana, Madera, and Silzer, then to those due west – Aquila, Opala, and Ulysses, due east – Glendor, Qoral, and Sli, and finally turned around to bow north to Drius, Hamel, and Flint.

Drius continued: "Merlin says he has a plan to save us. I want us to hear what he has to say, and then we can discuss it after, along with any other suggestions you all voice."

"Why should we trust, let alone listen, to a human?" Madera snapped. Eyes glanced up at her.

Drius growled. "You can trust him because I trust him. Do you really think that if he were of a bad sort I would let him stay in my mountains with my kind for so many years, let alone bring him here? Your objection is the equivalent of saying my judgment is bad."

Madera seethed through her teeth.

Liliana spoke then, her voice like sleigh bells. "We should listen to what the wizard has to say. If we all agree his plan is utter nonsense, then we can go about finding another way to live and will have wasted very little time and trouble on him. I trust Drius, and I have known Merlin for several years and have no qualms about him. If you still want to press the issue of trusting him, Madera, we can debate it after we hear him out." She smiled over her shoulder at the harpy, which stirred the fire in the bird-woman's eyes.

"Well spoken, your majesty." said Drius. "Thank you. Do you all agree then to hear him?"

Silent nods from the majority agreed, and Madera relented. She waved a winged arm for the proceedings to continue.

"You may begin, Merlin," said Drius and stepped back.

Merlin nodded. "Thank you, Drius." He faced the council and felt a chill run through his nerves. The butterflies fluttered again.

Steady, Merlin. You faced whole armies bearing down on you before. This should be so easy.

He took a deep breath and let it out slowly. He smiled, determined to show no fear or reserve. Under one arm was his Spell Book. The other arm, with fist closed, he laid across his middle and assumed the position of speaker.

In his most gracious voice, he said, "I do not take it lightly that I am allowed to be here. I respect the sanctity of the Great Circle and where it meets, and I revere every one of you and appreciate the seriousness of your situation. I can only imagine how you feel about me, a human, being here. I think then you ought to know the truth about who, or rather what, I am, if you are to hear me out.

"We are not so different, you and I. Each of you was born of magic, and so was I. I was born to a human mother, but I had no father. Magic sewed me together in the womb, for it needed an advocate amongst the people. I learned the arts of wizardry, how to cast spells and make potions, and I did my best not to abuse the gifts I was given. I served my country, raised a boy to be king…" He gulped. "And I watched him fall.

"But just as you and your own were pursued by human greed, so was I. Before Arthur, there were many would-be kings who begged, bargained, and threatened me to serve them, to make them rich and powerful and rulers of all. I know how it feels to be sought after for what you are, to be treated as a thing to possess and not as a soul with feelings. So when Arthur died, I was tired, tired of people and their villainy. I fled north and met Drius. I started a new life, out of sight, like the rest of you. I thought I was done…I wanted to be done with mankind, but here I am, once more, as magic's advocate, its warrior, and even its defender."

Merlin thought he saw waves of understanding fall over the council, as so many faces looked back at him with empathy. He was building a bridge of trust, and many were crossing it. But still, he glanced up at Madera, who continued to glare, and over at Sli, who was impassive, showing no emotion at all. Nor could he guess how Silzer felt, seeing only the back of his head. He betrayed nothing in his frame, his coils rising and falling with each breath. Merlin did not waver to wonder but continued his speech.

"When Drius told me of your plight, my heart broke. There is pain here." He put a hand over his heart. "The world cannot lose you. You are why the world is wondrous. You are part of its charm and mystery. Without you, there is nothing but sense and reason, and while those are good, the world needs the fantastic and unexplainable, and also magical. I feel the magic within me reaching out to you, and I believe it is my duty to help you. Some of you may not trust me, because I am human, or maybe it is not in your nature to trust. But believe me when I say that I want to help you, no matter your feelings about me, and"—he held his Spell Book out in one hand and placed his other hand on top of its cover—"I swear to you, by my magic, that if you let me, I will do everything in my power to help you."

There was a glow beneath his hand. His magic stirred, binding him to his oath.

"Should you dismiss my plan, I will think of another, and then another, and so forth till you dismiss me entirely. I beg you not to though because I do care about you and your own and the future that awaits you. I seek no favors in return. I only want to help because it is the right thing to do."

The glow faded. He then waved his right hand in a half-moon circle over the grass, and fresh shoots sprang up to form a pedestal upon which he set his Spell Book.

"My plan came to me in a strange way. After you left me, Drius, you gave me much to think about, and often when my mind is troubled, I go for a walk along the beach. There, I hoped to think better on how I might save you all, when I stumbled upon this." He pulled the bottle from his satchel and held it up for all to see. Only one parchment was rolled up inside.

Most stared at the bottle with confusion riddled over their faces, all save one.

"What isss it?" Silzer asked, his hiss sharp and impatient.

"A bottle," said Madera.

"A bottle?"

"Yes," said Merlin, "I found it buried in the sand with this rolled-up parchment inside, perfectly preserved and untouched by the sea." He uncorked the bottle and produced the parchment.

"A bottle and a piece of paper? What isss ssso sssignificant about these?"

Merlin put the bottle on the green pedestal and unfurled the parchment. It was the sketch of the unicorn and sleeping child. He had left the drawing of the knight and dragon back at his cave, thinking it might stir up bad feelings with the Circle.

"This parchment, as you will see, illustrates a unicorn standing guard over a sleeping child." With a wave of his hand, the parchment levitated, and he bid it pass itself around the Great Circle, so every creature, even Silzer, would see it. As this happened, he said, "The picture reminded me of a simple but significant truth. In all my years spent amongst people, never did I find more joy than when I was with children. Some of my fondest memories were spent in the village square, the children all huddled around me, eager to see magic. But their eyes would light up when I told them stories of dragons and mermaids and fairies, and so many other wondrous beasts. They were filled with awe and asked so many questions, and wished so much to see you. Children love you."

"So?" Glendor, the last to see the parchment, swished his tail. "What is your point?"

The parchment floated back to Merlin. He seized it and put it back in the bottle. "My point, lord griffin, is that children are innocent. Their hearts do not swell with greed and a love for violence. They would rather play, laugh, and have fun. They are enchanted by all that is magical, mysterious, and wonderful. So then, children are the answer. If children see you, their faith will keep you alive."

The idea stirred the Circle with excitement.

"Merlin is right," said Opala. "Children hold such a tender sweetness. I miss the days when my kind crossed paths with little ones. They would coo and marvel at us and beg to ride and be filled with such joy to be around us. Theirs is a love both simple and pure, and it does not want for anything, save only to be loved in return."

"I agree," said Liliana. "The fae have always held a special place in their hearts for children. Children love to laugh and play games, and so do we. Whenever a child was lost in our woods, we would entertain them and make them feel safe, then see the babe home. I know my kind misses the little ones."

"We miss them too," chimed Qoral. "The merfolk love little humans. Before our troubles, my grandmother told me that our own would guard the shores. We would keep little ones from drowning and often play with them, and even show them wonders beneath the waves." A tear fell from her lovely blue eyes. "It has not been easy for us to hide all these years."

Similar musings started, and Merlin smiled at their fervor.

A tree branch then snapped, startling him and others to silence. Eyes looked up at Madera, who patted the broken limb in her hand.

"Children, so sweet, so innocent, you all say. I agree. Children are kind, naive, and easily excited. So tell me, wizard, what happens when the little ones prattle on about us to their elders? Will they not become excited too, excited to hunt and kill us? And what is worse, those sweet babes will be forced to show them where we hide, and they will do it out of a misunderstood duty to and foolish desire to please those with authority over them. What then, wizard?" Her eyes glistened, and a wicked grin peaked the corners of her mouth, mocking him.

Merlin did not let her gaze ruffle him. Instead, he folded his hands and held her eye.

"You are right, your majesty," he said calmly. "The children would most certainly tell their elders. And why not? How could a child, after seeing any one of you, possibly contain his or her excitement? No, it is impossible. They would run home like little heralds, telling everyone who would listen of the wondrous creature they had seen. And unfortunately, yes, with great resentment, I predict their words would rouse hunters to come looking for you, if not in a foolish attempt to possess your magic, then out of some carnal love for the sport to kill, or worse, for fear of that which they do not understand nor wish to understand.

"People often have a limited scope of mind like that. They cannot fathom your intelligence, so they cannot, or perhaps will not, think an alliance can be struck with you. No. They are always quick to assume the worst, and think it better to strike first than be struck down. Foolish ignorance." Merlin's face darkened, and he wrung his hands, staring at nothing. "Perhaps that is why they have so many wars. Ignorance and greed. And so much that is good is lost, and even good men are struck down."

Merlin fell silent, feeling his chest tighten, and an old pang jabbed his heart. He stood there a moment, lost in a daze, until—

"Merlin?" Drius' calm voice pulled him out of the fog.

Merlin turned around to face the dragon, who looked at him concerned.

"I am sorry, Drius." Merlin looked at the Circle, seeing the uncertainty and confusion in their eyes. "My apologies. Just as you have lost so much to humans, so have I. Time has passed, but the wounds run deep, and I have not yet learned to let go." He cleared his throat and fingered the pages of his Spell Book. "Forgive me. I will move on."

He flipped through the pages till his hand fell on the page titled *Invisibility*.

"There is a way to keep you safe. Here in my Book of Spells, there is a spell for invisibility. I can alter it so that only children will see you. Not their parents nor any adult will see you. You could walk through a village, pass a caravan on the roads, and no man or woman will see you. Should you run by them, they will feel a gust of wind and think little of it. You can roar and shout at them, but they will not hear you. They will be blind to your presence, but their children will see and hear you and know you are real. They may tell their parents, but they will only think their child has a wild imagination. It will be something special for little ones, and I imagine the joy in their hearts will run over till the day comes when they are too old for wonders, and their minds fill with knowledge and learning which clouds their senses. Should be early adulthood, I imagine, for that is when they go to schooling, and young lads and lasses turn to other things, like battles and romance. The veil will fall over their eyes, and they will no longer see you, but then comes the next generation, and so long as children believe in you, you will remain in this world."

The marvel of Merlin's words fell over the gathering like a great wave, and he smiled to see the hope in their eyes and relief on their faces.

"What a wonderful idea," said Qoral, clapping her hands.

"But what is the catch?" Flint shook his feathers. "Magic is not free. It comes at a price, and most times it is too late to turn back when the trouble is finally realized."

Merlin nodded. "There is a catch, as you say, crown phoenix. If I cast this spell, there is no way, at least not that I know of, to break it. It will be permanent. You may prefer this, and that is fine.

"The only thing then is how do you feel about forming a bond with a child who will grow up to forget you? When the day finally comes that they cannot see you, and they pass you by. Can you handle the heartache?"

Madera laughed. "Little chance of that."

Merlin frowned at the harpy.

"Do not mistake me, wizard," she said. "What you say makes sense, and I am certain your plan will work for most who are here, but look at me. Do you really think a child will love me or want anything to do with a loathsome creature like me? A little boy or a little girl will take one look at me and run the other way, screaming in terror."

"You would be surprised, Madera, at the ways of children." Opala pawed the earth. "They have kinder hearts and more gentle spirits than their elders and are not so quick to judge appearances."

Madera glared at the unicorn. "What would you know of it, your grace – you, the most beautiful of all living things? No child has ever recoiled from you. I, on the other hand, have had grown men cry out in horror at the sight of me. No child will want anything to do with me or my own, and even if they did, my kind is not fond of humans."

"True." Opala shook her head. "But I have known the power of a child to warm even the coldest of hearts."

"We are a hateful race," Madera sneered. "It is in our nature to loathe and despise, just as it is with the basilisk. Tell me, wizard, how does he fit into your plan?" She pointed down at the great serpent, and Merlin saw his scales reverberate as he hissed.

"Ssspeak for yourself, harpy," said Silzer.

"But am I wrong?" She stared down at him. "Tell me I am wrong, Silzer."

Silzer said nothing, but his coils stiffened.

Drius stepped forward. "Madera, while it is true there are those here, yourself included, who are less fond of humans, is it not better to put aside your hostility for the sake of your survival? Surely your flock will understand and want to live."

Madera opened her mouth, but another voice cut her off.

"It is a matter of choice," said Sli.

The harpy stared at the sea serpent, bewildered.

"I am no fonder of humans than you are, harpy. My kind is known as the scourge of the sea, a terror beneath the waves. Man has hunted us for a long time, and we have sunken their ships in turn. But times are changing." His viscous eyes fixated on Madera, and she seemed nervous, folding her wings over her chest and looking away at the ground.

"Magic is change, but when the world changes, it is not always for the better. Change, then, is what we fear most. We want life to continue as it always has, but if we are to remain in this world, we must change with it. I speak for my own when I say we want to live on. If children are the only means to that end, then I will harness my nature and encourage my kind to do the same."

Madera closed her eyes and sighed in defeat.

"That isss all well and good for you to sssay, Sli," said Silzer, his head rising but not turning. "You and I are not ssso different. Our kindsss are not for the innocent, not for babesss. You can sssay you will play nice with them, and maybe you will, but I am cursed. Your ssspell, wizard, may render me invisible to adultsss, but ssstill, no child can look at me without dying. I do not sssee then how your plan will help me."

"You are right, king basilisk," said Merlin. "Invisible or not, you are still a threat, so long as you have eyes that bring death to any who look at them. But, I have a solution for this."

The basilisk cocked his head to the side.

"Really, wizard? And what might that be?"

Merlin took a breath, then swallowed. Fresh sweat prickled the back of his neck. "Please permit me to tell you the rest of my plan first, for there is more to it than making you invisible. When I am finished, I will tell you my answer to your deadly sight, and all will make sense."

Silence. All eyes turned to the basilisk, waiting for his response. His coils brushed back and forth, making a horrible grating sound, like cold water on hot metal. Merlin resisted the urge to cover his ears while others grimaced at the sound. Finally, Silzer became still and lowered his head. He sighed, and his forked tongue, just barely in view, flicked the air.

"Very well, wizard. Go on telling usss your plan, but I am anxiousss to know where my kind fits in."

"I promise I will not keep you in suspense, Silzer. Thank you."

Merlin flipped through his Spell Book again and stopped on a page titled, *Spells of Size*. His finger trailed the words, past *To Enlarge*, and stopped on *To Shrink*. He grabbed the bottle and continued.

"On my way home from the shore, it dawned on me that seeing you is not enough. Children need the chance to know you. The sight of you is inspiring, but it is the essence of who you are and what you are that is the true wonder.

"If I had never known Drius, my life would be very empty. The time I have spent with him and his own has made me a better man, as I came to understand and appreciate dragons more than I ever could without his guidance." Merlin flashed a grin at the dragon lord before saying, "Knowing you will mean a lot more to a child than catching a glimpse of you in the wood, the sea, or the sky. I also believe it will do you and your own a lot of good to know children in turn and make friends with them since they are your saviors."

"What are you proposing, Merlin?" asked Aquila, swishing her tail.

"Something strange and a little daunting. I saw this bottle, with its parchment inside, dry and safe, and thought it served well as a carrier. I then thought, what else can it carry?

"Here is what I propose, and I ask that you keep an open mind. You will each choose one of your own to go on a journey. The chosen will come to me, and I will make them small enough to fit inside a bottle—"

"Stop!" Madera glared at Merlin from her perch. "I do not want to hear another word. What you say is madness."

"I am not finished," said Merlin. He held her eye, not yielding.

"You have said enough. Does no one else agree this is absurd?"

Merlin saw the doubt and discomfort in their faces and worried he had lost their faith till Drius said: "Let Merlin finish."

Merlin turned around to look at him. The dragon lord was calm and spoke with confidence.

"Surely not," said Madera. "Even you must realize what he says is idiotic and foolish?"

"I will reserve my judgment till after he has finished telling us his plan. So far, I agree with what he has said, that children can alter our fate, and so they should know us better. And why not? How can a child appreciate what they see, if he or she does not know what it is? Let Merlin finish, and if the majority feel this bottle business is absurd, we can abandon it."

Madera sneered. She looked around for support, but the council was silent.

"Fine," she growled, withdrawing.

"Go on, Merlin," said Drius.

Merlin nodded to him, his grin a silent thanks, and continued.

"As I was saying, I will shrink the chosen, so each of them fits in a bottle. The bottles will have provisions – morsels of food and an enchanted seashell that fills with water. For those of you who live in water, your bottles will be filled as such.

"Each bottle will also contain a note, a note which I will write that tells a child what they must know to properly care for the creature they find. The bottles will be sealed and protected by a charm. Then, if Qoral is willing, the merfolk will ferry these bottles across the sea to new lands and keep watch over them till they are found by little ones.

"The child who should find one of these treasures will take it home and care for it."

"And what do you hope to accomplish by doing this, Merlin?" asked Opala.

"It will be a rare chance for a child to get to know one of your own, for them to form a connection, a bond that has more power, more meaning, in fact, than if that same child was only to catch a glimpse of you and think their eyes played a trick on them."

"You cannot guarantee that a good and kind child will always find the bottle," said the unicorn matriarch.

"No, I cannot guarantee that, but I think there is little need to worry. The magic that surrounds you, that is in you, will protect you, I believe. Magic may not stop the sword or spear of a hunter, but often, I have felt its hand in the little things. I cannot explain it, but I think you know what I mean."

Several nodded. They knew well how strange magic was, and how selective it was in its purpose and action.

"Will our fellows be small forever?" Liliana asked.

"No," said Merlin. "As the child cares for that creature they find, the bond between them and the child's

44

faith in your kind will restore your chosen to their original size."

"Again I ask," said Flint, "what are the drawbacks to the spell?"

Merlin winced. "Well, being so small makes one's voice inaudible for a short while. Only when that creature has grown some will the child be able to hear and understand them. That is why I will include the note so that a child can care for them without that creature struggling to tell them how."

"What if the child cannot read?" asked Glendor.

Merlin hesitated. He had not thought of that. He stroked his beard, thinking, and snapped his fingers when the answer came to him. "I will enchant the parchment. I will put my own voice to the words, so if a child cannot read, my magic will read the note aloud to them."

Glendor frowned. "Seems a lot of work."

"Yes, it is a lot of work, but I do it happily. Much of the workload is mine to bear. The only thing you have to do is choose one of your own for the journey."

"Can you really fit a giant in that tiny bottle?" asked Hamel.

Merlin smiled up at him. "Yes, I can."

"These notes, Merlin," said Liliana, "do you know all there is to know about each and every one of us to write them?"

Merlin blushed. "I must admit, your grace, no, I do not. So, should you all agree to what I propose, I request an audience with each of you so that I may gather the necessary details."

Several creatures nodded and voiced no protest.

"It seems you have thought of everything, Merlin." The fairy queen smiled. "I have no reservations then about your plan."

"Me neither," chimed Qoral. "I think this could work, and should the council agree to your plan, Merlin, my kind will lend you aid. The merfolk will safely carry the bottled treasures across the sea, and I promise they will be brought to pleasant shores and watched over till the children find them."

"Thank you, your grace," said Merlin, bowing his head to her.

"I think your plan is folly," Madera spat. "It may work for those pretty faces here, but what child will want to raise something so terrible and wretched as one of my flock? For ages, humans have done nothing but sneer at us and be afraid of how we look. Children will do no different."

Merlin frowned. Secretly, he thought, *I agree, you are hard to look at, and the way you speak and act is less charming, but...*

He approached the harpy in her tree. He saw the reservation in her eyes but made sure to sound confident when he said, "Madera, I have seen children do wondrous things, including show kindness to those who are different from them and the rest of society. I believe there is a child for every creature that goes on this journey, a child who will marvel and love them, care for them, and be sad when that creature is grown and free to leave them. If magic lets this plan work, then I think it will see to it that the right child finds the harpy you send."

He stared at her, his eyes soft and sincere.

She is frightened and uncertain. Everyone here is.

Madera gazed at him for a time, seemingly unmoved, then looked away and sighed. "Very well, wizard. I hope you are right."

Merlin nodded and returned to his spot behind the green pedestal.

"Thisss is all very touching, wizard," said Silzer, "but again I sssay, your plan will not work for me and my own. Never mind that the child who should find the basilisk I sssend will die on the sandsss of discovery, but you will perish before that when you make one of my own sssmall or put them in the bottle. Ssso let us get to that part of your plan that dealsss with my deadly sssight. Tell me your sssolution. Tell me *now*." His impatience was plain in every hiss.

"Of course, Silzer. Thank you for your patience. I will delay no further."

Merlin took a deep breath and flipped through his Spell Book to a page that read in big letters, *Forbidden.* He grasped the pedestal to keep his hands from shaking.

Heaven help me.

He turned the page, and there, scrawled in dark letters, was *Spells to Uproot Magic*. Merlin stared at it, and he felt an internal restlessness, as his own magic rattled him. A bead of sweat trailed his brow, fell on the page, and vanished.

"I have many spells in this Book. It should come as no surprise then that among them are spells that counteract, revoke, or unbind other forms of magic. There is a spell to remove curses, another that breaks most enchantments. These spells are difficult to use and require the talents of a witch or wizard with a lot of know-how and strength of magic. If one does not have the ability to use such magic, these spells will often throw the enchantment back on the caster and can even kill them.

"One of these spells is very dangerous, and I confess I have never used it, simply because it is unnatural. It goes against the laws and very nature of magic, forcing it to uproot itself."

He saw the discomfort and disapproval in several of the faces looking back at him. This was the sort of magic better left unmentioned and not even acknowledged.

But it is the only way that I see. It will work, if he is willing.

"Quit ssstalling, wizard, and get to the point." Silzer rubbed his coils together, slowly, so the grating sound was soft but no less unsettling.

Merlin's heart quickened. "You, Silzer, and your own were born of magic. A common serpent hatched a chicken's egg, and magic willed that you be its offspring, born with a deadly sight so that any creature which has the misfortune to look directly at you, eye-to-eye, is stricken dead. I find no joy or satisfaction in pulling up magic's roots, especially when they are old and run deep. Your kind has been around for centuries, so the roots are very deep, very old, but I could do it."

The grating grew louder. All around, the Circle became wary. Aquila brought her wings forward to shield herself and Opala. Qoral sank beneath the water, and Liliana was ready to flutter away. Flint spread his wings, ready to take flight, and Glendor was on his feet. Hamel reached for his club and Ulysses for his sword. Drius also stood ready, and Merlin could hear his low growl, as well as the crackling of fire deep within his breast. Even Sli and Madera became rigid, and the harpy moved to another limb and waited.

Merlin could hear his blood pounding in his ears. He took a step back, then firmly planted himself.

I am not a coward. Armies and mad kings…

The words seeped with hot wrath when Silzer spoke again: "You could do what?"

In one quick breath, Merlin said, "I could strip your fellow basilisk of his deadly sight and forever release magic's hold on him."

Everything happened so fast. Merlin had little time to react. He heard several others cry out, and there was a terrible sucking of air in one great *HISS!* A sword was unsheathed – its metal rang, and there was a terrible roaring heat, as Drius breathed fire at the deadly serpent. Merlin saw nothing, for he had turned away, keeping his eyes tightly shut. He thought the basilisk must be quick, for if he were burned, he would have cried out. No, he was fast, the air around him whooshing back. In that brief moment of chaos, Merlin thought his life was going to end.

But the blow never came. There was a sudden silence, and Merlin wondered if he might be dead, that it had come so quickly, he did not feel it.

That does not seem right.

He had seen men die, and most times it was not quiet, nor was it without pain. He opened his eyes and slowly turned around. His mouth fell open, and he stared wide-eyed. Above him was Silzer, his head caught in Hamel's great big hand. The giant's fingers were closed over his face, keeping his jaws shut and hiding his lethal eyes. All around, the Circle stared in amazement, eyes wide and mouths agape like Merlin, as the basilisk's body writhed and wriggled to no avail. For a moment, Merlin thought Hamel might squeeze and crush the serpent's head.

Below, the ground was scorched by Drius' fire. Liliana had flown aside and now looked over Ulysses' shoulder. The centaur held his sword with both hands, ready to strike the basilisk. Madera had come to the ground, the tree which had been her perch now charred, smoking and crackling. She stood close to Sli, a wing raised to shield her eyes from the harsh sunlight, seething and startled.

"Merlin?"

The wizard turned around to face Drius.

"Are you all right?"

Merlin's mouth was dry. His frame shook, and his nerves needed time to settle, but he tried to sound convincing when he replied, "Yes, Drius. I am fine, thanks to Hamel."

The giant did not seem to notice Merlin's words. He only stared at his caught villain. "I should crush you," he said.

Much to his own surprise, Merlin lifted a hand in protest and said, "No, there is no need for that."

Hamel and several others looked at Merlin in disbelief.

"He attacked you. It was not right of him," said the giant.

"No, it was not right, but I understand why he lashed out. I think you all can understand his anger. I told him the only way he and his kind fit in my plan is to strip his fellow basilisk of their magic. Their magic is part of their identity, part of their being. If I strip one of their magic, they become nothing more than a giant snake, terrifying and still capable of much harm, yes, but a great snake nonetheless. Their deadly sight is who they are, as it is for any basilisk. If I perform the spell, I will remove that one's identity and worse yet, I will break their bond with magic. That is it, is it not, Silzer?"

The basilisk lay still in Hamel's hand. Merlin was certain Silzer could hear him.

"I am sorry, Silzer. I meant no harm nor insult, and I am no less comfortable performing the spell than you are to have it cast on one of your own."

There was silence, then Drius stepped forward and leaned his head toward Hamel's fist.

"Silzer?"

The basilisk still did not move.

"I will ask Hamel to put you down beneath the tree, in the shadows, where you were before. He will face you due south, looking away from us. You will not turn around again, or I swear to you, my fire will not miss a second time. Show me that you understand."

There was a pause before the basilisk started to move. He twisted his body to form a knot in his tail. It was a self-crippling action, for with his tail knotted, Silzer would not be able to move or strike as quickly as he did before.

Satisfied, Drius nodded to Hamel, and the giant was careful to place Silzer back in his spot, beneath the smoking tree, facing south. He held his club high in the other hand as he unfurled his fingers from the basilisk's head, ready to crush him if the great serpent struck out.

With his head now free, the basilisk breathed deeply, his scales lifting and falling with each breath. He seethed, "Do that again, giant, and I will kill you."

Hamel still had his club raised, and he looked at Drius for a word. The dragon lord shook his head and said, "You attacked first, Silzer. We are allowed to defend ourselves. You do it again, and you will not be shown the same mercy."

"Nor will any of you. I had my sssights on the wizard when I should have looked on all of you."

"Enough!" Drius snapped, smoke billowing from his mouth. "Perhaps you should leave, and you and your kind can fade away. But if you are here to save your own, you will keep a civil tongue."

Silzer hissed. His body heaved, and his scales rubbed together with that awful sound.

It was then that Merlin stepped between the dragon and the basilisk, with his arms spread out, and, in a loud voice, said, "Stop this!"

The scales ceased to rub. The smoke dissipated, and Drius frowned at Merlin.

"I am sorry, Drius, but this has to stop. No one here needs to die."

Merlin turned to Silzer.

"Silzer, I would beg your forgiveness if I thought you might give it. I am well aware of your dislike for me and all humans. Even before I mentioned the spell, I felt your wrath coming off of you in waves. To this, I say I am here to help you and all those here, in whatever way possible, regardless of your feelings toward me. I took an oath, right here, with you all as witnesses. But if you and others of this council fight now, your races are lost forever.

"I understand your upset. I was born of magic, same as you. If I were stripped of it, I would feel lost and as though a part of me had died. I apologize because I spoke without sensitivity. But you said it yourself: if the child who finds your fellow basilisk looks at them, they will die.

"I do not want to be misunderstood: I do not suggest that you or your entire race go without your magic. I will only cast the spell on the basilisk you choose for the journey. You and yours, save that one, will keep your deadly sight. Let it then be the charge of the one you send to tell the child who finds them the truth. And perhaps, all those here can instruct their own to tell little ones about basilisks. What do you think of this?"

All was quiet in the glade. The only sound was the wind passing through the trees. All eyes were on Silzer, waiting. Merlin held his breath.

Finally, the basilisk's form relaxed, and he sighed.

"Good though your intentionsss may be, wizard, and it isss obvious you have friends here who trussst you, I am not your friend. I do not trussst you. You have a chance to render my kind forever vulnerable. You would do the humansss a great favor by blinding usss. Blind, yesss, for that isss how it would feel."

Merlin paused, then said, "If you want the truth, Silzer, the temptation is there, but I do not pay heed to it. Magic cast with immoral intentions often punishes the caster. I swear I will only cast it on the one you send. I will bind myself with another oath, if I must, to put your mind at ease."

Silence again. Everyone watched the pair – the wizard and the basilisk. Merlin stared at Silzer, his scales rising and falling. His temper may have eased, and his body was no longer rigid, but still, Merlin kept his guard up, a soft glow emanating from his hands.

No one need protect me. This is between me and you. I suspect I will lose, but I will leave a lasting impression on you.

Silzer spoke again in a low voice: "I offer a compromissse, wizard."

"What is it?"

"If the council agreesss to your plan, I will let you cast the ssspell on my fellow basilisk to render him blind, but you will also cast the ssspell on me."

Merlin raised a brow, curious, and waited.

"And I in turn will be allowed to look you in the eye."

Drius growled. "Why?"

Merlin did not look away from Silzer but lifted his hand for Drius to wait.

"I want to know what my fellow basilisk must endure. It isss only right, as I am king, to know hisss ssstruggle. It will also be a test of your magic, to sssee how powerful you really are. I will do the council a great sssservice in thisss way. For how do we know you can really do all that you sssay? You are a wizard but old, and I undersssstand you have not usssed your magic to its greatessst potential in sssome time."

Merlin said nothing to this. He kept a straight face so as not to concern the others.

"Deny it, if you wisssh, but if you are a wizard worth hisss sssalt, you will not mind thisss condition. If you refussse, then I should think you fear your magic will fail."

"Or that you might double-cross him," said Drius.

"I would never. Certainly not with the ressst of the council there. If hisss magic sssucceedsss, and I am sssstripped of my lethal sssight, I would be a fool to harm him, for then sssseveral of you will have the advantage to kill me."

"I accept." The words fell from Merlin's lips like stones, heavy and sure.

"Merlin—" Drius started.

"It is fine, Drius. His offer is more than reasonable, considering what will happen to him. I need only look at him for a moment, but he will have to live the rest of his days without his magic. And he makes another sacrifice in doing so. I presume, Silzer, that if you do this, you will lose your title as the king of basilisks?"

Silzer's tongue flicked the air, and he nodded.

Merlin sighed. "It is only fair then that I agree."

Drius frowned. "Very well, Merlin. It is your choice." He stepped back.

Merlin's heart quaked. He saw the pain this caused his friend, but what else was he to do? He needed the council to trust him, to believe in his magic, and if he objected to Silzer's demands, it might stir feelings of doubt. The basilisk was cunning, and he had laid a fine trap.

"So, we have a deal, Silzer?" asked Merlin.

"Yesss."

The tension in the Circle seemed to dissolve at once. Ulysses sheathed his sword. Hamel put his club behind him. Liliana grew a new flower to sit upon. The whole council eased, and Merlin, feeling the danger had passed, returned the bottle to his satchel and gathered his Spell Book under one arm. With a wave of his hand, the pedestal withdrew, its shoots going back into the earth and leaving no trace of the ground disturbed.

"Thank you, all, for hearing me. My plan is thus laid before you, and it is yours to do with as you please."

"I have a question, Merlin." Aquila raised her wings like one might raise their hand. She focused intently on the wizard as she spoke. "As much as it pains me to credit him, Silzer raised a fair point. He will test you to see if your magic is strong, but now I wonder, the spell of invisibility you hope to cast – how will we know it worked? There will be no child there when you cast it, and the nearest village is miles away. I would not dare make myself known to humans without some assurance. The risk is too great."

Several nodded.

"She is right," said Ulysses. "Not only this, but how will we know your magic reached out to touch our own who will not be with us when you cast it?"

Merlin frowned. Tears threatened, and he took a deep breath, forcing them back. He said, "You will have your assurance, Aquila. I promise you, when I cast the spell, it will be known to you if it worked."

"How?" she asked.

"Magic-born or not, I am still human and grown up. When I cast the spell, I will no longer see you."

A veil of surprise and disbelief descended over the Circle, stitched with remorse. Drius looked the most hurt by this confession, and he brought his great head down to Merlin.

"Merlin…" But he could not find the words to say.

Merlin saw his grief and tried not to cry. "It is fine, Drius. It is a small price to pay to make sure you are safe."

"But that is not fair," said Qoral. "It is like you are being punished for doing good."

Merlin smiled at the mermaid queen. "Not punished. Magic has its own rules, and I am no more exempt from them than any other witch or wizard. And sometimes, we must sacrifice for the greater good."

"A noble sacrifice it is then," said Opala.

"Thank you, your grace. When it is done, I will venture to the homes of your own, and I will declare aloud if I cannot see them. But should I see them, I will cast my magic again and again and again till all are invisible to my eyes. I promise I will leave none of yours without this protection."

This settled the matter. No one said anything more. Merlin bowed to the Circle, and Drius excused him so they could discuss it amongst themselves.

CHAPTER FIVE

The Decision

Merlin did not venture far. He could still see most of the Circle from where he waited but could not hear their conversation, only faint growls, splashes, and hisses.

He sat on a rock, cradling his Spell Book, and mused on what he had said.

I will no longer see you.

Inside, his heart was a well of emotion ready to burst, and as he watched the Great Circle and reflected on the wonder of its creatures, a silent tear traced his aged face.

His mind flurried, as he thought of times past with these and other fantastic beasts. He thought of magic, its pain and despair at the changing times, and how he himself was a relic of the era, he who might be the last wizard and great user of magic in this part of the world.

But I will not fade.

Through watery eyes, he stared at the Circle and set to mind their images.

What if I forget what they look like?

Every detail, every outline, every scale, fin, and feather. Surely, after enough time passed, his mind, old as it was, would misplace their features, forget the majesty of one and the innocence of another.

For my own sake then, I will sketch them.

It would not be the same though, a poor substitute. He put a hand over his heart, a new ache piercing then.

I may forget what it is like…

To see a unicorn. That feeling of conviction when he looked on the purest and loveliest of all creatures. Or the excitement to see a dragon take wing, soaring overhead. To hear the laughter accompanied by fairy antics and games. If he made them invisible, he would not take part in the joys of their existence ever again.

I will be alone.

He, the last magical being, seen but unable to see them.

He dropped his head and sobbed.

But they will be safe.

With a flick of his hand, he produced a handkerchief and blew.

I can save them.

He blew again.

Not only this, but the joy it will bring to children everywhere. How much more will they enjoy the thrills and wonder of these creatures? More than I, an old soul.

He grinned and dried his tears.

I have had plenty of time with them, I suppose. This is best…

He looked at the Circle and sniffed.

For the greater good.

When Drius called him back over, the sun was beginning to set. Most of the Circle looked tired and drawn out, but there was an air of satisfaction and reassurance.

"We have come to a decision," said Drius. "Though other suggestions were made, we see no hope in them. So we have decided to move forward with your plan, Merlin."

Merlin sighed his relief and bowed to the Circle. "I am honored. Thank you for putting your trust in me."

"The council thinks one month should be enough time for us to choose and ready our fellows for the journey, and for you to have your meetings with us and make preparations. Do you agree?"

"A month is plenty of time. Thank you."

"Good. And I want to assure the council that Merlin will not be alone when he comes to see you. I and several of my own will accompany him." Though he addressed the entirety of the Circle, Drius focused his attention on three in particular.

Sli grinned, dripping water from his jowls. Madera nodded, her face grim and arms crossed. And Silzer said nothing, but his scales moved ever so slightly to stir the air before he lowered his head.

A shiver traced Merlin's spine. The thought of seeing them in their territories, in their elements, was unsettling. It could be terrifying, and even dangerous, and he was grateful for Drius' promise of escort.

"Merlin," said Liliana, and he faced her, "you have our gratitude. If this proves successful, we will be forever in your debt." She bowed to him.

"Th-Thank you, your grace."

She lifted her eyes, looking into his. "From here on, our lives and that of our own are in your hands." She said this with a calm directness, like the launch of an arrow. It hit its mark.

Merlin tried to smile, but something old, a memory suppressed, chose then to come to the surface of his conscience, upsetting his composure. His brow furrowed as he tried to push it away.

"Merlin?"

The wizard rubbed his temple before looking up at Drius. He saw the concern staring back at him.

"Are you feeling well? You are suddenly pale."

"I am fine, Drius. Too much excitement at once."

He forced a grin, but the dragon lord stared at him, unmoved.

"Really, Drius, I am fine. More than fine, but it has been a long day, and I am tired. Looking around, I would say most of us are ready for sleep."

Several nodded, and a couple even yawned.

"Yes, I am eager to rest, but all the more eager am I to meet tomorrow and start my work."

No one else seemed worried after Merlin, but Drius still frowned. He was not so easily taken in by Merlin's words, and Merlin expected as much. Drius knew him better than most.

In a final, desperate attempt to settle the matter, Merlin nodded once to the dragon, a silent hint to let it go…for now. Drius looked displeased, but he nodded back and did not persist.

"We are agreed then," he said. "In one month's time, we will meet on the shore to bid our chosen farewell, and Merlin will cast his magic to draw the curtain on our fate."

There were no goodbyes or farewell pleasantries. The twelve went their separate ways without another word. It seemed so final, as if this silent, beautiful glen at the heart of an enchanted forest might never see them again.

CHAPTER SIX

The Flight Home

For most of the flight home, Merlin and Drius were silent. Below them, the trees of the enchanted forest gave way to rolling fields of summer grass, tall and swaying. A great distance west, the sun was setting beyond the faint blue rim of the sea, and the skies were like fire. Due north were the mountains, bare of snow, imposing and solemn. Everything was beautiful, yet Merlin could not appreciate the view.

The memory that reared its head at the Circle was still upsetting him. He shut his eyes, but behind their lids, he saw flashes in his mind's eye of war, panic, and death, and he heard a faint but sinister cackle. He was so caught up in it, in the past and his internal struggle to push it away, that he failed to notice Drius slowing up till the dragon settled in a field of heather.

Merlin opened his eyes and looked around, confused.

"Why do we stop here? Is something wrong, Drius?"

"You tell me, old friend." Drius looked back at him, his eyes searching for the truth.

Merlin fidgeted. He knew better than to lie to his oldest friend, and besides, Drius would not take them home till he confessed. With a heavy sigh, he dismounted. He sat in the heather and looked out over the fields. Some ways off, there was a pond, its waters calm and shimmering. All was quiet and peaceful.

Drius lay beside him, with one clawed foot crossed over the other and his wings folded back.

Merlin closed his eyes and put his hands flat on the ground. His spirit calmed with the strength of the earth. He listened to the breeze and felt it play with his hair. He took several deep breaths and quieted his aura before beginning.

"Drius, you know me well. You know my history, and I have told you a great deal about myself. You, in turn, have shared with me, and for a long time now, we have been able to tell each other most anything, and neither of us can hide much from the other. It does not surprise me that you saw something was amiss with me at the Circle."

A bad memory haunts me and makes me nervous, he wanted to say, but he hesitated.

He looked up at the dragon lord, but Drius did not look back. He stared ahead, out over the fields, at nothing. He did not see, but he was listening, Merlin knew.

"I am eager to save you and your own, and the others in the Circle and theirs, but I am also nervous. It is a lot of responsibility, and I know, I pledged myself to it. I worry though that I may let you all down, that I may fail in some way. Silzer is right. I am an old wizard, and my magic is old too." He then sat up and said with a little more mettle in his voice, "But that does not mean I am unable to cast it or that it will not work. I will do it, Drius. Everything I promised today, I will do it."

Drius still did not look at him. He stayed quiet for some time, and the only sounds to be heard were his breathing and the gentle rushes of the breeze. Merlin stared ahead and waited. When Drius finally did speak, he closed his eyes.

"I lost my temper with the council."

Merlin blinked at him. "What?"

"After I excused you, I opened the Circle so others could voice suggestions as to how we might save our kinds. Madera insisted we fight the humans and take back our territories. She wishes so much for bloodshed and revenge. I understand her want, but I also disagree with it, as does most of the council. Violence is rarely the answer in matters concerning humans and magic-born. Would you not agree?"

"Oh, most certainly." Merlin picked a sprig of heather and held it to his nose. Its rich scent was soothing, and he twirled it between his fingers.

What are you getting at, Drius?

Merlin did not want to seem impatient, but it appeared they had trailed off topic. He watched Drius as he continued to speak in a calm, controlled manner, his eyes still closed.

"We discussed approaching the humans and trying to talk to them, but as I told you before, unless people are willing to listen, they cannot hear us. And besides, the fiercer of the council would have a difficult time of it.

"We eventually circled back to your plan. Naturally, we thought over its drawbacks and pitfalls, but most agreed it is a good plan, and that you had thought of everything and seemed eager to help us in our plight. We were just beginning to settle our minds when Sli spoke up.

"He asked the council, as a whole, why we should trust you. I thought we settled the question before, and he assured me he meant no offense when he said, you being my close friend, I was apt to take your side. He said your oaths and promises were worth little to him, for he does not know you, and he wanted others of the council to testify to your character.

"I held my tongue at first to give others a chance to speak, but most had not met you before today. Liliana was the first to say that you have been her guest at many fae festivities in her forest, and that she had come to love you after you healed their Sacred Tree many years before. Then Aquila told us how you saved the foal, and Opala followed with how you saved her herd, during their migration, from a band of hunters who had laid a trap to ensnare them, but you snuck them by unharmed.

"Though he heard these stories, Sli was not convinced. He still wanted more, and that was when I lashed out at him."

Merlin recalled seeing, from where he had waited, Drius snapping his jaws at the sea serpent and Sli reeling back, his fins taut and teeth bared. He had wondered what had happened, but he rooted himself to his spot and swore he would not venture over, for one, he was an outsider, and these creatures handled disputes differently than people, and second, if a fight did break out, he might only get in the way. The event did not need much consideration though, for the moment passed just as quickly as it had started. Drius pulled back, and Sli settled. Drius then spoke, his mouth moving, and all eyes focused on him.

"It was my testimony that convinced him," said Drius. "It convinced them all, for no one asked again about your character. Can you guess which story I told them?"

Merlin looked at the scar on Drius' wing. "I think I can." He thought back:

It was a bitter winter night. The wind howled like a hungry wolf, and it shook my hovel so bad, I thought the roof might cave. I was hunkered down, wrapped in a heavy blanket, trying to sleep, when a light shone under my door. I felt a presence, neither friend nor foe, and I went to answer.

Outside, faring well in spite of the weather, was a will-o'-the-wisp. Its cold blue light hovered over the snow, and it danced around, beckoning me to follow it. Often I ignore these tricksters, but the way it carried on, I knew something was wrong. I grabbed my cloak and followed after it into the snowstorm.

I thought I was out of my mind. The cold bit at me, hungry and cruel. Ice crystals formed in my beard and on my brows. My teeth chattered, and I thought there was nothing worse than numb fingers and toes. But still, I followed, feeling compelled to, by what I am not certain, but if I had to venture a guess, I would say fate...or maybe magic.

The will-o'-the-wisp took me to the foot of a mountain and begged me to climb. I felt put out, and though the storm was starting to settle, I had neither the footwear nor the patience for such a feat. I was about to turn and leave when, over the wind and snow, I heard a low moan. It was sad and full of pain, and it came from up the mountain. The will-o'-the-wisp pleaded again. I was curious but also concerned. I am almost certain magic was afoot that night, directing my path. Something inside told me to keep going, so I rolled up my sleeves and started to climb.

It was a precarious ascent. One slip, and I would be gone. As I climbed, the wail got louder. It was mournful and broke my heart to hear it. I tried to ascend faster. The will-o'-the-wisp lit my way so I could better see my footholds and handholds. Finally, I came upon a cave. The source of the moan was inside, and the will-o'-the-wisp insisted I go in. My heart quaked, for there at the cave entrance were the charred remains of two men, their bodies smoking. Their weapons were melted and set into the ground, and I knew then a dragon was there.

Saying a silent prayer, I ventured inside, and there, giving me a fright, was a large silver dragon — a female — lying on the floor, a spear wedged in her heart and the vacant stare of death in her eyes. Behind her was a nest, disturbed and broken, and two crushed eggs, the lives in them snuffed out. There was also a great green dragon with golden wings — one wing torn, his breathing shallow. He cradled the last egg, still intact, and wept. He was the silver dragon's mate.

When the dragon saw me, he roared in fury but did not move. He could have burned me like the two lost souls outside, but he hesitated. He knew me, and I knew him. We had met before, in passing, and Drius, the lord of dragons, never forgets a face.

I sensed you were tired and had fought a good fight. You told me to leave, but I said no, and I explained how I had come to be there. The will-o'-the-wisp had disappeared without a trace, but I had no reason to lie, and I told you that magic, or fate, had brought me there with purpose.

You growled as I came forward, the sounds echoing off the cave walls, but when I laid my hand on your shoulder, you grew quiet. I mended your wing as best I could. I ventured down and back up the mountain with herbs and bandages to clean and dress the wound. Too much time had passed to cast a healing spell, so you were left with that painful scar. It was morning when I finished attending to you. I asked you if I could put the dead to rest, and you said yes. I carried wood up the mountain and built a funeral pyre for your mate and little ones. You lit its fire, and we watched them pass from this world to the next. For the villains who caused your grief, I dragged their remains down the mountain and buried them in unmarked graves.

I built a new nest for your sole heir, the egg you saved. You kept watch over it, kept it warm, giving your wing time to heal. I brought you food and water, and also changed your bandages, and when the day came that you were able to fly again, you invited me to stay.

Merlin smiled.

And I have stayed for many years now, and I gained a loyal friend.

"Thank you, Drius, for speaking well of me. I know it still pains you to think back on that night."

The dragon opened his eyes and looked up at the sky. The first stars were twinkling. Merlin saw a tear in his eye.

"I still miss her after all this time…my beloved. I miss my little ones who never had their beginnings. But at least I have Isla, thanks to you, Merlin."

Isla, Drius' only living heir, the sole egg that had not been broken.

"It was after I was well again that I called together the first Great Circle, for I was convinced then that the humans would not stop, that something needed to be done. And something must be done again, here and now, something permanent."

The dragon lord lowered his gaze and smiled at Merlin. "The council is convinced of your noble character, and no one dared to say another word about it. To have done so would have been a great insult to me, to Isla, and to my fallen."

Merlin said nothing. He made a gesture with his hand, placing it on his heart, and bowed his head to Drius. It was a sign of loving respect.

Drius stood up and fanned his wings. "No matter how frightened or nervous or unsure you feel about the task before you, Merlin, I believe in you. You can rely on my faith to give you strength."

Merlin beamed. The comfort of Drius' words radiated within him, warming him, and the memory that troubled him before was forced into a full retreat. He got to his feet, brushed the dirt from his seat, and placed a hand on the dragon's shoulder.

"Thank you, Drius."
"No. Thank you, Merlin."

CHAPTER SEVEN

The First Meeting

Merlin did not delay in his work. The following day, which was the first of the month given him by the Circle, he made a list of all the things he had to do and started checking them off with another walk on the beach. There, he gathered seashells which he would enchant to hold water so no creature grew thirsty on their journey.

When he returned to his cave, he made duplicates of the original bottle and cleaned them thoroughly, making them ready for their precious cargo. The original, with both its parchments still enclosed, he laid on his desk amidst other mementos.

All the while he worked, he hummed a merry tune, and his thoughts ran away with him.

I am as light as a feather. I am as happy as a child.

(But you are also sad.)

Sad, a little, yes, because I will miss them, but let's think on this: it is good work. If my plan is a success, then many years from now, these creatures will still be here, even after I am gone. It will be my last good work. My legacy.

Drius came to see him on the second day. He found Merlin at his desk, scrawling notes and studying his Spell Book, while all around him, there was activity. Papers floated in the air, each with its own dancing quill. The quills flew to the ink pot, dabbed their heads, then returned to the pages and scribbled in a frenzy. At the potions table, instruments of science hopped about as vials from the ingredients curio drifted over, and dashes and pinches and much mixing happened, with plumes of colored clouds spurting into the air.

The dragon lord laughed, for the cave had never been so alive with magic.

"What is all of this?"

Merlin lifted his gaze, his spectacles balanced on the bridge of his nose, and smiled.

"Chaos, I suppose." He laughed. "No, what you see here"—he indicated the papers and quills—"is a neat trick. I thought, since I will no longer see you or the others, I should make sketches so I remember what you look like when my mind goes. Oh, do not look so sad, my friend."

"I am sad for you."

"I am coming to terms with it. As I said before, it is for the greater good. But this is neat, do you not think so? The quills are tapped into my memory and draw each of you precisely. Then the paints, which are being made over there,"—he pointed at the potions table—"will color them. I admit some creatures, like Flint with his brilliant feathers or Qoral with her shimmering scales, are nigh impossible to capture in art. But then again, there is no substitute for the real thing."

Merlin beamed at Drius, his heart alight, and the dragon lord smiled.

"But what brings you here, Drius? A visit? I can put on some tea."

"No, thank you, Merlin. I only came to tell you that Opala has sent us word. She would like to see you tomorrow."

Color filled Merlin's cheeks. "Wonderful. I am looking forward to it."

"As am I. I will gather you in the morning."

The sun shone brightly, and there was not a cloud in the sky on the third day. Merlin stared up at the great blue overhead as he rode upon Drius' back.

"Have you ever wondered, Drius, what is beyond up there?"

"Only once, when I was young. Now I think it best to leave such mysteries a mystery. If I were meant to know, I would have been given the means to find out. At least I can see the blue, and the stars, and appreciate them."

They flew south to Greenwood, another enchanted forest. It was smaller than the wood where the Great Circle met but still lovely. It was home to Opala and the unicorn herd, but also to Liliana and her fairy kingdom. There were other creatures, too, like nymphs, brownies, and fauns, but Merlin could not remember the last time he saw one of them.

Greenwood was a wonderful place, so full of magic that when Merlin stepped foot on its grounds, he could feel it. It was like static, making the wizard feel all tingly, with pleasant goose pimples on his arms. The magic came from the unicorns and fairies. Together, they sealed the forest off from humans. It was not on any map, for those who had seen it would forget where it was, and when a person did stumble upon it, they would often run away in fear, claiming the trees were alive.

The unicorns and fairies also used their magic to help the forest grow. The trees, though younger than trees in other nearby woods, were two, maybe three times taller, and so thick around, you could not hope to link hands if you hugged one. Flowers grew in abundance, dabbing the woods with color. It was a charming place, and Merlin often thrilled to visit it.

But today, he felt a chill when Drius settled at the forest's edge. He took a few steps forward, but the trees did not even shudder, not a leaf twitched. That static feeling was gone, and the wood felt natural and less enchanted.

Opala stepped out from behind a great oak and bid them enter.

Merlin bowed to her, then said, "Opala, what has happened to Greenwood? The magic here is weaker since last I visited."

The unicorn tossed her head. "Follow me, and I will tell you what has happened here."

They passed through the wood in silence. The grass beneath their feet was still wet with the morning dew, and beams of sunlight glittered through the trees. They came to a clearing with a crystal blue pond. The unicorns were there, drinking and grazing and watching the foals play. Their heads turned when their matriarch appeared with her guests. The clearing grew suddenly quiet, and Merlin thought they might flee until Opala lifted her head and whinnied. A calm then descended, and the unicorns returned to their doings.

"Forgive them," said Opala. "We have never had a dragon here, and most remember you, Merlin, save the little ones. It is in our nature to be excitable. It may be why we have stayed alive for so long. But I am saddened to live this way, unable to trust and having to run away from everything. There was a time when we were appreciated and revered, and humans were proud to have our image on their coat of arms."

"I remember," said Merlin. "Some still have it, I am sure."

"But they know not its significance. Please sit."

Opala lay by the pond, tucking in her hooves, and Merlin and Drius did as asked. They looked over the waters at the unicorns, and Merlin marveled at them. Most were white, but one was as black as night – a stallion, and he played with the foals, chasing them, then taking turns at being chased. He was large, strong, and sturdy but gentle.

"My mate," said Opala, watching him fondly, "Obsidian."

"He is handsome," said Merlin.

"That he is."

"How long have you and he been a pair?"

"A pair?" She nickered at the word. "For many suns and moons. We can no longer count. But then time means little to our kind." She tossed her head, her mane shimmering in the sun. "But come, Merlin, you asked about the wood." Her eyes softened with worry. "You are not wrong. The magic here is not what it once was."

"It feels like it has grown ill or is dying." Merlin grimaced at his choice of words.

Opala nodded. "Merlin, the magic of my herd and Liliana's fairies for a long time has kept this wood alive and well, but now it withers. I believe it is because humans do not believe in us anymore."

"Truly?"

"It must be. After we went into hiding, the fairy queen and I noticed that as time passed, our forest lost more of its luster. We can still perform feats of magic. The fairies can make flowers grow, and my kind can still purify water, but we have not been able to wake the trees for some time, and I worry should a human come here and know how to return."

"I can cast my magic to help," said Merlin hastily.

"Thank you, Merlin. That is a kind offer, but if your plan works, our forest may not have to be hidden anymore. Liliana and I are discussing the matter, but if we are invisible, we may let humans come and go as they please and have little to worry over."

"Forgive me for disagreeing, your grace. A place like this, full of wonder and so beautiful, should last forever. I know how people are. I have seen them cut down many woods and plow many fields. It would break my heart if the same should happen here."

"You love Greenwood so much?"

"I adore it, and I adore you and your own, and Liliana and hers too. This place should remain. It is your home and a sanctuary to others."

"Others?"

Merlin nodded. "The nymphs, fauns, brownies, and the like."

Opala glanced at Drius. The dragon lord turned away and sighed. "Some are still here." She looked back at Merlin. "You will hardly ever see them, or they have changed. Like that tree over there, the one blossoming with pink flowers."

Merlin saw it. It was a small tree, and its branches, with their pink blooms, stretched over the water.

"That tree was a nymph once. Her name was Nyneve. She was lovely and liked to dance by the water in song with her sisters. But she was not as carefree as them, and she became afraid of change and uncertainty in the growing world. Then, one day, she said a prayer to become a tree. She spoke with me before this and said she would ask to be an apple tree so my herd could take of her precious fruit. A gift to us, she said, since she loved us so."

Merlin's eyes misted, and he batted at them with his sleeve. "Are her sisters still here in Greenwood?"

"They are somewhere. I doubt you will see them."

"I suppose not." Merlin looked around, and all he could see were the unicorns.

But that does not mean we are not being watched.

He reached into his satchel and produced a leather-bound journal, quill, and ink pot. He opened the journal to the first page, which had *Unicorns* scrawled at the top. He dabbed the quill in the ink pot and poised the tip over the paper.

"If it pleases you, your grace, I should like to ask you about your kind so that the letter I write tells a child all they need to know to care for the unicorn they find."

"Of course. Where would you like to begin?"

He started with something simple: what unicorns like to eat, or as Merlin called it, their *diet*. He then asked where unicorns tend to live – their *habitat* – and how they slept – their *bedding*. He inquired about their nature and mannerisms, or *behavior*, and how a unicorn should be handled and addressed.

Once they had gone over all those details, Opala asked, "What else would you like to know, Merlin?"

He hesitated. The unicorn matriarch had been patient and very kind in answering his questions, with eloquence and an appreciative amount of detail. But he stared at a word jotted down in his journal and spun the quill between his fingers.

"There is something else? Do not hold back," she said.

He looked at her, and her eyes were calm and full of peace.

Merlin asked, "Can you tell me about your magic?"

Her manner did not change, but she stared at him, maybe into him. Merlin thought she could see his heart and its intentions and believed no secret was ever safe from her.

"Do you worry I will say no?" There was a lilt in her voice.

He nodded.

"A child can know such things. Even if you did not tell them in your letter, the unicorn they should find would no doubt reveal the truth on their own. But I have one condition."

"Name it."

"You must convey in your letter what so few know. Humans hunted us because they thought that by taking our horns, they could wield our magic. This is not so. Our magic is for us. Only we can use it, and once our horn is cut, we die, and our magic dies with us. You must put that in your letter, so no child misunderstands like their elders."

"I will mention it."

Opala then told Merlin about her magic, and how her kind could heal sick trees and superficial wounds. She told him that where a unicorn stayed, it was always spring and summer, and her own had never known a winter. But most important though was her kind's ability to purify water.

"Take a drink, Merlin," she said, indicating the pond.

Not one to refuse, and feeling parched, Merlin got up and walked to the bank. He stooped, cupping his hands to lift the water to his dry lips. It was cool, pleasant, and refreshing. One sip, and he was no longer thirsty, but more than this, Merlin noticed the aches of old age melt away. His bones did not creak when he stood up. His back no longer hurt, nor did his knees. He felt as much as he did in his youth, and he thought he might weep, for it had been so long since he had not felt his age.

Opala and Drius watched him be overcome with joy. He laughed through his smile and stretched his arms upward, twisting his torso left then right.

"There is no pain. None at all," he said gaily. "Thank you, your grace." He took a knee before the unicorn matriarch. "Tell me, what is this? When you said your kind could purify water, I did not think this. There is something more here."

"My herd purified this water a long time ago, and every year we touch it again with our horns to keep it so. This is the only pool of its kind. It is not a cure-all. It will not heal fatal wounds or illness, but it can make one feel better."

"I should say so. Remarkable!"

"Take some with you. I am certain you have means of doing so."

"Oh, I could not accept such a generous gift."

"Yes, you can, and you will, or it would be a great insult to me."

Merlin smiled at her wit. He retrieved a goatskin from his satchel and filled it with the precious water.

"As I said, you will not find another pool like this. A single unicorn cannot achieve this feat. By itself, it can only purify water to drink. I thank heaven our pool is still so good when our magic over the wood has faded."

"Why do you think that is?" Merlin put the goatskin back in his satchel, as well as his quill, ink pot, and journal.

"My guess? The Great Creator, the greatest power and authority there is, watches over us and is kind enough to let us keep it. Without this water, most of what lives in this wood would have nothing to drink, and it has kept most of us well."

Merlin thought on this, then said, "Well, I hope the blessing continues."

"As do I."

Their meeting over, Opala led them back to the edge of the forest.

"Merlin," she said, "what you hope to do for us is noble. I assure you that none of mine think little of it. When all is said and done, I hope you will come back to Greenwood often. You may not see us, but we will see you. You may not hear us, but speak aloud, and we will hear you. You will never be alone."

"Thank you, your grace. That is comforting to know. I will come back. I promise."

"Good. Take care of him, Drius."

"No need to worry for that," said the dragon lord, hunching down to let Merlin climb aboard.

"Till we meet again." Opala reared up, kicking at the air with her hooves, and whinnied. She then turned and galloped out of sight into the wood.

CHAPTER EIGHT

The Secret Garden

Early the next morn, Liliana sent her messenger to retrieve Merlin. The messenger was a spritely fellow dressed in blues and wore a jaunty blue cap with speckled feathers. His name was Nut, short for Nutmeg.

He blew a small trumpet and proclaimed, "Her majesty requests an audience with you and Lord Drius. You are both invited to tea."

Drius, with Merlin astride, followed Nut back to Greenwood, to another part of the forest. They landed in a glade surrounded by lesser trees with a magnificent 500-year-old wisteria tree at its center. The hefty boughs reached out like many arms, each one blossoming with thousands of purple flowers. This was the Sacred Tree of the fairies. In its thick twisted trunk, there was a hidden door that opened with a spoken word from the fae. Its bark would then peel back into a smile to reveal the tree was mostly hollow, with little shelves and beds carved out and dressed with leaves and flower petals for the fairy folk to sleep upon.

Beneath the tree, there grew an abundance of flowers of many colors, as well as mushrooms and toadstools. Here, the queen sat with her husband, the king, her children, the little princes and princesses, and several figures of her royal court. Before them was a blanket of moss, and on it sat teacups of different sizes, three teapots, and several plates of goodies.

"Welcome, Merlin. Welcome, Drius," said Liliana. "Please have a seat."

"Thank you, your grace," said Merlin, being careful of the flowers and mushrooms as he sat down.

Drius sat, too, and folded in his wings, being mindful of the fairies that were flittering about, coming and going from the tree, or waiting to serve their guests.

The queen clapped her hands, and several fairies dressed in pink with yellow buttercups on their heads poured the honeysuckle tea and passed teacups to their guests. There was a very large teacup for Drius, and the fairies struggled to carry it, but he was quick to relieve them.

The lavender cakes and posy tartlets were delightful, and Merlin had to stop himself from eating too many strawberry scones. It was a beautiful spread.

As they sipped their tea, Merlin asked Liliana his questions about the fairy folk and jotted down her answers in his journal. Every now and then, she consulted the king, asking him if he agreed with what she said, to which he always said, "Yes, my dear," or "I could not have said it better, my love."

The children grew antsy and asked if they could go play. Liliana excused them, and for a while, she, her court and guests watched the youngsters get caught up in fox races. Each prince or princess had a fox – two reds, one silver, and one white, and they would sit astride them and race around the Sacred Tree three times. Whoever came in first won bragging rights for the fastest fox.

"Merlin," said Liliana after the third race, "what other questions do you have for me?"

Merlin looked over his scrawling and said, "I think you have told me everything, your grace. I look forward to writing this letter. I admit I did not know even half as much about fairies as I do now."

"Excellent. Then I would like to ask you something."

"What, your grace?"

She turned to the king. "Darling, will you and the others excuse us?"

"Of course, my love." He kissed her cheek and, with the court following his lead, floated back to the tree.

"Merlin, do you know of my secret garden?"

Merlin's eyes lit up. "Yes, I do, your grace. Your fairies often speak of it, and you yourself once told me its whereabouts. You said it grows underground, beneath your Sacred Tree. A garden that grows without sunlight, all aglow in the dark. Its flowers and plants thrive on bottled moonlight, a sprinkle of fairy dust, and your own magic. You also told me it is a sacred place, and only you and your fairies can visit there."

"I did say that." She smiled. "But now I wonder if you might accept my invitation to see it?"

Merlin's mouth gaped in surprise, and he leaned forward, his voice shaking with giddiness. "Really, your grace?"

She nodded.

"It would be an honor. But uh, how do I get there? I am so large, after all, and the way there is so small."

"Well, I thought you might cast that spell of yours, the one you hope to use on our fellows to make them small? Surely you can cast that on yourself, could you not?" Her eyes gleamed.

She tricked me!

Merlin would have laughed at her cleverness, but he held it in to not be rude. The bitter truth was, and he did not want to let it out, that he had never cast the spell on a living thing. He had shrunk large, inanimate objects but never a person or beast.

Well, I cannot refuse, or she may lose faith in me, and then word could spread to the others.

Drius did not look pleased about this but said nothing.

"Certainly, your grace," said Merlin. He folded his hands, with his pointer fingers directed at himself, bowed his head, and closed his eyes. He cleared his mind and thought only of the spell which was back home in his Spell Book. He knew the words, and he chanted them under his breath.

The immediate sensation was strange and nauseating. Merlin felt himself descending, being compressed, and he did not open his eyes till all manner of motion ceased.

"Merlin?" That was Drius.

Merlin opened his eyes and was startled to see the flowers and mushrooms so big.

"Merlin?"

Merlin looked up and fell over when he saw Drius' great big snout looming over him.

"How do you feel?"

Merlin caught his breath and patted his chest for his heart to stop racing. "I feel queasy."

Liliana floated over to him. "Drink this." She offered him a teacup with golden liquid.

"What is it?"

"Pure nectar. It will help you feel better."

He sipped it down. It was very sweet, and when it found his center, he felt warm inside. His stomach settled, and the dizziness passed. "Thank you, your grace." He put a hand to his throat. "Is that my voice?" It had gone up a couple of octaves and was now light and tingling like a bell.

"I am sure your voice will adjust," said Liliana. "He is fine, Drius. His voice is a bit high, so it may be difficult to hear him."

The dragon lord nodded.

Merlin stood up, planting his feet, and found he was only a hair shorter than the queen.

Good. I made myself the proper size. It would have been rude to still tower her.

He stared at her, enchanted by her beauty and outward charm – how her magic glistened in her skin and danced in her hair, the lilt in her smile, and the gleam of gold in her eyes. All those things he vaguely noticed as a grown person, he infinitely appreciated when small.

"I am pleased to see your spell works, Merlin. I am a queen of my word. Take my hand, and I will show you my garden. But first, take off your sandals."

"My sandals?"

"Yes."

He did not question her further. He kicked off his sandals and scrunched up the dirt between his toes.

"Excellent." She offered her hand, and Merlin took it. "Do not fret, Drius. I will not keep him long." She gave the dragon a reassuring smile. "Now take a breath, Merlin."

She beat her wings, stirring up a cloud of fairy dust in Merlin's face. He sneezed. Then he felt her lift him off the ground by his hand, and the pair floated toward the Sacred Tree. He laughed as the earth passed beneath them.

"This is incredible," and he was pleased to hear his voice returning to its usual pitch and quality so soon.

The queen smiled. "I suppose I take it for granted, but it is wonderful to fly." She put a hand on the tree and spoke a word in a language Merlin did not know.

The bark parted, showing the many shelves with their astonished occupants, all watching, fascinated by their queen and her guest. The pair floated down into the tree – down, down – till they left the shelves behind and descended into darkness. Merlin fidgeted and tried not to squeeze the queen's hand. He wondered how many leagues beneath the ground they were and, still descending, thought if he were left there, it would be a prison he could never escape.

But soon his feet touched on cool, grainy soil, and Liliana said, "We are here." She gave his hand a gentle squeeze and let go.

Merlin panicked at her sudden absence.

"Your grace?"

"Trust me, Merlin." Her voice floated through the air. She was no longer beside him.

Merlin tried to keep his breathing steady, but it came out shaky. The air was cooler down here, and he rubbed his arms.

Suddenly, a soft glow broke the darkness, and when his eyes adjusted, Merlin saw it was Liliana. Her fair skin and wings emitted a golden light, and he watched with fascination and curiosity as she touched a flower, and it glowed a pale blue. At once, the light spread till the whole of the leafy, budding bush illuminated. The queen touched another flower, a lily, and it gleamed white. Each time she touched something, its life illumined, and the light spread throughout the underground till Merlin found himself surrounded by a luminous garden of white, blue, and violet glowing flowers.

He gaped in wonder, misty-eyed before its splendor. Some flowers glittered while others sparkled. Overhead, the Sacred Tree's roots could be seen, dressed with splotches of soft glowing moss. It was a new world down there.

"What do you think of it?" Liliana asked. She stood beneath an arch of silver vines.

"I…I have no words. To say it is beautiful does not do it justice."

"Truly?"

"Truly, your grace. No garden above can compare with the splendor of this one."

Her smile brightened, and she walked amongst the flowers. "It took many years of patience and love and magic to get it to look like this. Most of these flowers I made myself, enchanting seeds from above to change their properties. These are my favorite."

Merlin walked over to her, and before them stood several bright stalks bearing brilliant five-petaled flowers of light blue and purple, with white anthers at their centers. They shimmered and looked like fallen stardust.

"What are they?"

"Delphinium. They grow on the surface too, but these ones are special. They possess my magic." She knelt and reached her hand deep in the soil to bring forth a glowing bulb full of seeds. "If the flowers are harvested at the peak of their bloom, they can be used to make a potion that will help one sleep the final sleep with no pain." She stood and offered the bulb to Merlin.

Merlin stared at her, stupefied.

"Take it, Merlin. It is my gift to you. You can enjoy the beauty of its flowers, and when your time draws near, as it does for us all, you can use those flowers, if you wish."

Merlin took the bulb and stared at it with wonder.

"Your grace…" He struggled to find the right words. "Thank you. I only wish there was something I could give you."

"You already have, Merlin. You have given me hope."

They returned to the surface, and with Liliana's gift in hand, Merlin cast the spell to grow big again. The sensation of rising fast and being stretched out did not bother him so much as the feeling of becoming small, and he sighed his relief when he was his actual size once more. He was also delighted to see the bulb had grown several times its original size with him and was careful to pack it in his satchel before climbing aboard Drius' back.

As they gathered air, putting distance between themselves and the Sacred Tree, Liliana, the king, and their court waved them farewell.

CHAPTER NINE

A Heavenly Ride

That night, Merlin was in his cave, eating supper, when he heard the soft beating of wings, followed by the clopping of hooves. He stepped outside to inquire and was surprised to see a great black winged horse.

"Merlin?" His voice was deep but gentle.

"Yes?"

"My name is Orpheus. Aquila wishes an audience with you tonight. I am here to collect you."

"Now?" Merlin looked at the moon, full and bright, creeping up in the sky. It was not late yet, but even if it had been, he supposed there was little chance he could, or would, refuse. He nodded once and said, "Let me grab my things."

He scurried back inside to gather his satchel and put on his sandals. He hesitated when Orpheus whinnied till he heard another pair of wings, more powerful and familiar.

"No need to fret," said Merlin, returning outside. He looked up and smiled to see Drius' silhouette gliding across the night sky. "The lord of dragons does not sleep when the moon is high. No doubt he saw you coming."

The dragon lord settled to the ground before them, dust whirling beneath him.

"A late-night visitor, Merlin?"

Orpheus snorted.

"This is Orpheus. Aquila sent him to gather me for an audience."

"I thought as much. Welcome, friend."

Orpheus bowed low to Drius. "My lord dragon, I did not mean to disturb you. I am only here for the wizard."

"It is well you did disturb me, for I am coming with him."

Orpheus shook his head. "My matriarch—"

"Your mare matriarch will not mind, I am certain. She and I get along well enough, and I swore at the Great Circle that I would accompany Merlin on these visits, so do not try to shake me off." He peered down at Orpheus, who took a couple steps back, but Merlin saw no hostility in the dragon's eyes. He was calm and spoke with emphasis.

Orpheus snorted again. "As you wish, lord dragon. But we must hurry. The night is young, but its hours fly fast, and there is much Aquila wants to show the wizard." He walked over to the edge and spread his wings.

Merlin raised a brow. "Show me?"

The winged horse looked back, his eyes deep and thoughtful, and nodded before leaping off and taking flight.

"Well then, I best not keep her waiting. Ready, Drius?"

They flew through the still night in pursuit of Orpheus. Below, the earth slept, and so did most of creation. Somewhere, a wolf howled, and its fellows returned its call. Shadows crept in the moonlight, sneaking and sliding over the landscape. Above, the air was crisp and clean, and the sky was clear and bejeweled with a thousand stars. Merlin marveled at it.

Look at them all up there. If heaven were a mine, and the dwarves could reach it, no substance on earth could compare with what is buried up there.

"Beautiful," he said under his breath.

"What is?" Drius had excellent hearing.

"The sky. I have flown with you by day several times now, but this is my first night ride. I think now I like it better than the day rides. The night sky is full of wonder. I wish I could reach up and touch it. How about you?"

Drius chuckled. "When I was a hatchling, I would gaze up at the stars and flap my wings so fast, so hard I would tucker out. When finally I learned to fly, I went as high as I could go, but still the moon laughs, and the stars tease, for I cannot reach them. Now I think, if I was meant to reach them, I would have been made to do so."

"I suppose that is true."

"It is, but I was made with eyes to see them and therefore love them, just as you, and that is enough for me."

Merlin smiled.

"I wish I could say it is enough for me too, but I think I will always dream of more." Merlin said this as he gazed at the moon, that beautiful orb of silver which shone so bright it purged the world below of cold darkness.

He was pulled from his thoughts when Drius began his descent. Below them was a small vale surrounded by mountains. They had not flown far. Drius and his fellow dragons occupied the east end of the mountains in the Dragons' Keep, while Aquila and her winged herd occupied the west end in this little valley that had come to be called the Valley of the Skies.

Drius settled on the lush grass, careful not to make too much noise. Most of the winged herd had lain down to rest. The mares had their wings spread around themselves and their foals to keep warm. Standing guard over them were three stallions, all big and strong. They watched the dragon and his passenger with mild interest.

"Wait here," said Orpheus. He walked over to the stallions. They nickered softly and spoke to each other in their own language. It was not long before he came back and said, "Our mare matriarch is in the valley over. I shall fetch her. Please continue to wait here."

"We will," said Drius.

Orpheus turned and got a galloping start. He beat his wings, was up, and then disappeared over the crest of the mountain.

Merlin slid off Drius and looked around. The valley was green and full; the tender blades of grass reached over his sandals and tickled his toes. The rigid rock faces of the mountains made a high wall, keeping enemies out. The herd slept soundly. Every now and then, a curious head poked through its mother's feathers to look in their direction, but its mother would nicker, no doubt telling the foal to sleep. Above them the stars twinkled, and there was a feeling that settled in all at once: peace.

"It is so calm, so tranquil," Merlin whispered to Drius. "I do not remember a time or place where I felt so at ease. I must sketch this scene when we return home."

Drius grinned. "I agree. It is serene, and it is good to see others safe and happy. This vale has been home to the winged horses for over a hundred years, and no human can reach it, for the mountains are too steep to climb."

"That is good."

He heard wings again, and over the crest appeared Orpheus with Aquila beside him. They swooped down and found the earth beneath their hooves, first cantering, then trotting, and finally walking over to Merlin and Drius.

"Welcome, Merlin. Welcome, Drius," said Aquila in a warm, quiet voice.

Drius bowed his head, and Merlin did the same.

"Thank you, Orpheus. Go join the others."

Orpheus tossed his head and trotted over to the sleeping herd. He took his place and stood guard with the other stallions.

"We will not speak here," said Aquila. "We will speak as we fly. Climb on, Merlin." She folded her wings and took a knee beside the wizard.

"Fly?" Merlin was dumbfounded. They had just come here, and she wanted to leave? Leave the quiet and stillness of her vale? "I do not understand."

"You will. Hurry. The night is short."

Merlin looked back at Drius for reassurance.

"Go on, Merlin. I will be waiting here when you return."

"I thought you said you would accompany me on my visits." Merlin grinned.

"I saw you here. Where you go now, I cannot follow." He looked at Aquila, his eyes gentle and full of understanding. "Is that not right?"

Aquila nodded. "Come, Merlin. And leave your satchel."

Merlin dropped his satchel beside Drius. Then, careful of her wings, he hoisted himself onto Aquila's back. He had ridden horses many times before, but there was a distinct difference in how he felt astride a winged horse. He could feel the muscle and softness of her, her grandeur, and her strength. When she spread her wings, her body quivered, full of anticipation, and the way she tossed her head, excitement. She blew hot air, her sides rising and falling beneath him. She was power and grace.

"Hold tight, Merlin," she said.

Merlin dug his fingers into her mane and held on. His heart pounded with the rhythm of her hooves as she began to run. When she beat her wings, he held his breath, exhaling only after she left the ground. Up they went, and he held tighter for fear he might slip off.

Aquila galloped on air, her hooves still running, her wings beating. Higher and higher they climbed, and Merlin dared to look back over his shoulder. He caught his breath, shocked at how high they had ascended. The mountains looked so small.

She is fast. She covered so much distance so quickly.

She suddenly turned, no longer rising, and flew north.

"Where are we going?" Merlin asked, looking over the winged horse's shoulder as the mountains swept behind them.

Aquila nickered. "You will see." She sounded happy and almost proud. "How do you feel?"

"Stunned." He laughed. "A bit faint but full of excitement."

Aquila chuckled. "So I did not frighten you?"

"No, no, well…" He looked over her shoulder again. The ground below was flat and green, fields of grass interspersed by forests and lakes. A snaking river, a farmer's field, and little towns, their lights snuffed out. Everything was so small, so far away, it looked like a map or a war table without the markers for its armies. "We are just so very high up. I have never been this high. Drius stays lower to the ground."

"I am certain he does that for you. He could venture this high with ease. But where we are going, even he cannot go, for only my kind can ascend to greater heights. Tell me, are you having trouble breathing?"

"No." His answer was hesitant, nervous.

"That is good, but we are not done climbing."

Merlin's eyes widened, and he gripped her mane before she could tell him to do so.

There was a rolling wave of clouds up ahead, and Aquila charged at it, ascending again, beating her wings with a great deal of force. They entered the clouds with a silent whoosh! Merlin had never touched a cloud before. All around him was dark, and the air was damp.

Like being in a great fog.

He could just make out Aquila's white head, high, direct, ears forward, bracing against invisible, natural forces that hinder most from ascending any higher. With every beat of her wings, she breathed out, hot and heavy, like a war horse charging into the fray. As they rose, the air thinned, and Merlin struggled to take a breath.

"Aquila?" He choked on her name. It was hard to speak this high up.

"Do not be afraid. I have you." Her voice was calm and reassuring, like a mother to a child. She whinnied, and a soft light emanated from her. It spread over Merlin, starting with his legs and climbing his frame, till he marveled at his glowing self.

"By the powers—" He gasped. He could breathe. His lungs filled with the cool night air, and he had goose pimples all over. "Your magic?"

"Yes."

She whinnied again, and they burst forth from the clouds.

The glow around them faded, but the wizard was too occupied to notice. Surrounding them was a new world, a world of cloud towers, rolling fields of cloud, and great waves of a cloud sea. Some were thick and bulky, others thin and flat. Some made strange shapes, like beasts and ships and great hands.

Merlin laughed through his smile, his merry eyes looking this way and that with wonder. Then he saw the moon.

The clouds shone white and silver under its brilliant gaze, perfectly framing it. It hung there in space, so big, so full, and so bright, a precious orb, a world of mystery so close but still beyond his reach. It had smudges on its lovely face. Maybe those were mountains and craters across its silver fields or islands floating in a shining sea.

Merlin opened his mouth to speak, then closed it again. He had no words.

Aquila flew steady now, with a gentle loping gait. Over their heads was a sea of blackness, with thousands of curious stars looking on at them. They twinkled and winked; those sky crystals flirted. Merlin wished he could pluck one down and keep it in his pocket. He was so happy, like a child. Never in all his years had he supposed he would get a view like this. It would be a shame to return to the ground when they did. So he would lap it up, soak it all in, every spectacle, every wonder, and be glad for it.

When the clouds began to thin and break, he looked over Aquila's shoulder and stiffened.

"What is wrong, Merlin?" She had felt him shift.

Below, there was a blanket of black. The earth had disappeared, and Merlin wondered if they flew in space. He saw then a bright dot below, churning and wavering. It was silver, then white.

"Where are we?"

"Over the sea."

"The sea?"

So that mere speck of light dancing below was the moon's reflection, a lost, lonely blip on vast inky waters.

"I want to show you something special, Merlin. I think you will appreciate it."

He had no qualms with that. He only wondered how far they had flown.

"How far are we from where we started?"

Aquila nickered a sweet laugh. "Very far. My kind can cover more air space in less time than most birds and fliers. We have bested dragons and griffins, much to their sore pride, and phoenixes come very close to catching us. Flint and I have raced many a time, all in good fun, and sometimes we call it a draw. But when I am up this high, no beast can catch me. Only a winged horse can fly so close to the heavens."

Merlin smiled. The lilt in her voice suggested she was proud but not vain. He understood. If he could fly this high every night, he would be pleased with himself, and below him would be all those fellows who either dream of reaching such heights or go about life unable to fathom it.

"We are close," she said.

In the distance, something glimmered, and Merlin peered out from his old eyes. It was a strange light, wriggling, dancing, fading, and coming back.

"What is that?"

Aquila, full of mirth, said, "You will see."

Closer they came till they were on top of it, then in it. When he saw it, Merlin wept. All around them was living light. A celestial parade of shimmering, gleaming, spectacular illumination. It shone forth in gamboling waves, which rippled and capered, leaped and swayed. Their colors wildly changed, from green to red to blue to purple, all at once or intermittently, whatever they fancied. The lights frolicked with no music, a cosmic dance in the silent night.

Stunned and full of awe, Merlin asked in a quiet voice, "Is this heaven?"

"No. Heaven is well beyond this. This, I like to imagine, is but a taste of what awaits those going there."

Merlin was baffled. Her voice was calm and full of certainty, like she knew.

"How do you know heaven is beyond this…" He waved a hand at the lights. "This empyrean display?"

Aquila was silent for a time. She loped alongside and through the lights with quiet grace. When she did speak, she said, "It is time we head back." She turned around in a great arc and gathered speed.

Merlin lifted a hand to touch the lights. The rays slipped through his fingers.

Incredible.

When they were back amongst the clouds, the lights well behind them, Aquila slowed once more.

"Merlin?"

"Yes?"

"You asked how I know where heaven is, and I thought it better, at first, not to tell you. Some mysteries are best kept secret, but maybe you are the exception. I am not sure children should know the truth. It may be too much for their small, fragile minds. Even you may be left confused and bewildered, but I will tell you."

Merlin leaned closer, curious and eager but also a touch nervous.

"My kind is charged with a special keep. We do not often need to answer it, but when we do, we are serious, and we cherish it. This is how I know heaven is real. When a body dies, its soul goes there or the other place. Sometimes, though, a soul gets lost between here and there, and it wanders, lonely and afraid. It is our charge to help those lost souls find their way home. I cannot say how we know which ones are deserving of heaven. We just do.

"When I find a lost soul, I ferry them upon my back, carrying them high over the earth, beyond the clouds, and as near the vault as I am allowed. Once they are there, outside heaven, they find the rest of the way. During these flights, the souls say things to me. Some say they smell warm bread. Others say they see a face they have not seen in a long time. One child's soul told me she saw a white-robed figure with wings greater than my own. So yes, heaven is real, and winged horses know this better than most."

Merlin was speechless. Goose pimples had broken out along his skin. His heart beat fast, his whole being shaken. His mind reeled, and he put a palm to his forehead, trying to focus the wild roving thoughts.

"It is all right, Merlin." Her voice soothed him. "As I said, some mysteries are best kept secret."

"It is a lot to think on all at once," he said.

"Then think on this: I told you a truth. You can choose to accept it or deny it. But then, what reason do I have to lie?"

"I would never say you are dishonest."

"That is good. It is not in me to lie. Be calm, Merlin. Think on what I said later, if you really feel you must. All I ask is that you decide if a child should know this truth. You must decide if a thing of such magnitude should be omitted from your letter."

Merlin nodded.

What would a child think?

"I will say this, though," Aquila continued, "children have a better faith than most adults. Grown persons want to see to believe. Children can believe without seeing."

Merlin gave a weak chuckle. "That seems to defeat the purpose of my plan."

"No. We beasts of magic are the exception. We are bound by the laws of magic. But heaven will never fade, even if all the lives on earth stop believing."

The herd was still asleep when they returned to the Valley of the Skies. Drius rose to meet them, having lain down but not slept. Aquila landed close to him, her hooves drumming the earth.

"How was it?" he asked as Merlin dismounted.

The wizard stood a moment, leaning against Aquila to steady himself till he found his feet again. "It was spectacular," he said with a brilliant smile. "Like nothing I have ever seen or could imagine."

Drius nodded. "I thought it might be."

Aquila looked to the east. A breeze caught her mane and played with it. "The sun will be rising soon. Merlin, there is still much to tell you, so let us speak fast. Then you and the lord of dragons can go home and rest."

They stayed at the vale only a little while longer. Merlin sat on the grass beside Drius, his journal in his lap and his quill writing fast, as Aquila, who lay beside them, spoke on the care of winged horses.

The sky was just beginning to tint over when they finished. The stars were fading, the moon descending, and the winged herd waking. Merlin, overcome with the wonders of his night flight, asked permission first, then hugged Aquila. He then struggled to climb aboard Drius, feeling the fatigue of a long night in his old bones. Drius reached around and lifted the worn wizard with his nose till Merlin found his seat.

"Hold tight, my friend," said Drius. He spread his wings and took flight.

Behind them, Aquila and several of her own whinnied farewells.

When they returned to Merlin's cave, the sun was over the horizon, and the sky was a light blue. Merlin dropped his satchel and kicked off his sandals. He was so tired, he almost failed to notice he had a visitor.

A red-brown kestrel perched on his desk. The bird of prey swiveled its head to look at him and screeched.

"Seems you have another visitor," said Drius, and he yawned.

Merlin approached the bird and saw a note tied to its leg. "This one is a messenger."

He carefully removed the note, unfurled it, and grinned.

"It is from Ulysses. He says we are invited tomorrow to attend the centaurs' annual Amare Feast. There, he shall tell me all I need to know and hopes we will enjoy the festivities."

"I am certain we will, but first, sleep. Rest well, Merlin." Drius left for his cave.

Merlin smiled and stroked the back of the kestrel's head. "I agree. Sleep first."

He walked over to the curio, opened it, and reached into a jar of dirt labeled, *Worms*. The one he got wriggled wildly.

"Here you go, my little friend."

The kestrel gladly ate the worm while Merlin wrote his response, accepting Ulysses' invitation.

CHAPTER TEN

The Amare Feast

The centaur village of Briar was in a wood many miles south of the Dragons' Keep. When Merlin and Drius arrived, they found the place a bustle. Centaurs – studs and mares – were prancing about with excitement, making ready for their biggest festivity of the year.

Ulysses was waiting for them. Behind him stood eight centaurs, all studs, each one with his arms crossed or a hand on the hilt of his sheathed sword and frowning.

"Quite the welcoming committee," said Drius to Merlin as he started his descent.

Merlin chuckled. "It is customary, I think. Most kings have an entourage when they receive guests. Arthur would have his best knights behind him."

Drius settled in a small clearing, the village applauding and cheering as he did. Merlin was taken aback by the mass greeting and laughed as he dismounted.

"Feel better?" He winked at Drius before turning to see Ulysses approach them, a proud grin on his face.

"Welcome, friends, to Briar." His voice was bold and well-pleased, not like before at the Circle, where it had been hard and reserved.

"Thank you, chieftain." Merlin bowed.

Drius nodded toward Ulysses but kept an eye on the centaurs behind him.

Ulysses must have seen this, for he lowered his voice so only the dragon lord and wizard could hear.

"I apologize for their lack of enthusiasm. My council was not pleased when I went over their heads and invited you to our village. I told them it was decided before they even had a say in the matter." He puffed up and spoke louder so his fellows could hear. "Besides, today is the happiest of our year, and we are honored to share it with friends." He looked over at his council, and they yielded, putting their hands down and bowing their heads toward their guests.

Ulysses shook his head at them but still grinned. Looking back at Merlin, he said, "Come. There is much to see."

Walking alongside Ulysses, Merlin's eyes lit up at the woodland setting. The centaur village was quaint and charming. They had not cleared the trees to make room for their village but instead wove themselves throughout it. Every other tree had a log hut built around its middle, with a roof covered in thick moss. Woven canvas covered the doors, each one embroidered with a symbol to identify the house family. There was a great log hut at the center of the village, with splashes of red paint on its walls. This, Merlin later learned, was where Ulysses and the council met in private to discuss those things which were of great importance.

Drius, being so big and the trees so close together, was unable to join them. He waited in the clearing, but not alone. The centaurian youths were fascinated to see a dragon in their wood, so many of them loped up to him with wide, enthusiastic grins and chatted him up. The little foal girls brought him a large chain of flowers to put on his head, and the little colt boys marveled at his wings, his claws, his teeth, and his massive tail, all without a trace of fear. Their mare mothers did not seem to worry or fret; they looked on briefly, then went back to festivity plans, no doubt happy to have their little ones entertained and no longer under hoof.

As they moved through the village, Ulysses explained to Merlin the significance of the Amare Feast.

"The Amare Feast is our most important festivity of the year." Ulysses waved his hands to encompass all the activity taking place. "Right now, everyone is making preparations. The studs must ready their bows and spears for the great hunt, which will happen soon. They will gather meat for the feast. Most times, when our hunting parties go out, they bring back a couple deer or maybe a large boar, and that is plenty to eat for a day or more. But on this day, we feast. While the studs hunt, the mares prepare breads, cakes, fruits, mead, and other delights. Except for the shield mares: they keep watch over the village while we are away on the hunt."

As if spoken into being, a shield mare came up the path toward them, dressed in leather armor and linen, with a sword at her hip, a bow across her shoulders, and a quiver of arrows at her other hip. She beat her chest once with her fist as she passed the chieftain, and he did the same.

"Those mares who are not warriors," continued Ulysses, "also set the tables and make ready the games—"

"Games?" Merlin raised a brow. He liked games.

"Not the sort of games you might be thinking. The Amare Feast is not just about the feast itself, Merlin. Today, all the young, eligible studs and mares will have a chance to marry."

"Really?" Merlin's wonder at this was in his voice and his delight in his smile. "That sounds exciting."

"It is, very much so. The studs will compete in games to prove who is the strongest, the fastest, the wisest, and so on. Those who are victorious will have first choice of which mare they wish to propose marriage."

A bit nervous, Merlin asked, "What if the mare does not want to marry the winner? Not that I am saying anything is wrong with the winner."

Ulysses grinned. "We are not cruel. If the mare's heart is not won by the victor, she can say no to his proposal. Understand though, the mare runs the risk of being passed over and waiting another year till she can marry. If she is chosen the next year, that is."

"So what happens if a mare never marries?"

"She finds her place in the clan. Most become shield mares. They hunt and fight and become a confidant to other mares. It is an honorable path."

"Can only those mares who never marry become warriors?"

"Certainly not. If a mare feels called to trail the path of a warrior, she can do so, whether she chooses to marry or not."

Merlin nodded, pleased. "So these games you mentioned?"

"You will see them later. After the games are played, and the studs and mares have chosen each other, there is a mass ceremony, and the couples are married. After that, we feast late into the evening."

"It all sounds marvelous. I am delighted to be your guest and thank you for welcoming me on such a special occasion."

"I thought it important that you be here. You see,"—he halted and placed a hand on Merlin's shoulder, looking him in the eye—"most humans think we are barbarians, an inferior race. I want at least one man to understand this is not so. We are civilized and have our traditions, just like humans. We fight, we love, we survive, but we do not commit the heinous acts that people so often portray of us. I hope that by the end of this day, you will know this and be able to convey in your letter who and what we truly are."

Merlin nodded, grinned, and placed his hand over Ulysses'. "I promise I will do right by you."

A horn was blown to gather the studs for the hunt. Ulysses was chief among them. All those who were not going, including Drius and Merlin, gathered for a proper send-off to wish the hunting party luck. Merlin would have liked to go with them, but he was no hunter and feared he would only be in the way.

Several more horns blew. Cheers were lifted. The hunting party hooped and hollered. Many of them reared up and beat the air with their weapons and hooves. Then, together, the studs charged off into the wood, and all those who stayed back looked on till they were out of sight.

Merlin was then in the care of Nora, Ulysses' mate. Beautiful and fierce, the shield mare had long, dark hair that fell in curls around her shoulders, wonderfully framing her face. Her fearless jade green eyes looked upon her husband's guest with kindness and reverence. She wore a black leather jerkin with matching bracers, and her sheathed blade was strapped to her waist. Her equine form was a sleek dapple gray, and on this day, her tail had many braids with white flowers and silver bells.

"While they hunt, the shield mares keep watch over the village," she explained, "and those mares who do not fight make preparations for the feast and games. As the chieftain's wife, it is my task to supervise all activities. Come, you can help us."

Merlin marveled at all there was to be done. First, the mares had to clear the path that ran the length of their village. They pulled material things inside their doors and swept the path free of stubbing stones and old leaves. Then, with formidable strength, the mares carried several large slabs of redwood, cut in half, and laid them on smaller cuts of the same trees to make five long tables, with the ends touching together. These tables were cleaned and set with wooden plates, goblets, and utensils, as well as flourishing centerpieces of flowers, wishing stones, and candles.

Once the tables were ready, the mares grabbed their bows and several large baskets of white flowers. The children, Nora told Merlin, had braided the flowers into long chains, which now the mares tied to their arrows and shot high over the tree limbs. When they finished, the flowers fell in cascades, dangling from the trees, like a delicate, white rain.

"It is lovely," said Merlin, admiring the scene from the head of the furthest table.

"We are not done yet." Nora smiled. "Now we ready the games."

There were five games, she told him, each one meant to test the skill and strength of the studs.

"First, there is a race. The studs run three great circles around our village, jumping laid obstacles. This tests their speed and stamina. It gets a bit rowdy, as you will see, but the studs are not allowed to cheat. No forced stumbles or shoulder jabs, or they will be pulled from the race."

"What comes after the race?"

"The hammer throw."

As she answered, Nora and Merlin watched a couple of mares carrying a box between them to a large stone. This they set down and opened to reveal the hammer inside. Its head was engraved with intricate knotwork and shone in the midday sun.

"The hammer is pure steel. Each stud must swing the hammer over his head several times, and then, without moving forward, throw the hammer for distance. The game proves their strength and focus."

Next came archery. The targets, made of straw, were set fifty yards away, and each stud had to hit his target ten times, with at least three arrows shot through the center mark. This proved their marksmanship, a key skill if a stud was to hunt and provide for his family.

"After archery is hand-to-hand combat." Nora led Merlin to a circle of stones. "Each stud will face off with another here in the ring. The goal is to push their opponent out of the ring or force him to yield. They have no weapons, only their strength and determination."

"Sounds thrilling." Merlin tried not to sound giddy, but he was excited to see these games.

Nora smiled at the wizard's obvious enthusiasm. "Then there is the final game. Ulysses will ask each stud a series of three riddles. Not every riddle is the same unless one stud fails to answer, so the next has a chance to solve it."

"Fascinating," said Merlin. "I, myself, like riddles. It was great fun when jesters tried to stump me, but I sent them away with the echoes of my triumphant laughter." He chuckled, then hesitated. "Sorry, I do not mean to boast."

Nora laughed. "The riddles test a stud's wit and strength of mind. Centaurs are not all brawn. We have to be sharp and make fast decisions if we are to survive. Some of these studs will go on to be captains and must be competent in war strategy."

"I agree. So how do you pick a winner? Ulysses told me the victor shall propose to the mare of his choosing."

"There is a point system. In every game, a stud tries to get as many points as possible. Whoever wins the most points has the first choice when the games conclude. The studs will form a line, and across from them the mares will make another line. The grand victor will step forward and propose to the mare he favors – or loves." She blushed at the word, maybe remembering her husband's proposal. "The mare can decline his proposal, though it is rare for one to refuse the grand victor. If she accepts, she takes the stud's arm, and they walk down the aisle made by the studs and mares and stand to one side. Then the next stud with the most points proposes to a mare, and so on, till all are paired."

"Has there ever been a time when a stud or mare was left without a betrothal?"

Nora frowned. "Yes, but a mare can make herself available to marry for another five years, and a stud can compete for another three. Should a stud or mare be passed over so many times, then it is up to them to decide their place in the clan."

Merlin stared at his feet, his lips turned down. "Seems sad to miss out…on the companionship, I mean…and love. What if a stud or mare were to find someone after?"

Nora half-grinned. "It has happened. Rare though it is, if such a thing did occur, both parties must go before the chieftain and ask his permission to marry. But come. We have set the games, so now we must ready the feast."

She led him to a great hut surrounded by five fire pits. The mares raked the ashes, laid fresh kindling, and cleaned the spits that would skewer the game brought back by the hunting party. Inside the hut, the mares were bustling, and Merlin leaned his head in, attracted by the aromas wafting through the air.

"Mmm…cakes," he said.

Indeed, there were cakes, and fresh breads, cookies, and pies. Three large clay ovens were at the center of the hut, glowing hot. Plumes of smoke puffed forth from their chimneys outside, and from those hot mouths came the mouthwatering delicacies.

Outside, several mares walked up with baskets filled with fruits and vegetables from a nearby garden. These they set down and started to clean meticulously.

"Make way," came a voice.

Merlin jumped aside as some mares walked past with three large pots.

"Merlin, are you good with your hands?" Nora asked.

Merlin grinned. "What would you like me to do?"

She set him to work on peeling potatoes, which were then boiled. He rather enjoyed the work and talked with the mares about their husbands and children, about the hunts and their everyday lives. The mares enjoyed Merlin's company, saying he was funny but also kind and very helpful.

Suddenly, a horn blew, and in the distance, there was singing.

The mares put down their work and laughed for joy because the hunting party had returned. Merlin walked with Nora while the other mares and their children ran ahead to welcome back the party. Ulysses was in front, carrying a great boar over one shoulder and leading the studs in a song of victory and mirth.

The hunt was successful. In all, they had caught six deer, four boars, a dozen pheasants, and seven rabbits. Some mares happily freed the studs of their game and carried it off to be cooked for the feast.

"Well, Merlin, has my wife taken great care of you?" Ulysses kissed Nora. He looked at her with more fondness than the stars look on the moon.

"She has been a wonderful hostess," said Merlin.

"Good." Ulysses faced the hunting party. They were a rowdy bunch, elated and filled with excitement after the hunt, jabbering with young mares and tussling the hair of little ones. He reared up and hollered, "Come now, studs. Ready yourselves. For it is time for the games."

They all cheered at once, pounding the air with their fists. The mares clapped their hands and laughed gaily. The little ones jumped around, unable to contain their excitement.

Merlin sat with Drius throughout the games. They had a great vantage point to see everything, from the race to the hammer throw to the archery to the wrestling matches. Ulysses and three of his captains were the judges. They determined if someone cheated, which no one did that day, and how many points each competitor got for his efforts.

"Fascinating," said Merlin. "It reminds me of the days at Camelot when knights would joust and combat fight in tournaments. They did it for honor and bragging rights, mostly. But every so often, there would be a romantic lad who hoped to earn a lady's favor."

"We dragons are less complicated in winning our mates," said Drius.

Merlin nodded. He was aware, having witnessed many a mating season at the Dragons' Keep. A dragon's way of courting was a lot more exciting, in that it was frightening, compared to the centaur games. Without saying so, Merlin preferred the centaurs' way, for there was more mirth and spectacle, and he clapped his hands for the victors.

When it came time for the riddles, Merlin raised a hand to his ear to hear. If he knew the answer, he would grin and shuffle his feet. If he did not, he held his breath for the answer.

Soon after, the points were tallied, and the victors were announced. There was little time for celebration, as Ulysses called the young, eligible mares to step forward.

A dozen studs to a dozen mares. The mares wore new jerkins, sewn the night before, of brilliant colors. Flowers and bells were braided in their tails, and shiny ribbons donned their hair. They all smiled brightly, and their cheeks blushed.

One by one, the victors stepped forward. Each took a knee before the mare of his choice and promised her his hand, his sword, and his life. To Merlin's relief – because he could not stand the thought of seeing a lonely heart, every mare said yes.

A horn was blown, and everyone clapped their hands and raised happy voices. The forest echoed with their glee, and Merlin could not help cheering as well.

Ulysses, with Nora at his side, called the new couples to gather in a line. All others stood aside.

"What happens now?" Drius asked Merlin, knowing the wizard had been told.

"A wedding." Merlin beamed. "I love weddings."

Nora walked the line of new couples, and each couple offered her their clasped hands so she could tie them together with a white ribbon. Each time she did this, she said to them, "Your lives and hearts are bound together," and the couple would say in response, "We are bound to each other."

Once all hands were tied, Nora returned to her place beside Ulysses. In a great voice, the chieftain centaur proclaimed, "We are witnesses this day to the pairing of these couples. Each stud has asked his mare for her hand, and she has accepted. Mares, do you swear to love your mate and keep him at your side forever?"

The mares all said yes together.

"Studs, do you swear to love your mate and keep her at your side forever?"

The studs all said yes together.

Ulysses raised his arms. "Do we, as their village and family, accept their unions and promise to support them?"

The crowd cheered unanimously.

"Then, by the power vested in me, as chieftain of this clan, I now pronounce you husbands and wives."

The studs eagerly embraced their mares and laid passionate kisses on them while all around them, their friends and families shouted hurrahs.

Merlin clapped with such enthusiasm, his hands became sore, but he did not care, and happy tears glistened in his eyes.

"Are you crying?" Drius stared at him with a fond grin.

Merlin wiped his eyes. "As I said, I love weddings."

With the wedding ceremony complete, it was time for the feast. The sun had begun to set when they stood around the tables. The candles at their centerpieces were lit, casting warm glows on all their faces. Ulysses was at the head, with Nora on his right and Merlin on his left.

Ulysses raised his hands for attention, and all fell silent. He then clasped his hands together and bowed his head. His clan did the same, and not wishing to be rude, Merlin did so as well.

Ulysses prayed: "To the one who gives all life, we thank thee for this bounty we are about to eat. We thank thee for the forest we call home, for the beasts we hunt, and for the earth that grows what we need. We thank thee for our victories and our losses. We do nothing alone. Hail thee."

All the centaurs spoke as one: "Hail thee" in a solemn, heartfelt manner.

Ulysses grinned and clapped his hands. "Bring on the feast!"

They all cheered and sat down. At once, several mares appeared with plates of fruit and bowls of bread. These they set down along the centers of the tables, and many famished hands plucked the foodstuffs from their wooden cradles. The mares came again with pitchers of water and sweet honey mead, which they poured for the parched parties. They came a third time with bowls of greens, chopped and mixed, dressed in oil. Next, the potatoes, which had been boiled and mashed. Merlin blushed when Nora told her husband the wizard had lent a hand with the dish. Then came the main course: the meats, which had been mindfully and delicately cooked over the fires, were carried out by two mares at a time on spits. The aroma was mouthwatering.

The mares carried the spits in a full circle around the tables, so all could see and get excited. Then they retired briefly and came back with the meat served on platters, which they added to the centers of the tables.

As was customary when hosting guests, Ulysses served Merlin his first course of meat, dropping a little bit of everything on the wizard's plate. Then the chieftain left his seat and called for the mares who were serving the food. They appeared with a whole deer and a whole boar still tied to their spits and followed Ulysses out to the glade where Drius was.

Merlin could not hear them, but he saw Ulysses wave a hand at the game as he addressed the dragon lord. Drius looked appreciative, grinning and bowing his head in apparent thanks. Ulysses returned, smiling, to his seat, and Merlin watched the mares over yonder serve Drius the deer and boar. They left and came back to the dragon again with several pitchers and two very large wooden bowls. In this way, they served him both water and mead.

With everyone served, the lovely mares who had done so much work to prepare the delicious feast were applauded before they took their seats, and everyone dined well. As they ate, several studs regaled their audience about the day's hunt, and this gave way to others, both studs and mares alike, telling stories. Even Ulysses got caught up in the merriment and told the tale of the bear that tried to take his arm.

Intermittently, the chieftain would speak with Merlin about centaurs and tell him what he needed to know for the letter. Nora would speak up now and then, lending her thoughts to the conversation, if she felt her husband forgot something. Merlin, still eating, listened, but at his side, his enchanted quill scrawled every word the couple said in his journal.

They finished this formal business just as the mares got up again to remove the dinner plates. They took away the potatoes and greens, the meats and bread as well, but left the fruits. They snatched up the pitchers of water and mead, now empty, and disappeared. Merlin wondered if the feast was over, but no, here came the mares again, with fresh pitchers and plates. Shortly, they returned with all those cakes and pies and cookies Merlin had been desperate to try. The wizard's eyes lit up as the sweet, heartwarming aromas tickled his nose.

There were so many delicacies, and Merlin tried them all without a hint of shame. His favorites were the elderberry pie, closely followed by the glazed peaches and the flour cakes topped with rowan berry jam. He also liked the hazelnut cookies, plum tarts, and blackberry custard. There was also a cake soaked in mead, rich and moist, and if Merlin had not already been drinking mead, he might have appreciated the cake more.

As he scooped up the last of the peach jam with a shortbread cookie, a young stud piped up from some ways down the table.

"Will our guest do us the pleasure of regaling us with some of his own stories?"

Many centaurs expressed their enthusiasm for this, saying "Yes" or "How wonderful" and "That would be a treat," and banging their fists on the tables. Ulysses raised a hand to quiet them.

"How about it, Merlin?" The chieftain smiled with warm encouragement.

Merlin, feeling good with a full stomach and a bit cheery from the mead, sat up in his seat and, with a great big smile, said, "It would be an honor."

The centaurs were quiet, and they listened intently, some with their hands to their ears, to better hear the wizard. Merlin was a great storyteller, and truth be told, he liked to tell stories. Every emotion that played across their faces urged him with fresh enthusiasm to go on to the next tale and the next one after that. They laughed at King Vortigern, the scoundrel, and his ever-falling tower. Their eyes lit up when he spoke of the Lady of the Lake, that beautiful enchantress of mystery. Fascination gripped them with stories of magical beasts, both familiar and some unheard of, which Merlin had encountered over his many years. Each time he finished a story, they raised their goblets to toast him and asked for another.

After they hailed the mention of Excalibur, a stud with rosy cheeks raised his goblet and said, "Tell us about King Arthur."

Many cheers followed. Many fists banged the tables. Voices piped up: "Tell us about his Knights of the Round Table" and "Camelot" and "The lovely Guinevere" and "The King's last battle."

An immediate change came over Merlin then. The cheer and warmth withdrew from his face, and he slumped in his seat, staring down into his empty goblet.

He did not hear the crowd anymore. Their sounds became muffled, as his mind started to drift away. He did not hear Ulysses speak his name till the centaur laid a kind hand on his shoulder.

"Merlin?"

The wizard lifted his gaze. He saw the worry on Ulysses' face, Nora's too.

"Are you feeling well?"

Merlin nodded slowly, then tried to laugh, but it hitched in his throat. "Too much mirth, I think." He set the goblet down on the table. "Forgive me. It has been a long time since I enjoyed a party."

His hosts did not seem convinced.

It was then that Drius stood up and said, "I think it is time we went home." Many heads turned to look at him, eyes sad and confused. "The hour is late. I speak for my friend when I say we are tired but much cheered by the warmth and kindness of your hospitality, Ulysses. I, myself, must ask pardon, for I must return to take my watch over the Dragons' Keep."

Ulysses looked from Drius to Merlin then back at the dragon lord and nodded. "Of course." He rose and clapped his hands. "We must bid our guests farewell. Raise a cup with me."

The clan did, each of them raising a goblet in silence.

"To you, Merlin." Ulysses and the clan took a drink, then, "To you, Drius, lord of dragons," and took another drink. "May the days ahead be kind to us and bring us good fortune. May our futures be bright."

The clan hailed, drank, and slammed down their goblets.

Nora stood up. "The moon is high. It is the hour to say goodnight. Newlyweds, take your place under the stars."

Arm-in-arm, Ulysses and Nora escorted Merlin back to Drius in the glade.

"I apologize if I cut the party short," Merlin said with a frown.

"You did nothing of the sort, Merlin," said Ulysses.

"If anything, the festivities ran longer because you were here." Nora smiled. "You tell such enchanting stories. You had us spellbound, and we might have stayed up all night to hear more."

"You are too kind." Merlin tried to grin but was too embarrassed and sad. "I must also apologize for my strange behavior a moment ago. I—"

Ulysses cut him off by placing a reassuring hand on the wizard's shoulder. "We understand."

The centaur chieftain's eyes conveyed deep thought with a keen line of perception. A hunter who could see through the brush and bramble to the heart of a matter.

When they reached Drius, Merlin thanked the couple for their warm and generous hospitality.

"I really did have a wonderful time and am honored to have been here for your beautiful Amare Feast. Thank you, lord chieftain and lady." He bowed low to them.

"We are glad to have had you," said Nora.

"Indeed." Ulysses grinned.

Behind them, the newlywed couples approached hand-in-hand. They fanned out to circle the perimeter of the glade. Merlin watched them, fascination bringing a little shine back to his eyes.

Nora, with a gentle smile, said, "Once you depart, the couples will sleep under the stars."

Ulysses nodded. "Our ancestors, the fallen, who were good and just and well-loved – they are the stars, immortalized in the next life. They watch over us."

Nora again: "And this night, the couples will sleep under their watch so they might have their blessing."

Merlin smiled and gazed up at the twinkling, bejeweled heavens.

A beautiful thought.

Drius said nothing on their flight home. This surprised Merlin, for he was certain his friend would question him about the incident at the feast.

Perhaps he is paying me a kindness by not mentioning it.

Merlin was too tired for words besides, so he kept quiet as well. He only wanted to collapse in his bed and get lost in sleep.

In sleep, I can forget for a time.

When they came to his cave, Merlin slipped off Drius' back. He was prepared to go in without a word, but he hovered at the entrance. He could feel the dragon's eyes on him. He slowly turned and looked back. Drius stared at him. His eyes were gentle but shrewd. He was searching, waiting for something – an explanation. He was not going to ask for it, but his thoughtful look spoke volumes.

Merlin opened his mouth, then closed it again.

I cannot…

"Goodnight, Drius." Merlin struggled to say it, and he felt worse when he saw the disappointment in his friend's eyes.

Crestfallen, Drius turned to the ledge. He spoke gently, "Goodnight, Merlin," and dove off the cliff.

Merlin watched him ascend and disappear. A silent tear rolled down his cheek.

CHAPTER ELEVEN

The Glimmer of Gold

The following day was quiet. There was no summons, and no messenger came for Merlin, so he spent the time writing the letters and wondering after Drius.

Last night could have gone better, he thought.

In his mind's eye, Merlin could still see the downcast look on Drius' face, and this upset him so much that he often stalled in his writing. Instead, he would pace about the cave, rubbing his temples. His mind might be soothed long enough to jot down a few words here and there, but like the waves rolling in on the shores of his memory, he'd see the dejected dragon again and again.

I am a fool.

He had done a great wrong to his oldest friend.

We've known each other for so long and shared so much. There should be no secrets between us, yet I struggle with this one... He faltered in his step and shook his head. *I am certain I hurt him by saying nothing, and it was cruel of me to say a cold 'goodnight' and shut him out the way I did.*

All day, he paced and wrote, wrote and paced. It was a grueling cycle, more so on his mind than his being. When nightfall came, he sat by the fire with an untouched bowl of soup in hand and stared at the flames. They danced and threw up sparks which flew this way and that like dizzy fireflies. He was so mesmerized by this and far lost in thought that he did not hear the heavy beating of wings outside.

A steady, low growl shook the wizard's bones and broke his trance. He looked through the flames and saw a red dragon with bronze wings and plated belly gazing in. Its eyes were sharp, golden, and fierce, and it had many scars along its hide.

"Merlin." His voice was deep and chilling.

"Godan?" Merlin put down his bowl and went outside to receive his guest. "To what do I owe the pleasure of this visit?" He tried to sound light and cheerful, but there was an undertone of dread.

The dragon snorted. "I am to inform you that Glendor, the lord griffin, has summoned you. My lord, Drius, will fetch you in the morn' to fly you to Griffins' Point. Be ready."

Merlin was taken aback. "I appreciate the message, Godan. Thank you."

The dragon turned to leave.

"A question, Godan."

The dragon hesitated.

"Is something the matter with Drius? Up until now, he has come to me with such news."

Godan glanced back at Merlin, his eyes unfeeling and reserved. "Busy, I suppose." Then he leapt off the cliff.

Busy?

Merlin returned to his seat by the fire and stirred the flames with an iron poker.

"Busy my foot." He frowned.

In all his years at the Dragons' Keep, Merlin had never received word from Drius through a messenger.

And of all the dragons he could send, he sent Godan.

Godan was intimidating, reserved, and not a social beast. Merlin had never seen him look anything but stern, always frowning with a stony gaze. Whether he liked or disliked the wizard was a mystery, but now that Merlin thought about it:

Tonight is the first time he's spoken to me.

He shook his head.

It does not help that his appearance is startling with all those scars.

He then winced, remembering Drius gave Godan most of his scars – first in the battle for leadership, then again for the love of Mira, the she-dragon who became Drius' beloved.

One might assume that Godan would be bitter and hateful of his leader, but he is quite devoted. He has fought alongside Drius more than once, and that is how he got the rest of his scars. But why did Drius send Godan to deliver me a message?

Merlin could not feign that he did not know.

I did this.

With the poker, he turned over a log and sent up a burst of sparks.

So how do I fix it?

It was bright and early when Drius appeared at Merlin's cave, looking solemn and withdrawn.

"Good morning, Drius." Merlin smiled and tried to sound merry as though nothing were wrong.

Drius, without looking at Merlin, said, "Good morning," in a low, impassive voice, and then, "We must hurry if we are to make good time."

Merlin frowned. "Of course."

Their flight was silent. Merlin dreaded the wall that had come between them. He wanted to say something, anything to break the tension, but he was at a loss for words. Soon they arrived at Griffin's Point, and there was Glendor, waiting for them outside his cave.

Drius settled, and Merlin dismounted. The rock face which jutted forth from the cave's gaping mouth was an overlook with a view both stunning and frightening. It was not the summit, but still a high place. Up here, the clouds were so close, Merlin could almost touch them. All around, the mountains rose and fell like stony waves. He stole a glance over the edge and saw the sharp jags and crags of the mountain's teeth far below. Those rigid fangs, waiting for perilous climbers to fall, still envied Merlin for escaping them when last he came here for the griffin's feather.

Merlin bowed as Glendor approached them. Drius, too, lowered his head, eyes closed, and the lord griffin did the same with mutual respect.

"Welcome to Griffin's Point," he said with a proud grin.

No sooner had he said this than a screech shattered the silence of the mountains. There was nothing to see at first. The screech was followed by several bleats of distress. Then Merlin glimpsed, beyond the overlook, another griffin, with something caught in its talons, descending toward a cavity in the side of the mountain.

"This is the hour to hunt," said Glendor with ease. "The pride left before the sun rose. We may hear similar cries of triumph as they return with their caught prey."

"And you?" said Drius. "Do we deny you a meal by coming so early? Your messenger said this was the hour you wished to see us."

"You deny me nothing, lord dragon. I hunted last night and brought back enough for me and my own."

A look passed between them, then Drius gazed past Glendor at the cave. It was deep and dark, and nothing inside could be seen. His nostrils widened, as he breathed deeply, closing his eyes.

Merlin watched, confused.

The dragon opened his eyes and grinned at the griffin.

"I believe congratulations are in order," he said. "Or am I mistaken?"

Merlin looked from Drius to Glendor and frowned for being left out.

There was a definite gleam in the griffin's eyes. "You are not." He then glanced at Merlin and chuckled, seeing the puzzlement and frustration thereof on the wizard's face. "You have come at a most joyous time for me and my Annora. Last night, I became a father, and she a mother."

Merlin beamed. "Congratulations, Glendor! That is most exciting news!"

"Indeed. Congratulations," said Drius. "How many?"

"Three healthy chicks. Two boys and a girl."

"May they be blessed all their lives and bring much happiness to you and yours."

"They have done so already, the moment their cries breached the world."

Merlin had never seen griffin offspring before, and he failed to contain himself. "May we see them?" The eagerness in his voice rang like a bell.

Glendor frowned. "You may come inside, Merlin, but I must ask you to remain out here, Drius, for our nest is laced with gold."

Merlin's breath hitched in his throat, and he watched Drius lower his head with the bitter weight of understanding.

The dragon lord sighed. "I will wait here then."

"You understand," said Glendor, "I wish I could let you enter, but I would never put my family at risk, nor Merlin nor you."

"I understand, and I appreciate that." Drius gave him a reassuring smile. There was no insult between them, no hurt feelings. He turned around so his back was to Glendor and the cave. He laid down, crossed his feet, and stared out over the rock face. "Merlin, if you need me, I will be here."

Merlin nodded, then prattled, "Thank you, Drius." He turned to Glendor and said with better control, "I will follow your lead."

As he followed, Merlin could not help but muse: *A nest laced with gold? By saying as much, Glendor has saved all our lives. Heaven forbid that Drius should ever turn rogue.*

Rogue was a term Merlin coined the first time he saw a dragon consumed with greed for all that glitters.

Humans think dragons are born with a love of treasure. That false thinking led many fools to ill fortune, as they snuck to dragon caves, seeking wealth, but most times found them empty, 'cept for the angry dragon that rages when intruded upon. No one, save me maybe, knows the truth.

When a dragon first looks at a gilded trinket or a glittering gem — not with a glance but with a long stare, a change, a terrible twist of nature, comes over them, and the dragon loses its senses. It suddenly, desperately wants riches of the earth and nothing else. So it seeks out treasure, steals and hoards it, and when it is not out looking for more, it guards its precious mound, forsaking food, water, and sleep, and in time withers and dies from lack of care. Dragons cannot help the change: their true self dies in the shadow of the horrible beast they become, and there is no hope for them, no cure unless they be slain before they starve, and before they burn countless souls for the cursed treasure.

Merlin shook his head, warding off these unpleasant thoughts in time to see a precious scene unfold before him.

Glendor's cave was a dusky gray when they entered, but outside, the sun was climbing, and its rays reached inside to warm the place. There was another griffin, a female, laying in a large nest, with her wings spread around her. Merlin's eyes wandered over the nest. It was a sturdy, interlaced construction of branches and twigs, but there — the light caught it — he saw the delicate threads of gold woven throughout. The nest glittered, and it was alluring.

"Annora, my love,"—Glendor rubbed her head with his, then stood to one side of the nest—"this is Merlin, the wizard I spoke of."

Annora's eyes fixed on Merlin, sharp but gentle, and instinctively, Merlin dropped to his knee and bowed.

"Rise, wizard," she said.

Merlin did as told.

"My mate told me of the last time you came here. How he almost killed you, and what saved you was your gesture of humility. I happen to agree with him: you must be daft to think you could make off with a griffin feather so easily." She grinned. "I appreciate you showing me the same humility."

Merlin said nothing but smiled.

"It means a great deal to us what you plan to do. If all you promise comes to pass, our little ones have a chance to live."

Merlin heard then a small coo, muffled beneath Annora's wing.

"I only do that which I think is right," he said.

"Is it not more than that?"

Merlin stared, not certain what she meant.

Her eyes penetrated him. "Do you do this because it is right, or because you want to?"

Merlin opened his mouth, then closed it. He thought about the question. The answer came fast, and color filled his cheeks when he said, "I do it because it is right, but also because I love you and cherish you. I do not want you to fade, nor do I wish it for Drius and his dragons, the unicorns, the fairies, or any other magical creatures. In truth, your grace, I believe the world needs you."

Annora's eyes softened, and she grinned with admiration and approval. "That makes you noble."

She pulled back her wing to reveal the hatchlings. They were small, no bigger than pups. Their fur was a light golden brown, and their down feathers were white. They slept close together in a ball, surrounded by gray-blue eggshells. Their tiny tails swished to their dreams.

"My goodness," Merlin whispered, not wanting to wake them.

"What do you think?" Glendor asked.

"They are beautiful."

Annora nuzzled them. "Come now, my little ones," she said in a soft voice. "We have a guest."

The hatchlings raised their heads, yawned, and opened their beady black eyes. They blinked several times, looking groggy and dreamy. One let out a tiny screech, perhaps in protest to being wakened or to say it was hungry.

Annora beamed at them, as did Glendor. Proud parents.

One hatchling got to its feet and peered over the edge of the nest. When it saw Merlin, it jumped back and fell over its siblings. Another shoved the first hatchling off, squeaking its displeasure. It then saw Merlin and scrambled to its feet. In a fierce yet adorable stance, with its feet planted and head down, it shrieked at Merlin with as much ferocity as a kitten. The third hatchling, now awake because of the commotion caused by its siblings, looked up at Merlin and did not react but stared in fascination.

Annora chuckled, drawing their attention. "Go say hello."

At the suggestion of this, the first two hatchlings hid behind their mother. The third made its way to the edge of the nest and tried to pull itself over but could not because it was so small.

"Our little girl is the bravest," said Annora with a smirk, eyeing their father. She lifted the hatchling over with her beak.

The little one slowly approached Merlin, hunched and low, her tail swishing with charged curiosity. Merlin knelt and extended his hand, palm up. She sniffed his fingers and recoiled to look at him with her deep, dark eyes. She did not seem afraid, only alert. She came closer and pressed her head against the tips of his fingers. Gently, he rubbed behind her ear, and she purred. She pressed into his palm for more, so Merlin sat down to pet her, running his fingers along her soft feathers and fur.

Her brothers peered out from behind their mother to watch.

"Come now," said Glendor to his sons. "You are made of braver stuff than that." He reached over and nudged them out of hiding.

They protested at first, but seeing their sister unafraid and even enjoying herself, seemed to convince them. They clambered over the nest and stalked over. Merlin extended a free hand to them, still petting their sister with the other. Like their sister, they sniffed first, then pressed their heads into his palm. Soon, all three hatchlings were purring.

This went on for a while, and Merlin felt he was a richer man for it. Experiences such as this could not be bought but were earned or gifted. His heart swelled with love for the little tykes.

When the hatchlings started to climb his shoulders or lay in his lap, batting at his beard, Annora called them back to the nest. They were reluctant to do so, squeaking their protestations, but came when their mother gave them a stern look. Glendor lifted the hatchlings into the nest and laid beside his family.

"Now, Merlin, what shall I tell you about griffins?"

Merlin got out his journal, quill, and ink pot, but before he could rattle off the first question, the glitter of the gold throughout the nest caught his eye again.

"Forgive me," he said, his cheeks full of color, "but your nest...why is it laced with gold?"

Glendor looked at Annora, and she at him. A silent thought seemed to pass between them before she tended to the hatchlings. Glendor, in a stern tone, said, "I am reluctant to tell you, for I cannot see how it is relevant to the care of one of my own."

Merlin put down the quill. "It may not be important. I apologize and admit that I am only curious and would like to know. But if you prefer to keep it a secret, leave me curious. I am curious about many things in this world, but I can live without knowing all the answers."

Glendor looked again at his mate, and she shrugged. The hatchlings curled up against her and drifted off to sleep.

"Very well. I say this only because I trust you. You do not strike me as one who is greedy, like others of your kind who would pay for this knowledge."

"I swear," said Merlin, raising his hand, "I will be careful with what you tell me."

"That is good enough." Glendor took a breath and let it out slowly. "Our kind has an innate ability to smell out gold. If it is close by, we can sense it. We can dig it out of lesser rocks, those stones that give way and crumble. We can also fish it out of streams."

Merlin's eyes widened with fascination.

"We do not profit from gold as humans or other beings do. Instead, we male griffins decorate our nests with the glittering substance and then gift the nest to our mate in hopes that she will favor us with offspring." Glendor smiled at Annora, and she back at him. "You can imagine, though,"—he looked back at Merlin with displeasure—"how this talent of ours has led to trouble."

Merlin frowned. "Yes, I can imagine."

"Humans were bad enough. They would scale our ridges and peaks, hoping to plunder our nests. Griffins are strong and fast. We will fight to protect what is ours, and most times we are victorious. If we cannot win, we fly away and leave them the nest. But, when there is a family to protect"—he paused to look at his offspring, then back at Merlin—"there is no running away."

"The dwarves were worse," said Annora without looking up from her brood.

"The dwarves?" Merlin repeated.

"Yes," said Glendor, a shadow falling over him. "Dwarves became our worst enemies. Before they knew about us and our innate gift, they stayed underground, mining the mountain's belly for precious stones and metals, and used their wealth to build great halls in the caverns beneath.

"But when they learned griffins can find gold, they formed small bands that snuck up the mountainsides in the dead of night to find griffin families. We have a great sense of smell, but the dwarves, clever and scheming, covered themselves in mud to mask their scent. They would creep in, kill the parents, and steal the hatchlings."

Merlin turned pale, and his stomach turned.

"I know little of what happened then," said Glendor. "There were rumors, but it was those other creatures who dwell within the mountains who saw the truth and brought word of it to the surface. Rock goblins, knockers, and the occasional gremlin. They would relay terrible stories of how the dwarves caged the hatchlings and fed them scraps to keep them weak so they could not fight back. Many hatchlings died, and those few that grew up did not live long, only long enough to smell out some of the gold and then be cast aside." Glendor's voice deepened, and he grew rigid. "There came to pass between our races a great war, and we slew many dwarves. Then the dwarves struck a deal with humans to enlist their help. Our situation only got worse, and it was shortly after that the Great Circle came together, and we griffins agreed to go into hiding. In those first ten years, nary a human nor a dwarf found us, though they searched fervently, and soon their bands broke up. I am certain they believe we are all dead, for ninety years have passed, and we have known peace."

Merlin sat still. His quill hovered over his journal and its incomplete sentence. His mouth was dry, and his jaw clenched. His eyes threatened tears.

"I am sorry," he said in a struggling voice. "I had no idea such a thing took place."

"The dwarves do well at keeping their business to themselves," said Glendor. "I do not think they told their human allies the whole truth, that griffins can smell out gold, but rather they claimed we were a menace and offered to pay for any help. They certainly have enough wealth to throw around."

"So much tragedy, all for a shiny metal."

"The glimmer of gold does not appeal to a moral sense, but often to an irrational sense of greed."

Merlin sighed. "Gold is not the only thing that corrupts." He might have said more. His lips parted, and a word lingered there, but he stopped.

Seconds passed in silence. The only sound was the hatchlings cooing in their sleep.

Merlin lifted his gaze. "May I ask, what do you do with the nest when your brood is grown? Do you keep it?"

"Our hatchlings will grow up and leave to make families of their own. Annora and I will have no use for the nest then. I will disassemble it, discard the branches, and scatter the gold for others of my kind to find and use for their nests."

"Then what do you both do?"

Glendor and Annora touched heads. "We stay together for as long as the other lives. When one of us passes, the other will soon follow, for no griffin can bear to live without its mate. It will die of a broken heart." Glendor and Annora pulled back to look at each other, and there was a glow between them. "Gold means little when you know the value of true love."

Merlin decided and swore to Glendor he would make no mention of gold in the letter, and the lord griffin was no less than grateful. He answered all of Merlin's questions about the care of one of his own, and when they finished, he escorted Merlin outside. It was past noon, and the day was clear and beautiful.

Annora, with the three hatchlings in tow, followed them outside. The little ones halted at the sight of Drius when he turned around to receive the party. Again, the boys hid behind their mother while the little girl moved forward slowly. When she reached her father, she looked up at Glendor with hesitant, hopeful eyes.

"Go on," he said in a gentle voice, rolling his head in Drius' direction.

She went on, and when she was before the dragon lord, she gawked. He was so big that she craned her head up to see all of him, standing on her back paws, trying to meet his eyes, and fell over. Drius chuckled and laid his head down before her.

"Hello, little one. It is very nice to meet you."

The hatchling squeaked, and she rested her avian claws on Drius' nose and pushed her head against him in greeting.

Seeing their sister best them, yet again, the boys ran up to better see their first dragon. Soon, all three were climbing on him, sliding down his tail, and squawking with delight.

"You have a beautiful family, Glendor."

"Thank you, Drius."

The dragon and griffin bowed heads to one another, and then Drius bowed to Annora, and she to him.

"Merlin?" Annora approached and gazed into him with her golden eyes. "Thank you." She touched her head to his. Her breath was soft and warm. Though Merlin was not quite sure what it meant, he thought well of it and accepted her gesture. She then parted from him to stand by her mate.

Merlin climbed aboard Drius' back, and when the dragon lord took flight, the hatchlings praised the spectacle with high-pitched, piping whistles.

The flight home was silent too.

When they reached his cave, Merlin invited Drius to stay.

"There are things I must attend to," said the dragon lord without looking at him.

Merlin was desperate and tired of the wall. He stepped in front of Drius before he could leave.

"How about tomorrow then?" He stared up at his friend with pleading eyes.

Drius sighed, looking off into the distance. "Perhaps." Then, after a pause: "Yes." He then turned and dove off the cliff.

CHAPTER TWELVE

Secrets and Friendship

Tomorrow came, and it belonged to Merlin. There was no messenger – no member of the Circle sent for him, and he put aside his work for matters closer to heart.

He had not slept well. Instead, he had paced by a dying fire till the sun's first light, all the while thinking about Drius.

"I must make amends with him," he said and left to find him.

The day was warm and pleasant. Scanty clouds drifted overhead, and the sun smiled over the Dragons' Keep. Merlin found Drius in the vale at the heart of the Keep. He lay at the top of a hill, observing his fellow dragons, his feet crossed and his wings fanned out to catch the sunlight.

The valley was a lush space, green and beautiful. There was a pool fed by a mountain waterfall, and here some hatchlings played, launching themselves into the cool, refreshing water and splashing one another. Others chased or wrestled, rolling around in the grass. A few practiced their fire breath, with whiffs of furious smoke wafting from their nostrils, but nary a flame was seen. The grown dragons were either basking in the sun or flying overhead. They paid little attention to the antics of the little ones.

Merlin sat beside Drius without uttering a word. He felt an air of tension between them but dismissed it. He wanted to be near his friend, and he wanted things between them to be good again.

"Beautiful day," he eventually said, dispelling the silence.

"It is." Drius' voice was low and dispassionate.

Merlin took a deep breath.

"Drius, I owe you an apology for the other night. When we came back from the Amare Feast, I am almost certain you wanted me to talk, and instead, I shut you out. Correct me if I am wrong."

The dragon lord said nothing. He stared ahead at the vale, blank-faced.

Merlin fiddled with the grass blades, pulling them and splitting them.

"Something happened that night at the Feast. You saw it. Everyone saw it. The moment they asked to hear about Arthur, I clammed up. I…" He faltered in his speech. Something lurched within him and held his tongue, and in the pit of his stomach, he felt ill. The words he might have said fell away, and he sat there with his head hung low as an internal struggle unfolded.

He might have been that way for a while, but Drius' calm voice pulled him out of the fray.

"You are holding back."

Merlin looked up at him, pale and shaking. The dragon lord locked eyes with him. Those eyes were sharp, piercing, and direct. They sought the truth.

"You have a secret that has become a burden. It hurts you. I have seen it. This is not the first time the name of your ward has caused you discomfort. Whatever you are hiding, it eats you up inside like a disease. I imagine you will never be free of its terrible grip till you finally expose it, cut it out by speaking it to light."

Merlin opened his mouth, then closed it again. He looked away, the intensity of Drius' eyes too much for him.

"Merlin, you and I have been close friends for many years. I have kept no secrets from you. It hurts me to know that after all this time you cannot trust me with yours."

"Oh, but I do trust you, Drius. It is not a question of trust."

"Are you sure of that? I believe it is one of two things: You either keep the secret because it is bad, and you fear judgment, in which case you question our friendship, or it is a secret that hurts you to think of, and those secrets should be told to ones who love you, or you may never heal. Are we not close enough for you to see that I love you?"

"I know you love me, old friend. I love you as well."

"Then what is this thing you cannot tell me? You should not fear judgment but look for relief when you tell me."

"I…" Tears traced Merlin's face, and he wiped them away. He took deep breaths to compose himself, then looked up at his friend. "You are right. A terrible secret ails me, and it concerns my ward, my king." His frame shook, and his fingers dug into the soil, feeling the cool, grainy relief of the earth. "I am sorry, Drius. I love and respect you, truly. Please do not question that. But this is something I am not yet ready to share. Maybe soon though."

They stared at each other, neither one giving an inch, but both of them thoughtful of the other.

"Our time together is waning, Merlin. If your plan works—"

"It will work," Merlin said desperately.

"I will be gone, and you will have no one close to you to share with. Promise me that you will tell me before our time is up."

Merlin's breath was shaky, but he felt compelled by the friendship and love between them to say: "Yes, I promise."

Drius nodded. "Good. Now, enough on that. Stay with me, and we will discuss more pleasant things."

Merlin cracked a smile. "Indeed."

They spoke freely about sundry things. First, the weather – Drius, like most dragons, could sense when a storm was coming, and he said there would be heavy rain by nightfall. They spoke about the dragons and sensitive matters the dragon lord attended to. Then their conversation shifted to the past few days and their audiences with members of the Circle.

"I must say, Drius, in all my life I never thought I would be so lucky."

"Lucky?"

Merlin nodded. "To meet and learn about so many fascinating creatures. Before this, I knew so little, but now I feel like a child who turns to learning, eager for knowledge, trapped in a swirling vortex of fascination and obsession."

"Sounds unhealthy."

"On the contrary, this is the best thing for me. It has been so long since I felt like this. Any opportunity to learn is a gift. Knowledge is power. Did I tell you that, in my lifetime, I have read over ten thousand books? It is true, I swear. Some of those works were romantic and fantastical, but so many were about science and history, great discoveries and theories. I love to learn. But this, what I am doing now, is better than reading. What I have learned thus far cannot be found in a book or even a hundred books. Magical creatures have eluded humans for so long and kept their mysteries a secret, with good reason. Humans are not entitled to know such things. I suppose then that makes me feel special because I am human, but still, I get to know the wonders of these races. Am I carrying on?"

Drius chuckled. "You are enthused and getting lost in words."

"My apologies, my friend. It is exciting, though."

"I wish the circumstances that led to your growth of knowledge were better."

Merlin frowned. "Me too. Me too."

Before them, in the vale, several young adult dragons were roughhousing. They were split off into pairs and wrestled with one another. There was one, a beautiful white dragon with silver wings and plated belly, who tussled with a red dragon with black wings and underbelly. They tackled and shoved, bashed each other with their tails, and roared with laughter.

"It occurs to me, Drius," said Merlin, "that I have not made time to sit with you and learn more about dragons. Should I summon my journal, quill, and ink pot and ask you questions?"

"You have lived with us for so long. Have you not learned enough to fill a page?"

Merlin thought a moment. "I suppose you are right. I know your habits and behaviors, your diet, and even your magic. I have no questions then, save one." He looked up at the dragon lord with inquisitive eyes. "Who will you be sending on the journey?"

Drius kept staring ahead and sighed. "I have not yet decided."

"Oh." Merlin looked back at the tussling dragons. "I imagine it is a tough decision."

"It is. The dragon has to be fit for the journey and right for the purpose. I need a dragon who is wise and gentle, strong and resilient. Many of my dragons became parents this last spring, and they will be reluctant to leave their broods."

"I had not thought of that." A pang of guilt speared Merlin. To his surprise: "I had not considered I might be splitting up families."

"Do not feel bad for it, Merlin. I know you, and you let guilt run away with you."

Merlin half-grinned. His friend did know him well.

"What we are doing is essential," Drius continued. "We know what we ask of our own, and they, in turn, know the risks. They know we would not have come to this decision lightly, and other options pose great risks. To make our presence known could lead to more bloodshed, but none of them wish to fade. What you have proposed, as the council determined, is our best chance to survive without repercussions. Whichever dragon I ask to go on the journey, he or she will understand and be honored for the chance to save their own."

Merlin nodded. "I am sure you will pick the right dragon."

They stared forward at the brawling dragons. The white dragon dodged the red dragon's tail and leapt at him. They rolled several times, and the white dragon pinned the red one to the ground with a victorious roar. The red dragon accepted defeat, laying his head aside. The white one jumped off her opponent, fanned her wings, and breathed a blaze of fire skyward in proud triumph.

"Isla has grown strong," said Merlin. "I remember when she was small and lost her brawls. In the last month or so, I have seen her pin Vesper three times."

"Perhaps he lets her win," said Drius, a little mirth in his voice.

"I think not. He likes her, certainly, but I can only imagine what she might do to him if she discovered he faked a loss."

Drius laughed. "No doubt she would pull a wild stunt like her mother did with me. I made the mistake of letting Mira win once. She hounded me to fight fairly, and when I refused to tussle with her again, she knocked me from the sky."

"What?" Merlin laughed.

"It is true. I said I would not fight her again, and the next day she surprised me mid-flight. She came rushing down on me, caught my wings, and we spiraled toward the earth. I tried to shake her loose, and the two of us scuffled in a fast descent. At the last moment, she released me, and I had just enough time to catch the air to glide to a crash amongst some trees. I took chase after her, and we brawled for several hours. In the end, she won, and she was satisfied with the fairness of the fight. That was when I knew I loved her."

"That is sweet. Strange, but sweet."

"Have you ever been in love, Merlin?"

Merlin blushed. "Yes, once, many, many years ago. She was lovely." His eyes hazed over with a memory.

"What was her name?"

"Nimueh. She was not mine to have, but I loved her. It was a fleeting romance."

"What happened?"

A shadow fell over Merlin. "She disappeared one day, and I never found her again. But what little time we had together, I cherish it."

They were silent a moment. Below, Isla was picking at Vesper, splashing him with water. Perhaps she was hoping for another tussle. Vesper, still panting, managed to splash her back.

"She is getting more brazen, like her mother," said Drius. "But I fear she may be too proud. Vesper is a fit opponent, but should another dragon challenge her, they might get the better of her." His tone was serious, and Merlin could see he was concerned.

"You mean a real fight?"

Drius nodded. "There will come a time when I must relinquish my position. If she is to lead one day, she has to be ready. Otherwise, I will have to choose another."

Merlin twiddled his thumbs and thought a moment. "I remember," he said with a struggling voice, "a boy who was brazen. Put a sword in his hand, and he thought he was unstoppable. One day, he got in a scuffle with some bigger lads, and they sent him home beaten, his pride bruised. I sat him down and said to him that brains count more in a fight than brawn alone. That night, he stayed up late, reading books on war strategies. The next time he crossed paths with those bullies, he baited them to chase him down a narrow alley, where he could take them on one at a time. He won that day."

Drius grinned but still looked at Isla. "This boy you speak of, was it Arthur?"

"Yes." Merlin hung his head.

A clap of thunder sounded overhead. The pair looked up to see dark clouds rolling in. It was the storm Drius foretold.

"Your Arthur went on to be a great king," he said. "I hope the best for my Isla."

The first raindrops fell with a pitter-patter. Merlin was glad for them, for though he smiled, they hid his tears.

CHAPTER THIRTEEN

A Giant's Harvest

Merlin was in bed, sound asleep. He had a silly grin on his face, as he dreamt pleasant dreams. What he dreamt was a secret, but the dream was charming and peaceful. How strange then it was when a distant sound wormed its way in.

"Hooooooo, Merlin!" It was a male voice, jolly and full of mirth.

Merlin stirred in his sleep, the dream fading. He desperately tried to hold onto it.

"Hoooooooo, Merlin. Great wizard!"

Merlin opened his eyes. "Great wizard?" His voice was groggy, his throat dry.

"Hooooooooo, Merlin."

There was no one at the mouth of the cave, yet the sound came from outside. Merlin struggled to his feet, still feeling a bit hazy. He then heard wings, and Drius appeared.

"You have a guest," he said.

"I gathered as much." Merlin came outside. The hour was early, and the world was still dark. The sun was not over the horizon, but its creeping light paled the sky a smoky gray. He looked over the edge of the cliff, and down below, he saw a figure waving up at them.

"Ho, Merlin. Ho, Drius." It was Hamel, the giant.

Drius flew Merlin down. The wizard was still dressed in his silver sleeping robes and slippers, his white hair and beard a mess. The hour was too early to stand on ceremony.

"Good morning, friends." Even in the dark, the giant's rosy cheeks bloomed, and his eyes sparkled.

"Morning? There is no sun," said Merlin in a friendly, jovial tone.

"No, but there soon will be. That is why I have come to collect you."

Merlin looked at Drius, a tad confused.

"You could have sent a messenger," said the dragon lord, "and I would bring Merlin to you."

"Yea, but I like to walk, and I can carry him back. Today is a great day. It is harvest day. I want you"—he pointed at Merlin, then Drius—"to be my guests."

The sun was peaking over the horizon when they set off. Merlin had changed to his familiar blue robes, and his satchel was thrown over his shoulder. He sat in Hamel's open palm while Drius flew overhead.

"You will like Holly," said Hamel. "It is a pretty place."

"What is Holly?" Merlin asked.

"Why, my village, of course."

If a man were to walk the distance from the Dragons' Keep to Holly, it would take him three days. A giant, though, covered more ground. They arrived on the outlying borders of the village within the hour, and by then, the sun was up and shining bright. Merlin could see the charming huts made of timber and thatch, bordered by a crescent of great trees that were many times the size of ordinary trees. A great valley stretched out before the village, with many hills, and the ground had been tilled into many rows. Some of these rows were orchards with great fruit and nut trees. Others were vineyards with tall trellises of grape vines, and there were also berry, melon, and vegetable patches. The scene was serene and lovely.

"Splendid," said Merlin, his mouth agape.

"Said you would like it." Hamel smiled proudly.

The village was alive and bustling. As they approached, Merlin saw the giants – men, women, and children – stacking empty baskets, presumably for the harvest. They hummed a tune as they worked, all together in great harmony. When Hamel walked down the lane, several folks waved and wished good morning to him and the "Great Wizard." Merlin was surprised and blushed to be addressed in such a manner.

"Hamel, not that I am not appreciative of formality, and it is very kind of your folk to call me such, though I am not sure if I would call myself such, but um, why do they call me 'Great Wizard'?"

"Because you are." The boss giant smiled as though he were stating the obvious.

"I am honored you think so." Inside, Merlin thought: *'Great' might be a bit much.*

"He is a humble wizard, is he not, Hamel?" Drius said from overhead.

"Indeed, Drius. That he is."

At the center of the village was a rotunda that split into three paths, and in its middle was a platform upon which Hamel stood. He raised a hand to his mouth and bellowed, "Hooooooo."

Several villagers, in response, cried, "Hooooo," and all gathered in the rotunda around their leader.

Merlin stood beside Hamel, feeling very small, and beside him was Drius. Several giant children awed at them, their eyes agleam with fascination and curiosity.

"Heaven and earth have been good to us," said Hamel. "They gave us a bountiful harvest in the spring, and just now, as I walked up, I could see the summer bounty far off – the watermelons, the red tomatoes, the eggplants, and more. I have no doubts that our summer harvest will be plentiful. With that said, let us say grace."

He and his fellow giants all clasped their hands in front of them and bowed their heads. Not wanting to be rude, Merlin did the same, and Drius lowered his head with his eyes closed.

"We thank thee, Great Provider, for the bounty we are about to receive. We thank heaven for its rains and the earth for her good soil. Though we toil, with our hoes and spades and forks, it is you who makes the bounty grow. Thank you for the food you put on our tables. May we have what we need and plenty to share. Amen."

All together, the village said, "Amen."

Hamel then exclaimed in a jollier voice, "Let the harvest begin!"

The giants went out to the fields in several lines. Each line, with at least ten giants to it, walked a different row of crops. Every giant carried a dozen wicker baskets, and this was how Hamel explained the harvest to Merlin and Drius:

"Every giant must harvest enough food to feed his or her family. No more, no less. They have a basket for each crop. Once the basket is full, that giant has enough of whichever crop he or she picked and waits for their line to trade rows with another line. Come on, lads. Let us find our place now." Hamel lifted his baskets onto his shoulder and offered his hand to Merlin to step onto again.

Merlin, with a single brow raised, tilted his head and said, "Beg your pardon?"

"I must harvest my portion too. You will come with me. Help, if you like, and we can talk some more. Better yet, we can talk after and taste the spoils of hard work."

Merlin followed astride Drius. The dragon lord insisted, thinking Merlin too small to work alongside the giants. "You will be underfoot and might get hurt," he said, to which Merlin replied, "I never thought you

would mother me, Drius," and laughed.

Their line started in the orchards. There were bright, juicy peaches and plums and cherries and figs that hung heavy on the branches, and when plucked, the branches snapped back. Merlin, with his magic, cut several with the snap of a finger, and they fell into Hamel's basket.

"Impressive," said the boss giant. "Your magic makes the work easy, but I rather like my way, with the use of my hands and the satisfaction of hard work. Makes me grateful for what I harvest."

"I can understand that," said Merlin, humbled by the giant's words, and he thought, *He is a simple being with simple ways, and happy for it. I have grown used to using my magic for almost every little thing and perhaps spoiled myself.*

The children who plucked fruit alongside their parents giggled and applauded Merlin for his feats of spectacle. They had never seen a wizard, and he fascinated them. They also loved Drius.

"Dragons do not often come this way," said Hamel. "Maybe one or two a year, but they pass by overhead, so high up, they look like a bird. This is the first time, I think, the kiddies have seen a dragon up close."

When they were done in the orchard, the lines switched, and the trio worked along rows of watermelon and cantaloupe, eggplant and tomatoes, blackberries, boysenberries, blueberries, and strawberries.

"Hamel, I am curious," said Merlin while cutting loose a melon, "does your kind eat any meat?"

The boss giant was taken aback and made a foul face. "Certainly not. We are a peaceful village, and we grow plenty to eat. I admit with much sadness that there are giants who have a taste for"—he grimaced—"flesh. There is a tribe way up north, surrounded by ice, I hear, that eats plenty of fish and whales. And beyond the sea, far south, there are rumors of giants who raise giant cattle for their tables. Enough on that though, for it makes me ill."

The harvest took all morning. The work quickened when the giants broke out in song. It was a humble tune, pleasant, with a rising and falling tempo. Merlin managed to scrawl a couple stanzas in his journal before getting lost in it:

I came, I sowed.
The hearty seed, it grows.
I shovel, I toil,
Now the boughs bow.

Kind soil, gentle rain,
Bring forth the grain.
My table is full,
And also my belly.

When the work was finished, the sun was high. The giants clapped their hands and lifted praises. All the baskets were full, and there were still plenty of crops left to be plucked.

Cupping his hands to his mouth, Hamel shouted: "Faithful stewards, raise thy hands."

Merlin counted five hands raised.

"Take your baskets home, then return and gather what is left. Put it all in the storehouse."

The stewards pounded the air with their fists and bellowed, "Yi."

"We are blessed," said Hamel to Merlin and Drius. "Ten years now, every summer, our fields yield more crops than there are mouths to feed."

"That is a blessing," said Merlin. "I imagine no human has fared so well with his own fields."

"You think not?"

Merlin nodded. "I knew your kind to be great tillers of soil. But after today, I can say with little doubt that you and your people know the earth as though you were kin to it."

Hamel chuckled. "I suppose you can say that. It was not that way in the beginning. Our record keeper has scrolls written by the first Meadow Giants, noting their struggles, trials, and errors. They broke soil several hundred years ago, and each generation after learned something new. They passed on their secrets to their children, and so on, and now here we are with bountiful harvests."

Merlin smiled. *Humans think you are an overgrown monster of little wit and brain. If only they knew it is they who are foolish and lacking in wisdom. If they would put aside their differences and not judge appearances, your kind could help them to never go hungry again.*

"Here comes the hard part," said Hamel, tearing Merlin from his thoughts.

"Hard part?"

"Carrying my baskets home. Every year, I do it myself. I can carry two at a time without spilling."

Merlin looked at the twelve full baskets and frowned. "Well, that is not fair. Maybe I can help."

"How?" Hamel looked at him with inquisitive curiosity.

Merlin rolled up his sleeves, focused his attention on the basket of strawberries, and whispered an incantation. Nothing happened. He closed his eyes, concentrated harder, and recited the spell again aloud. The basket wobbled and shook. Once more, with sweat breaking on his brow, he raised his hands, pronounced each word of the spell loud and clear, and willed it to work.

Hamel and Drius watched the basket lift from the ground, and the giant gaped in wonder. It rose a few feet, then stopped. Merlin shook. He struggled to hold the spell. The basket wavered and started to tip. Hamel grasped it before it could spill, and Drius caught Merlin as he collapsed.

"Merlin, are you well?" There was a ring of panic in Drius' voice.

Merlin gave a weak nod and tried to laugh off his folly. "I am fine, Drius."

"What happened?"

A woeful growl sounded from Merlin's stomach, and he clasped his hands over his middle. Blushing, he confessed, "I am embarrassed to say that powerful magic should never be done on an empty stomach. We were in such a hurry to leave this morning, I missed breakfast.

"Lesser spells and incantations do not require so much energy and are easily willed with a strong mind, but it seems the basket, being so big and full of heavy fruit, requires more substance. It is very much like trying to lift a hill or a castle with only my mind. Sometimes a user of magic must put more of themselves into their casting than sheer want and willpower. Sorry, Hamel. I wanted to be helpful."

Hamel waved off Merlin's words and smiled. "Do not worry about it. You were plenty helpful with the harvest. I do not mind carrying my bounty. It is strong work." He made a fist, and the muscles of his arm became pronounced.

Merlin grinned, appreciative of the giant's words. "But I did not spill the berries?"

"Not a one. Even if you had, though, what harm is a little dirt?" The boss giant laughed and picked up the baskets of strawberries and blueberries. "Come. I will show you my house and fix you something to eat."

With Merlin astride him, Drius followed Hamel at a steady flight. They circled round the village, and perhaps the boss giant worried his company would find this strange because he said, "I live outside the village. Always have. Not by much. I am close but not next door to any of my fellows."

They turned the corner of the last village hut, and there, just a ways off, backed up against the crescent forest, was a quaint little house. It was built of timber and thatch like the others, but there was a charming garden out front, blossoming on both sides of a cobblestone path leading up to the door. The house and its garden were fenced in with slabs of pine split in half and wedged in the ground side-by-side. To enter the garden, there was a swinging gate with a latch.

Merlin gazed at the flowers – tulips, roses, and lilies of all colors and sunflowers, lined neatly in their beds, all blooming, as if they were happy to see their master home again.

"What do you think?" Hamel asked.

"This is a lovely garden. The flowers are so grand and colorful. I love it."

"Thank you. I love flowers. They keep me cheerful. Come inside."

Merlin and Drius followed him through the great door to his home, and inside, they found it simple and cozy. There was a kitchen, with a fireplace, and a bedroom. A modest supper table divided the rooms. A chest sat on the floor, at the foot of the bed, and no doubt stored the giant's clothes. What caught Merlin's attention, though, was a small shelf, high on the wall, with a half dozen books stuck between two bookends carved into the likeness of rabbits.

"Do you read much, Hamel?"

The giant placed his baskets on the supper table, turned, and followed Merlin's line of sight to the books. "Some, yes. Truth is, we giants do not have many books. Those ones are fairytales and giant folklore."

"Would you like more books?"

Hamel's eyes brightened. "That would be nice."

"Maybe I can bring you some on that day at the beach. I have so many books, and there is no telling how much more use I will get out of them."

"You mean it? You would give me your books?" Hamel smiled big, full of hope and excitement, like a child about to receive a gift.

"Certainly. Would you like more legends and folk tales like these?"

"If you have them, yes. But also, would you happen to have any books on…" He grew quiet and looked down at his feet.

"On what?" Merlin saw doubt and uncertainty on the giant's face. "I promise there is no request you could make that I would find silly or dumb."

"Well, if you have them, I would like books on flowers and"—he took a breath and spoke the final word softly—"inventions."

"Inventions?" Merlin was surprised.

Hamel nodded.

"Oh, my dear fellow, of course, I have books on inventions. They are some of my favorites to read. Why were you so wary to ask?"

"Because giants tend to shy away from newfangled things."

"Other giants, but not you?" Merlin peered at him with a wily grin.

Hamel nodded again. "Give me a moment to fetch my baskets, and I will tell you." He left before his guests could say another word.

"Strange and wonderful," said Merlin.

"What is?" Drius asked.

"Him. His character. His inquisitive mind. I like him. Anyone who wants to read and learn will achieve great things in life. I certainly have."

The pair settled on the supper table and waited for their host to return.

"Tell me, Merlin, what did you acquire from books?"

"Oh, a great many things. I learned herbology, which is the gathering of herbs to make medicine and potions. I learned geography, history, war and battle strategies. It was also in books that I discovered the ways of magic."

"I thought magic came naturally to you."

"Some of it, yes. Little things, like changing a stone into a frog or making a branch grow, came easy. But I had to learn about magic to use greater feats of it. I will tell you truly, I was led to ancient scripts that held the world's oldest spells, and I studied page after page. I was so young then, and I still remember how excited I was, pouring over the words and trying the spells. Later on, I invented spells by reciting words and willing them to action. So I say again, the best way to learn anything is to stick one's nose in a book."

Drius chuckled. "Dragons cannot read."

Merlin grinned, knowing his friend was teasing him. "Well, if there was time, I would remedy that."

Hamel came and went from the house, bringing two baskets at a time, and after his fifth journey out, he finally brought back the last of his bounty.

"Sorry for the delay, my friends," he said, huffing. "Now, where were we?"

"Inventions," said Merlin with a smile.

"Oh, yes. But first, let me make us something to eat. It is past the lunch hour."

As much as Merlin was a wizard with spells, Hamel was a master in the kitchen. He revealed a cellar beneath the floor, where he stored onions and garlic and several jars of herbs. He gathered what he needed from down there, chose five freshly picked tomatoes, and prepared a delicious tomato soup. The aroma was tantalizing, and Merlin licked his lips in anticipation.

"I am sorry," said Hamel, suddenly red in the face. "I did not think. I have no bowls your size."

"Not to worry," said Merlin. "May I borrow two bowls?"

Hamel set the bowls on the table, and Merlin used his magic to shrink them down to sizes fit for him and Drius. Hamel laughed.

"You are full of surprises, Great Wizard."

Merlin blushed at the word "great" again and said, "Thank you."

Hamel filled his bowl, then, with some help from Merlin, filled the smaller bowls. He set them on a tray and headed for the door.

"Let us eat outside," he said. "It is better that way."

The trio sat on a hill that overlooked Hamel's hut, the village, and most of the fields and orchards. They sipped their soup, which was not only tasty but filling and sent a warmth down to the toes. When finished, Merlin patted his stomach.

"That was, without a doubt, the best tomato soup I ever had. You are a fine cook, boss giant."

"Thank you. My mum taught me."

"Tell me more about your interest in inventions. How did that start?"

Hamel blushed. "Well, it started when I was little. I did not have many friends, so I read books, grew flowers, and fiddled with things. If something broke, I fixed it. Papa said I was good at fixing things. Then, one day, I made something."

"What was it?"

"A timekeeper."

Merlin raised a brow. "A timekeeper?"

Hamel reached into his pocket and pulled out a round box. He shook out its contents into his hand. It was a small disc with numbers etched into its perimeter and a triangular shape fixed atop. He laid it on the ground.

"It tells me the time," he said. "Look at the shadow."

Merlin did. With the sun overhead, the point of the triangle's shadow fell on the number two.

"It is the second hour past noon." Hamel wrung his hands together. "Mum thought it was brilliant. Papa told me not to share it with anyone. He worried for me."

Merlin examined the device. He then looked up at Hamel, beaming. "You are clever, boss giant."

Hamel stared at him wide-eyed.

"What you have made here is called a sundial. This sort of timepiece has been around for centuries, but then I do not suppose you knew that?"

Hamel shook his head.

"And I suppose word or mention of most manmade contraptions does not reach your ears?"

Hamel frowned. "Humans are afraid of giants, so they do not share with us."

Merlin internally winced but smiled. "This is a wonderful thing you made."

"Really?" Hamel brightened, his eyes dancing. "You are not just being nice?"

"No, I am serious. This really is a great invention."

Color filled Hamel's face, and his smile was brilliant. "Thank you, Great Wizard."

Merlin felt a twinge. "About that: let us make a deal. You call me Merlin, and I will give you every book I have on inventions."

Hamel's smile did not falter. He nodded his head and said, "Agreed. Thank you,"—he paused—"Merlin."

The trio remained on the hill, and Merlin asked his questions about giants. Hamel left them momentarily to fetch a pitcher of honeysuckle peach water.

"My mum would make this toward the end of each summer. Drink up."

Merlin did not know how thirsty he was till he took his first sip. The water was cool, refreshing, and pleasant with its light hints of honeysuckle and peach nectars. He downed his glass and asked for another.

It was the third hour past noon, according to Hamel's sundial, when Merlin closed his journal.

"This has been wonderful," he said. "You are a delightful host, Hamel."

"Thank you. You both are welcome back anytime. You should return for the fall harvest. We have a great feast to celebrate the season and our labors. There are pies, so many they stack higher than our houses."

Merlin chuckled. "It sounds like great fun. I wish I could see it."

A pang of sadness riddled Hamel's face, as his memory dawned on him. "I am sorry. I forgot. Will you not be able to see the village?"

"I am not certain. Magic is a fickle thing, unpredictable. This is a giant's village, so maybe the spell will hide your entire village, the fields too. I will return to find out."

"Please do. I want to know if you see it or not."

"I am going to miss you, boss giant." Merlin looked up at him and smiled. "If I should never see this place again, I am grateful to have seen it today."

"It is not fair." Hamel sniffled. "I make a friend, and soon he will not see me. But maybe I can write you." His eyes brightened. "Yes. I could write you letters. I can make a box and stick it outside my home or yours. Inside it, I will leave you letters. How does that sound to you?"

A warmth filled Merlin's chest. "That sounds like a grand idea."

"Yes. That way, you will not feel so lonely. And if magic lets you see the village and my letters, maybe it will let you see our food. If so, I will leave you one of my pumpkin pies, my mum's own recipe." He seemed so jolly, his cheeks rosy and his eyes sparkling.

Merlin reached out and touched the giant's big thumb. "You are a kind soul, Hamel."

The gentle giant closed his finger over Merlin's tiny hand. "You as well, Great Wiz— I mean, Merlin."

CHAPTER FOURTEEN

A Journey Beneath the Waves

Merlin lay in bed, dreaming and snoring. He had retired early before the moon was at her peak, and now he slept so heavily, he did not sense the sunrise or the strange presence in his cave.

At first, all was quiet. All was peaceful and calm. Then he felt a weight on his chest. It was not so heavy he could not breathe, but heavy enough to penetrate the dream. Merlin tried to shift in his sleep, roll over and shake. The weight shifted with him, first on his chest, then his belly, and then his shoulder. Merlin laid flat on his back, and the weight returned to his chest. The dream hazed away and turned to the darkness behind his eyelids.

Slowly, he opened his eyes, the world a blur, and he saw a strange figure standing over him. It was mostly white and appeared to have a face with a yellow-orange protrusion that clasped something pink. He reached for his spectacles on his bedside table, put them on, and was startled to see it was a seagull standing on top of him with a salmon conch shell in its beak.

"Hello there," said Merlin. "Might that be for me?"

The seagull dropped the shell on Merlin's chest with a soft thud, mewed once, and hopped off to a corner of the bed, where it settled for a nap.

"Make yourself at home," Merlin chuckled, picking up the seashell. "But what do I do with this?"

As if in answer, Merlin heard a small voice echoing from the shell. He turned it over this way and that, studying it. The seagull mewed again, then stuffed its face beneath its wing.

"If only I understood seabirds. Owls, I can converse with politely. Eagles and hawks, they pipe like captains. And hummingbirds, their words fly as fast as they do and in high-ringing tones, but still, I understand them."

The seagull did not mind Merlin's words and slept soundly.

The voice in the shell spoke again, and Merlin, thinking of nothing better to do, lifted it to his ear.

"Merlin." It was Qoral's sing-song voice, speaking from the depths of the shell. "Meet me at the beach at your earliest convenience. I will be waiting there with an escort of my royal guard."

A moment passed, and the shell repeated its message. Merlin lowered it from his ear and beamed.

"A visit with the merfolk. I have been waiting for this with much excitement," he said to the seagull, who did not hear him. "You can stay if you like, but I must get dressed and go see Drius."

In less time than it takes a seagull to fly, Drius and Merlin arrived at the seashore and settled on its warm sands. The seagull messenger hopped off Drius' back, having hitched a ride home, and mewed at the dragon.

"You are welcome," said the dragon lord to the bird.

The seagull flew off and joined a flock of gulls that was farther down the beach, digging in the sands for stranded fish and crabs.

Merlin's brow lifted. "You understand seagulls?"

"Some." Drius grinned. "Most times, they squawk about food."

Merlin laughed and shook his head. "You never cease to amaze me."

"Good. That means you are not bored of me."

"I would never be bored of you. What a terrible thing to say." Merlin feigned insult, and they both laughed. "At least we are in good spirits today."

"And your day is about to get better, I suspect." Drius looked past Merlin, and Merlin turned around to follow his line of sight.

There was the sea, blue and calm, the light of the sun glittering off its surface. The small waves lapped at the shore in friendly handshakes. In the distance, the gulls mewed, but the only other sound was the water, cresting and breaking, rolling and drawing back. Bubbles of sea foam gathered on the sands and silently popped to oblivion.

Then, without a sound, Qoral and her escort of six royal merguards rose from the blue. From the waist down, they stayed immersed. The merguards wore sea glass armor – breastplates and helms, translucent and beautiful, in shades of teal, green, and gold. Each was armed with a trident and shield. They waited, at attention, for their queen's command, with nary a smile or hint of expression.

Qoral, less formal or severe, beamed at Merlin and bowed her head to Drius. "Welcome, friends." Her voice chimed and bounced off the water to them. "Come closer."

Merlin walked to the water's edge, where the waves lapped over his feet. As always, the water was cool and inviting. It seemed to tug at him, begging him to venture out. Drius stood behind him, observant and waiting.

Qoarl swam up to them, as close as she could get. She stared at Merlin, or maybe through him. Her blue eyes were calm but earnest. "Merlin, I understand you harbor a great love for the sea. Is this true?"

Taken aback, Merlin smiled and said, "Yes, your majesty. It is a great and wonderful mystery to me. I come here often to sit on the sands and listen to the waves, the power and strength of them, rolling and crashing. I look out over the blue, and my mind wonders with great curiosity as to what lies beneath the surface. It is a thing of magic itself, I am certain, and holds many secrets."

Qoral grinned. "Do you know the translation of your name, Merlin?"

"Yes. It means 'sea fortress.'"

"Appropriate, I think." She reached out her webbed hand to him. "Would you like to see it?"

Merlin stared at her, confused and bewildered.

Those blue eyes bubbled with affection. "What you hope to do for us should not be taken lightly. Your kindness and devotion, your determination to help us live on must be recognized. This, then, is my gift to you, Merlin. I shall take you where no man has gone before, under the sea. There are so many wonderful things beneath the waves, things you could never imagine. I want to show them to you. I want you to see our kingdom, see us, and know us better. I want to give you this. Will you let me?"

Merlin was speechless. His heart pounded with great excitement. His eyes danced in his head. "Truly, your majesty?"

She nodded.

Merlin nearly took a step forward, eager to clasp her hand, but stopped. He looked back at Drius, his eyes searching, maybe for permission or blessing.

The dragon lord sighed. "I cannot come with you. You will be completely at her mercy." He said this without a hint of worry and even grinned at the mermaid queen. He then laid down, wings folded in and feet crossed. "Go. I will wait for you here."

Merlin nodded with much enthusiasm, his smile wide and bright. To Qoral he said, "Your majesty, I would be more than delighted to see the wonders of your home and wholeheartedly accept your offer." He kicked off his sandals and cast a spell to make his satchel and its contents waterproof. He waded out to Qoral, his hand outstretched and shaking with euphoria. He put his hand in hers.

She felt nothing like a fish. She was warm, not cold and oily. And yet, Merlin could feel a light roughness to her, much like the feeling of sand, caused by the most minute scales.

The webbing of her fingers was slick and resistant. She closed her fingers over his and led him out to where he waded. The water was pulling at him, trying to knock him off balance, but Qoral held him steady. She then pulled him in close and whispered in his ear.

"You cannot breathe underwater like we can, so I shall give you a kiss."

Merlin thought he heard her wrong, but before he could say a word, she pulled him under. Startled, he nearly gulped sea water, when her lips found his. It was a soft, sweet kiss and seemed to go on forever. He was so dazed by it, shocked and bemused, that he did not notice the change come over him. When she parted from him, he sighed many bubbles.

"How do you feel?" Qoral asked. "Take a breath."

Without a thought or question, Merlin did as told and was overcome with stupefied wonder to find he could breathe underwater. He patted his neck, searching for gills, but there were none. Nor had he grown scales or fins or become fish-like in any way.

"So this is the magic of merfolk," he said, little bubbles trailing from his lips. "Incredible."

"The spell will last so long as you remain underwater," said Qoral. "The moment you breathe the air above, the spell is broken."

"Incredible. Simply incredible."

Qoral laughed. "If a little kiss can leave you so entranced, wait till you see what else awaits you down here."

At the start of their journey, all there was to see was the white sand that stretched on forever, in all directions, beneath the vast blue of seawater. Qoral led Merlin by the hand, her royal guard following behind them. Merlin gently kicked to keep pace, and the water teased his hair and robes. It was quiet, the only sound being the tender beats of the merfolk's tails as their party glided through the water.

But after they had ventured a good distance out, the depths widened, and the sands dipped, and life and color bloomed before them. A stunning coral reef stretched out in front of them, as far as Merlin could see. There were many hues and shapes, so many colonies of coral fused together, lacing and neighboring each other to form a spectacular garden.

Qoral pointed to and named the wonders they saw. There were staghorn corals, leaf corals, carnations, sea whips, sea anemones, and an abundance of colorful fish, darting in and out of sight amongst the vibrant rocks and branches. There was an eel with its toothy grin and an octopus with its many unfurling arms. A herd of seahorses hitched their tails to the limbs of a tree coral, and dueling crabs scurried beneath the sea fans. Overhead, a pod of dolphins trilled and whistled as they teased and pushed a sea turtle between them with their noses.

"Naughty," Qoral said with a laugh. She rescued the sea turtle and sent it on its way. The dolphins, unbothered by the mermaid breaking up their fun, nuzzled her neck, and she chittered to them.

"You can speak to them?" Merlin asked, entertained by their exchange.

"Oh, yes. We merfolk can speak with most sea creatures, but some are too fierce to hear."

A dolphin then squeaked, alert and with panic, and the pod folded together.

"Here comes one now," said Qoral, and her guards encircled them. She pointed in the distance, where the water was open and murky.

A lone figure swam out there. Its dorsal coloring was a dark, brooding gray, but its belly was white. It was a very large fish with pronounced fins and a strong crescent-shaped tail, and even from where they waited, Merlin could see the sharp, triangular teeth protruding from its lax mouth. He had seen the like of this beast before, caught up in fishermen's nets.

"A shark," he said in a low voice, trying not to draw its attention.

Qoral nodded. "Yes. We call this one the great white. There is no need to speak softly. He knows we are here. He sought us out, for his kind is good at sensing prey over great distances. But he will not come any closer."

The pod of dolphins swam around them in formation, chittering warnings to the predator.

"We are protected."

"So you cannot speak to that one?"

"No. Most sharks have their ears closed. This one cannot understand me, nor I him. He is driven by instinct and little else, but still, we do not hold his brutality against him. We do not hate him or other sharks, for they are only animals and do as the Great Creator intended them to."

The great white swam closer, then drifted alongside to look at them. Merlin got goose pimples, staring at its black, lifeless eyes. It gave no impression of thought or feeling, only hunger and the potential to strike. Then, silent and without hesitation, the shark turned and swam away, getting lost in the blue.

A dolphin whistled to Qoral.

"He has gone elsewhere to find a meal. Good." She chittered to the dolphins, and they swam off in another direction. "Come." She took Merlin's hand again. "We are not far from the city."

They continued on, staying close to the sandy seafloor.

"Even with my guard," Qoral explained, "it is safer to swim down here and not up there where there is no cover, no protection from danger. This is how we avoid ships and fishermen's nets, as well as sea predators."

They came upon a dense kelp forest. Thousands of lanky green seaweed reached up toward the glittering sunlight beyond the water, swaying this way and that with the current.

"The city is on the other side," said Qoral, pulling Merlin along.

They brushed the seaweed aside, which was slick to touch and prone to tangle around a wrist or ankle, and it seemed as though the forest went on forever.

Suddenly, a strange sound drifted through the silence. Qoral put up a hand to stop their party. She held her breath and listened. The sound came again. It was a long, lulling tone, melodic and soothing. It started out low, then rose several clicks. Qoral beamed.

"Come, Merlin. You will love this."

She swam upwards, with Merlin in tow, and the guards close behind them. They brought their heads above the seaweed, and there, out in the vast open water, was a pod of creatures Merlin could not fathom. They were floating giants, dark with white bellies, and they glided through the water in a carefree manner. Merlin gaped when he heard the beautiful, haunting sound again and realized it came from these creatures.

"What are they?"

"Humpback whales," said Qoral. "These are some of the most peaceful giants in the sea. The song you hear is how they speak to each other. They sing most beautifully during courtship, but this is not the season for love. See? That mother has a calf."

Merlin saw a much smaller whale tucked under an adult's large flipper.

"Are they not beautiful?" Qoral asked with an adoring smile.

"Yes, they are," said Merlin softly.

The whales' song filled his ears. It was so strange, stirring, and lovely a tune, he was entranced by it, and he could have listened to it forever, but Qoral tugged on his hand, breaking the spell.

"We must go. There is still much to see and do."

They reached the other side of the kelp forest, where the seafloor suddenly dropped off, and they were left on a cliff. Merlin looked beyond the shelf at the valley below and awed in many bubbles.

"Is this—"

"Yes." Qoral swam to the edge and, with a wave of her hand, declared in a voice both eager and proud, "Welcome to Nerida."

Nerida. The mer-city beneath the waves. Merlin marveled at it. It was grand in every sense of the word. He could never have imagined its splendor.

"Come. I will show you." Qoral took his hand, and their party swam off the ledge.

A great wall encircled the city, and Merlin thought this funny because, *Fish and folk can swim over it.* But then he saw several royal guards stationed along the top of the wall, armed with tridents. He blushed under their gaze. *Maybe not.*

They entered through the grand archway, the gates open to receive them. The gates, Merlin stopped to admire, were made of twisted bands of blue sea glass and gold.

"Beautiful," he said, brushing his fingers along the bars.

Qoral giggled. "This is only the gate. There is more to see."

The great wall, as well as the houses and other structures it surrounded, were all made from white sea clay. The latter were trimmed with multi-colored sands, seashells, and sea stones. There were coral gardens everywhere, great and small, occupied by many fish and sea critters, but the grandest garden was ahead of them and surrounded the palace.

"This is home," said Qoral, bringing their party to a halt before the royal house.

Merlin stared, his mouth agape and losing bubbles. The palace rivaled any castle he had seen on the surface. It had several towers of varying sizes, all interconnected by bridges. Each tower had a dome made of gold, and there were many windows to look out from on the city. The largest structure, which housed the great hall, was round and at the center of everything. Its dome was striped with plates of gold and blue-green sea glass, which shimmered in the drowned light of the sun.

"What do you think?" Qoral asked, a hint of excited anticipation in her voice.

"What words can I use?" Merlin looked on at the palace, his cheeks rosy with mirth. "There is no palace on the surface that is its equal. Its only rival would have been the Camelot I knew, but then again, I am biased."

"Really? How so?"

"I helped draw up the plans for Camelot. But I do not believe that even in my wildest dreams I could conceive something as grand and spectacular as this." He gestured to the palace with a wave of his hand. "This could be a wonder of the world if the world knew about it."

Qoral frowned. "Better that it does not."

Merlin nodded. "True."

Without warning, a herd of seahorses came rushing out of the royal coral. They headed straight for Qoral and hid in her long golden hair.

The mermaid queen was startled but giggled. "What is the meaning of this?" she asked the frightened seahorses as they poked their faces out of her long tresses.

Merlin looked where they had come from, and out of the coral appeared another figure, this one very strange and peculiar-looking. It propelled itself forward, its undulating fins quivering, and it changed many hues – first, it had stripes, then it had spots, then it was black, no white, no red. Whatever it was, Qoral caught it in her arms and laughed with great mirth.

"Piper! You naughty cuttlefish. Are you terrorizing these poor seahorses?"

The cuttlefish, as Qoral called it, was riveting with colors and nuzzled her. It cooed and tickled her face with its arms.

"Stop that, you silly thing. I pardon you. But you are going to let these nice seahorses go about their business."

The seahorses, seeing their chance, darted from her hair and disappeared amongst the coral.

"This is Piper, my pet cuttlefish." Qoral held him out for Merlin to see, and the strange critter stuck its tongue out at him.

Merlin laughed. "Pleased to meet you, Piper."

Just then, the palace doors opened, and a couple of mermen appeared with trumpets. These they blasted in a merry, formal tune.

"They are ready to receive us," said Qoral, lacing her arm through Merlin's.

"Who is?"

"My family."

They entered the great hall, and Merlin was met with several composed faces. There were guards and royal servants on either side of the room, waiting in the light of glow fish lanterns. At the room's center was a long dining table, set low to the ground and surrounded by pillows. There were several dishes of odd but attractive food laid out and eight place settings.

Me and Qoral, Merlin counted. *That leaves six.*

Qoral led him to the foot of the table, where they waited.

One of the trumpet blowers swam forward, blasted his trumpet once, and announced, "Presenting the royal family."

At the back of the room was a multi-paned window of translucent sea glass. Before this appeared the members of the royal family, one at a time, as their names were called. There were Qoral's five younger sisters – Aerwyna, Serena, Cari, Kai, and the littlest, Lorelai – and their mother, Meribella, the former queen.

Meribella swam forward and clasped Merlin's hands in hers. "Welcome, Merlin." She then kissed his cheek. "Please, will you join us for lunch?"

Merlin, his face warm with color, said, "It would be an honor, your highness."

The food ranged from familiar to bizarre and all delicious. There were cracked oysters with their pearls still in the shell. Qoral served Merlin three, each one with a different colored pearl – one white, one black, and one pink. The pearls, she told him, were for keeps. There were clams and mussels, as well as shrimp and crab – the crab was Piper's favorite, as he greedily seized one with his tongue and scuttled off with it to a corner of the chamber. Lobsters, both blue and red, were served, though Qoral assured her guest there was little difference in the taste between them. Merlin wanted to try a little of everything, even those things that looked strange or had funny names. Things like seaweed sandwiches, moss jelly, and squid ink pudding.

Only one drink was served, a pink luminescent concoction called jelly juice. Qoral said it was made from sea plants and zapped by live jellyfish. Merlin took a sip and found the drink delightfully tangy with a lot of zip.

While they ate, Qoral, with help from her mother, answered Merlin's questions about merfolk. Meribella was very formal in answering, while Qoral spoke with great elaboration and excitement. Before this meeting, Merlin knew Qoral was young, but seeing the queens together made it plain, and he realized she was no older than Arthur when he had become king – fifteen, maybe sixteen years of age.

After he put his journal away, and the table was cleared of food and dishes, Merlin enjoyed polite conversation with the queens. The princesses chimed in when they felt like it but were otherwise preoccupied. The youngest, Lorelai, played with her doll, while Cari and Kai compared the pearls from their oysters, and Aerwyna and Serena stole glances at a handsome guard and giggled whispers between them. The presence of a land dweller made little to no impression on them.

It was not much later that a short, plump merman hastened into the great hall in a frenzy with a long parchment trailing from his hand.

"Your majesty," he said, his voice high, rounded, and formal, "I need you to review the guest list for your one-year reign celebration."

Qoral frowned, and Piper, who was in her lap, growled at the merman, changing fiery colors. The merman ignored the cuttlefish.

"Picard, I have a guest. The list can wait."

Picard regarded Merlin strangely, then turned back to the queen and waved the parchment about. "But I must send the invitations today," he half-whined.

Qoral turned red, and she threw him a sharp look. She opened her mouth to speak, when her mother suddenly rose.

"I can look the list over, dear. You tend to your guest."

Picard was startled. "But, but—"

Meribella put out her hand. "Give me the list, Picard. My daughter has more important matters at hand, like saving our kind. What good is a party if no one lives to attend it?" Her voice held a tone of sarcasm, but her piercing eyes made clear her point.

Picard handed her the list. Meribella took it and turned to her five younger daughters.

"Girls, let us retire to the garden for your lessons. I think we have taken up enough of Merlin's time."

Merlin stood and bowed to Meribella. "Your majesty, every moment with you and your family was delightful. Thank you for the honor of dining with you."

The former queen smiled. "It was our honor, Merlin." She clapped her hands, and the servants, with Picard, left, and she and the princesses took their leave as well. Only the guards remained with Qoral, Merlin, and Piper in the great hall.

Qoral sighed. "I am sorry," she said in a quiet, worn voice.

"For what?"

"For Picard. He was rude."

"Oh, him? Nonsense. I am used to such people. Most times, they do not realize what they are doing because they get so focused on one thing."

"He makes a big deal out of every little thing and is afraid to make any decision without me."

Merlin chuckled. "We had such a man in Arthur's court. A scraggly, thin man by the name of Francis. He would hound the king almost every day with this or that. He tried my patience time and again. In the end, though, he was not such a bad fellow."

Qoral still frowned. Her eyes hazed over, and she absentmindedly pet Piper. The cuttlefish purred in her lap.

"If you do not mind my saying so, your majesty, you seem troubled."

"You could say that."

"Well, if it helps, you can talk to me."

Qoral lifted her eyes to see him. The blue in them quaked with sadness, and he thought she might cry.

"Merlin, if I confide in you, you promise not to tell another soul?"

"You have my word."

A brief smile flitted over her face before she said to the guards, "Leave us."

They did, and Merlin was alone with the young mermaid queen and Piper.

"The list Picard has is actually a list of eligible suitors. He and my mother settled the guest list for the ball several days ago. Now it is a matter of choosing those mermen who are fit to attend and, or so my mother hopes, ask for my hand."

"I see." Merlin leaned back and twiddled his fingers. "And what is wrong with that, majesty?"

Qoral stole a glance around the room, leaned in toward Merlin, and whispered, "I do not want to marry."

"Oh." Merlin made the "Oh" with his lips, and Qoral drew back.

"At least, not right now. I am only sixteen, and I have no interest in mermen or love or marriage."

"Sixteen? My, that is a young age to be queen. Still, girls on the surface marry at your age."

"Maybe that is right for them, but not for me."

"Maybe, maybe not. Maybe a young suitor will come to the ball and sweep you off your, um, tail."

Qoral tried not to laugh. She laid back on the floor and stared up at the ceiling. Merlin followed her line of sight to a grand mosaic up there, showing Meribella beside a striking, crowned figure, a merman, who Merlin assumed was her late husband, the former king, Lir. Qoral and her sisters were also illustrated in pretty tiles, surrounding their parents.

"My parents married young. He was eighteen, and she was fifteen. They fell in love after one night together, at a ball like the one we are having. Mother thinks the same could happen to me, just as you suggest. She says neither she nor my father was looking for love. It just happened. But she does not understand. I want more out of life."

"What is more?"

Qoral sat up. "Adventure. Thrills and excitement. My father promised me that when I turned sixteen, he would take me out of the palace to see the wonders of the sea. It was going to be grand, my greatest adventure, and then I could settle, my heart being satisfied in knowing what is out there and touching it. But I was cheated." A tear traced her cheek. "Father died, and now here I am, a queen, the youngest in history to take the throne. I have no idea what I am doing, and everyone expects me to follow convention."

Merlin sipped his jelly juice and pondered a moment. "You have my condolences for your loss. I never had a father, so I cannot imagine your pain. As to being queen and following convention, you remind me of a lad who felt the same way when he became king."

Qoral sniffed. "You mean Arthur?"

Merlin rubbed his chest, feeling the familiar sting, but he went on. "Yes. He was young, no older than you, when he became king. And being king, a lot was expected of him, but he was still a boy. He had me there to help him, just like you have your mother, but he wanted adventure, thrills, and excitement, as you say. Can you guess how many times he snuck away to go hunting or joyriding? Countless. And there I was, chasing after him and bringing him home." Merlin laughed and surprised himself to hear the mirth leave him.

"I remember, too, when it was time for him to settle, to find a queen. You would not believe the stunts he pulled. Once, he convinced the stable boy to take his place at a ball. Of course, I knew it was a faux king, as did the royal guard and Francis, but the young ladies, who had never seen Arthur before, knew not the difference. That was a great night of embarrassment, and I had to summon all my strength not to laugh so as not to encourage his behavior.

"Then, one not-so-special day, he went for a ride and met a girl. She was beautiful and stole his heart the moment he saw her. He could talk of nothing else but her, and when she came to the king's birthday, he danced with her and no other lady the entire evening. They were wed a week later."

The whole while he spoke, Qoral rested her cheek in her hand and listened. When his story was over, she shook her head. "That is all well for Arthur, but I am not him."

"No, you are not. But you will find your way. You will get used to the customs of queenship, and you will find time to play. There will be time for adventure and time to rest. And when it comes to love, well, no one can tell you when or where it will happen. But I can tell you this: it will happen when you least expect it. Who knows? Maybe the merman who steals your heart will love adventure."

Qoral rolled her eyes. "I will not hold my breath."

There was a moment of silence between them. The only sound was Piper, purring in his sleep.

"What if I fail?" Qoral said in a quiet voice. "What if I fail as queen?"

"Why would you fail?"

"Unlike my sisters, I never cared for lessons. I often snuck away to play, and Father would send the royal guard to find me. He and Mother told me time and again that lessons are important, that I must learn them to be a good queen. Truth is, I thought I had plenty of time to learn and plenty of time before I became queen. I could not believe my ears when, from his deathbed, Father named me ruler of Nerida and all merfolk. I have never been so scared. It is frightening and overwhelming to have so many lives depend on me. My council, for instance. They are not happy with this plan of yours, and they were even less happy when I said I did not care about their objections, that I was going to see your plan through."

Merlin could not help but smile at her devotion.

"I have so many duties and responsibilities, I feel I am drowning in them. I am so unsure of myself and whether or not I can handle this, and I wonder if Father made a mistake."

"Stop right there," Merlin said in a firm but non-threatening tone. He seized her hand and looked her in the eyes.

"Your grace,"—he calmed his voice and tried to sound comforting—"Arthur was frightened, too, and certainly overwhelmed when he became king. When first he was crowned, he told me he did not want to be king and thought it better left to someone older and wiser. He even suggested I take the crown – what a foolish idea. I remember a day that came much later when he locked himself in his room and told everyone to go away.

I, of course, walked right through the door and sat with him on his bed. His face was stained with tears, and he told me most emphatically that a mistake had been made, that he was too young and stupid to be king. I set him right, and I will tell you the same thing I told him:

"You are no fool, nor are you stupid. You are young, yes, but age is not the issue. The real issue is fear, fear of being a failure. You can either let fear beat you, or you can conquer it. Yes, there are a lot of decisions to make as a king, or a queen, but wallowing in fear solves nothing. If anything, it guarantees you fail. You have to push past it and take chances. You might stumble now and then, but when that happens, you pick yourself up and try again. You learn from your mistakes, gain knowledge, and use it moving forward.

"As for the naysayers – Arthur had them too, ignore them. There will always be someone who thinks they know better than you. Move past them and keep your chin up.

"One day, I do not know how far in the future, you will realize you are a good queen. You will look back and see how far you have come, and on that day, you will see that it really was not so bad."

With tears in her eyes, Qoral threw her arms around Merlin, startling Piper out of her lap. She whispered, "Thank you," and hugged him tight.

"Why did she say to come again at night?" Drius asked, gliding through the silent air, the stars twinkling overhead.

"She did not say. She only said to do it and see something neat."

"Neat? This neat thing, I wonder why she did not show it to you when you were with her before."

"Perhaps it is something I can only see at night. I think her mother, Meribella, insisted, or maybe it was Qoral's idea. The queens conversed in private before I was escorted back to the surface."

Drius shook his head. "Strange. Very strange."

The dragon lord settled on the beach. Merlin clambered down and listened. The only sound was the rolling of the waves, breaking on the shore. The gulls and other seabirds had gone to sleep, and the wind was still. His old eyes adjusted in the dark, and the bright moon brought to light many shapes.

"What do you see, Drius?"

Drius, like most dragons, saw very well in the dark. He looked this way and that, his eyes penetrating the shadows to see – "Nothing. Only water. Wait." He took a step forward, his head high and listening.

Merlin peered out in the dark. Things became a little clearer, and he saw – what did he see? He was not certain, but—

"Someone is out there," said Drius.

"Who?"

"A mermaid."

"Blast it all. I hate being old." Merlin searched his satchel and pulled out a wooden box with a different pair of spectacles inside. He switched them out with the ones he had on, and suddenly shapes in the night became clear. Enchanted spectacles – his own design – brought to light everything there was to see.

He saw the mermaid. It was Qoral. He waved to her and thought she smiled. She raised a finger to her lips for silence.

"What is she doing?" Drius peered at her.

"I am not sure."

Qoral raised her eyes and arms toward heaven, and suddenly there were with her many mermaids, maybe twenty or thirty. They all raised their eyes and arms, basking in the light of the moon and stars.

Mermen appeared too and did the same. Some of them were the royal guard, and some were not. They were all spread out in the water, none too close to one another.

Merlin said nothing. He gazed in curious wonderment. Among the faces, he also recognized Meribella and Qoral's sisters, Aerwyna and Serena.

Suddenly, Qoral let forth a high-pitched note that echoed off the waters. Several mermaids followed suit, lifting high notes in unison. Then Qoral sang. Her voice tilted in a series of high and low notes – they were not

TREASURES IN A BOTTLE

words, but the sound was lulling, inviting, and soothed the world around her.

She took a breath, and several mermaids accompanied her in song, lifting their voices and then drawing them back, letting the echoes of their notes dance over the waters. Soon, the mermen joined in, and it was the most haunting, beautiful choir Merlin had heard in all his life.

He sat down on the sands, and Drius laid beside him to listen.

As the merfolk sang, the water glowed an ethereal blue. It started out small and began to grow. Soon it was all around them, this cascading, luminescent light that brightened and dimmed with the rises and falls of their song.

They sang for what seemed like an eternity, and time stood still for them. The whole world had gone away. All that remained was their song. Merlin felt his heart rise and fall with the choir, and there were happy tears in his eyes.

When the song came to an end, the mermen faded first and disappeared into the sea. Then the mermaids followed, letting their echoes fall on the tide. As they went away, so did the light on the water. Soon, only Qoral was left with her arms still lifted. The water was dark around her. Her voice rose and fell with the care of an otherworldly minstrel, and then she let out a final high-pitched note that rang like a bell. She bowed her head to Merlin and Drius, then disappeared beneath the waves.

When Merlin returned home, he found a new seashell on his pillow – a golden-white shark eye shell with a beautiful spiral. He held it to his ear and heard Qoral's voice:

"Now you can say you have heard the song of the sea."

Merlin held the shell to his heart, a wave of warmth rolling over him. "The song of the sea," he whispered.

He had heard the tale of it from fishermen but never quite believed it. No seafaring man had mentioned mermaids or glowing waters. They only said that on quiet nights at sea, they heard the waters sing.

This had been a gift from Qoral to him.

"A wonderful gift." He wiped his misty eyes with the back of his sleeve. "Wonderful."

He drifted off to sleep fast and heard the choir again in his dreams.

CHAPTER FIFTEEN

The Funeral Pyre

The following day, Merlin was given chance to rest. Eleven days had passed. Eleven days full of excitement and wonder, and fatigue had caught up with the wizard. He lay in bed, with his eyes open, thinking:

There are four left.

He made the number with his fingers.

Four beasts.

A kettle whistled over the fire, and with a wave of his hand, Merlin willed a cup to fly from the curio and the kettle to pour the tea. The steaming cup floated over to him. He sat up and sipped the hot brew, the aroma and taste of lavender soothing his ancient nerves.

Who will be next, I wonder.

He did not wonder long. That afternoon, as he scrawled at his desk, Merlin heard the piping of a strange song outside and went to see what it was. A red bird soared across the blue sky. Its vibrant wings and tail feathers looked like living fire, and it flew straight and swift like an arrow, beating the air around it. It sang a series of notes that sounded very much like those of a flute, but they trilled and frilled in echo. The song danced in Merlin's ears, and he suddenly felt inspired.

Inspired to do what?

He did not know. He only knew that he felt enlightened and eager to create.

How very strange.

The red bird was soon joined by Drius, and the pair settled before the wizard.

"Merlin, this is Haco. He bears a message from Flint."

The phoenix fanned his brilliant wings and stepped close to Merlin. "The crown phoenix would like his audience with you tomorrow. Come when the sun is high. He will speak with you, he says, and then you will see that which no other has seen, that which you have always wanted to see."

Merlin's brow peaked. "And what might that be?"

"Sorry. That is all I am allowed to say. I will come again tomorrow to show you the way. Lord dragon, I am certain you have never been to our garden before?"

"No, I have not had the honor."

"Without me as your guide, you never will. I will see you both when the sun rises. Good day."

Haco took flight. Drius and Merlin looked after him till he was out of sight.

"Tomorrow then?"

Merlin nodded. "Tomorrow. Drius?"

"Hmm?"

"Did you feel strange when you heard the phoenix's song?"

"Strange how?"

"Not a bad sort of strange, but good, euphoric even. A feeling of inspiration."

"I felt no such thing. I heard his song, and I came."

"Very strange." Merlin rubbed his chin with his thumb and forefinger, then smiled. "But wonderful." He clapped his hands together. "I feel like drawing."

"What will you draw?"

"Hmm…I know! I will draw all the wonderful things I have seen these past several days." He turned on his heel and strode up to his desk. "See you tomorrow then, Drius, unless you would like to stay for a cup of tea?"

The kettle whistled.

"Not today, thank you. I will see you tomorrow, Merlin." The dragon lord ascended out of sight.

Alone with his parchments and quills, Merlin set about his drawings, some by hand and some by enchantment.

When morning came, Haco was there with the rising sun, as promised.

"There he is," said Merlin, waiting astride Drius.

Haco flew toward them. It seemed he might stop to talk with them, but he suddenly swooped and flew aside, casting a light wind in their faces that smelled of myrrh and cinnamon. He piped a high-pitch call.

"That is our cue," said Drius. He dove off the cliff and took chase after the phoenix.

"So, we are going south," said Merlin, noting the sun was on their left, in the east.

Haco stayed ahead of them for the entirety of the flight. How many miles distance they flew, Merlin was not sure, but after what seemed like a long time, Haco soared upwards. Drius went up after him, and the trio ascended till they were in the clouds.

They went a little way at a gentle flight before Haco called to them: "Keep close." He then folded in his wings and dove, passing through the clouds like a red arrow.

Drius pursued him in the same manner, folding his wings back and diving through the billows. At once, what was a rolling cloud turned into a heavy mist. The air was thick and wet, and Merlin could not see his hand in front of his face. The mist concealed Drius from him, and though Merlin knew without a doubt he was still astride the dragon, he felt for a brief moment the unsettling sensation that he was floating-falling through the air. He held on tighter and resisted the urge to close his eyes.

The only thing he could see in the impenetrable mist was Haco's flaming tail feathers. There they were, weaving and threading through the haze, a bright red beacon for them to follow. Merlin fixed his eyes on them and tried not to think what might happen if Drius lost sight of them.

When at last they broke free of the mist, Merlin breathed a sigh of relief and was met with the stunning aroma of cinnamon, myrrh, and sage. He blinked several times as light and color formed into shapes. Below them was a tight cluster of white flowering trees in which several phoenixes roosted. They lifted their heads as the visitors approached.

Lush grass trailed around the orchard in a thin green circle, then opened up to a small field with a rising hill. Bordering the trees and greensward was a clear, babbling stream. Then around all of this was the wall of mist, tall and looming like a curtain, hiding the garden from the outside world.

Drius settled on the hill, and as he did, many phoenixes took flight in a wave of red.

Merlin found his feet and gazed ahead, his jaw slack. "I have never heard of nor read about this place."

"I should hope not," said a voice behind them.

Merlin jumped, startled. A shadow passed over them. He looked up, and there was Flint, gliding on the air. The crown phoenix settled before them.

"This place cannot be found, 'cept by those who are led to it."

Merlin stared at the phoenix in bewilderment. He looked so ragged and frail, and not at all as he did when last Merlin saw him – a mere twelve days ago – at the Great Circle. His color had faded. His eyes did not shine as bright. And there, as he fanned his wings, a feather fell.

Flint caught his eye and said in a calm, unruffled voice, "Yes, Merlin. Your eyes do not deceive you. Age has caught up with me, and I look worse off than when last we met."

"I am sorry. It is rude of me to stare. It only took me by surprise."

"Do not be embarrassed. My time draws near. Every phoenix looks the same when its end is in sight. In the days prior, we age more quickly. We wither. Our bones ache. Our feathers fall out. That is when we come here, to Pyre Wood. It is where my kind comes to rest, so to speak."

"To rest? You mean to die and be…" Merlin held out on the last word, a wave of excitement pushing through him.

Flint nodded: "Reborn." He turned around to look at the orchard. The valley echoed with the chirps and whistles of his kind, so many of them still perched among the branches.

"Yes, this is where we pass from one life to the next. For some, it happens sooner than for others. Each one's time is different. I, myself, am nearly five hundred years old. This has been my longest life yet, and only now do I feel the weight of all those years. I have built my pyre nest and decided that today will be my final day, but I will not go till you and I are done." He looked back at Merlin, a favoring glint in his eye. "Come. Sit. We will talk here, and then I will go to rest."

Flint lay in the grass, with his wings fanned out to catch the warm sunlight. Merlin sat beside him, and Drius lay alongside, so all three of them were looking out over the orchard.

Merlin dabbed the quill in the ink pot and was about to ask his first question, when another phoenix came out of the mist, piping a song like the one Haco had sung the day before. Once again, Merlin felt internally lifted, overcome with an impulse to do…something. But what, he did not know. His eyes twinkled, and his hand shook, spilling a drop of ink on the paper.

"What is that?" he asked aloud, more so to himself than to Flint.

But Flint answered, "Inspiration," with a fond grin.

Merlin stared at him, baffled.

"It is our gift, or once was our gift to the humans. Our song has the inherent ability, a magical quality, you might say, to inspire creativity in others. Our kind has inspired many artists, be they painters, sculptors, songwriters, or storytellers. Poets and architects. Seamstresses and performers. And now you."

"Incredible." Merlin felt the sensation run through him. It was uplifting and joyful and made him feel more alive.

"Yes. If only we could have shared it with others of your kind these past hundred years or more."

Merlin nodded. "If only." But then he smiled with new hope. "But soon you will again. Children need inspiration too."

Flint chuckled. "Yes, I suppose they do."

Inspired to do his good work, Merlin asked his questions and wrote what Flint said about the care of phoenixes. After, he inquired for stories, excited and hopeful to learn, for a phoenix could remember its past lives, and therefore knew much of the history of the earth, having seen so much of it.

Flint humored him as best he could, but the moment came when the crown phoenix fell silent and looked to the sky. The sun was high overhead, and the valley was warm.

"It is time," he said in a calm, definite tone. He stood up and fluffed his feathers, three more of which fell to the ground. "Gather those up, Sir Merlin." During their talks, he started calling Merlin "Sir Merlin". Merlin corrected him only once, insisting the "Sir" was reserved for knights, yet the phoenix persisted and told him that "Sir" was polite.

Merlin gathered the feathers, as told.

"Now put them in your satchel. You may put them to good use someday. I certainly have no need for them anymore. There is a potion you may try, should you or someone you know need it. A phoenix feather is the key ingredient, or so I understand, in making a potion to heal blindness."

Merlin's eyes lit up. "I have heard of such a potion." He folded the feathers in the pages of his journal and put them away in his satchel. "Thank you. This is a generous gift."

"It is a small thing, but you are deserving of it. Drius, will you remain here?"

Flint looked at the dragon lord as he spoke, and the pair stared at one another, their eyes searching and knowing, before Drius nodded.

"Thank you. Come, Sir Merlin. Follow me."

Before Merlin could inquire as to what might be happening, the crown phoenix flapped his wings most vigorously, scattering more feathers. He glided low toward the orchard, and Merlin took chase after him at a careful run.

At the edge of the grove, Flint settled. He breathed hard and seemed frailer still. Merlin reached him, a little winded himself but was quicker to recover.

"Flint, should I carry you?"

"That is very kind of you to offer, but no thank you, Sir Merlin. This is my final walk. A phoenix seeks no help in meeting its end."

Flint moved forward into the shade of the trees, and Merlin stayed by his side. All the phoenixes nestled in the trees looked down at them and quietly chirped.

"I have decided, Sir Merlin, that I want you to see that which is both sacred to my kind and personal to me. I invite you to see my death, and my rebirth. Before you think this is some sort of impulse on my part, I tell you it is not. I sensed your mind at the Great Circle, and I know you to be a curious man, always chasing after knowledge. So consider this another gift to you and perhaps the child who will find the bottle with my fellow phoenix in it, should you mention this in your letter."

Merlin was astounded. He heard himself say, "Can you read minds? Did you read mine at the Circle?"

"No. I only sensed it. We phoenixes can sense the nature of most humans, but in your case, since you are part magic yourself, I think there is a stronger link between us. Even now, I sense you want to see a phoenix be reborn and your eagerness for it, now that I have invited you to do so, but I do not hear the words you think."

"You are an incredible bird."

"Thank you. Magic made me thus."

Flint stopped at the base of a flowering tree. "Up we go," he said. "You can climb, I presume?"

Merlin looked at the tree and rubbed the back of his head. "It has been a long time since I was a lad and climbed trees, but I think I can manage." He grabbed a low-hanging limb and though his bones ached, pulled himself up. He found a foothold and another limb to grasp and hoisted himself up. Soon, he was at the top of the tree, and there amongst the branches was a great nest.

From the ground, Flint called: "Comfortable?"

Merlin settled himself between two heavy boughs that curved to form a seat. "Comfortable enough, thank you."

Flint flapped his wings with much determination. He rose up and plopped down in the nest. His breathing was shallow, and his color faded to a dull, dark red.

"This nest," he said between breaths, "is made from cassia bark, sage leaves, spikes of nard, cinnamon, frankincense, and myrrh."

Merlin could smell the spices and herbs. They enriched the air with their muddled fragrances.

"You gathered these and built the nest yourself?"

"Certainly. Every phoenix builds its own funeral pyre. It would be wrong to ask another to do it." He laid down, folding his wings at his sides. His chest rose and fell with each breath, and he appeared tired, ready to sleep.

"But why these spices? What is their significance?"

"Why do humans anoint the dead with oils and perfumes, but to cleanse them and ensure the person is welcomed in the afterlife. Though I am to be reborn, these aromatic spices will burn as incense, and the fragrance rise to heaven, so that but for a moment, I forge a connection with my Maker, and my ashes are cleansed."

Merlin was silent. He stared at the magical bird, feeling the significance of his words stack upon him like stones on a grave, and he realized there was more at play here than the coming and going of a life, but also a tribute to the One who blessed it to be so.

"Flint, I want to say, before it happens…" Merlin hesitated. Flint's fading eyes looked at him. "Thank you."

Flint stared at him, and it seemed then to Merlin that an understanding passed between them.

"Sir Merlin, a phoenix does not let a human or any other beast be near when it is reborn. It is the moment we are most vulnerable. We cannot defend ourselves before or after it comes to pass. Look around you."

Merlin did, and he saw the eyes of many phoenixes fixated on their tree. They were all silent and waiting.

"I have assured them that you mean me no harm."

"Of course not. I would never—"

"I know. As I said, I can sense your mind."

Merlin smiled. "I am humbled and honored to see what comes to pass here. Again, I thank you."

"You are most welcome, Sir Merlin."

Flint tucked his head to his breast and closed his eyes. All around them was quiet. Merlin and the flock looked on, waiting. Merlin felt his nerves quiver, but he held very still and barely breathed.

It happened most suddenly. There was a crack and a spark. Flint glowed from within, his breast brightening. He then opened his wings and cried out. It was not a cry of pain or fear or anguish, but lovely, like a cry of relief, of peace and release. He caught fire. His feathers blazed. The nest crackled and popped, and a plume of fragrant smoke drifted up to encircle him. The plume glowed with the color of the flames. The fire consumed him and rose very high, tongues of flame licking at the air in a frenzy.

No phoenix present made a sound. They all watched in silent reverence.

Merlin stared in awestruck bewilderment. His mouth hung open, and he breathed the burning spices. The blaze was so intense, his eyes watered, but he did not dare look away.

Soon the fire snuffed itself out. The smoke billowed and faded. All that was left was a singed nest and a pile of ashes.

For a time, nothing happened. Merlin rubbed his chest, feeling it ache. He feared something was wrong, and he was about to ask the flock if this much was so, when he saw the ashes shudder. He leaned forward, so close he could feel the warmth emanating from the smoldering nest.

There! The pile of ashes did move. He was certain of it. Yes, yes, oh he could see it now. From the ashes rose a tiny head. A baby bird, naked and new, gave a small cry.

Suddenly, another phoenix flew down to the nest. It was a female. Merlin knew because she did not have the three distinct tail feathers of a male. She nuzzled the chick till he opened his eyes. The eyes were dark, black as obsidian, and Merlin saw his reflection in them when the chick gazed up at him.

The chick shook off the ashes, and little red feathers started to show on his body. Oddly enough, he dove into the ashes again, came free, shook again, and still more feathers appeared. Three times he did this till he was covered in feathers. He was bright, his colors vibrant, and he moved about the nest with ease. He chirped at Merlin.

"My goodness," whispered Merlin. "In all my years, I never could have imagined it the way it is."

"Are you satisfied then?" The female's voice startled Merlin, and her eyes peered at him with gentle sincerity.

"Satisfied is not the word, but yes. Enlightened is more accurate, and grateful."

The baby Flint hopped over to the female and cooed against her foot.

"What happens now?" asked Merlin.

"I will care for him till he has grown strong enough to fend for himself."

"Are you his mother?"

"No. I am Tana, his mate. Each time one of us passes, the other cares for the newborn chick. It will not take him long to grow up. He will mature in seven days."

"Seven days? Astounding."

Tana nuzzled the chick and cooed. "He will see you again on the beach."

Merlin bid Tana and the baby Flint farewell and managed to climb down the tree without a mishap. Haco was waiting on the ground, and he escorted Merlin back to Drius.

"I will lead you through the mist again," he said. "Otherwise, you will get lost."

"Many thanks for your help, friend," said Drius as Merlin climbed aboard.

Going through the mist the second time was less unsettling than before, but it did not matter, for Merlin was lost in his thoughts. In his mind's eye, he saw Flint be reborn again and again. He did not even notice when they were free of the fog till Haco sounded a farewell cry. The phoenix circled round them once, then disappeared back into the mist.

"How was it?" Drius asked, flying toward home.

"You know, Drius, each experience I have had these past several days has been, in its own way, astonishing and wonderful. But there are no words for what I saw today. It was death and life."

"Take it to heart, my friend."

"I have." Then to himself: "I have."

CHAPTER SIXTEEN

Bloodberries and Other Provisions

For three days, there was silence. Merlin thought this curious, and he listened for Drius, half-expecting the dragon lord to appear at his cave door all of a sudden and tell him to drop his doings and come quick because one of the three that completed the Great Circle desired an audience. But no word came, which was fine with Merlin. He used the time to rest and, truth be known, he was becoming anxious about seeing those three.

Their silence also allowed him to finish the letters for those magical creatures he had seen. He sat at his desk, with candles lit and journal open, and scrawled them out, one after the other. There were times, between his writings, that he would go sit with Drius in the vale, and the two of them would converse about a myriad of things before Merlin went back to his work.

It was on the third day that he decided to gather provisions for those creatures making the journey. He had the seashells, which he would enchant to fill with water, but there was no food. Grabbing his satchel and several empty bottles, he left his cave to find suitable nourishment for each creature.

The task proved more difficult, however, than Merlin anticipated. He had no trouble gathering berries and nuts and grains for those creatures that ate plant life. But what about the ones that ate meat? There were beasts whose appetites preferred, if not required, a fresh kill. This caused Merlin to pace in the middle of the wood and rub the back of his head till his face was red with frustration.

"I am almost certain the last three prefer live food, but I am not about to shrink a mouse or some other poor creature and put it in a bottle with one of them. What a mess that would be.

"I also cannot put fish or red meat in the bottles. There is the question of preservation – how to keep the meat fresh till that day on the beach, and even after, on the journey. Oh, imagine the smell. At least herbs and beans smell nice or have no smell at all. The meat will become putrid and – oh, I hate to think of it. And the mess, the blood – it would stain the letter, not to mention make the creature icky, sticky, and smell foul."

He slumped down on a nearby rock and shook his head.

"A spell will not work. Magic is particular about preserving most things, but it will not stay the natural laws of decay. I must think of something. But what?" He threw his hands up in exasperation. "Tell me, powers that be, what do I do?"

Something hit him in the back and fell with a thud, and there was the sound of a scattering of things. Merlin leapt to his feet and turned around with fists up. There was nothing behind him, but then he looked down, and there, on the ground, rubbing her head and jabbering all kinds of unpleasant ramblings, was a fairy.

She was pretty and spirited, more vibrant and less delicate than other fairies. Her eyes were like emeralds wrapped in clover, and her wild, flaxen hair fell past her shoulders with two braids in the front. She wore a leafy dress and an acorn cupule for a hat, indicating she was a fairy scout. Her tiny satchel was flung aside, its contents

spilled everywhere. There were a couple of buttons, a thimble, a tiny mushroom, and several colorful beads.

She looked up at Merlin and gasped. From her tiny leather belt, she pulled free a sewing needle and brandished it like a sword. "Stay back," she said in a voice that chimed like bells but struggled to be brave.

Merlin put up his hands in surrender. "I swear I mean you no harm. I am Merlin, the wizard, friend to your queen, Liliana."

"Oh?" She faltered and then waved her weapon again. "How do I know you are who you say you are?"

"Well, I, uh…" He thought a moment, then grinned. "You know wizards perform magic. I will show you." He waved his hand, and the scout's belongings floated and packed themselves away in her satchel. The satchel then levitated over to her, which she promptly snatched.

"You could be another magic user trying to trick me. If you really are a friend of my queen, tell me, what is the stone in her crown?"

Merlin smiled. "An opal."

Surprise raised the fairy's brow, and she returned her needle to her belt. "I guess you are who you say you are." She threw the satchel over her shoulder. "But what are you doing out here in the woods alone?"

"I could ask you the same."

"No, you cannot." She flew up to be eye level with him and crossed her arms.

"Why not?"

"Because it is not polite."

"Well then, neither is it polite for you to ask me."

"Yes, but you were sitting there, a thing out of place, and I bumped into you. I know every rock, tree, and bush in this forest. I can fly here and there without stopping to think about where I am. Then you were there, out of place, and I, I…" Her little face was red with exhaustion, for she spoke so fast.

"We have gotten off on the wrong foot," said Merlin. "I am sorry I was not where I was supposed to be and that you crashed into me. Are you hurt?"

The fairy shoved her cupule hat back and huffed. "No."

"Well, that is a relief. I would feel bad if you were. Can I ask what your name is?"

She thought a moment, then sighed. "My name is Honeysuckle. Honey for short. I know it is a funny name. Mom named me such because I was born when the honeysuckle was in bloom." She pouted and dropped her eyes.

"I happen to think your name is lovely, cute even."

She rolled her eyes like she did not believe him. She was favoring her left side and clasped the satchel with both hands.

Merlin pointed at it. "Is it heavy? Would you like some help?"

"No, thank you." She blushed and looked away. "It is mine to carry."

"Suit yourself. It really is no bother. Seems only fair, since I made you fall. I could carry it some of the way, and then you the rest."

Honey fluttered there a moment, then held out the bag. "Fine. But do not think you can steal from me."

"Oh, I would never steal from a fairy, or anyone else for that matter. Which way are you going?"

She pointed west.

"I see. Lead on then, and I will follow."

The pair ventured through the wood in silence. Honey floated ahead of Merlin, constantly looking back over her shoulder to see if he was still there. She was a strange fairy, Merlin decided – full of substance and lively. He liked her.

He did not like the quiet between them though. It was unnatural and uncomfortable. So he broke the tension by saying, "Do you often collect baubles and trinkets? If so, I have several little things that are of no use to me, and you are welcome to have them."

She said nothing at first but stared ahead, her wings fluttering. She then hung back to fly by his shoulder.

"What kinds of things?"

Merlin smiled. "Oh, the sorts of things people toss in a drawer and never think twice about. Coins, pretty stones, and charms. Please help yourself to them. I have no need for such things."

Honey was quiet a moment, thinking, then said, "Maybe I will." Another pause, followed by: "The other fairies think it strange, and I only do this with the queen's pardon, but I like to treasure hunt. The first day of every seven, I comb the fairly traveled paths for those things humans drop. I have to be careful though not to be seen."

"Of course."

"But I also come to the wood to gather things we need back home. That is what a fairy scout does. We find and collect. It might be roots and shoots, mushrooms and moss. Whatever we need, a scout retrieves," She said this proudly, and her face beamed.

"That seems a noble job," said Merlin, happy to see her come out of her shell. "To tell you the truth, I was doing some gathering myself."

"Really? What were you gathering?"

Merlin told Honey about the bottles and the creatures and the gathering of provisions. She nodded as she listened and even said Queen Liliana had announced to the whole of the fairy kingdom that such a plan by a wizard named Merlin was to unfold. When he came to the part of his predicament though – that being the gathering of meat, she faltered in her flight.

"Something the matter, Honey?"

She had a strange look on her face, like she knew something but was not sure she should say it. She paced the air, twiddling her fingers, then said, "I know a thing you can gather, but it is frowned upon."

Merlin's brow peaked. "Frowned upon?"

She nodded. "We scouts are not supposed to go near it, not even touch it. It is not something the queen herself grew, nor is it a natural thing, I suppose."

"Now I am curious. Tell me, Honey, what is this unnatural thing?"

She twiddled and cast her eyes downward. She then shook her head and said nothing.

"I am sorry to put you in a moral predicament," said Merlin, "but if it is something that might help these creatures, perhaps this bad thing can be put to good use."

She stayed silent a while longer, then sighed. "Follow me."

They went to the deepest of the wood, where brambles and thorns grew. Even during the day, the thick canopy of trees let very little light touch the ground here. Jagged stones breached the earth like twisted fingers, draped in dead vines.

This place seems familiar, but I cannot place it, thought Merlin.

He mused over it a while longer, rubbing his chin and wondering.

Honey stopped just ahead of him in a clearing. He pushed his way through the bushes to get to her and stopped short when he saw what she was looking at.

In the clearing, the grass grew well enough, save at its center, where the ground had been disturbed. This spot of earth was a couple mounds of dirt, long and narrow. A strange tangle of thorny vines protruded from the mounds but not the grass. The vines were a dark, sickly green, almost black, and dangling from them were several hundred dark red berries, the kind of which Merlin had never seen before.

"They are called bloodberries," said Honey in a quiet voice. "They only grow on unmarked, shallow graves. The queen says magic grew them."

Merlin's eyes widened, and he put a hand over his chest.

Honey looked back at him and fluttered close. "Are you well?"

"Do I look otherwise?"

"You are pale like you saw a ghost."

"Close enough. I know this place."

Honey faltered in her flight and tilted her head at him. "How?"

"Because I have been here before. Those graves, I dug them."

Honey floated back, wary, and put a hand on her needle.

Merlin noted this and said, "I did not kill them, but they were bad men." In as few words as possible, he told her about Drius' family and the terrible tragedy. "These are the men who slew his family. I buried them this way as punishment for their crimes."

Honey sat on a nearby stone and tapped it with her needle. The sound was like a drop in a pail, solemn and light. She said nothing.

"Now it seems," continued Merlin, "that magic has found a way to bring a little good out of the bad. It often does." He knelt and peered at the berries.

They were small, plump, and round and had a glossy skin over a lush red interior. Indeed, they looked like drops of blood.

Merlin went over to Honey and handed her her bag. "I must examine these berries."

Honey watched him from her stone perch.

Reaching into his satchel, Merlin pulled a thin vial with a cork. Inside there was a white powder.

"What is that?" Honey asked.

"An acidic powder. I shall sprinkle it over the plant. If the plant has toxins, there will be a reaction. I made this solution a long time ago after a terrible run-in with poison ivy."

He delicately scattered the powder over the plant. Honey peered forward, expecting something to happen, but nothing did.

"That is fortuitous," said Merlin. "The plant has no toxins. I shall test the berries now."

He plucked a berry from its vine and laid it atop a flat stone. He then took a small rock and crushed the berry. A thick, sanguine juice was left behind, and over this Merlin sprinkled the powder.

"No reaction. So the berries are not toxic either. All that is left then is to taste."

"No!" Honey flew from her perch into his face. "You cannot!"

"But why not? I have to see if they are fit for those creatures. I am not going to give them something that might hurt them."

"But it-it-it is gross! And vile!"

"If you do not want to watch, you can leave, but I must test them."

Honey hovered in the air, flitting this way and that, muttering to herself. She then settled back on her rock. "I suppose I have to stay in case you faint or worse. Then I can fetch help, if it does you any good."

"Thank you. That is very thoughtful."

Merlin pulled another berry from the vine and popped it in his mouth without hesitation. The berry burst between his teeth, and the juice filled his mouth. He twisted his face, repulsed. The berry had a metallic taste to it, like iron, and it was thick and sticky. He turned and spit it out.

"It even tastes like blood." He spat again. "I am afraid there is only one way to know if they are suitable, and I do not look forward to that test. I do not suppose you have seen other beasts eat these berries?"

Honey shook her head. "No. As I said, we scouts avoid this plant."

"That is what I thought. Yes, I am definitely not going to like this."

He gathered the berries while Honey looked on.

"What test?" she asked.

As curious as Honey was, Merlin was still surprised she followed him home. She sat on his shoulder, clutching his collar with one hand and her bag with the other. They went straight to the vale, and there was Drius in his usual spot, watching his fellow dragons.

"Merlin, you seem to have picked up a straggler," said the dragon lord, eyeing the fairy scout.

"I am no straggler." Honey flew from Merlin's shoulder and floated several inches from the dragon's face. "I am a fairy scout!"

Drius laughed. "You are a sprightly thing. Her majesty is lucky to have you in her service."

Honey did not know what to say to this. Her face, which had been red, defused. She floated back to Merlin and hovered with her arms crossed.

"I will get to the point, Drius, because this is not easy for me to say." Merlin held up a bottle full of bloodberries.

In not so many words, he told his friend what the berries were and where they had come from. He told him he had tried one and the result. The entire time he spoke, Merlin saw no reaction in Drius' face. This surprised him and left him a little wary. When he finished, he waited for the dragon to speak.

Drius peered at the bottle. There was a fleeting glint in his eyes. He growled from within, but it sounded, to Merlin, mournful rather than angry. It stole the attention of those dragons in the valley, and they all lifted their heads to look in the direction of their leader.

Drius closed his eyes, his breathing steady, and winced. When he looked at Merlin again, his eyes were clear.

"So you want another beast to try these berries to see if they are any good?"

Merlin nodded.

"I see."

"I feel guilty for asking, let alone bringing them to your attention, but I know not what else to do, and I did not think it right to keep them a secret."

"No, I appreciate your honesty, Merlin. It is one of the reasons you and I are friends, remember?"

Merlin nodded again.

There was a brief silence. The other dragons looked on, perhaps wondering what the trouble was with Drius. Merlin did not look at them. He kept his eyes fixed on Drius, waiting for him to speak again.

"Give me the berries," was what he said.

Merlin's eyes widened. "Drius, you do not have to—"

"Yes, I do." His voice was edged but not aggressive. It was strong, direct, and not to be challenged. "Strange how magic brings things full circle. Seems only fitting then that I should try these berries."

"If you say so." Merlin uncorked the bottle and came forward as Drius lowered his head. "I have several tonics in my bag, should there be a nasty reaction. I am not dead though, so I suppose they are fine."

"That is comforting." The sarcasm in the dragon's voice was clear, but Merlin ignored it.

Drius opened his mouth, and Merlin poured the contents of the bottle onto his great red tongue. Drius brought his head up and chewed. Trickles of red oozed from between his jowls.

The valley was silent as all eyes watched the dragon lord.

He swallowed. His tongue licked out and over his mouth to catch the juice that dribbled. He waited a moment before speaking.

"They taste of blood, as you said. Strangely enough, my appetite has gone, and not out of repulsion. They will do, but do not tell the others where they came from."

"As you wish, Drius."

"That means you too, little scout." Drius eyed Honey. "Do not tell your queen where the berries came from."

"I cannot keep a secret from my queen." Honey screwed up her face.

"Fine. Then tell your queen if she wants to know where the berries came from to ask me directly. This is a personal matter."

"As you command, lord dragon. Now, if you all do not mind, I have to get home. It is late, and the queen will wonder where I am."

"Tell her you were with me and that you helped me gather provisions," said Merlin.

"Then tell her you came to the Dragons' Keep and that I wish her well." Drius grinned.

"She is not so easily fooled, but I will tell her. If I get demoted, I will be knocking on your door, Merlin."

She fluttered off, and Merlin laughed.

"She came here of her own choice," he said.

"That is the trouble with fairies," said Drius, "curiosity."

Merlin looked over the valley. The other dragons went back to what they were doing before, and all seemed well again.

"Drius?"

"Hmm?"

"I am sorry."

"For what?"

"For…" Merlin was not sure how to say it.

For dredging up the past?

"Full circle, Merlin." Drius looked ahead. There was no trace of anger or sorrow in his eyes. He was stone-faced but at peace. "Full circle."

CHAPTER SEVENTEEN

Serpents' Cove

The silence broke the next day. Merlin was at his desk, writing, and outside, Drius sat to keep him company. It was the seventeenth day of the thirty Merlin was allotted to complete his tasks.

A strange wind blew. Below, at the foot of the mountain, the rustling of the forest was so loud and rough, it sounded as though it were alive and angry. The whipping of branches, the splitting of leaves, the woeful groans of trees twisting and bending to the wind's will — all these sounds echoed through the air, up the mountainside, and pounded on the walls of Merlin's cave.

The wind also brought with it an unsettling chill, the kind that penetrates the skin and nips at the bones. It sent shivers down Merlin's spine, and he put on his silver cloak to fare better.

"This weather is strange for summer," he said, pulling the collar high around his face.

Drius stared ahead at nothing. His jaw was set. He looked every bit composed, but there was a glint in his eye that suggested something more. In a low, plain voice, he said, "A storm is coming, a terrible storm."

Merlin put down his quill and came outside. "When will it get here?"

The dragon lord closed his eyes and let out a long exhale, concentrating. "It will be here tomorrow. My guess, at an hour in the late afternoon. I suggest you roll that great stone of yours over here to seal your door." Drius indicated the very large, round stone slab which laid to the side of Merlin's cave.

"It will be that bad?"

"It will bring with it stronger winds than this and lots of rain."

"Very well. I will do as you suggest. What will you and the other dragons do?"

"Wait it out in our caves, like we always do. Should you need help though, you remember how to signal me?"

"Oh, yes. I remember."

If ever Merlin was in trouble and unable to reach his friend, he was to summon a plume of red smoke that could billow out of the cracks and crevices of his cave. The smoke would seek out whoever he willed it to find, and neither wind nor rain could dissuade it from its course.

"Good. Hopefully, it will pass and not linger."

Merlin looked closer at Drius and noted how rigid he was sitting there. His muscles were tight. His wings laid flat, and his tail did not flinch. "Drius, is anything the matter? You seem on edge."

The dragon lord said nothing but turned his head fast and listened.

In the distance, there was a roar, strong and searching. It echoed across the mountains. Drius called back, his roar so great and deafening, Merlin covered his ears. Over the crags and rises of the mountain, Godan appeared. He circled and settled at Merlin's door. He bowed his head to Drius.

"What did you discover?" Drius asked.

"He is ready for him, the foul beast. He came, as you said, and told me to pass along this message: 'My distant cousin of wing, bring your wizard friend, and we will talk of many things.' He said 'things' with a terrible gleam in his watery eye. He then said, 'I eagerly await your arrival at Serpents' Cove. Come tomorrow, and I will receive you.'"

Drius growled within. "Thank you, Godan. Gather others, those you think are best suited to go. I will not take any chances."

"As you wish." Godan leapt off the cliff and rose out of sight.

Merlin saw the displeasure on Drius' face. He did not want to ask – his stomach turned at the thought of it, but he had to, to prepare himself. "Drius, what was that all about?"

The dragon lord growled again. Merlin could feel the heat emanating from him.

"Sli." Drius said the name with much disdain. "I wondered why we had not heard from the last three who complete the Circle. There are not many days left. So I sent Godan and a couple more dragons to inquire. Godan went to Serpents' Cove and brought back this news. We go to see the sea snake tomorrow, but not alone. Godan and several more dragons will be with us in case something should happen."

"Do you suspect something could happen?"

"I am not sure, but it would be foolish to go alone, and the same is true, I feel, about visiting the harpies and the basilisks."

A thought lingered on the tip of Merlin's tongue, and he shuffled his feet.

Drius went on: "I now wait for the others to return. I will not be calm till they are back home, safe."

"I see." Merlin looked over his shoulder at the fire pit, full of ash and unlit. "Maybe I can help with that." He went over to the pit and scooped up a handful of ash.

"How?" Drius watched him with careful interest.

Merlin, with the ash in hand, made circles over the pit and muttered an incantation under his breath. He then threw the ash down, and a fire ignited in full blaze. With the iron tongs, he laid a fresh log in the flames, and with the poker, he spread the charred remains of the once-healthy wood. He said more words under his breath and blew on the embers.

Images danced over the flames, first of the sky, then trees, then water.

"Who did you send to the harpies?" he asked.

"Cadmus." Drius' eyes widened when the image of Cadmus suddenly appeared in the fire. "What magic is this, Merlin?"

"The flames show me what is happening at present. We best be quick though, for it makes me grow tired fast. It appears Cadmus is returning to us. See? He leaves the sea behind him and crosses the shore."

"I see. Can you show me Kadel? He went to see Silzer."

At once, Kadel's face danced in the flames. He looked angry and appeared to shout. He was circling a vast empty space, a barren land. Below him, there was a great pit, dark and impenetrable to sight. Though they played what was happening, no sound came from the burning images. Kadel stopped talking. He circled high in the air several more times, then turned for home.

The flames receded, and Merlin slumped on the north stone.

"It seems Kadel is safe too," he said between breaths.

Drius watched him. "Thank you, Merlin. Will it be easy for you to recover?"

"Oh, I will be fine." Merlin waved off his friend's worry. "I will feel better after I eat. But now you can be at ease for a little while. At least till tomorrow."

Drius nodded, but he did not seem comforted. "Till tomorrow."

A thought still lingered with Merlin, and he said, "Drius, may I confide in you?"

"Always."

"These last three, I am nervous to visit them in their lands. I am grateful you and others go with me, but…"

"But?" Drius urged him.

Merlin leaned forward and rested his chin on folded hands. "Well, I am supposed to be impartial in all of this – make good on my promise to help all twelve of the Circle and go on my way. In every audience I have had thus far, I have been eager to see those territories and open to what is told me, but now my stomach turns, and I think about what I have read in books and heard in stories about those three, and I quell within. It seems silly that I, a wizard who has been in danger more times than I can count, am afraid of them, and I find it difficult to be fair with them. Tell me, Drius, how I should approach them?"

Drius snuffed, a whiff of smoke leaving his nostrils.

"What is so funny?" Merlin sat up with wide-eyed disbelief.

"Forgive me, Merlin. But you ask one beast to give you its opinion of another beast. My instincts tell me not to trust them, but then I suppose their instincts urge them not to trust me, so you cannot truly go off what I say if you are to be fair in all of this. I advise you to be wary when we go and keep your wits about you. In the end, you promised to help them, swore by your own magic, and that is binding.

"But think on this: consider what you know about me and dragons and compare it to what you have read in books and heard in stories. Is it the same?"

Merlin shook his head. "Certainly not."

"Then my best advice to you is to approach these three with the same mindset. For as long as I have known you, you have been a man of study and knowledge. You have a rare, albeit dangerous, opportunity to know these three better than any person ever did before you."

In the firelight, a glow set in Merlin's features, as understanding dawned on him. He half-gaped, half-smiled at the dragon lord. "That is wisdom not instinct you just spoke, my friend."

Drius grinned. "And besides, I will be there to protect you."

Merlin woke to dark skies with rolling thunderclouds. The air was heavy and oppressive, and the winds blew hard with a bone-aching chill. He put on his cloak, grabbed his satchel, and waited outside for Drius.

Drius came with six dragons – Godan being one of them.

"Hurry, Merlin. The sooner we get above the clouds, the better."

As he clambered aboard, Merlin said with a shaky breath, "Should we wait another day to go?"

"No. Time is short, and I cannot say how many days this storm will last. Hold on!"

Drius dove off the cliff and climbed the air. The other dragons glided in a circle above them, and when Drius pierced the ring, they took after him. They flanked their leader, three dragons on either side of him, in a V-formation, with Drius at its crown.

"We must get above the clouds," he said. "Brace yourself, Merlin."

Merlin held tight, his cloak billowing behind him in the ferocity of the wind. Up, up they went till they broke through the black wall and plunged themselves into darkness. Merlin could see little of anything. It was like traveling through the mist to the phoenixes' garden, but worse. This dark veil was foreboding and frightening. It was as though they had been swallowed by a faceless beast. Its belly rumbled with thunder, and its nerves lit up with lightning. With each flash, Merlin caught the silhouettes of the dragons. They too looked menacing in this way.

He could hear Drius' heavy breathing between each beat of his wings. He was a formidable creature, putting up great resistance to the brooding storm. His muscles tensed with each straining blow of the wind. That tempest sought to knock them down. Though he could not aid him, Merlin laid a comforting hand on the dragon's shoulder.

"Almost there," said Drius between breaths.

When they finally broke through the bank, it was like having a heavy blanket pulled from their faces. Fresh air filled their lungs, and the sun was there, casting its warm light over everything. The sky above was a clear blue, and below them rumbled and flashed the dark creature which they had overcome. It was an angry force, hungry for their return.

Drius calmed and breathed the better air. He glanced back, seeing his fellow dragons still in pursuit of him. They did not look as weathered as he did, but then again, he was much older than they were.

"How do you feel, Merlin? I did not lose you?" He forced a chuckle.

"No. You still have me, and I am fine. You seem a bit worn, though."

"It has been some time since I fought a storm like this one. There is something strange and unearthly about it."

"How so?"

"I am not sure how to explain it, but this storm, when I first sensed it, seemed none too peculiar. Now that I have come so close to it, I sense an underlying menace to it as though it were alive."

Merlin did not know what to say to this. He looked down at the dark amorphous veil, how it stretched for miles in all directions, with no end in sight. The angry clouds which formed its crown rolled and crashed like the waves of a torrent sea. It did look alive but without purpose or heart – a dangerous thing.

"We should have a better time coming back and diving through its quaking breast," said Drius. "We will think on that later though. Our minds must turn to Serpents' Cove and who waits for us there."

He turned north, and the dragons followed.

Being above the clouds, Merlin was not certain how far they traveled or how much time passed.

"How much further, Drius?"

"It has not been long. We will be there soon."

The further north they went, the darker the clouds were beneath them, louder too, the thunder ramming as though it wished to break the doors of earth and heaven.

"Hold tight," said Drius suddenly.

Merlin did so, and down they went in a nose dive. Drius folded his wings back over his passenger and plunged into the darkness. Merlin was pelted by cold rain, and his eyes stung.

Lightning flashed, and thunder rumbled, but they were out of the belly of the beast fast enough. Drius opened his wings to catch the air and lift so as not to collide with a bed of jagged rocks below.

Merlin shook his head and blinked his sight back. The sound of raging water filled his ears, and he saw a dark, cold menace – the sea, frigid and deep blue, was alive and crashing its waves on a beach of black sand. The dark shore spanned a great distance, and many jagged rocks protruded from it like gnashing teeth.

Drius and the other dragons flew low, the lightning grazing over their heads. It was raining, and the rain was icy and sharp, penetrating. Merlin cast a spell to wrap himself in an invisible veil to keep dry.

"Drius? Would you and the others like protection from this terrible weather?"

"No, thank you, Merlin. We fare it well enough. Look, up ahead."

Merlin saw an imposing wall of stone stretching skyward. It cut through the sands and out to sea. The rock was many shades of black and gray, rigid and cragged. There was a grand, terrifying archway in it, and through it, on the other side, the black sands and waves still collided.

"That is it," said Drius, "Serpents' Cove."

"Looks menacing enough," said Merlin, feeling a chill run down his spine as their party passed through the archway.

Serpents' Cove was a bay. The grand wall of stone curved its way around like a hand, leaving only the break between its fingers, so they could look out to sea. The water came surging in but lost its momentum when its waves crashed against the fingers. All around, jagged rocks breached the sands.

Each time the wind blew, its torrents were trapped in the bay, and as they gusted around the rocks, they wailed an eerie cry that steadily grew, then faded. It was as though the bay had breath and moaned.

Drius settled on the sands with Godan and another dragon on either side of him. The other four took positions along the rock wall. Merlin went to dismount, but Drius blocked him with his wing.

"Wait." Drius' eyes narrowed on the outlet to the sea.

All the dragons looked that way, and for a time, nothing happened. Merlin saw only the sea, raging and crashing upon itself. Then one of the dragons above roared, the ferocity of its signal echoing off the walls of the bay.

"They are here," said Drius. His body became rigid, and Merlin felt him grow warm.

Goose pimples broke over Merlin's skin, and he was aware of a sinking dread as though a large stone had dropped in his stomach. He held tightly to Drius and did not breathe.

Suddenly, Sli burst from the water, giving Merlin a start. He put a hand over his chest, his heart pounding with fear. The sea serpent rose above them, the mass of him terrifying, the length of him imposing. At the Great Circle, he had seemed smaller because the pool which held him there was small, and much of his length had trailed back into the underwater cave. But here he was, out in the open, free to move about and strike fear in all who saw him. He was frightening, and yet his grandeur – the measure and terror of him – stole attention, and Merlin found it difficult to look away.

The waters split on either side of the king sea serpent as a couple more serpents breached the surface. This put Drius on edge, a low growl vibrating through him. These serpents were much smaller than Sli, each one maybe forty feet long but still thick around. One was a tarnished silver, the other a faded green, and its left eye was clouded over and scarred. They howled, their jaws dripping, their gills fanned, and they flashed hungry, vicious eyes at the gathering on the beach.

"Well, this is a wholesome welcoming," said Sli, his voice cutting the tension like a knife. He sounded amused and appeared to grin as he set his sights on Drius and Merlin. "Quite the party you brought with you, Drius."

"You came with yours," retorted the dragon lord.

The lesser serpents hissed, and the dragons bared their teeth.

Sli grinned. "So I did, so I did. But this is to be a peaceful audience with your wizard friend, yes? No excitement will come about unless you happen to start it."

"I will start nothing, but should you or one of yours do so, I intend to finish it."

Sli laughed, the sound of it chilling and grazing. "I am certain you do."

Drius did not let his guard down, and he kept his wings high over Merlin. "I said at the Great Circle that Merlin would never be alone during his visits."

"Yes, but from what I hear, your guard was never with you when you met with the others. Oh yes, I have my ways of knowing. Nary a secret can be kept from me. Besides that, you and I pretend at nothing, Drius. Our kinds have been enemies for ages. It stands to reason, then, that you do not trust me, just as I do not trust you. So I take no offense at you bringing your small band, and you should take no offense at me bringing mine. No, you and I think alike, and as such, we should have mutual respect for one another. Why then should anything change between us? In fact, if it were not for your wizard friend and what he promises to do for us, I am certain you and I would not get along this well. Hush!"

Sli snapped at his comrades, who had grumbled and hissed at their guests. A sharp word from him made them silent and drop their heads.

"So, Drius, do we have an understanding?"

Drius nodded. "We do."

"Excellent. Wizard?" His eyes penetrated Merlin and made him quiver. "Whenever you are ready."

Merlin nodded and laid a hand on Drius' shoulder. The dragon lord cringed and lowered his wings. Merlin's feet sunk in the sand, the grains cold and coarse. He took a couple steps forward, his body shivering, and Drius brought his tail around to stop him.

"That is far enough, Merlin."

Sli chuckled.

Merlin sat on the sands with Drius behind him, vigilant and ready. He pulled out his journal, which was still magically sealed from his visit with the merfolk to keep it safe from water, so the rain ran off it without staining. Quill in hand, he turned to a blank page and scrawled *Sea Serpents*.

"So, wizard," said Sli with a menacing grin, "where shall we begin?"

Time slowed down at Serpents' Cove, or so it seemed to Merlin. He gathered Sli liked to hear himself talk,

as the sea serpent answered each question with great elaboration and a formality that was unsettling in so frightening a creature. Truly, this beast, terror of the sea, savage and ruthless, spoke with wicked grace and royal execution, much like a tyrant king, but there lurked a steady, cunning mind.

All the while they conversed, Merlin struggled within. The sea serpent unnerved him and made him feel like his inner being might unravel. The way he spoke, with beads of water dripping from his fangs, and his tone and vicious grin all suggested he was proud of his race, of their cruelty and brutality. Nothing he said offered a shred of decency or moral sense.

But the worst came when Merlin asked Sli about the magic he and his kind possessed. The sea serpent grinned with great satisfaction and looked up at the dark, threatening sky.

"How about this weather?" he asked.

Merlin raised a brow. "What about it?"

"Does it not impress and frighten you? It does most sailors. Makes them panic and lose their composure, and their mind frenzies just before one of us strikes."

Merlin stared at the sea beast. His quill was low, and his hand shook. "Do you mean to say you control the weather?"

"No. We do not so much as control it, but rather we impress upon it. It is a strange marvel, one that even I do not wholly understand. You see, small serpents like them"—he regarded his fellows—"cannot hope to stir up a light rain. But a beast of breadth and age, like myself, can agitate the winds and make the heavens weep. But when all of us come together in one place for a long enough time, this is what you see: chaos across the skies."

Merlin's eyes widened. "All of you?"

Sli nodded. "Yes. Does that bend your mind, even a little? An image there forms. Perhaps you see a hundred of us, gliding over top of each other in the deep blue abyss. I will put your mind at ease and tell you there are no more than twenty of us in all the sea. That is right: there are only twenty sea serpents left in the world, and all came together here the night before. Under the light of a great moon, we fought and mated, and now we disperse back to the corners of the world from whence we came.

"No, we do not control the weather. But our nature, our presence is impressionable, and the skies heed, and because we are dark and fierce, so do the heavens become. This rain will last the day. The winds will howl through the night, and the sun will not gaze on you till tomorrow."

Merlin frowned and said nothing.

The king sea serpent looked pleased and continued: "But let me think. You want to know about our magic. Well, magic gave us heightened senses. I can rest at the bottom of the sea and still smell blood or hear a life in distress many miles off. More than this: if I draw close to my prey, I can hear their heartbeat."

Sli brought his head low, but Merlin looked away. Behind him, Drius took a step forward and growled. Sli ignored this.

"I cannot speak for my brethren," said Sli, "but when a heart races, pumping fear and dread through its host, I get excited. Much like a shark, how it goes after that which bleeds, I go after that which beats to the brink of madness. It is thrilling, especially when it is the crew of a ship. So many hearts at once."

Merlin put his quill down and breathed deeply, trying to stay calm and in control of himself.

"Then there are our eyes. Only at the end, after much taunting and aggression, do we show our prey mercy by looking them in the eye. I think you know of what I speak, wizard. In fact, I know you do."

Merlin lifted his gaze and tried not to quiver. The sea serpent's great head hovered just a few feet from him, wet and glistening. His fins fanned, and his eyes, the pupils sharp and penetrating, looked right into him. Merlin felt then, most suddenly, as though he were tied down and could not move, though nothing restrained him. The world around him started to fade away, and all there was were those terrible, viscous eyes.

"You feel it, do you not? Yes, you do." Sli's voice was calm and undulating, rolling over Merlin in waves. "You have a strong heart and mind, but if you want to know the full measure of my power, you need only surrender."

Merlin set his jaw and thought, *Drius is here. No harm will come to me.*

In a moment of weakness, supplemented by curiosity, he let go.

There was a sensation of falling, but Merlin knew he was not actually falling. He was still sitting there on the black sand, but he did not move. Only in his mind did it seem he was falling, and there was a great sense of dread. Sli was all he could see. Those eyes, those dusty, murky eyes – he drowned in them.

He will devour me.

This thought alone stirred his blood. His heart pounded in his chest, and his mind got into a tizzy. His whole being spun in a whirlpool of fear. Then suddenly, he was still. Everything in him was quiet, and he was calm. Those eyes still looked at him, and Merlin felt numb. It was as though he had gone under another trance, and no matter how great the fear had been before, it did not seem to matter now. He cared about nothing.

(Surrender.)

That is not me.

Merlin felt as though his mind were in a thick fog, and the fog was heavy, and it made him tired. That voice, with a single word, wrapped around him and held him tight. It feigned comfort, but something about it, something underneath, seemed a menace.

(Surrender.)

That is not me…that is not me…No, it is you!

Merlin reeled. Sli's voice was in his head, and it carried with it this overwhelming, compelling desire to give up, give in, and abandon all sense.

Wake up, you fool, Merlin internally screamed at himself.

A light pierced the fog, obliterated it in waves, and Merlin was drawn out of the spell.

He fell over on the sand. His eyes were open, but the world was a blur. He heard a mighty roar, deafening and fierce. Shapes formed, and he realized Drius was standing over him. The dragon glowed, and he breathed fire across the sand.

"That is enough! Release him from your hold, sea devil!"

Merlin propped himself up and watched the fire extinguish, leaving a trail of black glass.

Sli hissed and reeled back, and his companions shrieked. Overhead and below, the dragons bellowed.

"I do not have to do anything, dragon," Sli said. "He broke free of me all on his own."

"Drius?" Merlin's voice was a strangled whisper, and he laid a hand on his friend's knee. "I am fine." He coughed, cleared his throat, and said it again.

Drius moved aside and stared at Merlin with disbelief. "You lost consciousness. You were anything but fine."

"It was the exertion of my mind against his. When I came to my senses, it was like my spirit crashed into my body from a great distance. I am myself now. The only thing wrong is a queasy belly." He rubbed his stomach. "Nothing a little chocolate will not soothe."

Drius huffed. "This is no time for jokes."

"If I did not make light of it, you would know then that I was not well. Now, let me speak to him."

Merlin got to his feet and brushed the sand from his clothes. He stepped in front of Drius and eyed the sea serpent with new-found prowess.

"So that is what you call mercy?" He gathered his breath and gritted his teeth.

Sli was impassive. He showed no emotion, though Merlin thought he saw a smirk at the corner of his jaw.

"That is not mercy. That is a cruel game you play for your amusement and satisfaction."

Deep and non-threatening, Sli said, "Perhaps, but do you deny that for a brief moment, you felt calm and did not fear death?"

Merlin pursed his lips into a thin line. "I do not deny it."

"Precisely. You are magic yourself, and as I said, possess a strong heart and mind. You saw through my facade. Other humans are weak-minded and feeble. They succumb more easily, willingly even, and as such, meet their end peacefully. It is more than they deserve."

Merlin shook his head in disbelief and spat, "You are cruel and a menace."

The other sea serpents edged forward, but Sli stopped them with a hard glance.

Merlin continued: "You are a tyrant of the sea. You delight in bloodshed and destruction and terror. It is no mystery, then, why humans hunt you. You drove them to it. If you left well enough alone – but no, you and your kind cannot be reasoned with. You are beasts without sense."

"Careful, wizard," Sli hissed, his jaws wide, and the fins round his head fanning. "You know not what you speak of."

"Truly? Then enlighten me. What have you to say?"

"Only this: we did not start the war. Your kind did."

"What war?"

Their voices echoed in the bay, ricocheting off each other. These also merged with the sounds of the crashing waves and tumbling thunder overhead and the hisses and growls of the sea serpents and dragons till the cove howled with such a clamor, it shifted the sands.

Sli settled back and breathed a heavy mist. "You know so little," he said after the bay settled in a voice that cut through silk. "You want the truth? This is the truth: though your friend may deny it, and so may every creature in the Circle, we all fight a war with the humans. We struggle to survive but also to keep our place in this world. For most of them, their battles began over a hundred years ago. But our war started well over a thousand years ago.

"There was a time when humans revered and respected us. They looked at us as though we were gods. They prayed and made sacrifices to us before they sailed our waters. They wanted our blessing and favor, and we gave it to them. We let them sail. We let them fish and live off the sea we call home. We were good to the humans and kept to ourselves, for what did we care of humans? They were there and so were we, sharing the great waters and minding our own lives.

"Then, one fateful day, a man, both vulgar and a brute, harpooned a juvenile, not even big enough to put up a fight. He brought it back to his village and declared himself a hero, a great warrior who killed a mighty sea beast. Do you know what happened then? More men came with harpoons and nets, scouring the sea for us. Any man who killed one of us was called 'great,' and his feat 'a show of manhood.'

"But you see, wizard, there were not many of us in the sea to begin with. Out of a thousand eggs a female lays, only one hatchling is certain to survive. It takes many years for us to grow big enough to fend off enemies. So humans killed the juveniles, the next generation, too small and too weak to fight or flee. Some show of strength. And what followed then?

"Well, humans slew other sea beasts. The great sharks and whales and anything they thought was worth killing because they thought they were rulers of the sea and that everything was beneath their boots. What a surprise then it was when, from the depths of the sea, there woke a great serpent of immense size and strength, a beast of legend and lore, and it raged because it was agitated by the cries of its own and the smell of their blood.

"We have been at war with humans for a long time, but we did not start it, no matter what your books say – your books, written by people, people who lie. And, despite what you have been told,"—Sli looked past Merlin at Drius, who said nothing—"we have every right to live, wizard." Sli slid his eyes back over him. "Think what you want of me, that I am cruel, wicked, or a menace, but this was not always the way. We once were peaceful. Any hate and malice I have were bred into me by your kind."

The only sounds then were the rain falling, the wind cutting around the rocks, and the waves splashing. Merlin and Sli stared at each other – Merlin, his face pale and his lips pursed as if he were holding back words. He looked in those eyes, those vile, viscid eyes, and knew everything the beast said was true. He could feel it – another impression Sli put off on him, but he knew it was no lie.

He opened his mouth, then closed it. Instead, he gathered his journal, picked up his quill, and scrawled without a word.

Neither Sli nor Drius nor their fellows uttered a sound as Merlin wrote in his journal. When he finished, he packed it away in his satchel, took a deep breath, and let it out slowly. He looked at the king sea serpent with weary eyes. He was cold and tired and conflicted, thoughts and emotions surging within him. He then stepped forward.

"One more question, Sli."

Sli waited, swaying ever so slightly with the waves.

"Can you promise me that the sea serpent you send on this journey will not harm its child caretaker? If there is as much hate and malice in you as you say there is, and the same is true of your own, I worry that—"

"I promise nothing," Sli was quick to say, spitting water. He then soothed when he spoke again. "But you can rest easy knowing my kind wants to live as much as any beast in the Circle."

Merlin nodded and turned away. He climbed aboard Drius but put a hand on the dragon's neck to stay his flight.

"Sli? I suppose it would do no good if I say I am sorry for your loss and for the humans?"

The great sea serpent blew mist and said, "No, it would not, even if you meant it." He then slipped into the sea, followed by his fellows.

CHAPTER EIGHTEEN

The Shrieking Rocks

The rain fell in droves on their flight home. When they returned, Drius excused Godan and the other dragons and brought Merlin to his cave.

"How do you feel, Merlin, now that you are away from Sli and his merciless gaze?"

"Better. I will still have some chocolate because it soothes any temperament. You are welcome to some too if you – Drius, what is the matter?"

The dragon lord had raised his wings to prevent Merlin from dismounting, and his body became rigid.

"We are not alone," he said in a low, foreboding voice.

Merlin looked around, but in all this rain and shadow, he could see nary a thing. He wiggled his fingers, and the fire pit inside his cave roared to life, chasing away the dark with its light.

"I see no one inside."

"No, she is above us."

"She?"

Suddenly, Merlin smelled it – a familiar stench of odious filth and rot. He cupped his nose and looked up. In a flash of lightning, he saw her, a wretched figure with wings and a bony frame, crawling down the face of the mountain like a spider toward them. Her black eyes glimmered in the thunderlight, and she came down with her fangs bared in a terrible smile.

Merlin's heart raced. She looked intent to kill, but then Drius, not one for games, said in a voice both ominous and threatening, "Get down here, she-devil, and make it quick, or I will bring you down."

She hissed and glided down. "What a terrible thing to say." She knelt before them with one black wing crossed over her chest. "You would dare harm a messenger, oh lord dragon?"

"If the messenger is sent to do harm, yes."

"I was not sent with such an errand. I am only here to deliver a message."

"Then do so and be on your way," Drius growled.

"Touchy." The harpy gazed past him at Merlin. Her lips peeled back to show her fangs in a grisly smile. "Greetings, wizard. My name is Corvina. I bring you this message from my queen: come tomorrow after the sun has lit the sky. Come to the Shrieking Rocks. She will be waiting for you with our flock."

Drius exhaled a plume of smoke from his nostrils. "You tell your queen that he does not come alone. There will be many with him."

"She expected as much. To you, lord dragon, I am to say, do not think you can come to our island and make trouble without a fight."

Drius snapped at her, causing her to fall back, her arm raised as a feeble shield.

"There will be no trouble so long as neither she nor any of your own start it."

"Drius," Merlin soothed him and put a hand on the dragon's shoulder.

Drius retracted and looked down at the quivering bird-woman, who, though frightened, still gazed back with much ferocity.

"Tell Madera I will come tomorrow," said Merlin, "and I thank her for the chance to speak together. Now I suggest you leave before more heated words are said."

Corvina stood, her taloned feet scraping the rocky ground, her feathers ruffled and sharp. She snuffed at them and said, "Soft heart," and took flight.

Merlin sighed. "Tomorrow again." Then in a happier, lighter tone: "How about some of that chocolate?"

Drius looked after the harpy, his eyes fixed on her leaving image. Beneath his seat, Merlin could feel the lingering heat within the dragon's belly. He dismounted and went inside the cave.

He fetched the tin of chocolate from the cupboard and brought it near the fire. "Drius?" He took a bite, its rich, velvety sweetness melting in his mouth, and shook the tin.

The dragon lord turned around and gave a faint smile. "Maybe just one piece."

Merlin did not sleep well that night. Every time he closed his eyes, he saw Corvina's eyes glimmering at him, mean and dark, and her depraved smile – those pointy teeth, eager to cut and rip. He often woke in a cold sweat with his hand around his neck, worried he was exposed and vulnerable.

Later, Corvina's face changed, and behind his eyelids, Merlin saw Madera, scowling and hateful. He startled awake, sat up, and took several deep breaths to calm himself.

Why bother?

He threw back the covers and made himself a cup of tea to soothe his nerves. He sipped it by the fire, and that was where Drius found him when he came for him at the break of dawn.

"You look terrible," he said. "Did you get any sleep?"

"No." Merlin rubbed his eyes. "I had nightmares, terrible, winged ones."

Drius nodded his understanding.

"Maybe after today, you will rest easier. No harm will come to you, I promise."

"Oh, I am not worried about that, Drius. I know you and the others will keep me safe. It is just that I remember what was implied at the Circle, that children can look beyond appearances and accept. But these bird-women...I worry there may be no hope for them."

"Do not lose faith in your plan yet, Merlin. As Opala said, children have kinder hearts than their elders, so they are not quick to judge appearances."

"Yes, I know. Perhaps that is my issue: that I judge too quickly."

"Because you are old?"

The cup of tea hovered at Merlin's lips. He lowered it and stared at the dragon lord a half second before both of them chuckled warmly.

"No, Merlin. You are quite fair. If you were not, do you think we would be such good friends?"

Merlin smiled. "No, I suppose not."

The Shrieking Rocks were not on any map. Merlin looked for them, scouring his maps and books on geography, but not only was there no trace of them, there was no mention of them at all. It was a hidden place, lurking and dangerous. He decided then to chart their flight.

Drius knew the way because he had been there before. He led their party many miles south, then turned east, past hills and sandy shores, out to sea. Merlin tracked their course with his compass and transmitted by magic traces of his finger the art of cartography and the scrawling of words in his journal.

"I hate to spoil your fun," said Drius, looking back over his shoulder at the wizard, "but you best put those things away. It would be unfortunate if you lost something."

"Just a few more lines," Merlin said, licking his lips. "Besides, it has been a smooth flight. Why then should I suddenly drop—"

A strong wind, very much alive and blistering, suddenly hailed from the east and collided with their party. It hastened around them, causing them to falter, and they flew higher to be free of its force. This sudden rise made Merlin fumble, and the journal slipped from his hands. He went to grab it but missed.

Panic set in, and he was about to cast a levitation spell when Godan appeared beneath them and caught the journal in his jaws. Merlin let out a sigh of relief and put a hand over his racing heart.

"I told you," said Drius, not condescending but also relieved.

Godan rose over them and with great care dropped the journal into Merlin's open hands.

"Thank you, Godan," said Merlin, putting it away in his satchel along with the compass. "I suppose I will have to map the rest of the way in my mind."

"There is no need for that," said Drius. "We are here."

Merlin looked beyond him, down at the sea. "Oh my," he whispered, baffled and bewildered.

The sea was a deep blue, ominous and threatening, with churning waves, and there was a great wall of mist. A deep, impenetrable fog, swirling and ebbing, white and hazy, that stretched for miles in all directions.

"In there?" Merlin asked.

"Yes. Hold tight."

Drius and his fellow dragons descended and entered the mist. "Not too low," he said to the others. "Mind the rocks."

Merlin peered through the haze. *Rocks?*

There was one! It appeared so suddenly – a wicked, jagged stone, curling like a hag's finger out of the sea. There was another, and another, and another. Drius wove around these with little trouble. So did the other dragons.

"Why do you not ascend and fly over them?" Merlin asked.

"The mist is dangerous," said Drius. "The higher one flies in it, the more disoriented and confused one becomes. It weighs down on you and feels like it is choking you. You can slip into unconsciousness and fall to a perilous fate."

Merlin gulped. "None of your dragons ever..." He could not bring himself to finish the sentence.

"Almost. But it was raining, and the rain seemed to lessen the mist's effect, and there was another dragon who noticed the danger and urged to descend quickly. I was lucky then."

Merlin's eyes widened. "It was you?"

"Mmmm...yes. It was my first time visiting the harpies, and not I nor any dragon was aware of the dangers of the mist."

Merlin patted his cheeks and rubbed his arms. His nerves were getting the better of him, and he felt cold.

"That time, in fact," Drius went on, "was the last time I came here, all those years ago. It was when I invited the former queen to attend the first Great Circle. She was just as wicked as her successor but better tempered. She met her fate amongst these rocks, I think."

A shiver ran down Merlin's spine. "These rocks, how many would you say there are?"

"Hundreds. They surround the island like a gaping maw."

"A treacherous path for ships. The teeth would pick off any who enter the mouth."

"I imagine so."

It was then, as if he had spoken it into being, that Merlin spotted a rotting hull and mast lodged between two rocks. The shredded sails billowed, and crabs scurried along the deck. There was no sign of a crew, but those red stains – *Blood* – at the helm and forecastle and all along the main deck, though faded, told a story.

"I do not like this place," said Merlin.

"Nor do I," said Drius. "But take heart in knowing you are not alone and be brave, Merlin."

The mist began to thin, and Merlin could hear far-off screeches and cries like distressed seagulls but worse. His heart pounded against his chest, and goose pimples broke out along his skin. He felt queasy and quietly told himself to be brave.

The dragons broke free of the mist all at once. Before them was a towering islet with a yawning cave mouth. The islet was gray and dead. There was no sign of vegetation, no greenery. The sea, its waters so dark they seemed almost black, crashed against the imposing stone edifice.

Merlin gaped at the mist, which formed a great ring of towering haze and murky cloud, with the islet at its center, much like the eye of a storm. Sunlight could not penetrate it, leaving the air here gloomy and leaden.

Dozens of winged creatures flew out of and circled back into the cave. Others were hunched over or poised on the rocky bank.

Like vultures, Merlin thought.

One of them shrieked – a pale one with red wings, sitting at the edge of the bank, and she pointed at the coming dragons. This riled the others, and they all began to scream – a sound both piercing and paralyzing. Merlin covered his ears and hunched over. Their cries were shrill, worse than metal raked upon stone or if a hundred glasses smashed to the floor. Even through his hands, the sounds rattled his mind, made him dizzy and ill, and he felt warm wetness leach through his fingers.

One harpy, both familiar and daunting, came forth from the cave to screech at the others. Corvina flew around their heads, clawing at the air in front of them and batting her wings like a mad woman. She shooed many of them back inside and startled the others into silence. She then settled and watched, with that unsettling, toothy grin, the dragons alight on the rocky shore.

She spoke – Merlin saw her lips move, but her words were muffled. He drew his hands away from his ears and found them covered in blood. There was a faint ringing in his ears, and he realized his eardrums had ruptured.

A harpy's scream, he recalled reading in a book, *will shatter a man's ears first, then his sanity.*

Drius looked around at him, and his eyes widened.

Though he could not hear his own words as he spoke, Merlin said, "I will be fine, Drius. Give me a moment," pronouncing each word carefully and hoping he sounded calm.

Closing his eyes and lowering his head, Merlin mumbled under his breath an incantation and felt the damage in his ears mend. The ringing stopped, and his hearing was restored.

"There. Now say something."

Drius grinned. "Something."

"Very funny." Merlin rolled his eyes and dismounted. He walked to the edge of the shore and washed the blood away with the cold seawater.

"A neat trick, wizard," said Corvina. Her voice sent a shiver down his spine.

Standing up, he turned around to face her, drying his hands on his robes. "Yes, I think so. Shame I had to use it."

"I agree," said Drius, lowering his tone and narrowing his sights on the harpy. "Why did your flock cry out? Surely your queen announced our coming, or at the very least, you should have."

Corvina recoiled and bared her teeth. Those harpies still on the shore also seethed, and the dragons snarled at them.

"Enough," said a voice, and out of the cave approached Madera, walking on her taloned feet. The foggy light made her seem more threatening and imposing than when last Merlin saw her at the Great Circle.

Merlin came to Drius' side and watched. The harpy queen shooed Corvina away and faced her accuser. She stood tall, seemingly unafraid, except her jaw was tight and her body rigid.

"Explain," Drius growled, glowing within.

A wicked grin curved the corners of Madera's mouth as she said in a voice both polite and vile, "A misunderstanding. It is only natural that my flock should try to defend our rock when danger approaches."

"We are no threat."

Madera waved a hand at the dragons. "And yet you bring a small band with you."

Smoke curled forth from Drius' nostrils. "I told your messenger I would do as much."

"Yes, she told me, and it is an insult. You do not trust me, dragon."

Drius exhaled a great plume of smoke and relaxed. "It is not in my nature to trust a creature both fierce and unpredictable. Given what you know about your own, insulted or not, are you that surprised by my decision? Would you do differently if you came into my territory?"

Madera's lip twitched. She crossed her arms and looked every bit vexed, but then she threw back her head and laughed. It was a horrible sound, high and cackling, mocking and foul. She then calmed and said, "No, I suppose not."

She looked over at Merlin, and her eyes unnerved him, making his blood run cold. "Welcome, wizard," she said with a hint of disdain and a fanged smile. "We have much to talk about, I gather. So let us not waste any more time. Come inside."

Merlin whispered to Drius, "Your ears do not hurt?"

"A faint ringing, but it has passed. Merlin,"—he looked him in the eye and said in a voice so low only he could hear—"you do not have to follow her if you do not want to. You should demand she stays out here, where we can see her and you."

Merlin thought on this a moment, watching Madera walk away back to the cave. The cave was a great maw, cragged and rigid, waiting to swallow its victims. He sighed and shook his head. "You may think me daft, but I feel I must go in. It would be another insult to her not to, and besides, there is much to learn here, and I think my understanding of her and her own will benefit from going inside, seeing where they live. Though trust me, I wish it were otherwise."

"Then I am going with you, but the others will stay here."

"If the two of you are done whispering," snapped Madera, looking back at them with a sneer, "I should like to be rid of you sooner rather than later. Come!"

Drius growled. "Remember, harpy, he is doing you a favor by being here."

"I remember, and do not think I am not grateful, but that does not mean I have to take a sudden liking to him. Let us talk and be done with it."

"I am coming with him."

"Of course you are. I suppose I have no say in the matter. And what of your fellows?"

Drius looked back at Godan and the other dragons. "Wait here," he said. "Come at the first sound of trouble."

Godan nodded.

Merlin walked ahead of Drius, approaching the cave mouth with caution. It was then he noticed the stench wafting out of it. The smell was putrid, a horrible blend of rot and waste and dirty occupants. He covered his nose and mouth with his sleeve, but it was so foul, it oozed through the fabric.

Heaven help me. I fear I may retch.

He glanced back at Drius. The dragon wrinkled his nose.

You were here before. But after a hundred years, the smell is worse now than it was then, I wager.

He managed to cross the threshold and heard sniggering over his head. He looked up and saw many eyes glaring down at him. The harpies peered from their nests – large baskets woven from dried seaweed and kelp, laced with feathers and bones, perched at the top of rock spires and cairns or on the edge of erosional fins in the cave walls. They hissed and whimpered and spoke in a tongue the wizard did not know.

He did his best to ignore them and took another step forward. Only this step was followed by a loud, echoing *CRUNCH!* as something gave way beneath Merlin's foot. He was familiar with the sound, and he chided himself – *Do not look down. Do NOT look down.* But he did look to satisfy morbid curiosity.

The cave floor was covered with bones. Fish bones, seal bones, all sorts of bird bones, bones of livestock and deer, their horns and antlers scattered amongst the piles, and even turtle shells. Worst of all, staring out at Merlin with hollow eyes, their jawbones agape in long, silent screams, were human skulls.

His heart leapt into his throat at the sight of them, and he gasped – a terrible mistake! The rancid stench filled his nose and mouth like a foul poison, and he retreated outside only a few steps before he lost the contents of his stomach.

What he heard next was laughter – hundreds of odious females chittering and cackling at his misery. He stole a glance and saw Madera, her hand over her mouth, but he knew she was smiling and entertained.

I will not be made fun of nor served up for your amusement.

Without hesitation, he whirled around and shouted, "Absolve ventus!" A great wind was born from the still air, and it filled the cave, a mad gust, whipping and blustering, beating every corner and crevice of the cavernous belly.

The harpies howled within. Some flew outside to get away from the terrible zephyr. Others held onto their nests, afraid they might lose them. The rock spires and cairns tilted but did not fall, no matter how many times the wind whipped around them.

Madera stood her ground, shielding her face with her wings. She peered at Merlin with hatred anew, but there was something else, something besides loathing. If Merlin did not know better, he might have thought it was the flicker of unease. When he was satisfied the gale had done its best, he traced a line with his hand from the cave mouth to the sea. The wind followed and carried away the foul stench.

Merlin wiped his mouth with the back of his sleeve and dared to grin when he looked back at the winged women. He saw their fear and seething dislike of him, as well as many ruffled feathers. He took a deep breath and exhaled slowly.

Much better.

Madera came at him but faltered when Drius stepped between her and the wizard.

"How dare you?!" she shrieked, pointing a finger past him at Merlin.

"How dare I what?" Merlin looked at her with feigned surprise.

"How dare you use magic on us."

"It was not on you. It was at you."

Madera hissed, her bony frame shaking.

"Careful, Madera," said Drius. "He did not harm you or your flock."

The other dragons edged forward, but Drius raised a wing to stop them.

Merlin then stepped out from behind Drius and locked eyes with the harpy queen. In a voice that was less than contrite but still civil, he said, "If I offended, your majesty, I apologize. I tend to speak better, though, when my stomach does not intervene."

Madera's lips curled back, and her chest heaved with fury. Her eyes darted past Merlin at Drius and his dragons. Her clenched fists shook, but then relaxed as she came to her senses.

She took a step toward Merlin, ignoring Drius' growl. In a calm but edged voice, she said, "This is my home. I have a responsibility to protect my flock. I ask, then, that you refrain from using any more magic while you are here, wizard. Can you honor my request?"

Reluctant to do so, Merlin nodded.

"Fine. Now that we have an understanding, I ask you again to follow me inside." She turned on her heel and trudged back toward the cave.

Drius relaxed a little, but his eyes were sharp. "After you," he said to Merlin, extending a clawed foot in the direction of the cavern.

"Right." Merlin moved forward, his heart racing.

Once more, he entered the cave, but this time he minded the bones, shoving them aside with his foot so he would not step on them. He ignored the upset in his stomach and the quaking of his nerves when he saw again the remains of people past.

The cave was tall and wide. There were breaks in its ceiling that let in a hazy light, so the cave was not plunged into total darkness, but neither was it well-lit. Shapes and shadows crawled along the rock walls, and eyes peered down with a horrible gleam from their rock spires and cairns.

If I had to guess, there may be fifty of them all cramped together in this place, nesting and hating the world outside.

Merlin did his best not to look up or be concerned with them. He focused ahead on their queen, her hunched shoulders and the way she stalked with her great, taloned feet, each step heavy and determined.

She led them toward the back of the cave, where there was a grand nest, big and ornate, laced with several hundred bones, sitting on a flat rock bed on the cave floor. There was a small pool off to one side, its waters trickling down from a break in the cave ceiling. Bones lay everywhere in a ring around the nest. The cave floor was slick and edged, and the whole place was gloomy.

Madera plopped down in the nest, tucking her feet under her and covering herself with her wings.

"Sit wherever you like," she said.

She smirked at Merlin as he carefully pushed aside the bones to make room. He put himself between Drius' forepaws while the dragon lord remained standing, throwing glances over his shoulder at the flock.

Merlin got out his journal, dabbed the quill in its ink pot, and was poised over the page when he said, "Whenever you are ready."

With an intimidating grin, the harpy queen said, "I am ready."

She answered his questions with a gleam in her eye. She spared no detail, even the most gruesome. Her flock, she revealed with a sort of relish, was a flock of fiends, menacing and horrible, vengeful too, and Merlin cringed at her words.

All the while she spoke, he did his best not to look at her. Sometimes he did to assure her he was listening, but most times he kept his head down and was hunched over his writings. He did not want to seem rude, and it was discourteous, but then... *Why should she care?*

She was beastly, unclean, ragged, and foul-mannered. She was a winged terror, death trapped in pale skin and a bony frame. She breathed through her mouth to show off her fangs, those teeth – *That rip flesh from bone* – were stained from so much blood.

But her eyes, her eyes were the worst, most unsettling thing about her. Those red-blue, strained eyes – Merlin hated them. For a brief moment, he let himself think, *I wish she had no eyes,* then reproached himself for wishing her ill.

So lost was he in his thoughts about her looks he failed to notice she had become quiet, and the only sounds to be heard were the crashing of the waves outside and the chittering of the flock.

"Wizard?" Her voice was low and lost some of its edge.

Without looking at her and feigning to write more, Merlin said, "Yes, your majesty."

"Put down your quill and look at me."

Reluctant to do so, the quill teetering in his fingers, Merlin did as she asked. He set down quill and journal and, with a deep breath, raised his eyes to look at her. She stared at him, her eyes sharp but also – *Could it be?* – with a twinge of sadness.

He became rigid and blinked a lot, desperate to look another way but did not.

She frowned at him and raised a wing to hide half her face.

"Is it really so hard to look at me?"

Merlin gaped, and words failed to find his lips.

"All the time I spoke, you barely glanced at me, and you buried your gaze in your writing. Is it because I frighten you, or because I am frightening to look at?"

Merlin was silent, uncertain which answer to give. She lowered her wing fast, and her eyes bored into him like vengeful daggers. She cried out, "I know what a wretched thing I am to behold. We are all wretched. Horrid manifestations of magic."

There were several screams overhead, her flock in agreement with her.

Ignoring her sisters, Merlin was surprised and caught off guard by her behavior. She looked as though she might cry. She seethed, sucking air through her sharp teeth, and her frame shook with upset.

"But what would you know, you old fool?" She scoffed at him. "You were born a man, and for all the magic you possess, there is nothing strange or foreign about you. You look plain and ordinary. Why was magic so kind to you?"

Merlin swallowed. "Am I to understand that you believe magic made a mistake in its creation of you?"

"Did I say that?"

"No, but you seem resentful."

"Resentful? How I feel is beyond your understanding, wizard."

Merlin sat up then and met her eye. "Try me."

She stood up and spread her wings to reveal herself. "When you see me, you see a terrible thing, a monster. That is the only thing you humans see when you look at us. And why not, when there are more beautiful manifestations of magic – unicorns, merfolk, dragons." She peered at Drius, then looked back at Merlin. "Your kind, in turn, has never shown us kindness or decent understanding. Instead, humans came after us, time and time again, when all we wanted was to be left alone in peace. We were forced off the mainland and onto this islet. We were dying, sick and afraid. Then one of our queens determined that if the world is going to see us as ugly and monstrous, that is what we will be."

She wrapped her wings around herself and gazed through Merlin. "Count yourself lucky, wizard. You hide away from the world because you choose to, not because you have to."

Merlin said nothing.

"But you wonder," she said, "if I resent magic for making me thus. No, I do not." She went over to the small pool, staring down at her reflection. "I am beautiful in my eyes, and besides this, the Great Creator who rules over all, even magic, does not allow life without purpose, so I am meant to be here. I live and thus am most certainly beautiful, even if the world sees me as ugly. I have a right to live as much as any manifestation of magic, beautiful or horrible."

Merlin swallowed and said on a soft breath. "I am sorry."

"For what?"

"For misunderstanding you."

"You are human, magic or not. Of course, you misunderstand."

"I know being good is a choice though, and perhaps with this plan of mine set in motion, you and your own could change and not be so…ruthless."

Madera huffed. She returned to her nest and sat but trained her eyes on him. "Do you truly believe children will be so understanding and accepting of us?"

"Yes, but kindness begets kindness. You will fare better if you and your own change your nature."

She exhaled sharply through her nose. "You think it so easy to change? Our nature is born of centuries of cruelty by humans. What you suggest is no different than telling the centaurs not to be warriors or the fairies not to be kin to the earth."

"But it only takes one to make a change." Merlin held up a single finger to emphasize. "You could be that one, that change."

Madera stared at him, silent, and her eyes softened. "I will consider your words."

There was a long pause between them before she sat up straight and spoke anew: "Do you believe in fate, wizard?"

It was a strange question, and Merlin thought a moment before answering. "I am not sure. I suppose I do. I have seen strange, unusual things happen that people often cannot explain, and they wonder why such things came to be. Then that thing, be it a person or event, suddenly fits into the grand scheme of things. It or they were meant to be. I am not sure how better to explain it."

Madera smirked. "You did well enough."

Merlin, intrigued and curious, was compelled to ask: "And you?"

"And me?"

"Do you believe in fate?"

She stared at him, then sighed. "I did not before. It was not till I met you at the Great Circle, and you told us your plan, that I came home to find fate smiled on my flock."

Merlin raised a brow at her. "I do not understand."

Madera looked back over her shoulder. "Show them."

Merlin stared past her. There were shadows and stalagmites and more bones. There was no sign of life. But then, did he see it? Or were his eyes playing tricks on him?

Something moved in the dark.

Drius growled and became rigid, but Merlin put a hand on his clawed foot. *There is something there, but it is no threat.* How he knew, not even he could say. It was a feeling, a mystic sense he had.

"Stop being a timid bird and show yourself," Madera snapped, her voice edged and threatening.

Out of the shadows, a golden-taloned foot slid across the rocky floor, and out from behind a stalagmite appeared another harpy, but this one was small, dainty even, and right away, Merlin knew she was different from her sisters. She stepped into the murky light, her wings wrapped around her, the feathers a dusty, light brown, spotted white. On her head, she wore the skull of a giant bird.

She stopped beside the queen's nest. Her cracked lips expelled a shaky breath, hesitant and afraid. Her frame shook, and she did not lift her head, so only the hollows of the bird's eyes gawked at Merlin.

Several bird-women hissed and split the air with low shrieks, and this made the strange, timid creature before them flinch. She gripped herself more tightly in her own embrace.

Madera raised a hand to silence the flock and glared at the poor creature. "Take off your mask," she ordered, her patience waning, "and drop your wings."

The harpy turned to the queen as if to protest, but Madera gave her a warning look, causing her to recoil. With slow, trembling fingers, she removed the skull and dropped her winged arms to her sides.

Merlin's eyes widened, and even Drius raised his head.

She has no color.

She was thin and bony like the others but smaller in stature. Her skin was pale, like the last snow before spring, and she had many scars healed over. The undersides of her wings were a dusty white. Her face was triangular with hollow cheeks, and she had a full set of pointy teeth, but her eyes – they were dark and light, a gentle mystery, and full. There was no hate in them, no malice, but a great deal of fear and a gentleness pleading out from them beneath light feathery brows. Her light hair was roughly shorn, as if with a dull blade, to the nape of her neck, so her pointy ears showed. She looked like a child, afraid of everything and unsure what to do.

"This," said Madera, pointing at the winged girl with a repugnant sneer, "is the bird I will send on this journey. I am only too happy to be rid of her, for she causes me grief."

"Grief?" Merlin was taken aback. "I am an old wizard, but still, I sense no ill will from her, no malice or contempt like your other compatriots." He swept his hand back to implicate the flock. "So what grief does she cause you?"

Madera scoffed. "You are right. She is a pathetic thing. She cannot fight or will not fight, even to protect herself. She is a poor hunter, so we feed her scraps to keep her alive. She is weak and timid and not a true harpy. Nor does she contribute to the survival of the flock, and our strength is in each other. But also look at her. Do you see?"

"Yes, I see. So?"

"No color. She is cursed amongst us."

"Cursed? I do not understand."

"The pale ones, we call them, are embodiments of lost spirits ill-fated to tread the world a second time. They are a bad omen or a harbinger of great change. We do not want her here."

Merlin said nothing to this but thought, *I am less inclined to believe her superstitions,* as he briefly reflected on Aquila and the winged horses and their secret charge.

"What is more," said Madera, "the pales ones are often sickly. She grappled with illness twice when she was very young and almost died. She is fortunate not to have fallen ill under my rule, or I would have cast her out. I cannot risk the flock being infected.

"Her own mother, our former queen, hated her, but this was her only child. She could not have any more, so she reluctantly kept her. Then came the time for me to challenge the queen for the right to rule, and I won." Madera leapt and seized the harpy by the nape of her neck, causing her to cry out. "I trapped her in a dive, bashed her skull on the rocks, and cast her body into the sea. The first thing my flock begged me to do then as queen was do away with this creature. But somehow, I knew she would be of use one day, and that day has finally come." She shoved the harpy forward, causing her to fall to the rocky floor. Tears streamed down her face, and she rubbed the back of her neck.

The other harpies chittered and chuckled at her pitifulness. Merlin clenched his fists and did not take his eyes off her.

"You see, wizard?" Madera continued. "She poses no threat to a child. If she stays here much longer, there is a good chance she will have an accident. She's had several already." She regarded the harpy's scars with a wicked grin. "I cannot guarantee she will survive the next."

Merlin shook his head.

This is not right.

He glared at the harpy queen, but she was unfazed. She only smiled, showing all her teeth. He, in turn, was not intimidated. He got up and approached the poor creature who was the target of so much hate.

I will not stand for it.

As he drew near, the sobbing harpy recoiled, and her breath hitched in her throat.

"I will not hurt you," he said in a gentle voice and offered her his hand.

She did not take it but looked at it and then at him. He saw her fear and trepidation.

All was quiet around them. No other harpy made a sound, not even the queen. They only stared in amusement.

Merlin knelt beside her.

"I am Merlin Ambrosius, the wizard, as you may have heard. What is your name?"

Her lips parted to speak but then closed, and she shook her head.

"She has no name," said Madera. "Her mother never gave her one. We call her 'bird.'"

Merlin pursed his lips together.

No name means no identity. They robbed her of that.

He offered her his hand again. "I promise you can trust me. I only want to help."

Her sad eyes searched him, looked through him, and there appeared in them – Merlin saw it and grinned – the faint but familiar glimmer of hope.

Her hand crept out and touched his fingertips. Her fingers were cold, and Merlin put a warm hand over them.

"You need a name," he said. "You remind me of a dove – quiet and gentle. May I call you 'Dove'?"

Her eyes lit up and welled with fresh tears – tears of joy. She nodded. Faint color flushed her cheeks, and she smiled.

Merlin pulled her to her feet. The pair stood, facing each other, she a whole head taller than him. He pulled a handkerchief from his sleeve and encouraged her to dry her tears.

"You are soft, wizard," the queen ridiculed. "Call her whatever you like. Just take her and be gone."

Merlin's brow furrowed. "Take her?" He stared at the queen, puzzled.

Madera lowered her head, her grin fading, and shadows peaked beneath her eyes. "You heard me."

Merlin turned around to see Drius frowning, displeased. "You cannot make this request," he said.

Madera glared at the dragon lord. "Do not tell me what I can and cannot do in my own house, dragon." Drius growled.

"You want me to take her," Merlin repeated. "Why?"

"I told you why. I do not want her here. She is a burden to me and my flock."

"Strange, seeing how she is the victim of your abuse."

"You will never understand, wizard. Creatures like her do not belong, but if I can get some use out of her, this is it. So I need her alive, but my flock has put up with her for far too long. You either take her with you, or she may not make it to the beach."

"So then, you have no control over your flock?"

Madera glared at him. Hisses and cruel whispers pierced the air. Merlin turned around to see the gleaming eyes, all sharp and savage, looking back at him. He shook his head.

"Shame on you all," he said in a great voice. "Here is a creature that may be your salvation, and you dare threaten her still?"

Madera seethed, and Drius growled threateningly, a soft glow in his belly.

"Careful what you say here, wizard," the queen hissed. "Say only if you will take her or not."

Merlin faced Dove. She was shaking, frightened and wary. She looked around at the queen, her sisters, Drius, and lastly him. Her eyes pleaded for mercy, for help.

Merlin raised a finger for her to wait, and he strode back over to Drius. The dragon lord shook his head.

"You are not actually considering this request?" His voice was a low, harsh whisper.

Merlin sighed. "There are only eleven days left till the council and their chosen meet us on the beach. Eleven days is not a terribly long time to keep a house guest."

"Where will she stay?"

"With me, I suppose. I can weave some magic, make her a place to sleep."

"I do not like it. She is timid here because she is under the queen's thumb and oppressed by her flock. Once she is free of them, do you not think she will change and revert to her true nature?"

"No, I do not. I think this, how we see her now, is her true nature. I cannot explain it, Drius. I have this feeling about her and know she is not a threat. It is the same feeling I had when I met you."

Drius snuffed. "That is unfair."

Merlin grinned. "I know, but still true. I do not think she will be any trouble. Besides, it would be good to show her some kindness before she is sent away. She deserves to know that the whole world is not against her so that, at the very least, when she meets the child who finds her, she receives them well."

Drius sighed and shook his head. "I still do not like it, but you do as you please." He lifted his head to address Madera. "Even if Merlin takes her out from under your wing, you still have to meet us at the shore in eleven days to bear witness to the events."

"Of course. I would not want to miss the magic show." She chuckled. "Especially, wizard, the moment you blind the basilisk. I look forward to that." Her lips pulled back in a foul grin, showing all her teeth.

Merlin felt the hairs on the back of his neck stand up, and he forced away the image she conjured up in his mind. He did not want to think about the giant, deadly serpent when there were more pressing matters before him. He went over to Dove.

"Will you come with us?" He offered her his hand again. She took it, and in her eyes and tiny grin, Merlin saw a descending wave of relief. He led her away, back to Drius.

"I assume, your majesty," said Merlin, glancing back at their grisly host, "that we are finished here?"

"Yes. We are finished. You have what you need to write your letter, and you have overstayed your welcome."

Outside, Godan and the other dragons waited. They did not sit or lie down but stood, their bodies rigid and their manners on edge. Only when Drius and Merlin walked out of the cave did the tension subside in their hides.

"We have another with us," said Drius to Godan.

Godan looked past him at Merlin, then at Dove, wide-eyed and her mouth agape at the dragons. He snuffed. "A harpy? The Keep will not approve."

"Leave that to me. She has my permission to stay in our realm, and she will be in Merlin's care. Besides, it is temporary. She will leave with the others at the shore in short time."

Godan brought his head down for a closer look, causing Dove to shudder. "She is scrawny. Can she even fly?"

Dove pressed her lips together and fervently nodded her head.

Godan chuckled. "You are sure? It is a long journey to the Dragons' Keep."

"She will do fine," said Drius. "And if she tires, you will carry her since you are so concerned."

Godan looked back quickly at his lord and fumbled for words, but Drius shook his head at him, putting an end to their conversation.

"Come, Merlin," he said. "We have stayed here long enough."

Merlin was astride Drius when he looked back at the cave mouth to see Madera and a number of her flock standing there, watching the party make ready to leave.

Drius eyed the queen and reminded her, "Eleven days."

She nodded once and said nothing.

The dragons took to wing, ascending. Only Dove wavered, sparing a moment to look back at her sisters. They narrowed their sights on her, and many hissed through their teeth.

She shook her head at them and also took flight, leaving the islet behind her. In her talons, she held the bird skull. She flew ahead of the dragons, but not so far that she was out of sight of the cave, then turned around and hovered.

Merlin thought he saw a change come over her. Her eyes were clear and bright. Fear did not strain them, and her countenance, the look on her face, was calm, serene, perhaps even confident. She tossed the bird skull into the air and turned her back on the islet and the flock. Her past and former shame disappeared into the ocean.

CHAPTER NINETEEN

Lessons

"I still do not like it." Drius kept his voice low so only Merlin could hear him.

They were outside Merlin's cave, while inside, Dove stood by the fire, shuffling her feet and rubbing her arms.

Their party had returned to the Dragons' Keep just as the sun was setting, and now the sky was turning dark, and the first stars were blinking awake.

"You let me worry about her, Drius. Go get yourself some rest before you take your watch."

Drius stared at the harpy. She noticed and shuddered under his gaze, ducking her head and turning away so as not to see him. He shook his head.

"You will send a signal if there is trouble?"

"Of course. Goodnight, Drius."

The dragon lord dove off the cliff and rose over the crags, out of sight.

"Do not mind him," said Merlin to Dove as he joined her by the fire and warmed his hands. "He means well and is kind and fair once you get to know him. But he is lord of his realm and responsible for his own, so he has to be tough and sensible at first. I think, with a little time, he will not mind you so much."

Dove fidgeted and spread her wings so the fire warmed them. She was so pale, her skin glowed in the firelight, and her eyes, big black reflective orbs, mirrored the flames. Merlin noticed her tiny frame, thin and half-starved.

"I am famished," he said. "How about some food?"

A smile pricked the corners of her mouth, and she nodded.

"I am sorry you will have to settle for my half-baked stew. It is not great, but it sticks to your bones." He giggled, but Dove stared at him with a raised brow, confused. "That means it is filling," he explained and rubbed his belly and smiled.

It was a hearty stew with rabbit meat, potatoes, and carrots. He had one bowl, and one was enough for him, but in the time it took him to finish it, Dove had three. She gobbled each serving down, never minding using the spoon. Every time she finished, she licked her lips and stretched out her hands, cupping the bowl, to ask for more.

"You flatter me," said Merlin with a hearty chuckle. "Perhaps I am a better cook than I thought." He served her a fourth helping and watched her slurp it down. "Living off of scraps for so long, I imagine you never had a decent meal."

She faltered, glanced at him, and shook her head.

"It must have been difficult all these years past."

TREASURES IN A BOTTLE

She lowered the bowl. There was stew crusting around her lips, and she wiped it away with the back of her hand. All that was left was a frown.

"I am sorry. I did not mean to ruin your appetite."

She sat there, her chest rising and falling, her eyes fixed on the flames dancing in the pit. She seemed far away, lost in remembering, and the memories, Merlin supposed, were not pleasant, as her eyes hazed over and her frown deepened.

Merlin peered at her, leaning to the side to catch her gaze. "Do you know how to speak?"

She came back and met his stare. There was a glint in her dark eyes, a sense of knowing. She nodded.

Merlin bobbed his head with her. "You need not be silent here. The flock is many miles away, and I like conversation."

She continued to stare at him and gave no hint of her thoughts.

"We do not have to speak now if you do not want to. I am sorry for spoiling your meal."

She shook her head, grasped the spoon, and ate slowly.

Merlin chuckled. "Hearty indeed." He stood up and patted his belly. "I myself am full, so the rest is yours if you can stomach it. Save me from throwing it out."

She smiled with all her teeth and proceeded to finish her bowl and all that was left in the pot. She seemed to glow after with a new warmth, that of fullness.

"Well no one can accuse you of not having a healthy appetite," Merlin laughed. He waved his hand over the pot and ladle, twiddling his fingers as he did so, and they became clean. Dove stared at them, her eyes sparkling with fascinated curiosity.

"You like that?" Merlin asked.

She nodded and traced her fingers along the inside of the pot, finding no trace of food.

"'Tis but a small trick. Effective though. I have not cleaned the dishes by hand in many years." He chuckled again, full of mirth, and stretched his arms toward the ceiling. A great big yawn left him, and his cheeks were rosy. "Time for bed, I think. It has been a long day."

Dove lost some of her glow, frowning once more. She got up, went to a corner of the cave, and lay down on the hard floor. Merlin, half-stunned, went over to her, shaking his head.

"That will not do." He took her hands and pulled her to her feet. She looked back at him, baffled. "You are a guest in my home and as such, deserve a proper bed. I will make you one. I will make you a nest."

He went over to the white curio and searched its contents behind the glass. When he found what he was looking for, he exclaimed, "Ah-ha!", and came back over to Dove.

"This is all I need," he said, stretching out his hand to show her a large plant bulb.

She stared at it, then at him, looking all the more confused.

Merlin kept smiling. "I know it does not look like much, but just wait. I think you will like this, especially if you thought so well of how I clean the dishes."

He put the bulb on the floor, closed his eyes, and muttered under his breath. Dove peered around him and focused on the bulb. When Merlin finished speaking, he reached out a hand and touched the bulb with a finger. He then backed away.

"Watch," he whispered.

Dove did, and she gasped, unable to contain her wonder. The bulb shook, and from its head sprouted several green shoots, rising and falling, bending and twisting, twining over each other in many braids and circles, looping and skirting around the floor. They came together in the most intricate fashion to form a large nest. It was plenty big for Dove, with room to spare.

Merlin smiled, proud of his work. "What do you think?"

Dove knelt and was hesitant at first, but then she slowly traced her fingers over it. As she did, white flowers blossomed along the outer ring of the nest. She brought a hand to her trembling lips.

"I think it is rather nice, if I say so myself. The last time I built a nest – it was so long ago – was for Drius, and I used less magic than this." Merlin might have carried on but was cut short when, most suddenly, Dove rose and threw her arms around him.

156

"Thank you."

Merlin became very still. Her voice was raspy and weak from so many years of no use. Still, her words fell on his ears like the ringing of a bell, for they were wonderful to hear.

He patted her back. "You are most welcome."

Dove curled up in her nest, her wings spread around her for warmth.

Merlin snapped his fingers. A blanket appeared from under his bed and floated over to them. He set it down beside her nest and said, "If you feel a chill, wrap this around you."

Dove pulled the blanket into the nest and smiled up at Merlin.

She seems content and happy. I am glad. I do not think she had a nest before. She was so quick to lie on the floor. I suppose that is what she did back on the islet. No matter. She is here now.

"Sleep well, Dove. Goodnight."

He turned on his heel and went to his bed. He got under the covers and dimmed the fire with a wave of his hand. In the faded light, in the silence of night, he heard her whisper, "Goodnight," and smiled.

Merlin woke to the shuffling of pages. His tired eyes blinked open, and he saw Dove at his potions table, studying one of his books.

The sun was up, its light pouring into the cave, and there was the sound of birds singing.

He yawned and stretched his arms, feeling the aches of his tender age.

I could do with more sleep.

But he got up and shuffled in his silver slippers over to her, this curious bird-woman who held the book so close to her face, the words must have been a blur.

She literally has her nose in a book.

Merlin smiled at this and said, "What do you think of it?"

This startled her, and she dropped the book with a loud THUMP on the ground. She was quick to pick it up and brush it off. Her apologetic eyes were soft and full of guilt.

"It is fine. That book has suffered worse than a mere fall. And there is nothing wrong with being curious. You are welcome to any of my books except my Spell Book. That is for my use alone."

Dove glanced over at the Book on its pedestal. In the morning light, it glimmered, and her eyes were like those of a raven when it sees a shiny pebble or bauble.

Merlin draped the red velvet cloth over his Spell Book, and it was like the trance was broken, and Dove blinked several times.

"I know it is a thing of great curiosity and wonder, but only a witch or wizard can cast spells without repercussion...most of the time. I speak from experience." He gulped and forced himself to continue. "My ward once thought he could perform magic. He wanted to be invisible. The spell turned on him, and instead of being invisible, it gave him influenza. He was terribly ill for several days. I say this as a warning. Even you, who was made by magic, can suffer a terrible consequence for messing with what you do not know. Promise me you will not fool with my Spell Book."

Dove nodded and turned her attention back to the book in her hands. She pointed at the page she was open to and showed it to Merlin. It was a picture of a bolete or penny bun mushroom, but it had teeth and a body. Better known as the bolete drake, it was one of several species of magical lizard that had the appearance of a mushroom or fungus. It could not be eaten, being quite toxic, but to get one to give up its spores or one of its growing mushrooms was critical to some of Merlin's potions. That was what she had grabbed – a potions book, one of the more sophisticated ones, in fact.

"You want to know what it says?" Merlin raised a brow.

Dove nodded.

Merlin wavered, then said, "Do you know how to read?"

She frowned and looked both ashamed and downcast. She lowered the book and stared at the floor.

At once, Merlin put a hand on her shoulder for comfort. "I meant no offense. I did not expect you to say 'yes.' I suppose your kind never had use for knowing how to read." He thought a moment before saying, "Would you like to learn?"

She looked at him, a glimmer of hope in her eyes, and nodded.

"Wonderful. Let me boil some tea, and we will start your first lesson."

With a flick of his wrist, the kitchenware floated through the air. The kettle filled with water and sat on the fire. Teacups and saucers sat nearby at the ready. Bread on plates was smeared with butter and jam, and the pair ate this while they waited on the tea.

"You are not my first student," said Merlin between bites. "I had to teach my ward to read and write. I had to teach him many things. Reading was not so difficult once he learned the sounds each letter makes. You will have to put your voice to use to learn. Here. This special brew will soothe your vocal cords and open up your throat so that you can speak better. Do not look so worried. Speaking is not a shameful thing. It is how most folks and creatures get on in the world."

He added a dollop of honey and two cubes of sugar and passed Dove the cup. She sipped the tea, the steam curling around her face, and smiled, pleased with its warmth and rich taste.

"Now say something, anything," said Merlin, leaning forward expectantly.

She thought a moment, perhaps on what to say, then croaked out, "My name is Dove." Her hand found her throat, and she frowned.

Merlin chuckled. "Do not be discouraged. You sound better already. Keep drinking the tea."

She finished her cup and tried again. This time when she said, "My name is Dove," it came out melodious and sweet. She beamed with surprise.

"See? Did I not say the tea would help?" Merlin was pleased and poured her another cup. "Let me get the lesson book. I am, I confess, a bit of a hoarder. I have a terrible time throwing things out, and I was never sure why I felt inclined to hold onto this book." He pulled a dusty, thin book from its place and patted it. "Now I see I was meant to use it again." He smiled and brushed it off.

He sat beside Dove and opened the pages to a chart of letters. "We will begin here. I will point to a letter, pronounce it, and you repeat the sound. Let's begin with 'A'."

Dove was a fast learner. She copied Merlin's pronunciations, and when they read simple sentences, she had little trouble putting the sounds together to form words. The entire time she smiled, even when she struggled with big words, and her eagerness to learn made Merlin smile, happy for a vibrant student.

Later he stood up and stretched his arms and said, "We have been at this all morning. It is time we took a break. How about we go for a walk and visit Drius?"

Dove frowned.

"What is it?" Merlin inquired.

"He, the dragon, does not like me."

"Oh, no. It is not like that." He sat beside her and looked her in the eye. "He is wary of you, but he has not cast judgment on you yet. You have done nothing to warrant dislike. Come." He offered her his hand. "You will see. Once he knows you, all will be well."

Dove hesitated before taking Merlin's hand. He hoisted her to her feet.

"There we go, and when we get back, we will have lunch and continue the lesson if you like."

Her lips curved into a small grin. "Yes, thank you."

Merlin walked outside and breathed the fresh mountain air. The sky was clear, and the sun shone brightly, its light warm and comforting.

"A nice day, is it not?"

There was no answer. Curious, Merlin turned around and saw Dove wavering in the shadows of the cave. She nervously held her arm and stared at the sunlit ground.

"What is it?"

"The sun. I cannot…" The light crept toward her, and she stepped back. "My kind cannot."

Merlin recalled Madera at the Great Circle and her own aversion to sunlight, hiding in the shadows of the trees and then again, raising her winged arm to hide her face from the daylight. The queen had made mention yesterday, and he had jotted it down in his journal, of how bitter the daystar's light was to her kind and how in shadow or under the cover of night they fared better, though she had not said why.

"I see. Is it that the light cannot touch you? Or that you cannot see well, like a bat or other creature of the night?"

Dove shook her head. "Not sure. Never left the cave. Was told the sun is bad."

"It is not bad, I assure you. Without it, nothing would grow, and the world would be a cold, desolate place. But for some creatures, the sun is not for them. Are you willing to try, though, to see?"

She chewed her bottom lip, thinking, then nodded.

"I promise you," said Merlin, "there is a spell or potion to remedy the sun's sting should it bite you." He reached out his hand, and she took it.

With caution and trepidation, she eased one taloned foot into the light.

"It is warm," she said and came out further.

Merlin saw no boils or burns appear along her skin, and her feathers did not singe. It was when she brought her face into the light that she cringed and shaded herself with her wing. She hissed and blinked several times.

"You did well," said Merlin. "You have not burst into flame. But you have been in a cave all your life, and I imagine your eyes need a moment to adjust. Try again."

She winced and did not look too sure of the idea but complied. She lowered her wing, her eyelids shut.

"Try looking at the ground first," said Merlin. "Then tilt your head up to look at the trees out yonder, then at me."

She opened her eyes into tiny slits but shut them tight again and put up her wing.

"It is bright, like fire," she whimpered. "Hot too."

Merlin sighed. "I wonder…keep your wing up and let me see your eyes."

Under the cover of her wing, Merlin saw her pupils dancing, very small, like the heads of pins. Around them was faint scarring, singed and ashen.

"No, you cannot look at the light. Either you waited too long, having grown accustomed to shadows, or magic made you this way. The latter is quite possible."

"So I will stay here and wait for you." She stepped back into the cave, its shadow blanketing her in a cool embrace. She rubbed her arms and sat on the west stone by the fire pit.

Merlin stood there, rubbing his chin and thinking. A faint glimmer passed over his eyes. "Do not give up hope yet," he said, moving toward his desk. "I may have something that will help you." He searched the shelves and drawers, shuffling items around, till he raised a triumphant "Ah-ha!" Then he went to the curio and took something from there as well.

He came over to Dove with a vile of clear liquid and something wrapped in linen.

"First, if you will let me, I will treat your eyes. There is some scarring from the sun, for which I am sorry since I encouraged you."

Dove nodded.

"Thank you. Tilt your head back." He put a drop of the strange liquid in each eye and watched the scarring fade. "Did that hurt?"

"No."

"Good. Now, here is what I want to show you."

Dove leaned in close as Merlin unwrapped the linen to reveal a pair of spectacles. The rim was a plain metal, but these glasses were not like those he wore around his neck. Those were shaped like half-moons, but these were full and blue.

"What is it?"

"Tinted glasses. An old friend of mine – he was a great craftsman, a glassblower, he made these at my request. At the time, I was practicing alchemy, which is the practice of transforming matter. I was trying, like so many before me, to turn lead into gold. Do not ask me why. I suppose I was curious and wanted to try my

hand at it. It was an utter failure." He chuckled and turned the spectacles over. "Some of my techniques created very harsh light, and I wanted to spare my eyes. So I designed these, and my friend made them. They worked well for the short time I needed them. I would like you to try them."

Dove's brow furrowed. "How do they work?"

"Well, you put them on, like so." Merlin gently placed the spectacles on Dove's face. She drew back, her eyes wide behind the lenses.

"Everything is blue."

"I know. Come with me." He took her hand and led her back to the mouth of the cave. "Now step outside."

She hesitated, rubbing her hands together, then did as he suggested. Merlin walked out in front of her and watched the expressions play over her face. First, she winced as if to prepare herself for pain anew. When it did not come, she opened her eyes, then gasped, covering her mouth with her hands, and stumbled back. She came forward to the edge of the cliff and looked out over the horizon.

"Well, how does everything look?" Merlin asked.

"Blue. Everything is blue, but I can see it. I can see all of it." A tear traced her cheek. Her talons gripped the edge of the cliff, and her muscles quivered, making her feathers stand on end. She suddenly dropped off, falling forward out of sight, and Merlin rushed over in time for her to ascend past him, laughing.

She flew in circles, giddy and full of mirth.

Her joy was infectious, and even Merlin chuckled at the sight of her play. When she finally settled, her face was wet with tears, but her smile was bright.

"Thank you."

"You are most welcome. Now let us go visit the dragons."

The valley was alive, full of sound and movement. Mother dragons basked in the sun while their hatchlings tumbled and played. Isla was there with Vesper, tussling again. And there was Drius at the top of the hill, watching over all.

It was not until Merlin and Dove approached that a great silence fell over the valley. All eyes set upon the harpy, who hugged her arms and hid beneath her wings.

"Pay no attention to them," said Merlin. "They are only curious."

"No. Angry."

Merlin saw what she saw. The mothers glared, and Isla and Vesper swished their tails. Only the hatchlings were oblivious to her presence, still frolicking with one another, till their mothers hissed to draw them back. They then looked out from between their mothers' claws, eyes wide and curious. Drius frowned as they drew closer.

"May we sit with you, Drius?" Merlin sounded chipper, giving no satisfaction to the ill stares of the others.

Drius looked past Merlin at Dove, and she lowered her head, submissive and vulnerable. The dragon lord nodded and curled his tail round the spot for them to sit.

"Thank you." Merlin sat beside Drius, and Dove beside him, still holding herself, anxious and shy.

Drius stared ahead again at the valley, and his consent for them to be there made the valley less idle. The hatchlings went back to their play, Isla and Vesper whispered, but the mothers still looked on, displeased.

"I suppose no one is too keen about it," said Merlin.

"I told them of her last night, and no, they are not," said Drius.

Dove sank her head lower and brought her knees up to her chest.

"Remember, Drius, how it was when you and I met?"

"Do not bring that up again."

"It is the same."

"The difference being that my kind is not known for cruelty to spite the world." Drius kept his voice low but there was a serrated edge to it that cut deep.

"That is not fair," said Merlin.

Dove lifted her head and opened her mouth to speak, but when Drius looked at her, she stayed silent.

"She is not like her flock, Drius. She is not hateful or bitter, despite all she has been through with her own. This morning she became my student, and I am teaching her to read."

"Have you lost sight of the task before you?"

"Certainly not. Most everything is ready – the bottles, the provisions, and most of the letters. I shall write the harpy's letter soon, and then all that remains is the basilisk." Merlin shivered at the thought. "I have the time to be a teacher, and it is quite thrilling for me to impart wisdom again."

Drius was silent for a moment, still frowning. "Send her off. You and I need to speak in private."

Merlin stared at the dragon lord, then shook his head. He turned to Dove. "Would you mind waiting over there?" He pointed to a shadowed corner where the valley met the hill. "It will only be for a moment."

Dove nodded but there was reluctance in her eyes. She flew over to the spot and stood, rubbing her arms.

"Now, what is it, Drius?"

"You seem quite fond of her."

"Should I not be?"

"She will leave with the others in a few days. You hope to change her nature by then?"

"No. Her nature is already different than that of her flock, and better even. What is eating at you, Drius? I have never seen you so on edge."

Drius looked at him, a fire in his eyes. "What if it is all an act? What if she is playing you? Maybe Madera wanted you to think one thing about her so she could get close to you. Maybe, once she feels safe here, she will turn on you."

"I keep telling you, Drius, I do not sense that about her. I trust my senses now as I did the day I met you. Can you not trust me?"

"I trust you, Merlin. But a beast like me knows how crafty other beasts can be. I have been around a long time, and keeping my suspicions has kept me alive."

"Well, I tell you, you are wrong about her. Give her a chance. I think she may surprise you."

Drius sighed. "What am I to do with you, Merlin?"

Merlin raised a brow. "How do you mean?"

Drius cracked a grin. "You drive me mad, my old friend."

Merlin smiled. "Someone has to." He put a hand on Drius' shoulder and leaned in. "Give her a chance, Drius. Just one, here and now, for me."

Drius gazed over at the harpy, who failed to look back at him.

"What does she have on her face?"

Merlin still smiled and said, "Ask her yourself."

Drius sighed again. "Very well, Merlin. You win. Harpy," he called to her.

She lifted her head.

"Her name is Dove," Merlin corrected.

"Right. Dove, come here."

She came and stood beside Merlin.

"No, come here and stand before me."

Dove looked at Merlin, who nodded, and she sidled over to the dragon lord till she was in front of him, still holding herself.

"Lower your arms. Let me look at you."

She did as told but stared at the grass.

"Lift your eyes and look at me." Drius' voice was calm, low, and not savage but direct.

Dove was slow to raise her head, but she did, and she shook all over as she looked the dragon lord in the eyes.

"What are those things you wear? Tell me."

She flitted a glance at Merlin.

"Do not look at him. Look at me. I address you, you speak to me. Tell me what you are wearing."

"Tinted glasses." Her voice was shaky, but she managed the words.

"Why?"

"The sun. It is too bright. My eyes cannot see."

Drius nodded. "How do I look to you?"

"Blue." She hesitated, then added, "And terrifying."

Drius snuffed a chuckle and grinned. "You fear me?"

She nodded.

"As you should. You know I am the ruler here?"

She nodded again.

"And as such, it is my responsibility to protect my kind from any threat."

"I am no threat, lord dragon."

"No? How can I believe you?"

"The queen, she told you of me."

"She told us you were abused and neglected because of your appearance and timid demeanor. But how do I know you will not turn on Merlin or one of my own? How do I know you are not pretending at everything that was said about you?"

Dove waited before answering, her lip trembling. She then took a deep breath and stood up straight with her arms at her sides.

"If you think as much, kill me now. I will not run. I will let you strike me down."

Drius leaned in close, his hot breath ruffling her feathers. "Really?"

"Yes. I am not afraid of death. Death was there, in the cave, always there. I did not think I would get away." Her stance softened, and she held the dragon's eye. "Till you and he came." She indicated Merlin with a tilt of her head.

She then got down on her knees. "Kill me if you doubt me. I will not flee. I am happy. For one night, I knew kindness from a stranger. I had a nest and food in my belly. I learned, and I found my voice. Kill me if you must, but I am happy."

Drius stared at her. She bowed her head to him and seemed to wait for the blow. It did not come.

"Rise."

Dove got to her feet.

"Look at me."

She did. Merlin noted her stance. Her trembling was gone. She stood very still, solid, and there was no fear left in her.

"Those were pretty words, and just now I felt their sincerity. A sense, as Merlin calls it. I will let you stay here till the day comes that you leave for another shore. You listen to me though and heed my words: should you play us for fools and do us harm, I will kill you, and it will not be swift. For your sake, I hope all you said is true."

"It is."

"Very well. Take your seat beside Merlin, and the three of us will talk."

They talked about many things. They talked about kings and monsters and saints, about heroes and villains, good and evil. Merlin and Drius told stories while Dove listened with great enthusiasm, her eyes wide with hooked attention. Later, they discussed the journey she was to go on, and Merlin told her of his time spent with children.

"Children are my favorite people. They are innocent in their youth unless they are forced to grow up too soon because the world is hard and cruel. There is a short window of time where, till they are perhaps thirteen, all they want, all they dream about is fantastic. They cherish the impossible, the inexplicable, and love magic and anything born of it. Or most things, I should say." A grim shadow fell over his face. "The darker things they fear, as well they should. But still, there is no helping their curiosity."

"Darker things, like me?" Dove asked.

Drius eyed Merlin.

The wizard fumbled, "Well, no, that is to say…" He took a breath and found his bearing. "Dove, your kind, I am sad to say, was impressed upon long ago by human failure. So it is with the sea serpents as well. But there are other beasts that I have read about and seen that do terrible things for no other reason than that it is their nature. You are an anomaly, it seems. You are not like your sisters. I think it was fate or fortune, or maybe something more, that made you so for the purpose of this journey. You may, however, have to tell your child the truth about your kind."

"For their sake." She already comprehended.

Merlin nodded. "Yes. So that no child is misled or harmed by one of your own. But as I told Madera, it takes only one to make a change. She may surprise us yet, and perhaps she will bring about a change in her flock. So I suppose, then, it takes two – you and her, and together, you will alter the fate of your own."

Dove sighed and dropped her head. "They would do it," she said, her voice low and sad. "Harm a child, I mean. They do not care. Young or old. Those ships on the rocks carried people. I heard their screams. They would carry on the waves back to the islet. It frightened me."

Merlin put a hand on her shoulder. "No need to say more. I do not like to imagine what took place out there."

"Nor do I," said Drius. "We will talk about something else."

"Will the child who finds me like me?" Dove stared at Merlin, her eyes soft and gleaming and hopeful.

"I am certain, Dove," said Merlin, "the child who finds you will wonder at you, be fascinated by you, and take good care of you."

Dove tried to smile but said, "I hate to leave you. You are so kind."

Merlin blushed. "Thank you. I, um…" He looked at Drius, who shook his head. He was not going to speak on it.

"Dove,"—Merlin thought well before he spoke—"I promise you, your child will be kind. I am not the last friend you will ever have."

At that moment, some hatchlings ran up to them, playfully growling, chasing each other, and puffing balls of smoke. They ran circles around Drius and Merlin, then butted their small heads against the dragon lord's massive claws.

"Settle, little ones," said Drius with a laugh and satisfied grin. He then brought his head down and growled at them in a friendly, non-threatening manner.

The little ones snarled back and leapt at his face. They were very young, only a week or so old, and did not care who they got to play with them so long as they did play.

Merlin cast his magic to turn blades of grass into dragonflies that zipped this way and that. The little tykes took after them, trying to catch them between their teeth.

One of the babes then faltered in its play and stared at Dove. The harpy had been smiling while watching the small dragons play, but now she looked nervous as the hatchling approached her. She glanced at Drius, then Merlin, as if for guidance, but neither of them said anything – Merlin, because he was curious to see what the little one might do, and Drius, with a sharp eye, was perhaps testing her.

The hatchling came up to her and pressed its scaly head against her palm. Dove, with little assurance, stroked its head, and it cooed. The hatchling then sat in her lap, looking out toward the valley at, Merlin noticed, a disgruntled mother.

Dove continued to pet the babe, making it coo and flap its tiny wings. Soon the other hatchlings, curious about their sibling's pleasant murmurs, came over and climbed on Dove, licking her face and begging her to play. At one point, she fell over, and they were on top of her, squeaking and tickling her with their snouts, and Dove laughed.

"No better proof than this," said Merlin to Drius, "that children know and are eager to love those that fascinate them."

It was not till close to sunset that Merlin and Dove started back for the wizard's cave.

"You made many friends today," said Merlin, "with the hatchlings."

"Yes. They are, what is the word? Cute?"

Merlin chuckled. "Yes. That they are. Mischievous too. Once, Drius brought his daughter, Isla, by my cave to say hello. She got curious about the potions table, and we only had our backs turned for a moment. It was long enough though for her to turn over a hair tonic. She was the wooliest dragon I had ever seen. Drius was not too pleased, but I set her right with another potion."

Dove laughed. "It is strange to imagine such a thing."

"Well, hatchlings are no different than human children. Different species, yes, but both are curious, playful, and filled with wonder. They gravitate toward that which is unknown, and they are innocent."

"You mean they are good."

Merlin stopped and stared at Dove. She had a troubled look on her face, almost sad. "Good is a broad term. Children are kind, yes, but I have met a few bad eggs. One boy comes to mind. His name was Mordred." Merlin then faltered and shook his head. "But I do not want to discourage you. I will say this: most children, the grand majority of them, are good, yes, because they are not grown up and do not yet care about the things of adulthood – money, wealth, title, and reputation. They are just happy to be living in the moment and are drawn toward that which is a mystery and full of wonder. You are a mystery, Dove. You are a magical creature. You will stun and stupefy many children, and I suspect they will love you for it."

Dove grinned. "I hope you are right."

They made it back to the cave, and with a wave of his hand, Merlin lit the fire pit.

"What should we have for supper? I think I ran out of meat. Yes, I have. All that is left is potatoes, sprouts, and beans."

"I can catch us something."

Merlin raised a brow at her. "Madera said you are a poor hunter. Is that not true?"

"I can hunt. But I do not enjoy killing like my sisters."

"I see. Well, Madera said your kind requires meat, and if that is so, I will not ask you to eat only vegetables."

Dove nodded. "I will return." She went outside and dove off the cliff.

It was not long before she returned with a couple of squirrels.

"I promise they felt nothing," she said.

"I believe you."

Merlin prepared them a stew, and they sat quietly around the fire and ate. When done, he cleaned the dishware and put it away.

"Night is here," he said, stretching his arms. "Time for sleep."

Dove went to her nest and curled up under her feathers.

Merlin also withdrew to his bed but stopped short.

His heart pounded in his chest as he stared at a lump under the covers. It moved, slid this way and that, then stopped.

"Trespasser," he whispered. With a twitch of his fingers, the covers flew aside, and there, coiled and poised to strike, was a large black snake.

There was a rush of wind, and suddenly Dove was there, crouched on the bed, the serpent caught in her hands, its fangs wide with a terrible hiss. She too bared her sharp teeth and shrieked at the thing as it coiled its length around her arm.

Merlin stared stupefied. There was a fierce gleam in Dove's eyes as she focused on her foe, and she shivered with unfamiliar fury and instinct. In that moment, she seemed like her sisters, angry and wild, but when she looked at him, her obvious fear and worry for him shattered the image.

She started, "Merlin, are you—"

"I am fine. Thank you, Dove." Merlin put a hand over his heart and waited for it to beat at a less frantic pace.

"Strange I should have such a visitor as this," he said. "A black adder. Venomous. But they prefer low ground and not high elevations. And to be in my bed of all places. This is no mere coincidence. Do not kill it."

Merlin went over to his Spell Book and found the spell that enabled him to speak the tongues of beasts. He recited it and addressed the serpent.

"Why are you here?"

The snake ceased its struggle. Its dark red eyes stared at Merlin, angry and spiteful.

"I ask again. Why are you here?"

"The king of serpentsss sent me," it hissed. "He demands hisss audience with you. Tomorrow."

"The king? You mean Silzer?"

The adder hissed a laugh. "He isss anxiousss to sssee you."

"I am certain he is. I did not know lesser snakes answer to him."

"He is the king of all that ssslither and ssstrike. His word isss law."

"I see. And what was your mission? To deliver this message or do me harm?"

The adder was silent, but it seemed to grin.

"You know I could let Dove snap you like a twig. I imagine she can easily do so."

Dove nodded, and the adder glared at her.

"But then, how would I send word back to your king? Tell him I will meet him tomorrow, as he asks. But where am I to meet him?"

"At the Pit."

"The Pit?"

"Ask the dragon."

Merlin nodded. "I will. Dove, please drop him at the foot of the mountain. Be careful he does not bite you."

Dove carried the serpent away and returned moments later.

"Wicked thing," she said.

"Yes, it was. No more so than its king. I suppose I should consider myself lucky."

"Lucky?"

"Yes. He could have sent one of his own to deliver the message. Then we would certainly be dead." Merlin sat on the edge of his bed and patted his brow with his sleeve. It was wet with sweat. "You were most impressive. Thank you for saving my life."

Dove nodded but did not smile. "This king, he is the last you must see?"

"Yes. The basilisk, Silzer. He is the one I fear most. I will have to think on how I will meet him. If I go as myself, I may not return. I am not sure I trust him after this little exchange."

"Then why go?"

"My oath. I promised I would help him and his own, and a wizard never breaks his promise." He grinned at Dove. "I will not think on it anymore tonight but save it for the morning. We both need our sleep."

He got under the covers and dimmed the fire.

"Goodnight, Dove, and again, thank you. I am glad you are here." He then turned on his side and tried to withdraw behind his eyelids.

Dove stood in the dark, watching him. She was not convinced of all he said, but after a moment, she too went to her nest and tried to sleep.

CHAPTER TWENTY

The Pit

"You cannot go." Drius was outside Merlin's cave, watching the wizard pace.

Dove sat on the south stone, holding her knee to her chest. At Merlin's request, she had gone to the dragon lord before the break of dawn and told him about last night's intruder. Hot with anger, Drius followed her back to the wizard's cave, and now they were deciding what Merlin should do.

"It is too dangerous," said Drius. "He is the one creature no dragon can oppose. He has the advantage."

"I know," said Merlin.

"There is no telling what he might do, but you cannot ignore him either. It is his right as one of the Circle to whom you swore your help."

"I agree."

"But after his trick with the messenger, I wonder if it is not a sign of ill will."

"Who is to know?"

Merlin plopped down on a nearby stone and twiddled his thumbs.

"What is the Pit?"

Drius sighed and shook his head. "It is as it sounds. It is a great pit in the earth, many miles from here, in a desolate place. All around it, nothing grows. The ground is dry and dead. Though I have never seen the heart of the Pit, nor do I ever hope to, the one time I came near it, I heard many hisses and the rubbing of many scales within. My guess is a great number of basilisks live there, slithering over top of each other. A massive, writhing ball of evil. Any creature foolish enough to wander the dead valley or steal a glance at the Pit seals its fate."

Merlin gulped. He felt the prick of sweat on the back of his neck and his nerves shaking. He summoned a pot of tea to brew on the fire.

"Tea to soothe my nerves," he explained, though no one asked. "I agree with you, Drius. I cannot go there in person, but I must appear. I said I would. Otherwise, I fear retaliation will be in short order."

Drius frowned. "I do not disagree. He is quick to anger and easy to offend."

"There has to be a way," said Merlin, taking the cup of tea that floated to him. He blew away the steam and sipped. "Something I am not thinking of."

Dove's voice piped up then: "Spell Book?"

Both Merlin and Drius looked at her, then at each other.

"Maybe," said Merlin. With a flick of the wrist, his Spell Book floated over to him. He set down his tea, took the Book, and flipped through its pages. "I am not certain what I am looking for. I suppose I will know when I find it."

"You think one of your spells can deflect the basilisk's sight?" Drius asked.

"No, nothing like that." He paused in his page turning. "This reminds me of a story I heard in Greece of a man who faced a gorgon."

"What is a gorgon?" Dove asked.

"Imagine a woman with snakes for hair. If anyone looked at her, they were turned to stone. A young hero used a shield as a mirror and cut off her head." He frowned. "But the basilisk is no gorgon. It is far more dangerous. Its reflection alone will paralyze a person."

"So no shield. No mirror." Dove frowned.

"No." Merlin perked up then, sat up straight, and pulled at his beard.

"I know that look," said Drius. "An idea?"

"Maybe. What are the four selves of a person?"

Drius shook his head, and Dove only stared.

Merlin raised a hand and counted off. "First, there is the body. Second is the spirit. Third, our reflection. And fourth, our shadow." He flipped through the pages of his Spell Book and stopped on a page titled, *Shadow Casting.*

"Yes, here it is. I used this spell once to eavesdrop on visitors to the king's castle. I discovered them to be traitors with a plot to kidnap the queen and hold her ransom for the crown."

"What does the spell do?" Drius asked.

"It allows me to move about, speak, and hear as my shadow. My body remains stagnant and appears asleep all the while. If I remember well, this spell requires a great deal of energy and strength of mind. I only used it that one time."

"Will it work?"

"I believe so. My shadow does not see as I see now. Rather, it sees dark masses and other shadows, and the scenery is mottled grays and blacks."

"You are certain then you will not see the basilisk's eyes?"

"Quite certain. When last I used it, I did not see the eyes of the king's traitors, his servants, or anyone's, not even the palace cat's or its victim rat's."

Drius nodded. "Very well. I trust your judgment."

"Thank you. I must prepare a special brew that will help me sleep. Dove?"

The harpy left her stone seat and came to him.

"Will you watch over my body while my shadow is away? I will be completely helpless."

She nodded.

"I am not going anywhere," said Drius. "I will stay as well."

Merlin smiled. "I did not doubt that for a moment."

Merlin lay on his bed, the steaming brew in his hand. Dove sat beside him, her eyes wide and nervous. Drius was still at the cave mouth, solemn and blocking most of the daylight with his massive body.

The cave was illuminated by a thousand candles. Most of these were set in crags and recesses along the cave walls but also on the furniture and even along the cave floor. The tiny lights flickered and danced, casting many shadows. Merlin's own shadow lay beside him, mirroring his every move.

"Everything is ready," said Merlin. He patted his Spell Book, which was open to the page on *Shadow Casting.*

"This is not like most spells. I will read and sip, read and sip, then down the rest of my brew and read the spell one last time before slipping into slumber." He was looking at Dove as he spoke but said it loud enough for Drius to hear. "You cannot wake me while my shadow is away, for my mind goes with it, and all that remains here is my body, still breathing and heart beating. There is no telling how long I will be gone, but for as long as that is, stay here and look after me. The exertion of my power may weaken my body, and if I get hot, take the washcloth and basin here and dab me over with cool water."

Dove nodded her understanding.

"I admit there was no one with me the last time I performed this spell. When I came back, it took me some time to find the strength to stand again. I am comforted knowing you both are here with me." He smiled at them, then raised his cup. "Cheers."

Each time he read the spell, he pronounced the words carefully, and his voice was low and sacred, and he concentrated all his thoughts on his wavering shadow. When sleep took him, Dove eased him down on the pillows, then she and Drius waited for what seemed a long time.

The first time the shadow quivered, neither of them saw. But then Dove, with her keen eyes, held her breath as its hand twitched, then rose and fell.

"Lord dragon," she said, "something…" but she did not finish.

The dark silhouette bounced and wavered, then its hands pulled at its feet as though it were trying to tear itself away.

"What is it? What is happening?" Drius could not see and was becoming agitated, nervous even.

"It moves."

The shadow pulled away from its master's body and slithered along the floor. It then stood flat against a stone wall, and a familiar laugh, Merlin's laugh, echoed from it. His laugh sounded far away – it was strange, and Dove tilted her head, staring at the dark shape.

"It worked," said Shadow Merlin. "Everything looks just as it did the last time. I see your dark shapes but not your faces. Are you surprised?"

Dove only nodded, at a loss for words.

Drius looked fixedly at the shadow and said, "I have known you for so long, Merlin, I thought your ability to surprise me had gone. This is an impressive feat."

"You like it?"

The dragon lord nodded. "How do you feel?"

"It is strange. I feel displaced and broken. I know my mind and shadow belong with my body, and the longer I am away, the more I will feel torn apart."

"All the more reason not to be away too long."

"Yes. But I also confess I feel a tad exhilarated and even delighted."

"Delighted?"

"In this state, I am free of the aches and pains of my withering shell. I can move about with ease. I can jump and skip, run and fly, and not feel the weight of my mortality. I do not hunger or thirst or feel fatigued, like when I am in my skin."

Drius said nothing at first, then sighed. "I like you better as a man than a shadow of yourself."

"Yes, I know. Do not fret, my old friend. I will return to myself. The sooner, the better. Now, how do I get to the Pit?"

The Pit was many miles south and then to the east. Shadow Merlin was swift, passing over mountains, valleys, and streams and through forests, moving along the ground faster than a deer can run, for a shadow cannot fly, being strangely bound by the laws of gravity, same as its master's body, but it is nimble and quick and can squeeze into tight places.

It was not long before he noticed a change in the earth. There was a recession of plant life, and he found a long track made by something big with no legs. It left a trail of death – withered flowers and scorched grass, even the trees drooped and browned.

"I must be close."

A little further, and then all manner of life was gone. All that was left was dry, cracked ground spanning many miles. Shadow Merlin felt a quake in his being. If he were with his body, his stomach might have butterflies, but as a shadow, it felt different, like electricity was running through him.

"Be quick. Be nimble."

He floated across the dead valley. As a shadow, he saw it in many tones of gray and black. There were plenty of large rocks and lots of fissures snaking the ground. Everything was dry and dusty.

Everywhere was quiet. No birds flew overhead. No insects crawled. Not even the wind blew here. All life was absent from this place. It felt unnatural and made him nervous.

Then there was a sound, faint, unpleasant, and chilling. He had heard it before at the Great Circle. The sound of cold water on hot metal. The sound of scales rubbing together.

He passed over a great pile of rocks, and there, it came into view so suddenly – a large black hole, the Pit. It was wide and gaping, like a terrible mouth, ready and waiting to swallow lives whole. It was so vast and immense, it could consume an army – cavalry and infantry, a small village, or even a castle, and there would be no trace left, everything lost in the darkness below. To look at it was enough to cause Shadow Merlin fear, but the sounds that emanated from within would have driven a lesser man to madness.

Rising from the heart of the Pit was a cacophony of hisses and the sliding of many scaled bodies over top of one another. The sound was almost deafening, and if he could have, Shadow Merlin would have covered his ears. Instead, he inched closer to the Pit, the dread in his heart begging him to turn back.

"I am safe like this," he assured himself with a whisper. "He cannot harm me as a shadow."

He came to the edge and dared to look in. All was black. He could see nothing, but the chaos below was loud and steely, cruel and unsettling. It made him retreat to a nearby rock pile and catch his absent breath.

"Easy, Merlin. You can do this. You have faced worse…I think."

Again, he went to the Pit's edge and looked in and, with a deep voice, shouted, "Silzer!"

All manner of sound ceased at once, and Shadow Merlin quivered, for the silence was more terrifying than the hisses and scales before it.

"It is I, Merlin. I have come, as you requested. I am up here, waiting for you. Let us talk."

He retreated to the rocks and soon heard the gliding, the pushing, the sliding of one scaled body up and along the rocky teeth of the Pit.

Silzer emerged from the great hole quite suddenly, his mouth agape and a hideous hiss resounding. Then his figure looked this way and that, searching.

He cannot see me.

"Where are you, wizard?" the great serpent spat.

In a calm voice, edged with bravery, Merlin replied, "I am right here, against these rocks. Do you see me?"

He waved at the basilisk, and when the great serpent saw his shadow, it was then, at that precise moment, back home on his bed, that Merlin's body was run over with chills. Shadow Merlin doubled over, grasping his middle. Strangely enough, he felt nauseated, and his silhouette quaked with nervous fright. It was like being dumped in ice water and set on fire at the same time.

What magic is this? His sight? Even the shadows feel it?

"What trickery is thissssss?" Silzer slithered forward and towered over Shadow Merlin.

"It is not- It is not-" Shadow Merlin struggled to catch his breath, to muster words into sentences. "It is not a trick. Merely a precaution."

"So you do not trussst me?"

"It is not a matter of trust, king basilisk." Shadow Merlin paused and heaved and thought carefully of what to say.

"Then what isss it?"

Shadow Merlin forced himself to stand up straight and look at Silzer, his shape a dark, imposing silhouette against all the shades of shadow he saw. "I hoped to come here in a way that meant no disrespect to you," he said with caution. "At the Great Circle, you must turn your back, but here, in your house, where you are master, your guest should submit to you, but still, I must be able to walk away alive. I apologize if this way offends you, for that was not my intent."

Silzer's tongue licked the air, a thin wisp of gray. "Quite the clever wizard you are," he said.

"I beg your pardon?"

"Ssspinning wordsss to flatter me. Whether you ssspeak the truth or not, I have no way of knowing, but I will allow it. But tell me,"—he peered at Shadow Merlin, and the silhouette crumpled ever so slightly—"how do you feel? You ssseem to ssstruggle."

"Nothing escapes your eyes. I do struggle. I feel- I feel terrible, if you must know. For though I cannot see your eyes – I see only the dark silhouette of your body, I still feel the power of your sight so long as you look upon my shadow."

Silzer chuckled. "Fassscinating."

"Truly?"

"Yesss. I had no way of knowing my power goesss beyond ssshape and form to pierce the shadowsss. How delightful."

"Delightful?" Shadow Merlin repeated the word in disbelief. "Do you really delight in wreaking such havoc?"

"Ssshould I not delight in my power? In what I am?"

Shadow Merlin wavered, irresolute and unsure how to answer, so he remained silent.

"I thought you might understand, wizard, being a magic user."

Shadow Merlin looked away, the power behind the basilisk's eyes too much for him, and he struggled to say, "I understand the thrill to use magic, yes, and I have a deep appreciation for my bond with magic. It is a gift for me to bend and use according to my will. But I do not delight in the misuse of it."

"Misssuse? How can I abussse my power, wizard? All I do isss exist. Instead, you should blame magic, how she misssused her power to create life when she made me."

"Blame magic?"

"Yesss. Think on it: how cruel wasss magic when she conceived me? How angry did the world make her that she sssewed me together and gave me the mosssts vengeful power of all her children? Everywhere I ssslither, death isss with me, if not in my presssence which makesss the earth wither, or my breath that shrivelsss the green, then my eyesss, for no man or beasssts can look at me and not perish, not even you. Only the ssshadow of you can ssstand before me, barely, and even so, it quiverssss."

Silzer edged closer and leaned in, his dark frame imposing, so close, his breath blew dust from the rocks where Shadow Merlin lingered. "I am curiousss to know how long you can hold thisss ssshape. No doubt it is difficult, even without my ssstaring at you."

"It is a feat…" Shadow Merlin struggled to catch his breath, "like any magic."

"An impressive one at that. I commend you on your sssharp thinking. To come to me as a ssshadow – I do not sssupposssse you had any other choice?"

"Choices were limited and few."

"Hmm…Tell me, jusssst to sssatisfy my own curiosity, what elsssse could you have done to keep thisss audience with me?"

He stared intently, and Shadow Merlin trembled. There was a growing pain, like many tiny cuts opening and closing and opening again, and an invisible hand seemed to close around his throat, making it all the more difficult to breathe.

"Why does it matter?"

"It doesss not matter. I only want to know." Silzer exhaled sharply, and his tongue reached out to touch the wizard's shadow. This brush of contact caused Shadow Merlin to recoil, feeling as though he had been burned.

"I will not say, and I ask you, Silzer, to please look away. I cannot withstand your power any longer."

"Tell me what I want to know, and I will."

"I- I will leave then."

"And break your promissse? You bound yoursssself in an oath to me with your magic to help me and my own. What will the consssequences be if you break it?"

Shadow Merlin clenched his fists in frustration.

"Come on, wizard. I asssk ssso little."

"You ask too much," Shadow Merlin cried. "Please look away."

"No."

Shadow Merlin fell to his knees, the pain and suffocation so great, his body at home paled, and he was aware of it all these miles away at the Pit.

"Fine then," he shouted. "The only other way to come here that I could imagine but would never entertain was- was-" He gasped, his breath leaving him, and he forced the last word: "Necromancy."

Suddenly, he was at peace. Shadow Merlin's struggle ceased, and he felt a faint cold dampness as, back home, Dove batted his brow with the washcloth, and over here, his strength rolled over him, returning in waves. He lifted his head and saw Silzer had withdrawn and turned away.

"Necromancy," the great serpent repeated. "Black magic."

"Yes." Shadow Merlin coughed and strained to stand up. "It is dishonorable magic, shameful even. Forbidden."

"How would it work?"

"Must I tell you?"

"I want to know."

Shadow Merlin paused, thinking.

No good can come of telling him, but he may look on me again and torture me with his stare till I give in, and I can go nowhere since I am oathbound.

With a heavy, reluctant sigh, he said, "I could have- I could have borrowed a body for a spell."

"A dead body?"

"Yes, you know as much."

"And then what?"

"I would have sent it here, in my place, and"—he internally cringed—"spoken through it."

Silzer hissed with vile laughter. His forked tongue snaked the air as he did so. "The great wizard, Merlin, a kind and sssimpering old man, would have gone againssst nature and heaven and dabbled in the Black?"

"No, I would never," Shadow Merlin snapped with anger. "I would sooner come here as myself and risk death than use such foul sorcery."

Silzer continued to chuckle and raised his head. "And yet, you know of it. How?"

"Pardon?"

"You know the waysss of dark magic. How?"

Shadow Merlin withheld his speech till Silzer started turning to face him. He then said in a low tone, stopping the great serpent, "I studied a lot in my youth and, in my ignorance, thought it wise to learn the darker ways of magic so that I might know how to fight them." Then, in a quieter voice, "A lot of good it did me."

"Ahhh, I sssense a terrible missshap befell you then, did it not?"

Shadow Merlin clenched his jaw and said through his teeth, "It does not matter, and I will ask you not to press any further."

Silzer tasted the air, his head high as though he were contemplating. He then coiled up in a ball, his scales lightly grazing each other. "Very well, wizard. I will be kind. I do wonder, though, if my sssight, my power, hasss any effect on the dead?"

"I doubt it."

"Who isss to know? It will remain a myssstery."

Shadow Merlin shook his head, and perhaps Silzer saw this out of the corner of his eye, for the basilisk then said, "You do not agree with my musssingsss, wizard? My dark fassscinationsss, which you musssst find dissssturbing?"

No, Merlin thought, but he said, "I do not understand them."

When Silzer spoke again, there was a lilt in his voice that razed Merlin's spirit. "Do you know how it feelsss to take a life?"

Shadow Merlin hesitated and, with hard reluctance, said, "Yes, I do."

"Do you regret it?"

"Yes."

"Of courssse you do. You only regret becaussse you know how it feelsss to look at life and sssee it move forward, while I do not. I have never sssseen a life look back at me and continue that wasss not one of my own. Fear and death are my companionsss. They go before me and ensssnare the livesss of thossse who are not another basssilisssk.

"Ssso I regret nothing. When I look at a life, and it extinguisssshes in an insssstant before me, how can I regret the lossss of it? I never knew it. Thisss is what I am…and I am proud to be asss such." The last he said in a sharp whisper, and Shadow Merlin wondered if he was being sincere.

"Your kind," he started, "are they all as proud and ruthless as you?"

"Certainly. We musssst be to get along in life, and why ssshould a basssilisssk regret what he isss? We are all hard and pitilessss. To be otherwisssse is to be weak."

Shadow Merlin stiffened as a thought, a sudden realization, settled on him. "Would you say then your kind is unfeeling toward all life?"

"Yesss."

"Even each other?"

Silzer hesitated. Shadow Merlin pursued.

"Tell me, king basilisk, are you and yours callous and insensitive toward each other? What goes on in that Pit?"

Silzer rubbed his scales together, the sound grating a warning, but Shadow Merlin did not let up. Courage gripped him and propelled him forward.

"I pity you."

The grating ceased, and Silzer faced the accusing shadow, his eyes piercing, but Shadow Merlin did not waver. He held his stance. "You pity me?"

"Yes."

"Why?"

"Because I see now and understand: your deadly sight cripples you. I never thought it before, not till I heard you speak. Am I right to suppose your own are not kind to one another? You do your best by them as king, but you are not fond of them, are you? If anything, you tolerate them."

Silzer's tongue split the air, but he said nothing, waiting.

"If the only life you can look on is one of your own, but your own cannot appreciate nor care for one another, then neither you nor they understand the sanctity of life. You do not know its value, how precious life is, how important, because you only know death. Your sight robs you of the chance to form any sort of bond with another living thing beyond death bringer and victim. So you know nothing of compassion, friendship, or love, all the good things that make life significant and worth living. So, actually, you lead a lonely existence, and death is a miserable companion. I see that now, and I pity you."

Silzer rubbed his coils ever so slightly, agitated and unnerved. "Sssave your pity," he said, the venom dripping with each word, and looked away.

Time slunk by as Shadow Merlin and Silzer conversed about the care of a basilisk. Silzer answered most questions with grim detail. Some particulars he told with cadence and a grin, revealing his morbid pleasure, but still, his rigid figure and sharp hisses gave proof he was riled and displeased and wanted to be rid of the wizard's company.

Is he upset because I pity him, wondered Shadow Merlin, *or because I revealed a truth that causes him discomfort? A truth that, perhaps, he was not even aware of? Or maybe he was aware of it but had buried it deep within himself, and I brought it to light. Fierce beasts like him cannot afford to be exposed, even unto themselves.*

In the middle of their talk, Silzer said, "I am looking forward to our deal, wizard."

"Our deal?"

"Yesss, where I get to look on you after you hope to ssstrip me of my sssight."

Shadow Merlin gulped but said nothing.

"I am assshamed to admit there isss a part of me that hopesss you sssucceed becaussse then your plan will be ssset in motion, and my own will have a chance to live. But then there isss another part of me, ssselfish and indignant, that hopesss you fail."

"And why is that?"

"Becaussse if you manage to do it, I will have to look at life all the time, and it will look back at me. I will no longer be myssself, what I have been for well over a century. No more a basssilisssk. Jussst a great ssserpent."

When their conversation concluded, and Shadow Merlin was about to take his leave, Silzer said one thing more to stay him from fleeing.

"Do you hate me, wizard?"

Surprised by the question, Shadow Merlin stammered, "Wh-why do you ask?"

"I want to hear you sssay it." The basilisk's tone was insistent and had a subtle edge, as though he were convinced he knew the answer.

Shadow Merlin was silent for a time, searching himself for the truth. He let out a long sigh before answering. "I have done my best not to hate any living thing, not even bad men. I admit that before I came here, I had formed an opinion of you based on what I knew about your kind in books and stories and my first impression of you at the Great Circle. After speaking with you, I still think you are cruel, and you delight in the misery of others and relish your power. Still, for all of that, I would like to think you are redeemable, that you can be otherwise, but maybe it will not happen till I strip you of your sight, and life finally looks back at you. As I said, I pity you because you do not know how precious life is or what there is beyond death and solitude. Not yet. But no, I do not hate you."

Silzer said nothing, and his silhouette did not move. Shadow Merlin continued:

"Hate poisons life. It can turn a man against himself, corrupt and spoil the spirit, and turn all that is good into evil. It clouds good judgment, mottles sense, and spurs bad actions with terrible consequences.

"I do not know how much longer I have to live on this good green earth, but I will not ruin my remaining days by letting hate turn me and spoil my vision. I choose to accept you for what you are and nothing more."

Silzer's tongue flicked the air and withdrew. He still said nothing.

Shadow Merlin did not wait for a response. He found strength in his words to take his leave and concluded their meeting with, "For what it is worth, I bid you good day and goodnight, king basilisk. I will see you again on the beach."

CHAPTER TWENTY-ONE

The Others

"I do not hate him."

Shadow Merlin was slow to return home, for as soon as he left the Pit, his mind waged battle with his conscience, and ill thoughts distracted him.

"He intimidates me, and I have a healthy fear of him, and I respect him, for I would be a fool not to. I am not fond of him, certainly, therefore I do not like him, nor do I have to like him, but I do not hate him."

Yet, in the pit of his stomach and at the back of his mind, something turned over and did not feel right. He held up by a stream to sort it out and paced, his silhouette darting amongst the trees.

"I do not hate Silzer or his kind—"

The eye of his memory recalled a couple visages, both equally terrifying.

"Nor do I hate Sli nor Madera nor their own. I understand them better after our meetings. I understand why they are the way they are toward the world, but still, I worry. I worry about those they send – except for Dove, she having a kinder disposition, but if she were not here, Madera would send another, less pleasant harpy, I imagine. I worry for the children who will find the others, and I worry about those that stay behind, who will be invisible and able to move freely throughout the world."

His mind reeled, and worry sank in him like heavy stones, dragging him beneath the surf of his conscience.

"I pray they do no harm. I know they want to live and for their own to survive. Hopefully, that will stay any violent impulses."

A new thought then surfaced, coming up for air, and it left a bad taste in Merlin's mouth as he said it aloud.

"How is it they joined the Great Circle? Why were they allowed in when the others – Drius, surely – knew better and could see how they are?"

How? Why?

Those two questions repeated in his mind over and over again, but no answer came.

"Drius…"

He looked up and saw the world darken. Day was turning to night, and he could see the pale scythe moon rising.

"I must get home. He and Dove will worry."

Still, as he moved over the terrain, his mind pounded those two words in a steady rhythm, like the steadfast beat of war drums.

How? Why?

When at last he was home, he said nothing. He made no sound to alert them of his return. He saw Dove dabbing the brow of his sleeping figure, and Drius sitting at the cave entrance. Most of the candles had burned down to almost nothing, and their fading lights flickered.

He floated over to his body, and Dove gasped when she noticed him, knocking over the bowl and splashing water on the floor.

"He returns," she said, a joyful lilt in her voice.

Drius lifted his head to see better but was silent.

Shadow Merlin rejoined himself to his body, and then Merlin sat up, gasping. He broke out in a cold sweat, and tears streamed down his face.

Dove knelt beside him, looking frightened and scared, not sure what to do. He sobbed but patted her hand.

"I am fine," he wheezed, then coughed. "Fine. Water, please."

Dove fetched him some and brought it back in a tin cup.

He downed it quickly, its cool freshness soothing his dry throat, and then he coughed again.

"I forgot how painful it is to return to my body after a spell like that, especially now, being as old as I am."

"Were you successful?" Drius asked.

Merlin gave the dragon lord a cryptic look and said on the cusp of a breath, "Yes."

Drius peered at him and frowned.

Despite his labored breathing, Merlin attempted to stand up. His knees wobbled, and he dropped the tin cup as he started to collapse, but Dove caught him and steadied him.

"Thank you. It takes a moment for everything to work again," he said, trying and failing to laugh.

Dove helped him cross the cave floor, with him leaning on her shoulder and her arm around his torso to hold him up.

"I must get warm," he said.

She led him toward the fire, its embers still glowing, friendly and inviting.

Once there, Merlin insisted, "I can manage now, Dove. Thank you."

She was hesitant to let go of him but withdrew. He tried then to lift the tongs to place fresh wood to burn, but the tongs were heavy, and Dove, seeing his struggle, did it for him. She then sat on the north stone, and he on the west stone. He stared into the pit, its embers red hot and breathing sparks. He muttered a few words, and the fire raged anew. He rubbed his arms and stretched out his hands to catch the warmth.

Drius still stared at him and said, "How do you feel?"

Merlin looked over at him and saw the concern in his friend's eyes. He noted his solemn stance, suspicious brow, and careful observance of him.

"I feel cold, Drius." His voice was weak and feeble, almost like a child's, and he was ashamed of it. "I feel I shall never be warm again." The words then spilled forth without control. "The basilisk is more powerful than I thought. When he looked at my shadow, I felt the force of his power. It shook me, made me tremble. I felt a pain I cannot describe, a pain I never thought possible. I realize now that, though I was away from my body, the bond with my shadow is strong, so when Silzer looked at my shadow, my body was chilled over a hundred miles away."

Merlin threw a handful of stardust on the fire, making it glow and burn more brightly. He leaned closer to the flames, not caring that he sweat or that his blood boiled. He felt the heat – it was plenty hot, but still his core, perhaps his heart, but most certainly his soul was cold.

He rocked back and forth, still rubbing his arms, and fresh tears trailed his cheeks.

"Dove?"

Drius' voice was low but gentle. The harpy raised her worried eyes. She too was rubbing her arms, nervous and unsure, for Merlin acted and spoke so strangely.

"Will you leave us for a short while?"

Her dark eyes widened, and she frowned, hurt.

"I must speak to Merlin alone. You understand?"

She stood up but wavered beside Merlin.

Without looking at her, Merlin said, "I will be fine, Dove. You did very well. Thank you."

Dove looked from him to the dragon lord, and she may have felt trapped, pushed out even. She was slow to move, and she stopped beside Drius, looking up at him with pleading eyes.

Drius softened and said to her, "I am glad you were with him, but now it is my turn. You can wait in the valley. When we are done, I will come fetch you myself. The view is nice, and you should see the stars and moon at least once here before you cross the sea."

Dove grinned, childlike and simple but understanding. She understood she was not being thrown out or unwanted.

She patted Drius' claw as if to say good luck, then ran off the cliff and soared out of view.

A moment of silence passed between the dragon lord and his wizard friend. The only sound to be heard was the crackling of the fire.

Then Drius said, "Will you not say what bothers you? It is obvious you are troubled."

Merlin stopped rocking. He stared at the flames, his eyes still wet with tears.

A log fell, sending up a burst of sparks.

"How could you let them in?" His voice was thin, his tone dry, and he struggled to speak.

He turned his gaze on Drius, his eyes wet and shattered. His face did not crumple but was plain and hard. "How could you and the others at the Great Circle, the good ones, the kind ones, let them in?" He stood up and stumbled toward the dragon lord.

"How could you let the sea serpent, the harpy, and the basilisk…how could you let them into the Circle when their natures are less pleasant and often prone to violence? I do not understand."

He paced, drawing near the fire for its warmth, then coming back to Drius to accuse him further.

"These last few days have left me worried. With each one I have met, this feeling in the pit of my stomach quakes all the louder, making me wonder if I am doing the right thing. I admit Dove is the exception to her kind, but her kind is no exception to cruelty and callous behavior. The same is true of Sli and Silzer, those serpents of sea and terra, and I doubt the serpents they send are any different. And those who stay behind, who will be unseen except by youths, will have the advantage. There might later be stories about haunted places and bad spirits, when it might be something else, a beast I enabled to roam about freely, hidden in plain sight. I only pray and hope such terror will not come about.

"And though I have come to understand the plights of these creatures better and know why they act the way they do, I cannot fathom why, why you let them in. Well, answer me, Drius. How could you? Tell me why?" His voice was high and pleading, and his eyes searched his friend's, desperate for an answer.

Drius only stared at him. His great eyes were soft and full of compassion. There was no flicker of anger or resentment for being accused.

There was a loud pop from the fire, and a burst of embers flew up like crazed lightning bugs. Drius looked past Merlin at the flames, and his eyes seemed to glaze over and become lost. He was suddenly far away, lost in thought and time.

Merlin watched him, and his upset withdrew a little. He sat on the south stone and waited, hunched and rigid, his hands clasped together, his fingers turning white.

Without looking at him, Drius spoke in a low, somber voice:

"You were not there, Merlin. You do not know what we suffered. The dark ages…that is what man has called these last couple hundred years. Dark for whom? Dark for them? It was dark for us. We had no hope. The humans wanted blood, and they came in full force. Greed, cruelty, and hatred were their coat of arms.

"So much loss, and for what? Humans wanted our magic and our splendors, but we are only great while we are living. Pointless slaughter – hundreds of magnificent beasts and folk lost in a great sea of blood.

"You came to me at the tail end of it. You saved me, and it was after that that I called together the first Great Circle. I sent my dragons far and wide to give an invitation to any creature that would listen and wanted to live to join the Circle. There were so many, others you do not know about, that did not come."

Merlin leaned back, his eyes bright and widening. "Others?"

Still Drius did not look at him but went on without loss of rhythm:

"Some thought they could get on with the humans, belay their smite, and pay off their avarice. The dwarves, great tillers of the mountains, are the only race I know to succeed. But have they really? They spend and gamble the riches of the earth on the human's feigned respect. Do you think humans see their equals in the dwarves? No. They see slaves, a means to an end. Humans are only too happy to let another, what they call a lesser race, mine the cold, dark wombs below. They trade mead and pleasantries and, in return, are given gold and precious stones. The dwarves' halls used to be great and sparkle with splendor – the riches of their work, or so I am told. Now those halls are dull and lackluster."

Drius glowed within, and he blew thick smoke on the cusp of a heavy sigh through his nostrils.

"Some were too naive and carefree and did not want to concern themselves with anything too serious or grim. I am referring to the nymphs, fauns, and satyrs and those like-minded creatures that spend their days and nights in frivolity. They would rather play and dance and be lost in fun than think for a moment that it could all come to an end. They thought the humans' bloodlust and treasure hunting would pass like a strange cloudburst, and all would go back to the way it was before. Foolish! I, myself, tried to reason with them, to get them to see the truth, but they would not listen.

"I cannot think of when last I saw one of their kind. Opala said some still live in Greenwood, but there was the one nymph, she said, who prayed to become a tree, her spirit crushed by fear. I wonder how many trees were once vibrant beings. The rest of them – the fauns and satyrs and other merry folk of the like, I think, will fade in the passing of another year or so."

The fire crackled and popped, and its light cast strange shadows throughout the cave and over Drius' face. Outside, the night was calm and quiet and without troubles.

"Some could not be talked to at all. There are beasts in this world, magical and mindless, who have no sense or intelligence. They cannot speak or understand speech. They live on raw instinct and are fierce. To try to reason with them is futile. Take, for instance, the Kelpi, that deadly water horse, or the fire drake, my small, volatile cousin. To approach them is to be met with resistance and even aggression. They do not know what we say, and others of the like will fight or flee, not knowing our intentions are good."

Drius closed his eyes and breathed deep and long before continuing:

"Finally, there was one race who accepted their fate. The elves, those immortal beings, as beautiful as they are wise and good of heart. They saw in their far-sight that their time was over, or so they said, and that the age of man is here to stay till the world ends. They passed on, and I have not seen an elf since."

Merlin sat there, silent and stupefied. He was pale, and goose pimples pricked his skin.

"You see, Merlin?" Drius opened his eyes and gazed at the wizard. "I invited many to the Circle. I invited every child of magic, beautiful and frightening, to join us. Those who came were desperate to survive, and who am I to turn them away?

"We were united in the face of a great threat. No matter how much we may favor or dislike each other, who are we to decide who should live or die? If we ban even one, we are no better than the humans. We all deserve the chance to live."

Silence.

Drius was finished talking, and all there was then was silence.

The fire was low. The candles burned out one at a time, sending up brief ribbons of smoke.

Merlin kept his head down, cradled in his hands, his mind heavy with everything Drius had said. Thoughts flashed –

When was it last that I saw an elf? I do not remember.

What about goblins or brownies or redcaps?

I have not seen a troll in so long, nor an ogre.

– and went out like the candles.

Is Drius right? Was he right back then?

Yes.

Then who am I to say differently? Shame on me.

But I am only…human. But I know better.

He lifted his gaze and saw Drius looking back at him. The dragon lord showed no malice or disappointment. He was reserved and dignified, and his eyes were forgiving.

Merlin got up and walked over to his friend. He put a hand on his clawed foot and, without saying it, thought, *Forgive me?*

As if he heard him, Drius grinned.

Merlin nodded. "I understand now, Drius. Thank you."

CHAPTER TWENTY-TWO

A Late Night Confession

Nine days remained till the Great Circle would come together on the beach. In those nine days he had left, Merlin buried himself in work. He readied the bottles, checked the provisions twice, then three times, finished writing the letters, and still found time to complete Dove's lessons.

Dove was a welcome distraction. In the short days they had left, she blossomed. She gained confidence and was an astute observer, full of intrigue and curiosity. She took to her lessons like a fish to water – natural and spry. Merlin liked having a student who was eager to learn. He often praised her progress, hoping to instill in her better feelings about herself and wipe away the smudges of cruelty left by her flock.

When they were not busy with lessons, and Merlin said he must tend to his other work, Dove would fly off and explore what was nearby. On her first outing, she found a quiet, shaded spring and cleansed herself of the lingering malodor from the harpies' nesting cave that clung to her feathers and hair. She liked it so much she bathed every other day, usually at night, because, as she told Merlin, the stars were nice to look at, shimmering in the sky and on the water.

Sometimes she would go to the vale and sit with Drius. Drius would later tell Merlin that the dragons had come to accept Dove and that the hatchlings adored her.

"You were right about her," Drius said one afternoon to Merlin as he and the wizard watched the harpy play with the baby dragons.

Merlin nodded. "I will be sad to see her go."

"I think the feeling is mutual."

As the last day drew near, Merlin frowned a lot, and his eyes would mist over. He tried to hide it but failed, and all the time he thought, *What I am doing is the right thing. It is the right thing to do, to save them.*

Then, one day, Drius said, "I worry about your heart, Merlin."

They were outside Merlin's cave. Dusk was falling, and the sun was going to bed. Dove was inside, nestled in her nest with a book about birds and winged beasts, reading each line with a trace of her sharp finger and pronouncing big words aloud.

"My heart?" Merlin tried to sound jovial and blew on his hot, steaming cup of tea.

"Do you deny it hurts giving us up?"

Merlin stared ahead, his feet dangling off the edge of the precipice, at the mottled colors of gold and purple and red across the horizon.

"No, I do not deny it. The closer the day comes, the more ill I feel. My heart hurts, and I know it is a great sacrifice I am about to make. I will miss seeing so many marvelous creatures, with some exceptions."

Drius grinned.

"But I will miss you most of all."

"What about your new pupil?" Drius tilted his head back toward the cave.

They were speaking low enough for her not to hear, not that Merlin thought she would eavesdrop.

"Of course, I will miss her. She has been a blessing these last several days. But you know what I mean, Drius. We have been friends for over a century. We have been through so much together. I will miss our adventures, our talks, and our visits. Life will not be the same without you."

Drius lowered his head so he could look Merlin in the eye as he spoke. "I feel the same way, Merlin. My heart aches too."

Merlin put a hand on Drius' clawed foot, and the pair said nothing more. They watched the sun slip past the horizon and night come forth with all its stars.

It was the night before the day at the shore. Merlin and Dove sat by the fire, sharing their last meal together – a hearty rabbit stew with mushrooms and potatoes. Dove was slow to eat, but Merlin ate only a couple bites before he gazed ahead, lost in thought.

Tomorrow…

Everything was ready. The letters were written and stuffed in their bottles. Each letter was enchanted to read aloud, in his voice, should a child not know how to read. Ten bottles had an enchanted seashell that filled with water when the occupant was thirsty, and two were filled with seawater. Each bottle had provisions for its destined passenger.

The twelve bottles lay nearby, and next to them were five great volumes of text: a couple on Britannia's folklore, one on gardening, and two on inventions. These he had set aside to gift to Hamel.

The Spell Book was on its podium, open to the page on *Invisibility*. For the better part of the day, Merlin had meditated over its verses, preparing himself. When it was dark, Dove stirred him out of his fog of concentration to eat supper. Now, as he stared ahead at the flames, his bowl full and tipping, she watched him and frowned.

"You do not eat because you are sad?" Her voice was careful and concerned, and her dark eyes searched him for the truth.

"Sad, yes." He nodded. "And nervous, I think."

"Why nervous?"

Merlin opened his mouth, then closed it again. He licked his lips and thought first of what to say so he did not worry her. "What I hope to do tomorrow will require a great deal of strength and focus and a lot of heart."

"Heart?"

"Yes. Sometimes what the heart wants is stronger than the thought or intent behind magic, and I admit I am sad to see you all go. My heart wants you and the others to stay, but I cannot be selfish."

Dove put down her bowl and brought her knees to her chest.

"I do not want to leave," she said. "I am sad to leave you and this place…It is home."

There was a tightness in Merlin's chest, and he took a breath to ease it and steady himself. "I see. I am glad you feel as much about this place. It is the first you can truly call home. Am I right?"

She nodded. "But still, I go."

"Because it is the right thing to do?"

"I think so." Her lips curved into a small grin before she pointed at his bowl. "Eat. For strength."

Merlin chuckled. "Right." He started to eat again, though his stomach was aquiver and his heart continued to ache.

He had a couple of bites left when Dove suddenly sat up and became very still, rigid even, and her feathers twitched. She then rose and stared at the cave entrance.

Merlin followed her line of sight outside and saw nothing, but that did not mean something was not there.

"What is it?" he asked.

She paused, the firelight glimmering in her dark eyes. "Company," she said.

Merlin put down his bowl and stood up. "I wonder who it is at this late hour."

The answer came first with the soft, powerful beating of wings, followed by the sharp, hollow clops of hooves outside. Aquila came forward into view, the moonlight dancing off of her, making her glow like an ethereal spirit. She shook off bits of cloud and folded her wings.

"Good evening, Merlin," she said, her voice calm and light, pleasant.

"Your grace?" Merlin, stunned, came to her outside, smiling. "This is a surprise and a most welcome one at that."

"We came to see you."

"We?" Merlin raised a single brow, seeing no one else.

Aquila turned, and there, holding small handfuls of her long, white mane, was Liliana.

"Merlin." The fairy queen nodded to him with a gentle grin.

"Your majesty." Merlin bowed his head to her. "To what do I owe the pleasure of this visit?"

"We—" Aquila looked past Merlin, and he followed her gaze.

Dove stepped outside into the night. In the moonlight, her pale skin glowed, and her dark eyes were striking. The way she half-hid herself with her wings suggested she was nervous, but still, she stood upright and held her head high.

Merlin gestured to her. "This is Dove. She is Madera's chosen for the journey. She has been staying with me, and she is my friend."

Aquila's muscles quivered, and her ears swiveled – one forward, one back.

Liliana patted the winged horse's neck and said, "We heard tell of you keeping strange company."

"Who—" Merlin started, but then he saw the fairy queen's smile and hushed.

"The fae have eyes and ears almost everywhere, Merlin. You should know that better than most."

Merlin nodded. "I suppose I should. If that is true, your majesty, you know then she is nothing like her flock."

The fairy queen let go of Aquila's mane and fluttered forward, coming within inches of Dove's face. Dove leaned back but did not look away.

"I heard as much," said Liliana. "It is nice to meet you, Dove."

Dove flitted a glance at Merlin, and he nodded his approval. She bowed her head to the fairy queen and said, "Nice to meet you."

She then sidestepped the queen and locked eyes with the winged horse matriarch. She bowed to her. "You too, your grace."

Aquila snorted but lowered her head in solemn reply.

Liliana smiled and flew to Merlin.

"My friend and I wanted to see if all is well with you, Merlin, before the big day tomorrow."

"Is that so?" Merlin tugged at his beard. There was something – he did not see it with the queen, for her beauty and smile masked her thoughts, but in Aquila's thoughtful eyes – oh how she looked at him, into him – and stern stance, there was something more to be guessed.

Before he had a chance to speak, another pair of wings beat the night air, and Drius appeared over the crags. He settled down beside the party.

"Good evening, Drius," said Merlin. "We have company." He said this with a jovial tone, still smiling.

"I can see that. One of my dragons, a lookout, said as much to me, and I came to investigate."

"We apologize for the late hour, and in truth, we had hoped not to disturb you, my lord dragon." Liliana spoke with a lilt in her voice, but beneath it, there was something grave.

Drius stared at her with a certain scrutiny.

"There was no better time to come," said Aquila. "We had to see Merlin."

"Had to? For what purpose?" Drius folded his wings and sat back.

Neither matriarch gave a response.

Merlin piped up, "The queen said it was to see if all is well with me before tomorrow. But forgive me for saying so, your majesty, I believe it is something more."

The winged horse looked at the fairy, and she in turn lowered her gaze.

"Your graces," said Merlin, "whatever the matter is, please say it outright and in the company of friends. Whatever it is you have to say can be said with them present." He indicated Drius and Dove with a wave of his hand, then folded his arms.

The fairy queen sighed. "Very well." She flitted back to Aquila and laid her tiny hand on the winged horse's muzzle. "We are concerned, Merlin."

"Concerned?"

Aquila pulled away and said, "We wonder if you are ready for tomorrow."

Merlin looked from one to the other and furrowed his brow. "Is that all?" He put up a hand to stay another word. "Let us go inside and sit by the fire."

He ventured back into the cave, not waiting for them to voice agreement. He took his seat on the west stone, and Dove sat to his left on the north stone. Liliana fluttered over and settled herself down on the east stone, and Aquila stood behind her. Drius, of course, remained outside but watched and listened to the scene unfold before him.

Merlin removed the pot of stew from its perch over the fire. He then threw on another log, sending up a scattering of sparks. They danced and flickered before snuffing out.

"Now, your graces, you want to know if I am ready for tomorrow?" Merlin's old eyes stared at them through the flames. He could see the worry in them looking back, but rather than press, he spoke lightly. "Take a look." He indicated the bottles with a pointed finger. "The bottles are there. The notes are written. I had my audiences with those leaders who make up the Circle, yourselves included. I gathered provisions so no creature goes hungry or thirsts during their journey." He paused, seeing no change in either matriarch. "But that is not what you mean, is it? I see your distress, your agitation. Speak plainly. What do you want to know?"

Aquila nickered to Liliana, and the fairy queen raised a hand to stay her.

"Know first, Merlin, that we are here of our own accord. We have not spoken to others in the Circle. None, save Drius, know we are here. We are acting on our own feelings, out of our own concern." She said this with caution, her eyes sparkling, but her glow diminished.

Aquila snorted. "Your majesty." Her tail swished, impatient.

"Steady, my friend." Liliana glanced at the winged horse, then looked back at Merlin. "We do not worry over your provisions. We worry about your magic."

Merlin felt his stomach turn over. The color in his cheeks faded, and he leaned back, his fingers pressing into his knees.

"We mean you no offense. I speak to you as a queen who cares for her own but is also your friend. I have known you for several years, Merlin. You have been a guest at my Sacred Tree many times, and I trust you with the knowledge of my secret garden. Know then that I have a deep love and respect for you.

"But now I must challenge you. In all the time I have known you, I know not of a time you cast a great feat of magic. I know the stories, the legends of those times before you came to us, before you left Camelot and your past. Back then, you did many astonishing things, and your name was whispered on the winds, and we fae heard tell of you each time it blew.

"But tell me, can you do what you have promised? Can you cast these spells which require a great concentration of will and power? These spells will demand so much of you, for it is true that any time a being casts magic, they put some of themselves in it — their energy or substance, if you will. You hope to cast magic to unbind the laws put here by magic long ago. Can you do it without failure, or worse, death?"

There was silence, save for the crackling of the fire. Merlin was hunched over, his folded hands pressed to his lips, and his eyes closed. He felt them staring at him, and he winced. He then lowered his hands and gazed ahead at the fairy queen.

"So that is it then? You wonder if I am capable of great feats of magic anymore." He swayed from side to side. He looked ready to crumple, and he licked his lips several times. Inside, the butterflies turned to heavy stones, sinking to the pit of his stomach. He inhaled sharply and said, "How terrible it must be for you then to hear that I am not so sure of myself."

Aquila raised her head. Her muscles twitched, and she flicked her tail. Dove pulled her knees to her chest and perched, nervous, on the north stone. Liliana, however, sat still and did not take her eyes off Merlin.

"I know shrinking and making myself big again at your Sacred Tree was not a great feat – impressive, yes, but not great, so I will not use it as a defense. You wonder about the other spell, the one of invisibility, and whether I can actually cast it on you and the others at the beach and all like creatures beyond the sands. I wonder too, for it has been, as you say, a long time since I cast powerful magic." He sighed heavily. "But I have my reasons."

From his pocket, Merlin brought out a small pouch. In it was a heap of glittering stardust. He took a pinch and sprinkled it on the fire, making it blaze with new life and light. He looked over at Drius, who stared back at him, calm, concerned, and a bit grave. Merlin attempted a grin, but it was weak and nervous. "I suppose it is never too late to tell a story, and I can keep my promise to you after all, Drius."

The dragon lord looked on, seemingly composed, but Merlin saw the brightness in his eyes, which conveyed he knew what the wizard spoke of.

Merlin waved a hand over the flames, causing them to leap, jigger, and dance. He clasped his hands together, turning his knuckles white, and took a deep breath before letting it out slowly. "What I am about to tell you I have never told another. No one knows, and I would like to keep it that way. It is my story to tell, mine to choose who should hear it. I would have taken it to my grave, 'cept here you are, asking me that which I worry about as well. So I must tell you.

"You know of—" The name caught in his throat, and he mustered it forth: "Arthur. My ward. My king. You know he died in battle, but no one knows what really happened 'cept me. I know because I was there.

"The king made a grave mistake in his youth, and from it came his illegitimate son, Mordred. The boy was wicked and cruel, a villain who, when he was of age, came for his father's crown, backed by an army of brigands and thieves. He demanded Arthur surrender his title, the throne, and all of Camelot. Arthur, of course, said no.

"With his knights and soldiers, he met his son on the battlefield. I was there, too, to aid and protect my king. I can still hear the war cries, the horses whinnying, and the men beating their weapons against their armor."

As Merlin spoke, the flames came to life, and in them were images, glimmering illustrations of all he said. There were two rows of men opposite each other, raising arms, and horses rearing, their hooves kicking at the air. Out of the fire came the faint, distant cries of battle.

"I do not know how long the battle went on. I remember it was morning when we set out from the castle gates, and the sun was not yet at its peak when we came to the hill. Mordred and his men were already there, dressed in tarnished metal and furs. He rode a great black horse, and Arthur was astride his white charger. Father and son, two opposite sides of the coin, different in every way, came to blows.

"As they and their armies fought, I stayed back, casting my spells. I cannot think of another time I spun so much magic in one place at one time. Spells of protection, of deliverance, even spells to give nature life so that it too turned against our enemies. Doing so much, it was easy to lose sight of what mattered.

"In truth, I underestimated our opponent. I thought victory was with Arthur. He had more experience in battle and studied the art of combat almost every day, and he had Excalibur, the magic sword that put all mortal-made weapons to shame. I think also that I was blinded by the foolish notion that fate and heaven would not let an evil man like Mordred win. How could they? For these reasons, and because there were so many bodies on the field, I foolishly let Arthur out of my sight.

"The battle was in Arthur's favor. His army slew many of Mordred's ruffians. They were calling to retreat, but Mordred would not fall back, and I am sure he threatened the life of any man who would be a coward. The field was painted red with the blood of both sides. Above all the clamor and chaos, I could hear the whine of Excalibur – that sword had a melodic strain only good men can hear – as it clashed with Mordred's blade.

"I remember I was in the middle of an incantation when a sudden feeling swept over me. It was cold and dark, threatening and sinister. There was another, another being like me, out there, with their hand in the fight.

"I concentrated my sights, looking past the battle, and there she was at the edge of the wood astride a

withered beast. She was cloaked in aged rags. The way they swayed in the wind made her look like a wraith, a demon come to feed on lost lives.

"Mordred had gotten himself a witch, an enchantress by the name of Morgana. I met her once before and knew then she was unredeemable. She practiced dark magic, forbidden and volatile – the kind that twists the mind and blots the soul. She was a hag, but she masked herself in beauty to lure men to her side. She had her claws in Mordred, and I am certain she promised him the crown and all the splendor that came with it. What she wanted in return, I cannot begin to guess. It did not matter.

"I noticed then a dark mist around Mordred, only visible to my eyes. The witch was casting her black magic to aid and push him on. I spurred my mount forward into the fray. I had to get to Arthur. I pushed my life force out to him, and I muttered spells, pouring all of myself into my magic, desperate and afraid for his life.

"Suddenly, an invisible force knocked me and my horse to the ground. The animal was on top of me, struggling. I looked over at Arthur and Mordred, throwing themselves into every blow. It was then I heard Morgana's wretched voice, rising over the tumult, and I, in turn, raised mine, all the while trying to get out from under my mount. When finally I could stand, it was too late.

"On the cusp of victory, Mordred mortally wounded his father, and Arthur delivered a fatal blow to his son. Their leader dead, and any hope for the crown lost, the last of Mordred's army fled into the wood, and Morgana withdrew into a fog."

Merlin stared at his aged hands, palms up, the rough lines in them like rivers of time.

"I fell to my knees beside Arthur and held him in my arms. I wept over him, this man, this boy I had raised as my own. I called him son, and I was torn apart within, for it was I who had brought him to this point. It was I who brought him to the Stone, where he pulled Excalibur, making him ruler of Britannia. It was I who helped him build Camelot and be its king. He was a good man, not by my doing alone. No, he was kind, generous, and forgiving all his own, an honest ruler who led with a firm but steady hand. His knights, his people, they all loved him. But I loved him most of all.

"I spilled my tears over him, begging his forgiveness, for I had failed to protect him. You know what he did?"

Tears streamed down Merlin's face, and he struggled with his next words: "He put his hand on mine and said, 'No, you did not fail. Victory was not certain, and this is the end of my time, so says heaven. Thank you for all you have done for me, my friend.' Then he bid me take Excalibur and not let another possess her. I told him I loved him, and I held him till his last breath."

Merlin sobbed, his tears pattering on the ground between his feet. The flames cast no more images. He kept his head down, holding it in his hands. Through gritted teeth, he continued:

"Ever since his death, it has been a struggle for me to speak Arthur's name, to tell stories of him, or to even think about him, because I feel pangs of guilt every time I do. But I do him a great disservice by not speaking of him, by not telling his story. Camelot is gone. It was to be his legacy, but lords, full of greed and desperate for power, brought it to ruin. I am all that is left of him, his time, and his history."

He wiped his face with his sleeve and tried to catch his breath. His body trembled, and his face glistened in the firelight, wet and salty. "You have every right to question my abilities. After Arthur, I came here a shattered man. I left my past behind and put as much distance between it and me as I could. I put away my Spell Book, veiled it so I did not have to look at it. I was angry and bitter with myself for my failure. Though he assured me with his dying breath that I did not, I could not shake the feeling.

"I determined that I would never use my magic again to alter fate. But then…" He paused and looked over at Drius. The dragon lord stared back at him with faithful compassion in his eyes. "Drius came to me and told me of your plight, and there was a stirring in my heart." He looked at Liliana and Aquila, and his voice grew stronger. "I felt called, by heaven or magic, I do not know which, to step in and change what can happen. I admit I fear failure again. I am terrified by my memory. My self-doubt is a plague, a tormentor that stirs up quakes within me. But despite all of this, I feel also, buried beneath the dark waves of self-reproach and weariness, a tiny flicker of hope. It is small, like a candle, but it gives me reprieve and rest.

"I am old. I am withered and out of practice. But I say this: I feel it here." He laid a hand over his heart. "I feel there is a chance, and I must be allowed to take it. This is right, my striving and hoping to save you. I will not let you down. Even if it takes every ounce of my strength, every fiber of my being, even if it takes my life, I will not fail again."

He stared at the matriarchs and saw their pity looking back at him. Aquila, her eyes soft in the firelight, still appeared to look past him, into him, at his aching heart. Her gaze was tender and empathetic, and all of her was relaxed now — all tension and urgency lost. Liliana only stared, with no plain expression, her hands still folded in her lap, but there was a tiny tilt of her head and a twitch of her wings that suggested she was moved, her feelings rubbed.

Merlin's frame tilted, and he lowered his head, his eyes misting over. He breathed low and deep, feeling run down by the past and the strength of his words. Fresh tears traced his face and fell with quiet splashes on the cave floor. He covered his eyes with one hand and shook, trying not to weep aloud.

Suddenly, there was a bright light. It was golden white and blinding. It filled the cave all at once, touching everything. Merlin, with his hands up, reeled back in silent awe.

He then felt a hand rest on his head, and the light withdrew. He blinked several times, and when his sight came into focus, there was Liliana, now a full-size woman, standing before him. Her gown was full and shimmering. Her wings caught the firelight and reflected it in glimmering bows. Her skin glistened, full of magic. She was beautiful and radiant.

Her lips curved into a soft grin, and her eyes were gentle and full of compassion. She cupped Merlin's chin, holding his gaze.

"I believe you, Merlin." Her voice was low but musical, dancing on the air. "But if you are to be successful tomorrow, you must forgive yourself. You did not fail your king. Arthur was right to say so. His time came, as it does for us all. You did your best, and that was enough. It is the same with us. We are grateful, humbled even, that you want to help us, and all we ask is that you try. Forgive yourself, and your power will be restored to you in full, unheeded by your guilt."

She touched his temple, and a tiny light beamed beneath the tips of her fingers. Merlin closed his eyes and trembled. He felt her light within him, and he lifted a silent prayer to heaven. Most suddenly and inexplicably, his guilt and disappointment and sadness crumbled, were reduced to dust and swept away, and his heart beat fast and light, and hope blazed within him.

He gasped and opened his eyes, looking at the fairy queen. He saw the understanding in her eyes. She knew of the change that had come over him. With all the grace and formality he could muster, he kissed the back of her hand.

"Thank you," he whispered.

She nodded and stepped back. Another bright light exhaled from her, but this time Merlin saw through it. He saw her change back to her small, petite self, and when the light died, she fluttered back to Aquila.

"We have learned all we need to and then some. I think it is time we let our wizard friend sleep. He will need his rest, and so do we all."

Aquila nickered and shook her head. "Agreed."

The matriarchs went outside, both bright in the moon and starlight. Liliana grasped Aquila's mane as the winged horse fanned her wings. She seemed ready to gallop forth and leap into the night until she turned and looked back at Merlin, who stood at the entrance of the cave, watching them.

"Merlin, after tomorrow, and perhaps after you are rested, go to Avalon and visit the Lady of the Lake. I think she has much to tell you."

Merlin raised a brow, curious. "What do you mean?"

"I can say no more, but I think you should go forth and discover. She is often lonely and would be glad to see you. Farewell all, till tomorrow." She reared up, whinnying, then turned on her back hooves and charged forth. She leapt from the cliff edge and seemed to run on an invisible path through the air, climbing higher and taking wing south to Greenwood.

Merlin looked after them till he could not see them. He stood beside Drius, and Dove was behind them, leaning on a cave wall.

"Quite a night," said Drius after a long silence.

"Yes," said Merlin. "Unexpected."

"How do you feel?"

Merlin thought on this a moment, then smiled. "Relieved."

"Good."

After a brief pause, Merlin looked up at him and asked, "Did you know?"

Drius nodded.

"And all this time, you said nothing?"

"It was not my place. If I had made mention of it, you may never have spoken to me again, or it may have done you more harm than good to be faced with it sooner. For reasons such as these, dragons do not interfere in the affairs of others. Each other, yes, but not others, beast or human. I figured you would tell me when you were ready. I am glad you are finally free of your past."

Merlin put a hand on Drius' clawed foot. "Me too. And I am glad you were here to witness it."

Drius grinned. "As am I."

Merlin looked over his shoulder at Dove, who cradled her arms, awkwardly off to the side. He went to her and laid a hand on her shoulder.

"You too."

She smiled, warmed by his inclusion.

"If there is to be no more excitement," said Drius, raising his wings, "I think it best we all get some rest, as her majesty said."

Merlin nodded. "Agreed. See you bright and early, Drius."

The dragon lord left them. Dove curled up in her nest, and Merlin put away their supper and the dishware. He warmed himself by the fire before willing it to dim, then went to his desk and opened a small compartment. Inside was a wooden box carved with the likeness of two dragons facing each other, their tails entwined.

Merlin sat in his chair and traced a thumb over the dragons. He sighed and opened the box. Inside were various trinkets and tokens, items from his journeys and adventures. He fiddled around them till he found what he was looking for – a painted portrait laid in a gold frame. He bid a single candle on his desk to light and held up the portrait to see it.

The image staring back at him was of a young lad on a white horse, and next to him was a younger, less gray Merlin on his chestnut mount. Merlin smiled and traced the edges of the miniature painting. One lonely tear gleamed in the corner of his eye before falling and catching the edge of his smile.

"Rest peacefully, my king…my son."

He placed the portrait on his desk and returned the box to its compartment. He bid the candle to sleep, and it snuffed itself out, leaving a curling wisp of smoke.

CHAPTER TWENTY-THREE

Farewells

Merlin rose with the sun. Rather than busy himself right away, he spared the time to stand outside, a cup of tea in hand, and watch the golden globe imbue the sky with brilliant colors.

He had seen hundreds of sunrises, but this one was peaceful, comforting, and shone on a better day.

He heard shuffling footsteps behind him.

"Beautiful." Dove's voice was soft and fragile, and she yawned.

"Yes, it is. Awe-inspiring, really, and completely normal."

"Normal?" She came to his side, and he noticed she held the blue-tinted glasses in front of her eyes so as to blot the sun, but beyond the rims, she could see the dazzling hues.

"Yes, normal. We know the sun will rise and fall each day, but each time it does, the colors are different. It is a new sky every time. It is nature's magic."

"Hmm." Dove grinned and kept her eyes ahead.

"Nothing I hope to do today is normal," Merlin said on the tail end of a breath. "For centuries, humans and magical creatures have lived side by side, at one time, in harmony, but now in discord. I will undo what has been for so long. It is chilling, but when I think of the reason, I feel a wave of, of…" He waved his hand as though he were trying to summon the right word.

"Color?" Dove asked.

He looked at her and blinked several times, astounded. He then laughed. "Yes. A wave of color. Beautiful."

The pair watched the sun till Merlin was finished with his tea.

He smacked his lips and said, "Best get things packed. I do not want to make us late."

He returned inside and grabbed his satchel.

"Want to see a neat trick?" he asked Dove.

She nodded and joined him.

He waved his hand over the satchel and mumbled a few words under his breath.

"Watch," he said with a delightful grin.

One by one, he took the bottles with their notes and shoved them in the satchel, followed by the books he had set aside for Hamel. The satchel was not all that big, yet each bottle and volume of text disappeared beneath the lip, and the satchel did not grow any wider. Dove's eyes widened though with fascination.

"That is not all," said Merlin. He retrieved his Spell Book and put it in the satchel with as much ease as everything else.

"How?" Dove asked.

Merlin chuckled. "That is one of my favorite spells. It lets me pack as much as I want in the satchel, but it is never full, nor does it weigh any more than when it is empty. See?" He handed her the bag, and she lifted it up and down, gasping at its lightness. "It was a handy spell when I moved from place to place till I settled here."

He walked around the cave, drumming his fingers over various surfaces. "Let's see: I have the bottles, and they have their notes and provisions. I have my Spell Book and the books for Hamel. What am I…oh, yes." He took a crystal rock from his desk and slipped it in his pocket. "I think that is all I need." He turned and saw Dove frowning. "What is wrong, Dove?"

Dove shuffled from one taloned foot to the other and rubbed her arm. Merlin came to her.

"What is it? Do you not feel well?"

She shook her head, then forced a tiny grin. "I feel the same. I will…miss this place. Miss you."

Merlin felt a sudden pang in his heart, and he put a hand on her shoulder.

"I will miss you too. You brought an old man a lot of joy and comfort these past several days. You are gentle and curious, a good student, but beneath the surface, you are fierce and loyal."

She looked at him as though he were telling a joke.

"I am serious, Dove. You saved me from that serpent. In that brief moment, I saw a brave soul who can fight and defend when it matters. All that time you spent with the flock, they did nothing but tear you down. They muddied your spirit and made you feel less than you are, but I tell you, you are made of greater stuff than any of them.

"You are their savior. You, who will go on this journey and do what is frightening and uncertain. I think it takes a lot of character to do what you are about to."

He leaned in close and said further, "When you see Madera on that beach, hold your head up and do not let her intimidate you. For without you, she ceases to exist. You are better than her, better than all of them, in my humble opinion."

Her grin widened, and she threw her arms around him in a charmed embrace. He patted her back, holding her hug.

They parted when the sound of wings could be heard outside.

Dove held Merlin's eye a moment more and said, "Thank you," in a low, sweet whisper.

"You are welcome."

Drius appeared at the cave entrance, and Merlin hovered to see which of his dragons was with him. His breath hitched when Isla touched down beside her father.

Isla? He chose her?

Merlin was stupefied, and he gaped.

"Good morning, Merlin," bellowed Drius.

It is better I say nothing, and Merlin smiled as he came outside to greet them.

"Good morning, Drius. Good morning, Isla."

The young dragon nodded in the wizard's general direction, then looked at the horizon. She was small beside her father but also sleek and elegant, lithe and nimble, and as Merlin had seen in the vale, a strong, graceful challenger. She looked so much like her mother, but she had her father's set jaw and far-seeing gaze and a spark of his temper. While she looked at the view, Merlin saw her frown, her eyes glazed over with thoughtfulness.

"How did you sleep?" asked Drius.

"I slept very well, thank you. I think last night helped tremendously."

"I thought it might." Drius grinned, then looked past his friend at Dove. "Good morning, Dove."

"Good morning, lord dragon and lady dragon."

Isla did little more than huff to acknowledge the greeting.

She is in a terrible mood.

Merlin pulled at his beard in thought just as Drius threw his child a sideways glance, and she lowered her head in reprimand. He then shook his head and pressed on.

"Are we ready to leave?"

Merlin nodded. "Yes, I think so. Let me grab my satchel and something to eat."

He went to the curio, searched amongst its jars and ingredients, and pulled out a small bag.

"Dove and I have not eaten yet, and I think it best she not be famished before her trip, nor I before my feats of magic." He unfurled the bag and offered it to Dove. "Try this."

With mild hesitation, she reached in and pulled out a thin strip of something dark and veined. It was tough but giving, and she held it to her nose to take a deep whiff.

"Meat," she said, a little astonished.

"Yes, dried meat. I have been perfecting my technique. I hope it tastes good. It is venison."

She took a bite, a light color filling her cheeks as she chewed. She swallowed and grinned.

"It is good."

"Wonderful." He took a few strips for himself. "Take as much as you want so you are not hungry."

Drius shook his head but was still grinning. "We really must be going, you two. Come."

Merlin got astride Drius, his satchel clutched in both hands and a couple strips of dried venison held between his teeth. Dove put on her blue-tinted glasses and, while munching another strip, leapt off the ledge and soared into view.

Before taking to wing, Drius looked back over his shoulder at the crags and mountains. Merlin noticed a faint sadness in his eyes, but before he could ask, Drius let out a mighty roar that shook the stony ground and summits. On the echo of her father's roar, Isla raised her own – not as deep or as powerful but still moving, sending tremors through Merlin's body.

The pair waited, the echoes of their roars rolling off the peaks. In response, a great many roars were lifted, shaking the heavens. The other dragons, all of them, Merlin wagered, even the hatchlings, returned the call.

Isla took flight after the harpy, and Drius behind them.

Merlin looked back over his shoulder. No dragon was in sight, but the reverberation of their cries hung in the air and in the fibers of his being. Never had he heard such a lamentation.

"Drius?"

"Hmm."

"What was that just now?"

The dragon lord hesitated, then, in a solemn voice, said, "It was goodbye."

Their flight was without conversation. Merlin glimpsed at Dove every now and then, amused at her flight pattern – how she swooped to the left, then to the right, catching drifts of air that pushed her up. But most times, he stared at Isla.

She cut through the air like an arrow, straight and deathly quiet. Her tail swayed behind her, and she clutched her claws. Her gaze was forward, her eyes narrow, and Merlin thought, *She is perturbed.*

How could Drius choose his sole heir for this journey? Surely there are dragons better suited for the task. He has invested so much in her, so much time and effort, training her, readying her to take over after him. Besides, it will break his heart. She is all he has left of family.

But still…a dragon's decision is not to be questioned. I have no right to object to or say anything about it. It will only complicate things and make it worse for him if I voice my concern.

The sun glittered off the horizon, and Merlin saw the sea, twinkling and winking at them. That vast blanket of blue, wet and salty, was resplendent and pleasing.

The corners of his mouth turned up, and he sighed his contentment. He then took a deep breath, smelling the briny air, and let it out slowly.

May it all be as it should be, he prayed with eyes closed. *Those who go, may honor be theirs and victory, too, in saving their own, and may their sacrifice never be forgotten. I certainly will not forget.*

"Father." Isla's voice was calm but upright.

Merlin opened his eyes.

"They are here," she said. "I see them."

They passed over the trees and green earth, and suddenly the long stretch of shoreline was beneath them.

Their shadows rippled and played over the golden sands.

Merlin looked ahead and saw several figures forming a wide circle. Most waited on the sands, but others were in the water, the waves curling around them. Heads turned in their direction.

They passed over the Circle and came around slowly, gliding on the air. Merlin saw the eleven and, save for Madera, who was alone, their chosen standing beside them. Floating aside the Circle were also twelve merfolk – six mermaids and six mermen – who, Merlin guessed, were charged with ferrying the bottles across the great blue.

Drius settled a ways off from the Circle, and Isla alighted beside him. Dove stayed with them and helped Merlin dismount, holding his satchel for him.

"Thank you, Dove," he said, taking it back once his feet were on the sand.

"Are you ready, Merlin?" Drius asked.

"As ready as I will ever be." Merlin patted the satchel, and the four of them moved forward.

The Circle was silent as they approached. Merlin met their eyes, and he saw many things – kindness and welcome from most, mixed with nervous excitement, while others lacked any emotion but were rigid with impatience.

He noted Madera's grim composure, her winged arms folded across her chest, and her stern face devoid of feeling. Her red eyes stared in their direction with intense focus, but she was not looking at him. Merlin stole a glance at Dove and grinned to see her approach with her head up and her eyes, behind their glasses, shimmering without fear. He looked back and saw the harpy queen's feathery brows furrow, then ease, and a dull sheen passed over her eyes as understanding dawned on her. He was not sure, but he thought she nodded – a slow, minute dip of her chin – as though she admitted the change in her sister.

The basilisks, Silzer and his fellow, kept their backs turned, but when Merlin laid eyes on them, he remembered that terrible chill and proceeded to clench his hand into a fist and release it three times to get hold of his nerves.

He saw Flint and how brilliant he was in the daylight. He and another phoenix perched on Hamel's shoulders, observing, waiting. Seven days past his rebirth, the crown phoenix looked vital and healthy, new and mature. He was fully grown, as Tana said, vibrant and striking. His eyes were bright and alert, all-seeing, all-comprehending. His feathers were shiny and smooth, and when the ocean breeze ruffled them, they resembled tongues of fire, the air became spiced with the perfumes of his funeral pyre. It did Merlin's heart good to see him this way.

He looked at Liliana last. She had summoned another lily to sit upon, and she looked at him with a polite, all-knowing smile. In her eyes, he saw a sparkle – hope and trust mingled together, and the color in her cheeks made him feel warm within. She did not nod, nor did she move, but the way she batted her lashes, a single blink, slow and with purpose, told him that she still believed in him.

When they closed the gap, completing the Circle, Drius looked around at all who were present. His eyes held them, and no one uttered a sound. He then spoke in a solemn voice with great mastery of attention:

"Welcome all. A hundred years ago, we came together like this, the twelve, and made a choice. It seemed the right choice, and perhaps it was at the time, but this is now. You all know the threat we face. We face extinction. Magic gave us life with limitations, the most important of which is we cannot live by sheer want. We exist because humans believe we do, but after being gone for so long, that faith has wilted.

"We fear bloodshed if we reveal ourselves, and there is no telling which is the lesser evil – to die on the edge of a sword or to fade into nothingness. So we turned to Merlin, the wizard and my dear friend."

Drius looked at Merlin, and Merlin grinned, rosy and full of encouragement. Drius then continued, looking back at the Circle:

"He gave us an idea. It is bold and uncertain, but in the face of greater uncertainty, it is our only way. Those of you who were chosen to be here, I am sure your leaders told you of this plan. I, for one, am proud of you all. Whether you volunteered for the journey or were told you must go, what you do now is a brave thing, and it is not to be taken lightly.

"There is no telling what waits for you at your journey's end. Hopefully, it is a child, full of mirth and love, who will find you and be charmed by the wonder that is you. That child will then care for you, and I hope you will care for them. May you bond with them and teach them about your kind, thus planting the seed of belief. That seed may then spread, and for the rest of us who remain here, we will do our part too, or so I hope.

"I hope each of you has considered what you and your own will do should you cross paths with a child. Though their forebears, those who came before them, were our enemies, the children we may encounter are not. They are innocent and only capable of awe and admiration in our presence. Most of you, at least those of you who are willing, should be capable of loving and understanding in turn."

His eyes moved over the sea serpents, Madera, and the basilisks.

"It is a choice. Hopefully, you will do what is best. I believe this: faith bound in love is strong and brings with it joy and splendor and all that is good. Faith bound in fear and hate is also strong, but it brings destruction. Think on that when you live out the rest of your days from this day forward."

Drius paused to let his words sink in. Most of the faces looking back at him seemed to understand and agree. But without seeing the basilisks, though their bodies were still and their heads low, and looking over at Madera, then Sli, and noting their grave expressions, Merlin ventured a guess and thought, *They know he is right.*

"If no one has anything to say," said Drius, "I will turn things over to Merlin."

Silence. Merlin stepped forward and, same as before, bowed north, south, east, and west to all the leaders and their fellows. He then pulled out his Spell Book and flipped through the pages to that which read *Spells of Size.* He traced a finger over the one that shrinks, paused, and closed the Book. He looked at their faces again, and in his heart, there was a fluttering.

"I have something to say before I begin. These past thirty days, I have had the honor to meet with those of you who form this Circle. I had the pleasure of seeing your homes, meeting your own, and learning more about you in a month than I ever could have hoped to in a lifetime. I want to say thank you, thank you for the opportunity to become a richer man.

"I know some of you may not like me. Others love me, and I dare think respect me, for which I thank thee. I cannot express…there are no right words for how I feel about your faith and trust in me to deliver on what I have promised. I admit that being faced with so much responsibility and having your fate and future laid on my shoulders put me off balance for a spell, but then some of you set it right."

He smiled at Liliana and Aquila.

"I know in my heart that what I do today is right. I hope and pray the best comes out of it and that you and your own live on for centuries till the world's end."

There was a strange tingling then within him, beneath his skin, racing in his blood, from his fingertips to his toes, behind his eyes, and on the edge of his tongue. It was magic, his magic, alive and full of purpose, awake and ready to spill forth.

He put a hand over his heart, feeling it beat more strongly, forcing loud pulses in his ears, and he smiled.

"But pretty words can only do so much. Let me prove myself to you. Silzer?"

The basilisk lifted his head. His forked tongue split the air.

Merlin then sighed with relief, for he did not feel the chill this time. On the contrary, he was warm all over, his magic causing internal friction and blazing with excitement. He said in a strong voice, "Will you still permit me to cast the spell to remove your deadly sight? Yours and your fellow basilisk's? First, so he does not bring death to the child who finds him, and second, so I may prove myself a worthy wizard to you and all who are here?"

The king basilisk hissed his delight, a lilt of laughter poised on each hiss. "Certainly, wizard. But remember our deal: I ssshall look on you firssst when the ssspell isss complete. Should you fail, your time will be over."

"I did not forget."

He flipped through his Spell Book again and came to that page entitled *Spells to Uproot Magic.*

"Shall I then?"

"Mussst we do anything?"

"No. Just stay there, and I will do the rest."

Merlin pulled the crystal from his pocket and laid it on the open page with its tip pointed at the basilisks. It was to help focus his magic.

"I must say this one thing, Silzer. There is no way for me to know how the spell will perform. This sort of magic has a will of its own. It may work in the blink of an eye, or there may be some spectacle for all to see. I ask then that after I recite the spell, we wait a time."

"Not too long."

"No, not too long."

The king basilisk nodded his consent.

Merlin closed his eyes and cleared his mind. He took a couple of deep breaths to center himself, then lifted a hand, palm open, and recited the spell three times, each time a little slower, in a deep methodic voice.

All the while he spoke, the magic within him grew bright. No one could see it, but Merlin felt it. It was like a white-blue fire, blazing forth to engulf everything and nothing, coming out of him like a spear to strike its intended targets.

But nothing happened. There was no brilliant flash, nor did a glittering bolt of power leave his fingertips. There was a charge in the air and little else, but that could have been the combined energy of so many magical lives in one place.

There was an invisible struggle. Merlin held onto the spell. He grasped its tail and did not let go. He willed his life force into it and bid it work. It was after a brief silence, trailing his third recitation of the spell, that clouds rolled in overhead to blot out the sky. All eyes looked up, and many quaked when, after a crack of lightning spidered its way along the dark, rolling nimbus, loud thunder shook the earth and made the waters ripple.

It started to rain. It was cool and crisp and seeped into Merlin's robes. He did not lower his hand nor take his eyes off the basilisks. The crystal glowed a pearly luminescence and then cracked.

It was at that precise moment, when most of them were confused and unsure of what was happening, that both basilisks fell over, crashing to the sands, writhing in pain.

Merlin came to, as though out of a trance, and watched, his mouth agape. The basilisks reeled and retched, wriggled and convulsed. They gnashed their fangs. They screamed an unholy sound that split the air – it reminded Merlin of the cries of dying men, and he resisted the urge to cover his ears, grimacing. They were in pain. Their eyes were shut tight, but a white smoke seeped from their lids and dispersed in the rain.

Silzer bashed his head into the sands several times, seething. "What have you done to usss, wizard?" The agony was sharp in his words. "I will kill you!"

Dove pulled Merlin back, and Drius put them in his shadow.

Many of the others looked on, eyes wide and fearful. Madera had leapt aside so as not to be crushed by the serpents. She crouched on the sand, her winged arms lifted as though ready to flee, but was paralyzed with terror. Sli and his fellow sea serpent slunk back into the waters but watched with anticipation. No one else moved, and none uttered a sound. All of them were struck silent with terrible awe and dismay at the scene before them.

Merlin gripped his hands tightly, wrenching them till his fingers were white. He could still feel his magic, how like a stag it had leapt forth from him and touched the basilisks, and how it held them tightly and without mercy, intent to complete its task. All the while, his magic managed a link between him and them, and he was acutely aware of their suffering, with dread and upset at heart.

I am sorry, he internally appealed and dropped his head. There was nothing he could do to stop the spell or make it less severe for them. All he could do was watch and hear their agony like the others.

The unpleasant spectacle seemed to go on forever, so when the clouds finally dispersed and the sky cleared, the tension of the Circle broke but was not eased. The sun shone brightly, and all of nature was calm again. It was as though nothing unearthly and unnatural had happened, but all of them remained on edge, anxious and uncertain.

The basilisks lay still on the sand. The Circle watched them and waited with apprehension. Their eyes were still shut, but Merlin, for the first time, could see their faces.

They looked like most snakes, 'cept their snouts were sharp and came to a point. Their horned brows made them look more sinister, and they had massive jaws, able to swallow a man whole. The deep pits edging their jawlines flared as they breathed, and those long, black forked tongues hung limp.

Neither moved, and no one dared go near them.

Silzer then hitched his breath and hissed out, seething with venom: "Where isss the wizard?"

His agitation and obvious fury caused Hamel to brandish his club, and the centaurs their swords. Others became rigid, and some recoiled or crouched, ready to flee.

Before Merlin could speak, Drius put a wing in front of him, shielding him.

"What do you plan to do, Silzer?" he asked.

"Kill him! I will kill him!" the king basilisk shrieked.

Drius growled. "You will do no such thing. I will kill you first."

"He mutilated me!"

"He did nothing."

"But hisss magic did."

"And he warned you he did not know what his magic would do. He told you, and you accepted the risk."

Silzer screeched but did not move. After a brief pause, he said, "I mussst look at him."

Drius did not move. He planted his feet, his body unyielding. "No."

"He and I have a deal! You cannot protect him."

"I can and I will if I think you intend him harm."

Merlin put a hand on Drius' wing and came out from behind it. "Drius," he said in a quiet, unperturbed voice, "it is all right."

The dragon lord looked down at him, unsure.

"Silzer is right. He and I have an agreement, and I must uphold my part. Do not worry. I am not afraid."

"Merlin—"

Merlin held up a hand to stay him. "He has every right to be upset. We saw what my magic did, and I confess I did not think it would be so frenzied and ruthless. It caused me deep regret and made me ill to watch. I am sorry for how bad it was, but a deal is a deal."

He stepped forward but was held up. He looked back and saw Dove, clutching his sleeve. There was a desperate pleading in her eyes, asking him not to do it. He grinned and patted her hand.

"It will be fine. You will see."

Reluctantly, she let go.

"I am coming forward, Silzer, slowly."

His steps crunched in the sand. No one made a sound.

A sense of unease gripped Merlin's stomach, and his knees were like balls of lead, but still, he held his head up as he approached. He stopped close to the basilisk, near his tail.

"I am here, Silzer."

The basilisk rose, bits of sand falling from him like ashes. With his eyes still closed, he turned toward the Circle. He breathed deeply and tasted the air with his tongue. He was catching Merlin's scent. The pits at his neck, Merlin knew, mapped out his hot blood. Silzer brought his head low and close, and his tongue brushed against Merlin's robes.

The great serpent cracked his jaws open, venom dripping from his fangs. The malodor of his breath made the hairs on the back of Merlin's neck stand up. It was poison and death entwined together – it stung, causing Merlin's eyes to water.

In a low voice, the basilisk hissed, "I can sssmell you, wizard. I can sssmell your fear."

Behind him, Merlin heard Drius emit a low growl that rolled over the Circle. It shook him, and without turning around, he was certain the dragon was glowing within. The heat of his internal fire, faint but there, laid a warm hand on the back of his robes, assuring him.

Silzer shut his mouth and tilted his head up, his eyes still closed. He said nothing, but the way he frowned, as though he were robbed of his hideous amusement, and how his tongue flicked the air like a whip indicated his displeasure.

"Get on with it, Silzer." Drius said these words through his teeth.

Silzer's tongue slipped out once more, his head hovering, and then he returned to Merlin, so close the wind from his nostrils disturbed Merlin's hair.

Merlin never looked away. Those dark eyelids rolled open, drawing back to reveal a grim, repulsive truth. Merlin quaked within but did not show it without. Staring back at him was a sickly, timeless omen, that thing which all creation fears. Death looked at him. The eyes were yellow and thin, and fixed in each one was a black, bottomless pupil, slender and sharp. The pupils widened, gazing deeply at Merlin, and it was as though an invisible force leapt out of them into him.

He felt the cold again, but it was tinged with sorrow and grief, with feelings of loss and despair. The force, like a hand, grasped his heart and squeezed. It was a terrible truth, the truth all souls fear and hate. It was ugly and wretched. Merlin saw a vision of himself gripping his own heart, but it was not him. It was all that was bad within him – his malice, his deception, his sin. This version of him was gaunt and skeletal – it was him, but dead. It yawned, peeling its faded lips back into a hideous smile.

So this is your curse. When life looks at you, it is stricken dead. Death seems swift, but in that instant, all of this plays out. Your victim is faced with their sin and all that is evil within them the moment they look into your eyes.

Merlin saw and even felt his dead-self squeeze his heart, and with its other hand, it grazed his skin, causing it to prickle and the hairs to stand on end. He felt he was becoming petrified, that his body was turning to stone. Strange and crippling as it was, his mind glimmered, and he bid his fingers curl. Sweat broke from his brow as he forced all his effort into complying. It was like his hands were frozen, and his fingers did not conform, not at first. He focused past his grisly self and, without looking at his hands, willed them to move.

It was when his pinky finger twitched and curled in on itself, touching his palm, that Merlin sighed, having not realized he had been holding his breath the whole time. Suddenly, the ghost of himself disappeared, evaporated into mist, and was gone.

Merlin put a hand on his chest. His heart beat loud and unheeded. His blood danced within him. His mind reeled with a thousand thanks to heaven, for his soul, a little shaken but bright, was still with him.

Filled with relief and joy, he smiled at the basilisk and laughed within. Silzer then frowned but did not dare show surprise.

"Can you see me, Silzer?" Merlin asked. "Can you still see at all?"

The king basilisk flicked the air with his tongue. "Yesss, I can sssee you." He lifted his gaze, and his pupils widened, taking in the scene before him and seeing all those lives look back at him and not perish. His eyes glazed over with disbelief. "I sssee everything."

"It worked!" Qoral's voice was like a bell, breaking the silence.

Several voices muttered their wonder. They all stared at the great serpent, still deadly with his fangs and venom, his sheer size and willpower, but he was stripped of the magic that had made him intimidating and without weakness. For the first time in his life, Silzer was vulnerable.

Merlin caught a flash of something in the king basilisk's eyes. He gazed around the Circle at those creatures which at one time had feared him, and he did not like what he saw. He retreated to his place in the Circle and coiled upon himself, agitated and upset, but he never looked away from them.

Just as I thought...

Merlin frowned.

Forever he has held authority over vitality, but now life looks back at him, and it is less afraid of him. He is not certain of his future, not sure he will get along without death as his companion, as miserable a companion as death was. It was all he knew. Now he starts over.

"Come here, Merlin," said Drius, his voice crackling with embers.

Merlin did, walking backward, never taking his eyes off Silzer. Internally, he winced, and he pitied the creature's new predicament.

We had a deal. He knew what could happen, and it has. Without his deadly sight, he is nothing more than a giant serpent, and I wonder, can he look at another basilisk without dying? No more a king of his kind, he will wander forever. And I did it to him...but he sacrificed so that his companion would not suffer alone.

Merlin halted in Drius' shadow. Dove was at his side again, hovering, relieved.

"A basilisk stripped of its sight," Sli mused, water dripping from his fangs, his lips curled back in a horrible grin.

Silzer glared at the sea serpent with boiling silence.

"But what of your companion? Is the same true of him?"

"I will test him," said Ulysses, approaching the second basilisk, who still lay on the sand with his eyes shut.

The centaur chieftain kept a firm hand on the hilt of his sword, and his muscles quivered with anticipation. "Recover fast and look at me, basilisk."

When his companion did not move, Silzer hissed, "Get up, Azrael."

The basilisk opened its mouth in silent protest but did as told. He lifted himself from the sand and searched out the chieftain, tasting the air with his forked tongue, the pits at his neck flaring after the hot blood of the warrior. He found him and looked at him with the same unsettling eyes as his king.

Ulysses tightened his grip on his sword, but he did not fall or sway. He held his stance and engaged in a long staring match till Liliana broke the tension by saying, "It seems Merlin has proved himself. He turned magic against itself and was successful."

Ulysses returned to his place in the Circle. Waves of relief and wonderment washed over the majority, and only Madera, standing again with her winged arms crossed, glared at Merlin.

"Let no one be fooled," said Merlin then. "These basilisks are still deadly and deserve your respect, if not more so for what they have endured."

"Sssave your wordsss, wizard. They do not sssoften the blow." Silzer said this with sizzling anger, and drops of toxic spittle dripped from his jaws, turning the sand black where it fell.

Drius growled. "But now the one you send has a better chance to save you and your own. Does that not make your sacrifice noble?"

"Noble? Tell me, dragon, how would you feel if you were ssstripped of your fire breath or your wingsss for all eternity? You would be nothing but an overgrown lizard. I feel incomplete, lossst, and not myssself anymore." He stared intensely at Merlin, his horned brows caving, his eyes sharp and eager to gouge out Merlin's own. "I am no more a basssilisssk. Jussst a great ssserpent. But if it givesss my kind a chance…" He paused, seething, then said in a low, steadier voice, "No, it doesss not feel noble. I hate it. But ssso it isss and will alwaysss be."

Merlin observed several in the Circle looking at the basilisk with uncertainty but also sympathy. Silzer noticed, too, grimaced and hissed at them, "Sssave your pity. It isss empty." Then to Merlin, "Get on with it, wizard. You did your worssst."

Merlin's chest tightened, and his heart seemed to slow as he felt the bitter sting of Silzer's words, and he lowered his gaze.

"Most noble acts are noble because they involve self-sacrifice," said Liliana. "Just as Merlin plans to do today when he gives up seeing us from this day forward."

Merlin blinked and looked at the fairy queen, sitting poised on her flower and smiling up at him.

"So go on, Merlin. Do your best."

New warmth bloomed over him, and color filled his cheeks. He nodded, grinning at her, then walked over to Qoral.

"Your majesty," he said, bowing his head to the mermaid queen, "with your permission, I would like to speak with your merfolk and you about their role in all of this."

"Of course, Merlin." She waved her hand, and the twelve merfolk swam over in silent rushes through the water.

Merlin knelt on the sands to be level with them. "My plan cannot work without you. Each of you is charged with ferrying these creatures across the sea. With your queen as my witness, I ask that you find good shores for them, where humans often pass, and a child is sure to find them. If your queen permits it, I would like you to stay and watch the shore till the creature is found, so you can tell her as much when you return. Do you agree, your majesty?"

Qoral beamed a bright smile. "I agree, and it shall be so." To her kin, she asked, "Do you still accept your charge?"

All twelve nodded, certain, and several of them spoke up:

"It is a privilege."

"An honor."

"To serve you, my queen, and this council."

"And a higher purpose."

Merlin grinned, stood up, and bowed to them. "I thank you for your willingness."

He returned to the middle of the Circle and flipped through the pages of his Spell Book till he found again that page with *Spells of Size*.

"I suppose there is little left to say. But forgive me as I divert a moment."

Many stared, curious, as Merlin brought forth from his satchel several volumes of text and presented these to Hamel.

"These are for you, my friend, as promised. But here, let me make them your size."

He recited the spell opposite the page *To Shrink*, that was *To Enlarge*, and at once, the volumes began to grow till they filled Hamel's hands. The giant's cheeks turned rosy, and his smile could not contain his cheer.

"Thank you, Merlin. I will love them always because they came from you."

Merlin bowed to the giant and returned to his Spell Book, ignoring the baffled looks of the others in the Circle. Only Drius looked at his friend with an all-knowing grin.

Merlin reached again in his satchel to bring forth the twelve bottles and laid them on the sand.

"Each bottle has its note so the child who finds you will know how to care for you. With the exception of those bottles that will carry creatures of the sea – those bottles are filled with seawater, the others have an enchanted seashell that fills with water when you thirst, but it will never spill. And there is also food that is to each of your likings. I wanted to be sure you were well taken care of on your journey.

"I pray your journey will not be a long one, that the merfolk will find friendly shores to leave you, and a child will find you shortly thereafter.

"This spell is tricky in that, being so small, your voice is so high it cannot be heard. But as the child cares for you, and they believe in you, you will grow, and your voice will deepen, and in little time, I imagine, you will be heard and, a while later, restored to your true stature.

"So who will be the first?"

The centaur, whose name was Brom, stepped forward. He was a dapple gray stallion, and his long silver tail had several braids, one of them interweaved with a token of good fortune from his clan. His sword laid across his back, and he had a shield strapped to his side and a belt around his middle with many pouches. He was as battle-scarred as Ulysses, with old wounds mapping his torso and arms. He stood before Merlin with his arms crossed.

"I will be the first," he said in a voice that was proud but reverent.

Merlin nodded. He remembered Brom from the Amare Feast. He should have been part of the games but did not participate because, as Ulysses had told Merlin at the feast table, he had volunteered to go on this journey the day Ulysses returned from the Great Circle with news of Merlin's plan.

Merlin could not help but admire and respect the centaur. "As you wish," he said.

Ulysses came forward and slapped the warrior on the back. The studs took hold of each other's strong arms, the muscles tight, the veins prominent, and tipped their heads till their foreheads touched.

With his eyes closed, Ulysses said, "Honor is yours, brother. Victory is ours."

Brom grunted and beat his chest twice with his free fist.

Ulysses parted from him and went back to his place in the Circle.

Merlin bowed once to Brom and placed his hand on the centaur's shoulder. He closed his eyes, channeling his magic. He still felt it, leaping and dancing within him, awake and ready to spring.

He opened his eyes and read the spell only once. Before many gasps and widening eyes, the equine warrior grew smaller. He descended, and all he carried became small with him. He fit in the palm of Merlin's hand and was not frightened but stout and brave.

Merlin picked up the bottle with the centaur's care note.

"Let me help you."

He uncorked the bottle, and the neck was wide enough for the centaur to walk inside.

"I assure you, you will never run out of air. I enchanted the bottle. For now, I will lay you here." He set the bottle with its precious cargo down on the sand. "And I will do the same with the others till all are inside their bottles. Then I will cork them. Nod if you are fine."

The centaur nodded once and crossed his arms.

"Excellent."

To the Circle, he said, "Who is next?"

The creatures came forward in this order: phoenix, griffin, mermaid, winged horse, unicorn, sea serpent, fairy, giant, and basilisk.

Each one Merlin shrunk, he helped into their bottle.

Some of the leaders bid farewell to their chosen in a moving way, most with the touching of heads and the parting of sweet words. Hamel shook his compatriot's hand, a good fellow named Bantuck, who carried with him a satchel filled with seeds from the harvest. Liliana hugged her fairy subject, a pretty, rosy thing named Mari, short for Marigold, who had a red marigold tied up in her long red tresses and wore ferns and ivy leaves. She also had a pouch strapped to her hip, perhaps filled with trinkets or some other fairy provision – Merlin was never to know.

After the basilisk was in his bottle, there were two bottles still empty. Merlin turned around to face the dragons and Dove.

Dove frowned and held her arms in a self-embrace, just like when she first came to them. She looked up at Drius, and he indicated she go ahead with a single nod. She took a reluctant step forward, almost shaking, and it was then that Drius brought his great head low and said to her in a tender voice laced with gentle sincerity:

"Best of luck to you, dear one. You proved this old dragon wrong, and for that, you have both my love and admiration."

Dove managed a small grin. A faint bloom filled her cheeks, and she bowed to him. "Thank you," she said.

She looked at Merlin again, and her grin faded.

Merlin knew what she was feeling. He felt it too. He put on a brave smile, hoping to encourage and reassure her.

She came forward and stood in front of him. Her eyes then flitted past him, and she hesitated. Merlin turned around to see Madera approaching them, and he was reluctant to step aside but did so when Drius motioned for him to comply with a tilt of his head and a clearing of his throat.

The harpy queen stopped before her sister and gazed at her. Dove did not waver or crumple but stood upright and looked back at her, a gleam in her eyes.

Something is different, Merlin thought.

Madera did not look at Dove with reluctance or hostility but with silent recognition and regard. The bitterness had left her eyes, and her jaw was slack. She was calm and unruffled, and without looking away from the one she had cast out, she nodded to her, then turned and walked away, going back to her place in the Circle, and crossed her winged arms.

Merlin came to Dove and whispered, "What was that?"

"She acknowledges me." Dove stared at the harpy queen as she answered, her voice subdued with disbelief. Merlin wondered if she might cry or be upset, but when she looked at him, he was both relieved and pleased to see her eyes were still bright behind her glasses.

"This is it," he said.

She nodded. "Merlin—"

He put a hand up to stop her. "I know. We said much at the cave. I think there is little else that can be said without saying it a different way."

She suddenly threw her arms around him, surprising many – Merlin heard them gasp, and he thought he stunned them again when he returned her hug.

"Thank you for everything," she whispered.

"You are most welcome," he said, trying not to let his voice crack.

She held him a moment longer. Her final word fluttered at his ear like a butterfly: "Friend?"

"Yes. Friend." He squeezed her gently, and they parted.

He had to will himself not to cry as he made her small and put her in her bottle.

Eleven in their bottles. Only one left.

Merlin had butterflies in his stomach as he faced Isla and her father.

This will not be easy, separating them. I still cannot believe he chose her of all his dragons.

"Isla—" he started, but then the words hitched in his throat, as Drius shook his head at him.

Drius turned away, and Isla followed him. They left the Circle and stood apart from all who were there. A hundred feet away, maybe more, Merlin could not guess, the two dragons faced each other and spoke in inaudible tones – their lips moving, but the words lost between them.

Merlin and the Circle only watched, and he could not help but notice the trouble and upset in Isla's deep, catch-all eyes. She grimaced. Her body was rigid, and her tail curled around her back heel. Her wings drooped, but she never lowered her gaze. She held her father's eye, seeming to be brave.

Drius was like a statue, unwavering and without obvious emotion. He spoke to her, his head bobbing, but there was an air about him that was calm, determined, and sure.

At last, he reached out to her, brushing his head against hers. Low rumbles resounded in their throats as they entwined their necks in a loving embrace.

There was a twinkling of something in Isla's eye – the sun caught it, and Merlin saw it was a tear.

The dragons began to glow, their plated bellies flaring, their scales gleaming. They parted and raised their heads toward heaven and let forth tremendous roars that shattered the shores and waves. The hot light within them rushed, and the flames breached the air with explosive force, raging and booming like thunder. Their fires spiraled, climbing toward the sky and casting a warm light over the sands, the water, and the Circle.

Merlin felt the heat but raised no hand to fend it off. He could only watch, finding the spectacle beautiful and powerful but also commanding. It demanded feelings be moved like mountains and that any who saw it be shaken within like tremors in the earth. It inspired awe but silenced all manner of thought. It shattered time, being eternal, and yet it passed in a fleeting moment.

The dragons ceased their ignited breaths, and the pillars of fire extinguished. The sun was the only light again.

Isla bellowed once and shook her head, looking offbeat and sad. She threw her wings open and lumbered away, beating the air till it was whipped and at her command. Up she went, gathering space between her and them, climbing, soaring. Her last roar descended on them like a gentle rain, and they could feel her sorrow. She turned for home and was soon out of sight.

Drius looked after her, even after she was gone. A veil of woe and heartache draped over him, and in his eyes, it was clear that he hurt.

Merlin went to him, his lips trembling, his hands shaking.

"Drius?"

He put a hand on the dragon's foreclaw, and his light, gentle touch seemed to pull Drius out of a trance.

"Merlin."

"Drius, why?"

Drius sighed. The breath tussled Merlin's hair, feeling cold and broken. "It is her time to lead. She is ready. But she could not stand to watch me leave."

Merlin shook his head. "But, Drius, there are others, good dragons, who can go. Why must you?" The tears sprung forth and ran down his face.

Drius brought his head low and stared at Merlin. "Who better than me?" His eyes were gentle, full of wisdom and tenderness. "I am over a hundred years old, Merlin. I have always been here. I can still do some good in the time I have left, however long heaven deems that to be. If I can do one thing more for my kind,

then it is my honor to serve. I know everything about my own, and I am not young and hot-blooded, quick to temper or anger. I know patience and how to love a human. You taught me that."

Merlin tried to manage a grin, but his face was shattered with sorrow and upset.

Drius nuzzled his snout in Merlin's hair.

"Do not be sad for me, old friend. I go on to do something great, also your doing."

"If I had known it meant losing you—"

"Enough." Drius hovered, pulling away and staring at the wizard. "You would lose sight of me. You said so yourself. Did you not stop to think that I would be sad to see you each day and know you can neither see nor hear me? I want to remember you here in our final chapter together."

Merlin shook all over, his shoulders slumped, his head low. His stomach turned itself over in knots, and his heart felt it might beat itself to shambles.

"Oh, Drius." He hugged the dragon's face, and Drius pressed into him a little, breathing warm air over him. "You are my best friend. Losing you is like losing a part of myself. You have done so much for me."

"And you have done much for me, Merlin. You saved my life. You saved the life of my daughter. And now you hope to save my dragons as well as these creatures here and their own beyond the shore. You are a wonder among men."

Merlin glanced at the scarred wing, and the memory came swiftly back to him. He wept anew, his tears spilling over Drius' scales.

Drius moaned a low rumble that shook Merlin's blood.

"I suspect we will never forget each other."

"No. Never." Merlin hugged a little tighter, then parted.

Drius straightened up and, to the Circle, announced: "You are all my witnesses. I have made Isla, my only living heir, the new leader of the Dragons' Keep and its dragons. I have chosen myself for this journey, and I want to say that it has been a privilege to know you all and be a part of something bigger than ourselves. To be united and survive. I wish you all farewell."

Ulysses unsheathed his sword, planted it in the sand, and knelt in reverence. Aquila and Opala also bowed, with a foreleg out and the other bent. Liliana touched her lips and parted the dragon with a kiss. Qoral brought her hands together, lifted them high, and bowed her head. Hamel, Flint, and Glendor dropped their heads, eyes closed in respect. Even Sli, a great enemy of dragons, without taking his eyes off of Drius, bowed his head to him. Only Madera and Silzer remained motionless and without expression.

It was then that Drius looked at Merlin and, with a faint grin, said, "Isla wants you to stay with her and the others in the mountains. She will look after you even though you will not see her. I hope you stay, Merlin, for it will do my heart good to know you are safe and cared for."

Merlin nodded, unable to speak.

"Good. Then do it now, Merlin, while you still have the nerve and strength."

Merlin took a deep breath and grasped the spine of his Spell Book. His finger shook as he traced the words of the spell, and it took all he had not to lose focus or let his voice crack as he read it aloud, as he summoned his magic to bend to his will and do as he asked.

His heart then clamored as Drius became smaller, and it was difficult for him to keep steady hands as he helped his old friend into the bottle. When they chanced to look at each other through the glass, Merlin thought,

Goodbye then, great and wonderful friend. May the child who finds you be good to you, and may the winds tell me of you, should heaven show me one more kindness. Its last was when I met you.

The twelve were ready. Merlin corked the bottles and cast a charm of protection over them. Then, one at a time, with great care, he brought them to a mermaid or merman, who held the treasure close.

Drius was the last he parted with, to a mermaid, and he said to her, "Take good care of him."

She nodded and swam back to her fellows.

Merlin wiped his face dry and withdrew to the center of the Circle. He flipped through the pages of his Spell Book once more and came to the spell of *Invisibility*.

His hand hovered over the spell. He licked his lips and took several deep breaths, trying to calm his nerves.

He looked around at all the faces staring back at him. These were some of the most wondrous beings on earth, born of magic like him – the beautiful and fierce, the wise and sudden, the tempered and terrible.

Inside, he was quaking, his sorrow building. He was a towering figure of grief and woe, ready to fall with another shedding of a tear. He was fragile, but beneath it all, his magic was still stirring, ready to aid and bend and change.

"I have one last thing to say," he mustered, then cleared his throat. "If heaven and magic give their blessing for me to do this, then may fortune and fate smile on you as well. I am blessed to know you, and I will carry the memory of you with me forever. Thank you for letting me into your lives. I am the most fortunate of all people. My hopes and prayers are with you."

Liliana fluttered over to him and touched his chin. "It is we who are blessed to know you, Merlin. You, who gives us our second chance. Thank you." She kissed his cheek and flitted back to her flower.

All around then, Merlin saw her shared feelings amongst the Circle. Every creature, even Sli, Madera, and Silzer, bowed their heads to him.

Merlin's eyes were wet again. He raised a hand in farewell but also to center himself as he summoned his magic one more time.

With careful meditation and perfect pronunciation, he read the spell. The magic was ancient, the writing in a language he himself made up. As he said each word with focused intent and a determined heart, the air became heavy with a mist that soon turned to a hazy fog, light and luminous.

It swallowed the Great Circle, hiding their faces. There was a slight chill in the air that nipped, but Merlin read on, slow and purposeful. He felt his magic go out of him into the fog. It was running and racing like a rabbit with a fox on its heels, leaping and prancing like a gazelle in love. It did not stop there though. It grew wings and flew beyond them, over the sea and sands, the woods, and every mountain and valley further on. It sought out every creature like those in the Circle, found them, and wrapped around them in a gentle embrace. Merlin felt it – like a great hand that envelops all it cares for and yearns to protect, his magic found them and held them tight.

Even after he finished reading, the spell was still spinning. He grew tired and faint and fell to one knee, but his resolve, his purpose spurred the magic on. Then, just when he thought it might take his life, take all that was left of him, it was over.

The magic dissolved with the mist. Gasping for breath, Merlin felt his strength come crawling back to him. It filled his old frame and bid him to stand up, so he did. Within, his magic slept, worn and tired, but there was relief and a sense of completion.

The mist faded, and Merlin found himself alone on the beach.

He turned around a couple of times but saw no other life. He looked at the sands and saw the impressions left by them, but no grains stirred. He saw Liliana's flower, beautiful and solitary. He gazed out at the water and thought he saw a deviation, a ripple or two, but then the waves were churning, and he was weary.

"I see nothing," he said, soft and to himself. Then, in a loud, clear voice, with a great smile, he announced, "I cannot see you. I see nothing. Not a trace of you. Nothing."

He laughed as he bent down to pick up his Spell Book.

"It worked."

He brushed the sand from the Book and shoved it in his satchel. Tears of joy traced his face.

"It worked. My magic worked."

He then sniffled and wiped his face with the back of his sleeve.

Gathering himself up, he said more calmly, "It worked," and bowed to the vacant sands.

He then started for home, but when he was at the edge of shore and green, he turned and looked back at where he had been, where they were – he knew.

The beach was serene and quiet, 'cept for the sound of the waves rolling in. It was as though nothing of significance had happened there. Everything was as it should be.

With a parting grin, he said, "Farewell," and left.

CHAPTER TWENTY-FOUR

Never Alone

Merlin was slow returning home. His feet dragged, and his satchel was heavy. It ached his shoulder to carry it. He had lost a lot of his strength to his magic, and once more, he felt his age.

But more than his physical state of being, beneath it all, his heart ached, heavy with sorrow and loss. He could still picture their faces in his mind, and he held onto those images with desperate devotion.

I will go home. I will draw. I will sleep.

He would capture that final moment, that final scene on the sands, in ink. It would be all he had left to remember them by, along with his other drawings. He had done so many in his spare time, driven by fear of forgetting, of his mind turning dumb and losing its splendid memories. It could happen. After all, he was mortal and still a man.

When he reached his cave, the silence of the mountains was deafening. Every now and then, he heard a bird call or the wind pass through, but he did not hear the ramblings, roars, or wing breaks of dragons, sounds he had grown accustomed to, even fond of hearing – now gone. All was silent.

But they are there. I know.

Of course, they were there. They were there. He was there. They could see him, but he could not see them.

He hung up his satchel and put his Spell Book back on its mantle. It was too early for a fire, even though the cave appeared dark and felt cold in the daylight.

He lumbered over to his desk and flopped in his chair. His bones creaked, and his muscles strained. Every inch of him hurt, and he tried to summon from the curio a special root that, if boiled in tea, would soothe any pain. The curio quivered, and the glass rattled. One door opened, but nothing more happened.

"I am too weak even for this," he grumbled to himself.

He put his hands on the desk to push himself up, but it was then that he noticed something out of place. There, in plain sight, was an envelope, golden in color, that shimmered when Merlin held it up. It had a seal unlike any he had seen before: not made of wax or red like blood. It was a living flower, small and white, with tiny leaves forming a circlet around it.

"Strange," he muttered and opened it.

Inside was a letter on parchment made of white leaves sewn together. It was beautiful and seemed fragile, but when Merlin touched it, he felt its magic, strong and resilient. Written on it in delicate ink strokes was this message:

Dear Merlin,
If you are reading this, it means you were successful. I knew you would be.

On our last night together, I saw the passion and determination alive within you. Magic often comes to those with goodwill and purpose, who sacrifice for something greater than themselves.

You did us a great kindness and paid a terrible price to do it. Your sacrifice will not be forgotten. Your name will live on forever in our hearts and stories.

You are always welcome at Greenwood. When you visit, there will be tokens of our love and appreciation waiting for you at our Tree. I know how much you love our lavender cakes.

I know you met Honey, and she is quite fond of you. Therefore, I have given her a special charge. Notice the basket in your garden.

Merlin looked up, and sure enough, there was something cradled in amongst the plants of his garden. He went over to see. It was a small basket woven from birch branches and laced with flowers and acorns.

Whenever you feel alone, write me a letter. Leave it in the basket. Honey will fetch it and bring you one from me. In this way, I hope to stave off your loneliness.

I shall not be surprised if the others look in on you. So many of them have come to love you, and I think I speak for most when I say we care for you. None will forget what you did this day.

You are forever a friend of the fae.

Thank you, Merlin, for all your hard work. I am certain your king would be most proud of you.

Sincerely,

Liliana, Queen of the Fairies

A tear splashed on the letter. Merlin set it aside and dried his eyes.

"Thank you, your majesty."

Next to the basket was a small shoot in the soil of his garden – the beginnings of the delphinium the queen gifted him.

He smiled and gazed around the cave. There was no way for him to know if Honey was there, waiting, or if he was alone.

I will write her back. Most certainly.

He fetched the root from the curio, brewed his tea, and returned to his desk. While sipping from his cup, he read over the queen's letter again, and a single word leapt out at him like a falling star.

"Stories," he mumbled. "Stories."

He put down the letter and drummed his fingers on the desk. His sketches were strewn all about, and his eyes danced over them.

"Must it stop here?"

No.

An idea was forming, growing fast in his mind, and he got up and paced.

I want to do more, but how?

The falling star hit him, bursting with color and light, and he stopped in his tracks. He stared out his cave at the vast horizon and smiled.

"I will write our story."

He sat down at his desk and pulled from a drawer a brown, leather-bound book, its pages crisp and blank. He took his quill in hand and dipped it in its ink pot, turning to the first page.

Now, where to begin?

"At the beginning, of course," he chuckled and put to the page:

In olden days, when knights fought for glory, and kings ruled from great stone castles, fairytale creatures, both beautiful and frightening, roamed the land and sea...

A MESSAGE

My dear reader,

Did you like my story? It is true, every word of it.

Have you seen a dragon? What about a unicorn? I should not be surprised if you once saw a fairy dancing in the wood. There are fantastic beasts and beings all around you in this vast world of ours. Some are fierce and others friendly, some beautiful and others terrible.

I miss them, but I am happy should you chance to see a giant or a griffin or you happen upon a centaur or mermaid. If you should look toward heaven and see a winged horse galloping amongst the stars or hear the phoenix's song and be inspired, think of me and my story, and believe.

Some creatures may still be less friendly after all this time and history. I hope that is not so, but still, I caution you to be wary. Be mindful of sea serpents and harpies, but do not spurn them as the world has done. Be careful of the basilisk and his deadly sight but pity him because he can neither see nor understand life and is alone.

My parting words are these: believe, dear child. Believe so that magic is still here, still alive in this ever-changing world. We need magic so that life is still a wonder.

Your friend,
Merlin Ambrosius

LETTERS FOR THE CARE OF MAGICAL CREATURES

My dear reader,

I offer you one thing more: these letters for the care of magical creatures. These are copies of those same letters that accompanied the creatures on their journeys.

Though those creatures were found a long time ago, should you happen upon one of their own, and it needs your friendship and care, I hope you find these letters useful and a great source of learning.

– Merlin

LETTER FOR THE CARE OF A DRAGON

To the child who reads this letter, you have found a dragon. Do not shy away or be afraid. Dragons are not the monsters of fairytales and legends that were told to you at night. Dragons are indeed fierce and powerful, but they are also wise and thoughtful and loyal to those they love. These great reptiles are masters of air and fire, due respect and consideration, and great company to keep. This one has come to you to be your friend, and I speak from experience when I say there is no better companion in all the realms of magical beasts to know so well as a dragon. – Merlin

Diet (Food and Drink)

Contrary to fables, dragons do not eat people. Apparently, we taste bad. Besides that, dragons are averse to consuming intelligent life. For this reason, dragons do not devour other beasts of magic, being so much like them.

Dragons hunt other prey – deer, wild boar, bears, great cats, and the like. They do not eat meat raw but prefer it cooked, using their fire breath to smoke it till it is savory and easy to chew. This dragon is too small and vulnerable to fend for himself, but if you take great care of him and tend to his needs, he will grow and, in little time, be able to hunt again. And I should think that if you and this dragon become close, you will never go hungry again. Dragons have hearty appetites, so feed this one well.

It is a myth that water puts out a dragon's fire. Their fire is their magic, so it cannot be extinguished. Dragons, therefore, drink plenty of water but can also drink it sparingly in hard times.

Habitat and Bedding

Dragons can live almost anywhere, being hardy and resilient to most environments and weather. This dragon comes from a mountainous region in northern Britannia, a place that sees all the seasons. It is pleasant in the spring and summer and turns bitter in winter.

Mountains afford a dragon high elevations, rocky terrain, and snow, as well as precarious climbs and privacy from the outside world. This one's shelter was a cave, and he slept on the hard cavern floor. I am sure your home is more comfortable, and this dragon will have no trouble getting used to his new surroundings. He still needs a place to sleep, however. Where he rests should be warm and safe – a place from which he can survey the room, for a dragon never wants to be snuck up on. Do not fret if he takes to sleeping in the fireplace. Dragons are resistant to fire. Their wings are tough, their scales hardy, and no amount of heat or flame will ever burn them.

Behavior (Mannerisms)

Of all the magical creatures I have come to know, I am fondest of dragons. Imposing, formidable, and impressive, they fight with unmatched ferocity when threatened. But there is another side to dragons that most people do not see. They kindle tender hearts and care deeply about those dearest to them. They are wise and thoughtful, intuitive and conscious of changes in others. You cannot hide anything from a dragon. They always know if you are hurt or bothered, so you might as well tell them what is the matter. They will listen and advise, if you are willing to hear their counsel.

Dragons are noble, loyal, and true. A dragon that is your friend will not abandon you but will fight with all its strength and heart to keep you safe. Nor will you find a companion as honest as a dragon. It is not in a dragon to lie. Dragons are always to the point. Telling untruths is a waste of time, and though dragons live a long time – several hundred years, in fact, they see no point in hindering conversation. Actually, if you attempt to hide anything from them, dragons take this as a slight to your friendship and can be offended. The best thing for this is a sincere apology on your part, followed by the truth.

Most dragons are forgiving. You can mess up time and again and, depending on the slight, a dragon will still love you. I hope you have a great friendship with this dragon. Be patient though: you must prove yourself first and earn his trust and admiration. With time and good deeds, the bond between you will grow and strengthen, and you will be one of the lucky ones to say you have a friend in a dragon. You may even get the chance to ride upon his back in flight, which I must say is one of the greatest thrills in life.

One thing more: dragons are intelligent creatures and have feelings like you and me. As you bond with this one, there should often be an exchange of words and feelings, honest thoughts and opinions. If you have not guessed it after reading this far, I will tell you that this dragon, like most, has the power of speech. This one understands what you say, but his voice is soft while he is so small. Once he has grown some, you will hear him, and then, I imagine, you will learn a great many things about dragons and other fantastic beasts.

Dragon Magic

Most dragons can sense an approaching storm a great distance away. How it was described to me by a dragon is as follows: they feel the pressure in the air change, and the forces that create lightning and thunder begin to swell so that they can predict when the storm will come and how light or heavy it will be.

The magic you are probably most familiar with, however, is their fire breath. A dragon's fire can melt all metals and will never be extinguished or run out. How it is made, I cannot begin to imagine. It is magic, and magic cannot always be explained.

A Word of Caution

There is a truth about dragons I prefer not to share but must for your safety and that of this dragon. There are stories about dragons hoarding treasure, but the truth is dragons do not come by this naturally. Dragons are born with a terrible curse, that if ever one should see riches – be it gold or precious stones, the dragon is consumed by a desire it cannot shake, a disturbed form of greed. A shadow falls over the dragon's senses, and it is no longer itself. It becomes obsessed with treasure and steals and hoards it, often by terrible means, just like in the stories. The tragedy is it could steal all the wealth in the world, and still, it would not be enough. I call these dragons "rogues," and they often die from lack of sleep, food, and water because they keep a desperate vigil to guard their treasure. I have never known a dragon to be itself again once it has turned rogue, so I beg you do not let this one see riches, for that will be his undoing and yours as well.

LETTER FOR THE CARE OF A UNICORN

To the child who reads this letter, you have found a unicorn. The most beloved creature to grace the earth, she is beautiful and without sin. To look at her, your heart feels a pang of guilt, as you become suddenly aware that you look on the purest and most innocent of all creation. It may be no one is worthy of her save you. She has sought you out and sees the good in you. – Merlin

Diet (Food and Drink)

Like its simple cousin, the horse, a unicorn grazes when hungry. But unlike its cousin, a unicorn does not do this for the better part of the day. It will graze by morning light, taking to the grass that is sweetened by the morning dew, and then wander or frolic with its herd.

No unicorn has ever known a winter. The enchanted wood in which they live sees only eternal spring and summer, and wherever a unicorn is, winter does not come. Should this one encounter the bitter frost where you are, you must feed her well with hay and grain.

Unicorns also like apples and berries and most fruit that is sweet. You can also give this one sugar cubes or some honey, or better still, look for fondness in her eyes when you bring her a handful of honeysuckle flowers, for unicorns like their saccharine nectar.

A unicorn must drink water every day, but like its grazing, it only drinks enough to see the day through. Why unicorns drink and eat so little, I cannot say. I think it must do with their immortality. Living forever makes them worry little, and instead of being hungry for sustenance, they hunger for life and what there is to do each day.

This unicorn is small now, but she will grow. Till then, you are her keeper. You must feed her till she is big enough that you will then watch over her as she grazes and fend off any danger that threatens her. Only when this unicorn has grown to her full size will she be able to fend for herself. Most beasts revere her and stay away, but some are less good. With her horn, she can slay the ruthless but will sooner run, being swift and always outpacing the wind.

Habitat and Bedding

This unicorn comes to you from an enchanted forest in Britannia. Her wood is filled with great trees, and the ground is lush with soft grass. There are so many flowers of every color, you cannot hope to see them all. And there is a pond by which her herd stays, in a small clearing where their foals play.

A unicorn is not itself when it is removed from its forest and its herd. It takes time for it to adjust to its new surroundings, but I promise this one will grow fond of you and where you live, so long as you treat her well and do your best to make her less homesick. To help her along, make for her a bed of grass and flowers in a place where she will feel safe and not trapped. The sweet fragrance of lilac, lavender, and honeysuckle will help lull her to sleep. This bedding will need to be changed every seven days, and make certain she is warm.

After this unicorn has grown, do not try to shelter her in a barn with common animals. A unicorn is a free spirit, wild and untamed. It would be a great insult to try to harness her with reins and bit or stall her like her cousin. You then risk losing her trust and faith, and these are hard to regain after you attempt such things.

Behavior (Mannerisms)

In all creation, there is no beast so good and blameless as a unicorn. It has no ill intentions nor spoiled nature. It kindles a gentle heart and is fond of life. Often it tends to those animals that are hurt or frightened, using the magic of its horn to heal wounds and undo snares so that no beast in its forest is ever caught.

But gentle though it may be, a unicorn has a fierce spirit. No person can tame a unicorn, and no person will ever capture and contain one. It is quick to flee, but if cornered, will fight to the bitter end, never willing to surrender its freedom.

In addition to being so pure, the unicorn is one of the wisest creatures in all the world. You can learn a great deal from her, and yes, she can speak. Her voice is soft now, but give her time to grow, and you will hear her. Unicorns are immortal, and so learn a great deal over the ages, and they forget nothing. Knowing so much, they are thoughtful when making a decision, but once they know their mind, they cannot be swayed.

Lastly, a unicorn sees all. By that, I mean it sees a man or beast for what they are. No human can fool a unicorn. With one look, she knows your heart and intentions and knows if you are good. I said before that when you look at this unicorn, you may become frightfully aware of your past wrongs. Be comforted, for that means you are worthy of her and can become her friend, for only humble hearts can be made aware of their transgressions and do better.

Unicorn Magic

With its horn, a unicorn can undo locks, purify water, and heal sick trees and superficial wounds. These may be burns or cuts or blows from a weapon, but a unicorn cannot mend broken bones or bring a soul back from the edge of death. Even magic has its limits.

All the magic a unicorn has is anchored by its horn, and know this, dear child: its magic cannot be wielded by another. For ages, humans have been misguided by the notion that if they possess a unicorn's horn, they possess its magic. This is not so. When its horn is removed, a unicorn dies, and so does its magic. Then the earth weeps over the loss of that which was so good and innocent.

A Special Word

So you do not misunderstand: a unicorn is not a horse. This is not a domestic beast you can harness and ride. A unicorn is a wild creature. It is kindred to the earth and magic. It loves to run free, with the wind in its mane and the ground leaping at its hooves. Its heart belongs to the wood, and when this one has grown up, you must not hold her back from leaving. If you have won her heart, she will return to you and never stray far. But still, you wish to ride her, do you not? If she knows you, and you earn her trust and love, I am certain she will let you climb upon her back without saddle or bridle. When that day comes, hold tight to her mane. A unicorn is so quick and nimble, being the fastest creature on hooves, it may feel as though you outrun time and the seasons.

LETTER FOR THE CARE OF A WINGED HORSE

To the child who reads this letter, you have found a winged horse. A runner between heaven and earth, this winged equine knows the wonders of the empyrean and has her likeness forever fixed in the stars. Faster than the common horse and wilder than a unicorn, this beast cannot be tamed, nor her spirit broken, for she has great strength of will and is perceptive. She has come down from the clouds to find you, dear child, making you her north star. – Merlin

Diet (Food and Drink)

Like its wingless cousin, a winged horse grazes the better part of the day and rests at night. In the winter, when nothing grows, a herd will often migrate to warmer regions to find food and return home in the spring after the snow melts.

If where you live, dear child, knows the bitterness of a cold season, you must provide this winged horse with plenty of hay and grain till the first spring grass emerges. Winged horses also like fruits of the tree and vine, like apples and berries, and root vegetables, like carrots and sweet potatoes. You can give this one sugar cubes or, better still, pieces of honeycomb, for winged horses like its gooey richness.

Winged horses must drink water every day. They drink plenty so their muscles are supple and their wings limber so they can fight or fly without need of warning and never cramp or ache.

This winged horse is small but will grow if you take great care of her. Give her plenty of food and water, and when she grows big enough that she desires to graze, keep watch over her in the fields and let no harm come to her. When she is full grown, you will see her strength in the way she moves, in the beating of her wings, and in the kicking of her hooves. Take comfort then in knowing she will fend for herself.

Habitat and Bedding

Winged horses can be found in fields and forests, but they prefer to be closer to the skies, for the aerial plain is where they love to roam. This one's herd lives in a mountainous region of Britannia, bringing the sky so close you feel you can reach up and touch it. Living in higher, more precarious terrain also keeps the herd safe from most dangers.

In the mountain valley, the grass is lush and soft and makes perfect bedding for a winged horse to lay down and rest. While this one is small, gather for her handfuls of fresh grass and make for her a warm bed and put it in a safe space, high up, so she can look out over the room. You can also dress the bedding with wildflowers to make it nice and fragrant. The bedding will need to be changed every seven days.

When this winged horse is fully grown, do not attempt to stall her in a barn with common animals. It would be an insult to try or suggest it, for a winged horse is not common. She is a free spirit, made to roam, wander, and fly. You best then let her rest outside, wherever she pleases, under the sun, moon, and stars.

Behavior (Mannerisms)

Do not fret at the beginning if this winged horse is distant and does not interact with you. Understand she has left her herd and may be lonely and sad. You will earn her trust and favor through kindness and care, but be patient and tender. When she has warmed up to you, she will keep close, be protective of you, and tell you many things. Oh yes, a winged horse has the power of speech, and you will hear her voice after she has grown some.

Earning the affection and trust of a winged horse takes more time and patience than with a common horse.

Winged horses are quite perceptive and sensitive to people's characters. Though you may tend to her needs, it is most important that you be kind, courteous, and speak the truth. Tell this winged horse about yourself. Show her what kind of person you are and be vulnerable in sharing secrets. This winged equine will watch and listen, and you will know she accepts you when that first time she blows in your face and presses her head to yours.

After she accepts you, you will notice a change in her behavior. She will be more spirited, jovial, and playful when you are around. Winged horses often frolic together, running and jumping and taking to wing. In this manner, they bond with each other and keep up their strength and stamina. Do not shy away from this winged horse's antics because having fun together will strengthen the bond between you.

The closer you are to this winged horse, the greater her loyalty and fondness for you will become. You will know this if ever you become ill or get hurt. Winged horses are empathic and sensitive to the feelings of those they care about. This one will do her best to comfort and keep you safe till you are well again.

Winged Horse Magic
Should you have the chance to ride this winged horse, and that will only come about with her permission and invitation, and you rise to greater heights than the birds, you will find the air up there very thin and hard to breathe. But this winged horse can share her magic so that you breathe easy and enjoy the view.

If indeed you hope to ride this winged horse, do not attempt to harness her with a bridle or lay a saddle on her back. She will never be tamed like her wingless cousin. Besides, the euphoria of riding her bare, with your fingers tied up in her mane, the wind in your face, and the eternal ether all around you, is captivating. I know. I rode a winged horse once, and before that, I thought riding a dragon was the greatest sensation.

A Special Word
There may be times this winged horse goes away, but only for a little while, and returns quiet and solemn. Winged horses have a special charge from heaven. They can see those souls that are lost and wandering the earth in shadow. Though they do not understand it, winged horses know which souls are destined for heaven, and so will ferry these souls upon their backs across the skies till they are close enough to the vault that the souls can make the rest of the way. I caution you not to press this winged horse to speak about death and her glimpses of the other side. She would rather talk about life and watch yours play out.

LETTER FOR THE CARE OF A CENTAUR

To the child who reads this letter, you have found a centaur. Half-man, half-horse, the centaur is not a barbarian or inferior race, as you may have been told, but rather a noble creature, brandishing honor and courage in his sword and shield. He is a warrior, always willing to fight for a just cause or put down his life for a friend or brother. He has left his clan, his military rank, and his chance at love and marriage to find you, dear one. Do not shy away when he swears his sword and life to you, for you are his new charge. – Merlin

Diet (Food and Drink)

Though he has the body of a horse, a centaur has an appetite like yours and mine. Centaurs are excellent hunters. They can see at great distances, are strong and agile, and have acute hearing. Most wild game they can take down with bow and arrow, but they will not shy away from grappling with a boar, a wildcat, or even a bear, if necessary or when threatened. Centaurs are also great trappers and fishers. So it is reasonable to think, dear child, you may never go hungry if you are friends with this centaur, and he may teach you better huntsmanship.

Centaurs cook their meat, and with it, they also eat fruits and vegetables and bread and pastries. They eat three square meals a day – morning, noon, and night, and when this one is grown – his small stature is only temporary if you take great care of him, he will have a hardy appetite. His body burns energy in excess, and it is not in a centaur's nature to stand still and do nothing. He will be bigger than a horse, twice as strong and fast, and he will work and contribute to your wellbeing, for you are now his clan.

Centaurs also drink plenty of water to stay limber and loose, so they are less likely to injure themselves should they need to move fast or react in a situation. They will drink other refreshments, however, like tea or milk with honey, and on special occasions, wine or mead.

Habitat and Bedding

Centaur clans live in densely wooded forests, where there is plenty of wild game to hunt and natural materials for building their houses. Together, they raise their village. Using timber, they build log huts around the trees, pack these with clay and mud, and thatch the roofs with thick moss.

The inside of a centaur's hut is simple but comfortable, with spaces to store weapons, clothes, and other articles and a bed laid out on the floor. Their beds are made like so: first, they spread thick cuts of grass followed by a layer of pine needles and leaves. Over this, they lay a heavy canvas, and over that, several animal hides. Such intricate work may be difficult for you to imitate, dear child, but this centaur will need someplace to sleep. Perhaps, while he is small, you can share a pillow or, if you know how to sew, make bedding for him and have him sleep where it is warm and safe.

Behavior (Mannerisms)

Of all the creatures to grace the earth, the centaur is one of the noblest, proudest, and bravest. They are not rogues or half-breed scoundrels, but rather possess a quality of character that I often find is lacking in most humans. I spent a day with this one's clan in their village, and I was warmed by the camaraderie and openness with which I was received. It was in the midst of festivities, and there was much gaiety and fun, that the clan welcomed me at their table and shared with me their food. I never felt like a stranger.

In a clan, no centaur is more significant than another. There is a chieftain and his council, and there are warriors – both male and female, but the clan works together to stay alive. They raise each other's children, feed and clothe one another, and keep each other safe if there is danger. They have their own laws and code of conduct so if one centaur does wrong against another, the matter is settled quickly by the council, and order is restored.

The warriors, both stallions and mares, are skilled and fearless. They will run into the fray and pay with their lives to keep their clan safe. This centaur is a great warrior and will protect you at any cost as soon as he is able. Being small may damper his pride, so be sure to encourage him. As you care and look out for him, you will strengthen the bond between you.

Alongside civility, there is always good-natured fun. Centaurs can be boisterous at times, lively, and excited. They will kick at the air and cheer loudly, especially when there is cause for celebration. When I visited their village, it was the day of their Amare Feast – an annual event where the eligible stallions compete for the hand of the mare they wish to marry. There were games, a great hunt, and a marvelous feast. You should ask this centaur about it. Yes, he can speak, but you will not hear him till he has grown some. It was a splendid thing to witness, the Amare Feast, and it showed me the tender side of these strong, disciplined beings.

A Special Word

I write this with great emphasis, care, and consideration: a centaur should never be compared to a horse. Centaurs are intelligent and capable and do many things you and I do, perhaps even with better skill, fortitude, and patience. So they deserve your respect. And so saying, I advise against asking this centaur or any other for a ride upon their back. If such a thing were to happen, better if it was by the centaur's invitation rather than by your request, or you risk offending this proud creature.

LETTER FOR THE CARE OF A FAIRY

To the child who reads this letter, you have found a fairy. She is a fae, cousin to sprites and pixies, but less mischievous. Small as she is, she has much spirit. She is kin to the earth and its mysteries, magical, and estranged from feelings that are not light and joyful. Like a child, she delights in merriment. She left the fairy kingdom to find you and hopes to call you her friend and play till the sun goes to bed. – Merlin

Diet (Food and Drink)

Fairies eat that which grows from the earth. They know which plants are good or bitter and which ones can make you ill or feel better. They will eat some flowers and mushrooms but love berries and other fruits, as well as leafy plants like burdock, mint, and thyme.

But more than they like greens, fairies are very fond of sweets and delight in creating confections. You are in for a treat the first time this fairy makes you lavender cakes – so light and sugary, they stave off sadness with one bite.

Fairies take tea with their pastries, sipping brews mixed with sugar and honey. Tea is a favorite pastime of theirs. It gives them chance to rest after spending the morning waking their forest, tending to trees, and growing flowers, but also time to visit with each other.

While tea is nice, a fairy still needs water. Being so small, this fairy will not drink much, maybe a thimble's worth, and even after she grows – she will stand only a little more than a person's hand, a mere seven inches, if you take great care of her – she may not drink more than two or three full thimbles.

Habitat and Bedding

Any forest that is green and alive with lots of flowers is home to fairies. If you sit still, you may see one, but they are nimble and fly faster than a dragonfly. This fairy came from an enchanted forest in Britannia, and she has never known a winter, for her forest is also home to a herd of unicorns – ask her about them. She can speak, but first, her voice must grow with her stature.

Elsewhere, in woods where fairies are the only magical beings, when the bitter frost of winter sweeps over, the fairies retire within their Sacred Tree and rest till they hear the call of spring – a sound they say only they can hear, and it is like the chiming of bells, warm and inspiring. At that time, they come out of their tree and usher in spring growth.

Inside their tree, the fairies carve out little shelves and beds and dress these down with leaves and flower petals. This fairy needs someplace warm and safe to rest. Your dresser drawer, where you put away your socks and other clothes, might be a good place, left a part of the way open so she can come and go as she pleases.

Behavior (Mannerisms)

For one so small, a fairy has a lot of personality. This fairy may be shy and a little wary of you at first, but be patient and kind and take no offense. Fairies feel safe together, but this fairy is far from home and her folk and may feel lonely. Be friendly and tend to her well, and she will warm up to you fast.

Once she knows you, her true nature will blossom. Fairies are lively, sociable creatures – very sweet and innocent, full of laughter and fun. When they are not tending to their forest, they like to frolic and play games. They also love parties and will find occasions to celebrate those things that are dear to them, including the seasons, the flowers, and many a birthday.

Fairies are often curious and not shy to know more about the world. They think human things – our belongings, tools, and baubles – are peculiar and like to know how a thing works or what is its purpose. This fairy may ask you questions about those things that pique her interest. Answer her well so she may better understand them, you, and how you live.

Some fairies collect small items – a hairpin, a spool, an earring, or such – that humans drop or which become lost and fascinate them. They like shiny things, in particular – a pretty rock, a coin, or a ring, but if those things are missed, a fairy will return them if asked nicely. Sometimes a fairy will gift what they find to someone they are fond of. With this fairy, that may very well be you, and even if what she gifts you is yours, smile and say thank you, for it will make her feel good. You can also make her heart swell with greater joy if you gift her something in return.

Fairies become very fond of the one they are with, be it a person or animal. As the bond between you grows, she will want to stay close to you, and she will dote on you, be sensitive when you are ill or overcome with joy when you are happy. You are the only friend she has now that she is away from her folk and queen, and she will often look to you for guidance, direction, and kinship.

Fairy Magic

Fairies are kindred to the earth and thus are born with magic that ties them to the living world. Have you ever wondered how a fairy is born? The parents each bestow a part of themselves, their life force, if you will, into the bud of a new flower. When that flower blooms, resting within its petals is the teeniest baby you ever saw.

Fairies usher in three of the four seasons. In springtime, they encourage flowers to bloom and trees to leaf. During the summer, they make all lush and green, and at the turn of autumn, they dance along the branches, changing leaves to amber, scarlet, and gamboge.

Fairies understand the speech of most animals and are friends with many beasts of the forests and fields. These creatures, in turn, keep the fairies safe, letting them know if danger draws near.

I caution you, dear child, so you may be sensitive to it: this fairy may not be strong in her magic. Fairy magic depends greatly on their proximity to each other and is anchored by the power of their monarch. Away from her folk and queen, this fairy may struggle with those gifts. She may often meditate to reconnect with the earth and withdraw into herself. The best I can advise you to do is love her and be understanding.

LETTER FOR THE CARE OF A GRIFFIN

To the child who reads this letter, you have found a griffin. Having the head, wings, and talons of an eagle and the body of a lion and being so immense and impressive, he is the king of birds and beasts. No other creature stands on ceremony as he does, so I encourage you, dear child, to bow low to him, like you would the crown, on this, your first meeting. The gesture shows respect and humility, and thus, you will earn his esteem so long as you are sincere – and a griffin knows if you are not. If you are sincere, he will bow in return. Thus begins your friendship with one of the noblest and kingly of beasts. – Merlin

Diet (Food and Drink)

Griffins are excellent hunters. Strong and silent, they stalk through the air, and their sharp eyes see anything that moves along the ground. When they catch sight of their prey, the griffin folds its wings to its sides and descends at a rapid pace, and the animal below does not know its fate till a shadow falls over it, and it is too late. The griffin throws open its wings at the last moment of descent, catches the prey in its talons, and pins it with its paws. Not fond of blood sport or long sufferings, the griffin ends the life of its catch quickly, then carries it home before another predator tries to steal it.

This griffin is small but will grow if you take great care of him. A griffin eats raw meat or fish at least once a day, and it must be fresh. Spoiled meat will make the griffin ill. If this happens, you will need to give him a special brew of boiled ginger with sugar or honey. Once the griffin has grown big enough to fend for himself, he will hunt for his own food and may, if you are indeed good friends, provide for your table.

Griffins drink plenty of water to help them digest their food. Water is also essential in keeping their muscles loose and their bodies limber so they can fight or fly with less risk of injury.

Habitat and Bedding

Griffins prefer to live in isolation, close to the skies, so they are often found in mountainous regions where the clouds are so close you can touch them, and the cliffs offer protection and stunning views. Griffins are excellent climbers with their strong feline hindquarters, balance, and precision, and they can leap off a rock face and take flight at once, giving them the advantage in a fight or when hunting.

Griffins occupy caves in the rock face so they have shelter in all types of weather. Griffins can live in the same territory with each other but will keep to themselves and not share food or shelter unless it is with a griffin that becomes their mate. And on such occasion, the male griffin builds a great nest to woo the female, and if she is pleased, she will hatch their offspring in it.

This griffin needs a place to rest while he stays with you. You can either gather for him twigs and sticks so he can build a nest, or you can provide him with soft bedding made from scraps of cloth. While this griffin is small, his bedding should be placed high up, where he feels safe and can survey the room. As he grows, he may later occupy the foot of your bed, if you do not mind, then the floor, and eventually, sleep outside when he is his actual size again.

Behavior (Mannerisms)

Griffins are often solitary creatures. This means they keep to themselves and hunt and live alone. They constantly defend their territories from encroaching animals. Territories can include a popular hunting ground or fishing hole, and their defense becomes more aggressive if food is sparse, like in the wintertime.

But when courtship happens in the spring, and a griffin finds a mate, the pair stay together the rest of their lives, caring for and supporting each other. Griffins are one of the few magical creatures that mate for life, meaning they fall in love only once and spend the rest of their lives together. When one passes away, the other dies of a broken heart.

Griffins are fiercely loyal and protective of those they love. Whether it is their mate, their hatchlings, or even you, dear child, a griffin will fight to the death to save the lives of those dearest to it. So I encourage you to bond with this griffin. Tend to his needs but also spend time together, talking and sharing – and yes, this griffin has the power of speech. Right now, his voice is soft, and you will not hear him till he has grown some. Griffins are intuitive creatures, smart and thoughtful, so do not hold back when you speak to him. There is a lot this griffin can share with you, and you will be amazed.

How to Bow to a Griffin and Why

I know many magical creatures, but so few are as ceremonious during a first meeting as a griffin. This is not to say this creature is a snob or pompous. On the contrary, griffins are courteous and composed but also rightfully suspicious and careful of strangers and strange beasts.

A bow is often reserved for lords and ladies and is considered polite and respectful. The griffin is the king of birds and beasts, so if you want to earn his or another griffin's favor and trust, showing respect with this single gesture goes a long way. So what is the proper way to bow to a griffin? Humbly and sincerely.

Should you encounter a griffin in the wild, and it charges you, do not run, fight, or cry out. Drop to one knee, lower your head, and submit. Willingly leave yourself vulnerable to the attack, and this response will stun the griffin into stopping its charge. Do not lift your head nor raise your eyes till the griffin gives you leave to do so. Only then will it permit you to speak, and if you mean it no harm, it will let you go on your way. Griffins are perceptive and aware of our behavior and intent, so they can sense if a person is dishonest. If such is the case, I am not sorry for the liar.

A Special Word

Griffins are proud beasts, so I caution you, when this one has grown big enough, do not attempt or ask to ride upon his back. To do so is discourteous. Better to wait, and perhaps with time and patience and a growing fondness for one another, he will offer to show you the skies. It will be magnificent, I am sure.

LETTER FOR THE CARE OF A GIANT

To the child who reads this letter, you have found a giant. Do not laugh but spare his feelings, for though he is small, it is but an enchantment – a spell only you can break. Put out of your mind the stories told to frighten you, the ones about giants grinding human bones to make their bread and other such nonsense. This giant is the friendliest fellow, the kindest soul you will ever meet, and would no sooner harm you than he would any creature. He is a farmer, a skilled tiller of the land, and prefers to eat the fruits of his labor than fabled carnage. He left his fields and village to find you, dear one, to call you his friend. And what greater friend could you have than one who stands above the trees? – Merlin

Diet (Food and Drink)

It was told to me by a giant that there are giants in far-off parts of the world who fish and raise large cattle for their tables. That giant and this one, however, will not consider eating meat. The very thought discomforts them and makes them ill. They and their whole village are farmers, and their fields and orchards yield a plentiful bounty each ripe season, with produce several times the size of what human farmers grow. Truly, these giants know the secrets of the earth, and so can nurse sick plants, stave off hungry pests, and grow enough food to see themselves through the longest winter. I am sure, if you and this giant become good friends, he will teach you how to better cultivate crops so that your table is never bare.

Besides being excellent farmers, giants are also great cooks. They use what they grow to make hearty meals, and because they love to entertain guests, they take pride in what they serve. Perhaps, when this giant has grown big enough, he will prepare meals for you or walk you through the steps to make a tasty stew or delicious pie. So long as you tend to his needs and take great care of him, this giant will grow to be giant again.

Giants drink plenty of water, but they like to sweeten it with fruit juices and flower nectars so that it is more refreshing. They also enjoy tea and, on special occasions, wine or mead. Back home, this giant's village has a magnificent vineyard, and when it is time to pluck and crush the grapes and ferment the juice, the giants make excellent draughts that set you on your heels and redden your face.

Habitat and Bedding

This giant's village has houses made of timber and thatch, and their fields and orchards stretch out before them over many hills. It is a lovely place, peaceful and full of good nature. The inside of a giant's home is no different from your own, I imagine. There is a kitchen, a hearth, a dining area, and a bedroom, and the spaces are warm and comfortable.

While this giant is with you, he will need a place to sleep. Would it surprise you to learn that, in addition to being a farmer and cook, this giant, like most in his village, is a skilled craftsman? Giants build their own furniture, most of it simple and not too intricate but sturdy and dependable. I ask then that you supply this giant with materials to make his own bed. These can be sticks, stems, shoots, wood slices, bark pieces, and glue, if you have some. If not, giants can make their own glue from pine resin and charcoal – how clever of them. While he builds, perhaps you can sew for him a mattress, sheets, and pillow using scraps of cloth and wool.

Behavior (Mannerisms)

Again, I write, giants are not the monsters you hear of in fairytales. This is a gentle giant you have found. He and his folk do not care for violence or fights or disagreements. They prefer to keep the peace and are friendly to those who are kind and do not shun their size or appearance. Do not mistake what I say as any implication that a giant is weak, a fool, or a coward. This giant can be incited to fight, to brandish a club and bludgeon an enemy that threatens him or his own. He will not shy away when a friend is in danger, and that includes you, dear child. He will keep you safe.

Giants are not idle fellows. They enjoy hard work and like to keep busy, especially in the fields, where they can get their hands dirty with the good earth. No task is too daunting for them, I imagine, and they like to help each other with chores and tough labors because it is the neighborly thing to do. In this way, the giant folk get along and keep good relations. If ever you need help with something that is beyond your size and abilities, I am sure this giant will be glad to lend you a hand.

Giants are not all work and no play. They have their amusements too, same as you and I. As this giant grows in stature, he will be happy to play games with you or enjoy simple pastimes, like watching clouds drift or taking walks in the wood. He may even join you and your circle of friends in whatever sports you play. You should ask him what Mud Ball is – a game giant children play that is a lot of fun and very dirty. And yes, this giant can speak, but while he is small, his voice is too soft for you to hear.

A Special Word

Giants are proud of their natural height and strength and, as I mentioned, are eager to help any person or beast that is smaller than them. So it may embarrass this giant to be small and need so much help for a time. He knows he will grow if you take care of him, and that is a great comfort to him. Still, he has always been big, and for the first time in his life, he is seeing a giant world. In his heart, he is still big, and I ask that you encourage him so that he keeps his chin up and stays cheerful and hopeful. In turn, when he is giant again, he will have a greater fondness for you.

"How tall is a giant?", you may ask. Most giants, when fully grown, are fifty feet tall and stand with their heads above the trees. So much stature can make a giant clumsy in places made for smaller folk. Be mindful, patient, and understanding then as this giant moves throughout your house and is growing, and think how difficult it is for one who is used to bigger spaces and things.

LETTER FOR THE CARE OF A MERMAID

To the child who reads this letter, you have found a mermaid. A maiden of the sea with the tail of a fish, she is mysterious and beautiful, the heartache of many a sailor. Her kind is elusive and stays hidden beneath the waves, but she has surfaced to find you, dear child, and the ocean weeps in her absence. The great blue is all she knows, and it is strange and foreign to her to be on land, so be kind and thoughtful of her. She wishes to know you better and seeks your friendship and, in this way, might bring your worlds together, uniting the land with the sea. – Merlin

Diet (Food and Drink)

Merfolk have appetites like yours and mine in that they eat three square meals a day – morning, noon, and night, but all their food comes from the sea. They eat a variety of fish, crustaceans, and mollusks, as well as seaweed, kelp, and other sea plants, and make strange, wonderful foodstuffs that taste better than they sound – I know, for I have tasted and savored them. I recommend then the squid ink pudding.

Though you could try to fish and forage for those foods she likes, I caution you, the sea can be dangerous, and bringing back a haul of sea life may raise questions from your elders. Fortunately, this mermaid can partake of land food, be it meat or vegetable, till such time she has grown big enough to return to the sea and fend for herself. She will grow so long as you take great care of her, and sad as it is for me to write, you will have to let her go back to the waters she came from, for the sea is a part of her, and she a part of it. To be gone from it too long will break her heart, and she will die.

Living in water all the time, a mermaid does not need to drink it. Merfolk do, however, enjoy their own potations, and this mermaid might share a drink with you from her native waters, if she has the ingredients to make it. In turn, she might try your local refreshments. I recommend tea or milk with honey and sugar.

Habitat and Bedding

This mermaid comes from an underwater kingdom at depths no person can reach. It is a world of color and light, alluring and outlandish, but in all things wonderful. How do I know? I have seen it. I was only able to see it because the mer-queen brought me there, and no land dweller will ever see it unless a mer-person takes them there.

Imagine a city beneath the waves, with coral gardens everywhere. Every mer-person has a dwelling made of white sea clay, and inside are rooms like in your own house, only yours do not have fish and other sea critters swimming through them by way of an open door and windows.

The merfolk sleep on beds of sand and clay raised out of the seafloor. Over this they lay blankets of sea moss, followed by seaweed that is woven together, and their pillows are sea sponges.

For as long as she is with you, this mermaid needs a space to dwell and sleep. While she is small, a bowl or basin will do, but as she grows, you will need larger vessels to hold her till it is time to return her to the sea. Natural bedding may be difficult to gather, so if it is easier for you, sew for her a mattress, blanket, and pillow using scraps of cloth. You must also change her water every day so she does not become ill, and while seawater is preferable, she will not mind freshwater.

Behavior (Mannerisms)

Mermaids are the female of the mer-species, and mermen are their male counterparts. There are some differences between their behaviors and appearances. Mermen are often brave and do not shy away from a challenge, while mermaids are more cautious and likely to flee. Mermaids do not have the strength nor skill to fight, but neither are they helpless. A mermaid is armed with poisonous barbs along her tail, and the toxin is potent enough to paralyze most sea predators and kill a human. But do not fret, child, when you handle this mermaid. She will not strike you dead by mishap, for she is in control of her barbs and their sting and will only use them if threatened.

Merfolk, particularly mermaids, are social creatures. They desire attention, affection, and good company. Those who strike out on their own are often shy and wary of other persons and beasts. This mermaid may need time to warm up to you, for she is in a strange place, away from the sea she loves and the merfolk she has known all her life. Be sensitive to her feelings and comfort her in her loneliness. Take care of her but also talk to her often – and yes, she understands and has the power of speech, but her voice is too soft for you to hear while she is small. She must grow for that to change. Always be there for her, show her you are her friend, and her heart will lighten.

Once she knows you, you will see a change come over this mermaid. Her nerves will ease, and she will ripple with mirth and bubble over with excitement to be near you. She will, at times, be much like a child – glowing, carefree, and full of life. She will want to play and be desperate to swim, but I caution you not to take her to the sea or any other large body of water till she is of a size that deters most creatures from snatching her up – a most unpleasant thought.

Merfolk are often curious and fascinated by the world above the waves. They think human articles are peculiar and want to know their purpose. If this mermaid asks you such questions, do not withhold answers or hesitate to satisfy her wonderings. In turn, she may tell you about her underwater world, and perhaps, when it is time for her to go back, she will show it to you.

Merfolk Magic

Merfolk can talk with and understand most sea creatures. Only those predators, like the shark, giant squid, or juvenile sea serpent, which are driven by pure instinct – the natural impulse to act or react in a particular way without conscience, have closed ears, and so cannot be reasoned with or understood.

Lastly and perhaps most enchantingly, we humans cannot breathe underwater, but merfolk, by their own strange and wonderful magic, can bestow on us with a kiss the power to do so. If a mermaid or merman kisses a human with intent, that human will be able to breathe underwater without growing gills. The enchantment is temporary and breaks once the person breathes the surface air. The sensation of it is extraordinary though, speaking as one who was blessed with a kiss from a mermaid. There is no magic I would rather be under and wish so much to know again. I hope, dear child, you come to know the feeling.

LETTER FOR THE CARE OF A PHOENIX

To the child who reads this letter, you have found a phoenix. This magical avian is a beautiful mystery. Time is his slave and wisdom sits at his right wing. Eternity is his sigil, eclipsed with fire. No bird nor beast knows more about the world than he does, for he has lived several lives and seen much of history play out. He left paradise to find you, dear child, to kindle amity and goodwill between you. If you are caring and true, you may learn the secrets of the earth and times past, as seen through the eyes of your new feathered friend. – Merlin

Diet (Food and Drink)

Like most birds, a phoenix eats half of its body weight in food every day. It does not eat meat but prefers a diet of nuts and berries and seeds and flowers. It also likes most fruits, but those with soft skins, like pomegranates, peaches, and dates, are its favorite.

On its own, a phoenix will be cautious when eating, taking small bites here and there. Too much food at once can make it slothful, and idle senses are dangerous. Phoenixes live a long time because they are careful and have a keen awareness of their surroundings. Their sharp eyes see several times as far as other birds, and they can see behind themselves without turning their heads. Their acute hearing can detect a subtle breath in the brush. The moment danger breathes, a phoenix takes to wing, and this avian flies faster than any other bird and most winged beasts.

While he is in your care, this phoenix may ease and eat more casually because with you, he is safe. You need only care for him till he has grown big enough to fend for himself – and yes, he will grow, so long as you tend to him well.

Phoenixes are light drinkers and drink only water. Water helps them digest their food but too much can upset their bellies. If that occurs, they must fast till they feel well again.

Habitat and Bedding

This phoenix has traveled the world several times over, but his home is a secret garden that cannot be found by outsiders. Only a phoenix that is willing will show the way, and even then, the garden is not easy for most to reach.

The secret garden is warm, beautiful, and bright and has an orchard of white blossoming trees. Phoenixes go there to be reborn, making it a sacred place, and it has never known an autumn or winter but always spring and summer. Away from the garden, a phoenix has never known a cold, bitter day, and wherever it is, when the first leaf heralds the coming of fall, it flies, chasing the sun, and does not come again till the first budding of spring.

When roaming, if a phoenix grows tired, it will find a tall tree to roost, usually in a dense wood, where it is safe and out of sight. It need only rest for a little while because, being immortal, a phoenix does not need as much sleep as you or I.

While this phoenix is in your care, do not be foolish or offend him by trying to cage him. He is not a pet bird, and no cage will hold him. He needs no nest nor bedding, only a high place to alight to rest or watch what goes on in your house.

Since he has never known a winter, if the bitter cold catches up with him where you are, you must keep him warm and comfortable till the frost is over. If all else fails, light a fire, and he will lay beside it, fanning his wings to catch both light and heat so he can warm his blood and self. And there is no need to worry for his safety: being reborn from ashes and flame, a phoenix will not burn, nor his feathers singe, till it is his time.

Behavior (Mannerisms)

Being eternal and having seen so much of the world, the phoenix is the wisest bird in all creation. It does not insert itself into events wherever it is unless those happenings concern it. Instead, it is a gentle, careful observer, fascinated with how life turns – cause and consequence, reason versus emotion, and what people and beasts do. Thusly, the phoenix acquires a deep knowledge of things and forgets nothing.

Phoenixes are intuitive and able to sense the nature of most people, even if they attempt deceit. They have an innate sense of goodwill or bad and are a better judge of character than you or I. Even now, you are under careful scrutiny by this magical avian as he decides what kind of person you are based on feeling and observation. He has seen people fail time and again, seen the worst of them and what harm they can do. You, dear child, have a rare chance to prove that not all humans are bad, that you are better than most. Treat this phoenix with kindness, admiration, and respect, like the worthy companion he is, and he will not forget it. In turn, he will admire and love you.

Phoenixes are not violent by nature. They prefer to lead peaceful lives and will sooner fly away than fight an enemy. However, if a phoenix is cornered, or those it loves are in danger, and that includes you, dear child, those talons and beak can deal lethal blows, and the phoenix will become too hot to touch, its feathers graced by its inner fire. A phoenix is also surprisingly strong and can lift an assailant twice its size several feet in the air and will drop them in an effort to break them.

Phoenix Magic

The phoenix is an immortal bird. It can live up to 500 years at a time, and when its end draws near, it returns to the secret garden to build a nest with cassia bark, sage leaves, spikes of nard, cinnamon, frankincense, and myrrh – rich spices that produce fragrant smokes to cleanse its ashes. The nest acts then as a funeral pyre, and when the phoenix lays down to rest, its internal flame sets it alight so that its old self burns away, and from its ashes, the phoenix is born again a new chick. The chick then matures in seven days, becoming a young adult, but has all its memories of its past lives. How lucky you are, dear child, if this phoenix tells you all he has seen and lived through – and yes, this phoenix possesses the power of speech and can understand you. While he is small though, his voice is too soft for you to hear, but give him time to grow, and you will hear him soon enough. Then you will delight in his song as well.

The song of the phoenix is the most beautiful sound of any bird to grace your ears. It not only pleases and captivates the listener but also inspires creativity. Many artists – painters, sculptors, poets, songwriters, and the like, were lifted to a higher plain after hearing the phoenix's song and created wonderful, timeless masterpieces. You, too, can be inspired, dear child, and I can only wonder what works you will conceive.

LETTER FOR THE CARE OF A SEA SERPENT

To the child who reads this letter, you have found a sea serpent. Sea serpents are the ghosts of seamen's stories – the great antagonists of ships, terrors beneath the waves, beasts with no predator that prey on all. But I tell you, do not pay heed to the narratives. The truth you never hear is humans caused a rift between us and these creatures a long time ago, and war raged at sea. I will write more, but I implore you, dear child, do not fear nor toss aside this sea serpent. You have a rare chance to know him. He puts himself at your mercy, having left the deep blue, where he was safe, to find you. If you take great care of him and are kind, you may rectify past injustices and yield more good than you can fathom. – Merlin

Diet (Food and Drink)

Sea serpents are brutal, capable hunters. That much is true. The juveniles or adolescent sea serpents are voracious eaters and quick to strike at most prey that is no bigger than them. Mature sea serpents, however, are patient and clever and will stalk and ambush their prey. They also do not require nor desire constant feeding.

Though this sea serpent is small, he is a mature adult. If you tend to him well, he will grow and become a size where he can fend for himself after you return him to the sea – and yes, you must take him back to the waters from whence he came, for his actual bulk and breadth are greater than you can imagine, bigger than your house, I wager. And do not think to put him in a lake or pond or another body of water surrounded by land, for a sea serpent can live a long time – for hundreds of years, in fact – and will never stop growing. The sea is the only place that can hold him.

Sea serpents eat almost anything in the ocean – fish, crustaceans, mollusks, cephalopods, sharks, even whales. While you could try to fish and trap small sea critters, I warn you, the sea can be wild and treacherous, and returning home with a bunch of sea life may raise suspicion from your elders. Fortunately, this sea serpent can eat red meat and poultry, and though he will hungrily devour what you serve him, he will not crave too often and afterward sleep to ease the slow digestion of his food.

Habitat and Bedding

This sea serpent comes from a stretch of ocean that is cold, dark, and treacherous. Seamen do not venture there, for the waves thrash violently, and the wind chases and bites and howls misfortunes. There is solitude in the chaos, so this sea serpent and others occupy the deepest fathoms there – in the abyss, where sunlight cannot touch them, but still, they see in the pitch black.

Sea serpents live all over the world. The juveniles wander, being too small to steal or defend a territory from a mature adult. Adults are colossal and so occupy and stalk areas of the ocean as their own. In those places, they hunt, drift, sleep, and chase off trespassers or challengers.

Juveniles take short periods of rest between meals, being wary of danger, and will take up temporary residence in an underwater cave. Mature adults, being so immense and intimidating, rest on the seafloor and only stir if they sense disaster, like a ship caught in a storm, or another sea serpent in their territory.

While he is in your care, this sea serpent needs a submerged space to dwell and be contained. You can start with a bowl or basin, but whatever the vessel is, it will have to grow with him till such time he can return to the sea. Change his water daily to prevent him becoming ill, and while seawater is preferable, he will keep well in freshwater. Be mindful to put him where there is shade, for though the sun does not cause him distress or pain, he is used to the cold dark of the ocean floor.

Behavior (Mannerisms)

Sea serpents are fierce from birth. They must be to survive in the ocean, where threats linger above and below the waves. Juveniles are rash and impulsive, while mature adults are sly and cunning. As the stories suggest, sea serpents are not opposed to violence and even delight in wreaking havoc, especially for ships and seamen, but this was not always their way. Much of their behavior can be attributed to great tragedy.

The War between Humans and Sea Serpents

There was a time sea serpents shared the sea with humans. Ships could cross the ocean in peace because there was respect between our kinds. Then, one day, a foolish brute speared a juvenile and boasted he was a hero, and this spurred the slaying of many adolescents by others who wished to claim the title. This betrayal and butchery enraged the sea serpents, and the adults fought back, sinking ships and devouring seamen. It was war between us and them. You should ask this sea serpent to tell you about it. Yes, he can speak. His voice is too soft now for you to hear, but give him time to grow, and you will hear him tell of those war atrocities.

There were not many sea serpents before the war, and fewer exist today. Out of a thousand eggs a female lays, only one of her brood survives. Regrettably, the savage behavior for which sea serpents are well known was bred into them by our follies. There needs to be a change. I hope, dear child, that change starts here with you. Show this sea serpent a kinder love and respect and prove to him that there is still good amongst the human race.

Sea Serpent Magic

The ferocity and intense nature of a sea serpent can incite bad weather. Juveniles have no influence by themselves, being small and immature. An adult, however, can provoke violent winds and heavy rain, and when all sea serpents come together to mate under a great moon, the skies break out, and the heavens are chaos.

Sea serpents have a greater power than this that is deceptive. By way of their eyes – if they look at their prey, and the animal or person does not look away, a sea serpent can compel its victim to surrender to death. The sensation is strange and maddening, and only a strong mind anchored by a strong heart can break their trance. I suffered it once, and at first, there was great fear, so much fear, I felt as though I were drowning, and then there was a sudden calm, and I cared about nothing, not even death.

In spite of what I have written here, I swear, dear child, this sea serpent will not harm you. He needs you, and there is more to his being here that only he can tell you and concerns the survival of his race. Do not be afraid but take heart and be brave. In truth, as my magic stirs within me as I write this, I believe good things will come from this union, and you will have a fierce friend at sea.

LETTER FOR THE CARE OF A HARPY

To the child who reads this letter, you have found a harpy. Please, do not fear her. She is not the feathery fiend you hear tell of in stories. The truth none know, save me and now you, is that the nature of her race is the fault of human scorn and spurning. I will write more on this, but I beg you not to be cruel or neglect her. She has suffered enough, having been mistreated most of her life and cast out by her flock – they did not want her because of her passive nature and pale appearance. She is not cursed, nor is she a monster. Her name is Dove, and she is my friend. She left behind all she knew to find you, dear child, and I hope you will be her friend too. – Merlin

Diet (Food and Drink)

Harpies are hunters and scavengers. Do not let their thin, bony stature fool you. These bird-women can lift prey twice their size and will drop it from precarious heights to break it so as not to tire or risk getting injured in a struggle. Dove's flock lives at sea, so they often fish and pluck aquatic life from its waters, but they are also a short flight from the mainland, and so will go there to snatch up wild game or straying livestock.

Harpies eat their catches raw, for they do not know how nor care to cook, but fortunately, Dove's appetite is not so unsavory. She stayed in my company for a number of days and was glad to eat hearty meat stews with potatoes and vegetables. Her palate then is diverse. Also, unlike her sisters, she takes no pleasure in killing but ends a life swiftly and mercifully when she hunts. She is small now by way of enchantment, but if you tend to her well, she will grow, and I do not doubt then she will provide for your table and look after you.

Harpies drink only a little water at a time, for their stomachs are sensitive and prone to ache with too much drink. Dove also likes a cup of tea with sugar and a dollop of honey which soothes her voice – and yes, she can speak. Quite well, in fact. Her voice is too soft to hear while she is small, but once she has grown, you will hear her.

Habitat and Bedding

Dove's flock lives on an islet that cannot be found on any map. It is lost at sea, surrounded by a dangerous fog and jagged rocks. The sun does not shine there, and it is a cool, damp place. The islet has a cave – massive, dark, and dank, and inside, the flock nests in filth. The smell within is offensive and cannot be suffered without getting sick.

On top of rock spires and cairns or on the edge of erosional fins in the cave walls, the harpies build large nests of dried seaweed or kelp and branches. In these they sleep and hatch their young. When Dove came to stay with me, I made her a nest of living branches and flowers by way of magic, and she delighted in it. Before this, she had no nest but was forced by her flock to sleep on the cold, hard cave floor. I hope, dear child, you will build her something – a nest or a bed using twigs and scraps of cloth, and have her rest where it is safe and warm and near you.

Behavior (Mannerisms)

I will tell you first about Dove and her nature before I write more about her sisters, for she is very different from them. Also, I use the term sisters reluctantly. It is what a harpy calls her fellow harpies though there may be no relation between them. The flock, however, treated Dove cruelly and not as their equal and thought her a burden.

Dove is quiet and often shy, not fierce or incensed like her sisters. Such behavior, coupled with her startlingly pale appearance, provoked their shunning and mistreatment of her. They often hurt her, and she did not defend herself, so she has many scars. Because she did not want to thrill in hunting like them, she stayed back at the cave and ate scraps. It was after she came to me that she found her true self. In a handful of days, she gained confidence, found her voice, and even learned to read. She also proved herself to be brave and fierce enough when she saved my life from a deadly serpent.

Though her sisters do not bathe, Dove does and often. She likes to wash and favors fresh air and keeping dry and warm. Harpies are sensitive to daylight and see better at night, in the dark, but you will notice Dove wears blue-tinted glasses. These are my own design and invention and allow her to venture into the sun and not suffer to see.

So what of the harpies you hear tell of in stories? Those winged terrors that snatch up travelers and do unspeakable horrors. It pains me to write I cannot deny the narratives, but read carefully, dear child: harpies were not always mean and callous. They once were peaceful and kept to themselves. They did not bother us. But humans came after them because of their fearsome and beastly appearance.

Humans forced them off the mainland onto the islet. There, the harpies became sick and were dying. One queen decided then that if humans were going to treat them as monsters, than monsters they would be. And so, by human fault, malice and savagery were bred into these once docile creatures. Now the only hope for change starts here with you and Dove, if you are willing to accept and be kind to her.

The Pecking Order

In a flock, there is a pecking order. The stronger, more aggressive harpies bully their way to the top, and the queen rules over all of them. Should a harpy want to claim the queen's title and authority, she must fight her for them to the death. Dove's mother was a former queen, and when she was killed, the flock hoped the new queen would get rid of Dove. Instead, she spared her, and she did not know it then, but it was so Dove could be sent to you, dear child.

A Special Note

A harpy's scream will shatter the eardrums and inner ear, causing hearing loss. If her scream continues, it will drive a person mad, even killing them. I never heard Dove scream, but I imagine she would in defense or to get away from an assailant. Should it become necessary for her to scream, for example, if she were protecting you from a force she could not hope to fight and win, cover your ears and hum. Humming will lessen her shriek. It would be better, though, if you had earplugs made from beeswax.

A Final Word

Take great care of Dove for me. Do not be like humans past who shunned harpies for their appearance. You cannot judge the quality of a soul by how one looks on the outside. Dove is, at heart, a beautiful soul — kind, eager, and loyal. She became one of my dearest friends in such a short time, and though I may never see her again, my life is richer for knowing her. Yours can be too, dear child, so welcome her.

LETTER FOR THE CARE OF A BASILISK

To the child who reads this letter, you have found a basilisk. The deadliest and greatest of serpents – all lesser snakes give him way where he slithers. If you heard tell of him, you heard that with a glance, he has the power to cause death. This is true, but you need not fear nor look away from this basilisk, dear child. His sight is not lethal. By his leave and by way of magic, I removed his power from him so that he could come to you safely. You are the most fortunate of people to have found this creature. The basilisk has always been a mystery, but you have this one chance to know him without fear or risk of death, and he to know you. This exchange is a wonder for him, for he has never had a life look back at him that was not another basilisk. I swear no harm will come to you or yours by taking him in and caring for him. You have my word, as a wizard. – Merlin

Diet (Food and Drink)
Like all snakes, the basilisk eats other animals. He will stalk and ambush his prey, and once caught, he swallows it whole. While he is small, you can feed him worms, insects, and minnows, but if these are hard to come by, he will consume cuts of raw meat, though these must be fresh so he does not become ill. He will grow as you care for him and, in time, fend for himself. Then you will not have to worry about mice, rats, or other pests.

Fully grown, a basilisk is over thirty feet long, heavy, and powerful. Even without his deadly sight, he can take down big game with little resistance, wrapping his coils around a catch and delivering a lethal bite – his venom stops the heart in seconds.

After ingesting his food, the basilisk coils up and sleeps to conserve energy for the digestion of his meal. How long he rests and digests depends on how warm he is, his size, and the size of his meal. As winter nears and outside gets colder, the basilisk will stop eating altogether and eventually enter a state of dormancy called brumation that will last all the cold season.

A basilisk drinks enough water to help him digest his food. Too much drink will make him slothful or ill, and in hot, dry places, he can go several months without a sip.

Habitat and Bedding
This basilisk comes from a desolate land, a dead valley where nothing grows and there is no wildlife. There are only more basilisks, and all of them are in a great pit in the earth, slithering over top of each other, their scales rubbing together to produce a frightening sound like cold water on hot metal. You know when a basilisk has come by if you see a withering trail of earth where his body snaked over, but when many basilisks are in one place, their presence decimates the land, leaving the ground dry and cracked and unsuitable for other life.

Basilisks are resilient and able to survive in most places that are not cold. They like to keep warm and are not bothered by rain or storm. In your care, while he is small, I think the best thing to do is let him occupy your clothes drawer in the dark, muffled quiet, curled up in your warm clothes, and leave the drawer cracked open so he can come and go as he pleases. When he has grown big enough to fend off other beasts, he will search out a den outside your house but still close to you and where there is food.

Behavior (Mannerisms)
For ages, the basilisk has been a symbol of death and evil. I understand your fear of him and any reserve in looking after him. If you are like me and have heard the stories about this fatal ophidian, you think the worst of him. I did too, and so few magical creatures have caused me as much dread as him. However, I realized a

truth that absolved my prejudice, and now I pity the basilisk.

Though he may boast of his power and say he is proud of what he is, the truth is a basilisk's deadly sight cripples him. He can only look at another basilisk, but his race is unfeeling and cannot appreciate nor care for one another, so he cannot understand the value of life. He knows nothing of compassion, friendship, or love – those things that make life worth living – because his lethal gaze keeps him from bonding with another animal or person. So, for all his power and authority over the living, the basilisk leads a lonely life.

This basilisk, however, can look at you and you at him, and I imagine he may not like it at first. Without his fatal look, he feels he is not a basilisk but a great serpent and worries over the loss of his identity. Pity him all the more then, dear child, but do not let on to him that you do. Show him kindness and understanding, be patient with him, and be his friend, and with time, I think he will come around and learn much from you.

I must write you to beware though, dear child: this is the only basilisk you can look at and not die. All others still have their deadly sight and remain threatening, hard, and merciless. You do not want to meet one of them, or your life is over. Look for the signs when you venture out – withered earth, wilted plant life, and the absence of animals and natural sounds. Keep your hand level with your eyes and walk, do not run, or else you might attract his attention.

Basilisk Magic

A basilisk is not born by breeding, as with other snakes, but is conceived by magic when a common serpent hatches a chicken egg. This does not happen often, so there are not many basilisks in the world, and it is why all basilisks are male.

"Where goes the basilisk, death is with him." That is a verse from an old poem, and I quote it because the basilisk is more than his eyes. Where he slithers, the earth withers. His breath wilts plant life, and his venom blights the soil so nothing grows. Though I took away his power to cause death with a look, I did not take from him those other ways to inflict suffering. He is allowed them so as to remain a basilisk.

By now, you surely wonder why send a child such a dangerous creature? I will let the basilisk tell you – and yes, he can speak, only his voice is too soft to hear while he is small. Care for him so he grows, and he will tell you a story, at the end of which you can be the hero, dear child, if you only accept him, be gentle with him, and show him love and friendship he could not know before. A lot of good can come of this odd pairing, I think. Perhaps this basilisk will prove the narratives wrong and even become a symbol of life.

HOW A STORY WAS BORN

Being a Christian, I firmly believe that the good Lord leads us to opportunities that we ourselves could never imagine. This story was inspired by a picture in a book, a book that just happened to be at a garage sale that my mother just happened to visit, and this picture just happened to be in this book. But I do not believe in happenstance or luck. I believe things happen for a reason, and I dare to say that the Lord (or Great Creator) saw this book to me, knowing that a picture would inspire a story in a girl, who was maybe sixteen years old at the time, and that story would grow into what you just read.

The book is titled *In Pursuit of the Unicorn* by Josephine Bradley, and toward the front, there is a picture of a unicorn in a bottle washed up on a beach entitled *Beach Treasures* by Dale Rutter. In the distance, there is a small boy with a pail, and though his back is turned, we all know he is going to find the beach treasure. All the while I stared at this picture, I wondered, *How did the unicorn get here?* And so, a story was born. I admit it took me several years and several drafts to get it here, but I suppose that goes to prove you cannot put a good story down, not one you believe in, and certainly not one I believe I was led to write.